PUSH BACK

DISRUPTION - BOOK 2

A Thriller By

R. E. McDermott

Published by R.E. McDermott

Copyright © 2016 by R.E. McDermott

ISBN: 978-0-9837417-7-0

For more information about the author, please visit
www.remcdermott.com

Layout by Guido Henkel, **www.guidohenkel.com**

Printed in the U.S.A.

To my readers
You make it worth the effort

CAMILLUS

PROLOGUE
The Story Thus Far

THE EVENT
1 APRIL 2020

When a massive solar storm takes down the power grid, Captain Jordan Hughes opts to take his ship *Pecos Trader* and its precious cargo home to Texas despite formidable odds. Sailing from Wilmington, North Carolina, with a partial crew supplemented by a group of ex-Coast Guardsmen, Hughes eludes both corrupt government forces and Cuban gunboats to get his ship and crew safely home.

But as Hughes sails south, civilization crumbles. The President, head of an ill-prepared government with insufficient resources to sustain the population, makes a self-serving decision to keep scarce resources for 'government use,' and to seize private stocks of food, water, and fuel. Assisted by a corrupt Secretary of Homeland Security, POTUS squashes political opposition and arrests his most vocal opponent, Simon Tremble, the Speaker of the House.

In Wilmington, civil order collapses and gangs fill the power vacuum to terrorize a desperate and vulnerable population. But the ascendancy of the gangs is not unchallenged; a coalition of ex-Coast Guardsmen and the remnants of a National Guard unit seize the Wilmington Container Terminal and its massive store of cargo and establish Fort Box. As frictions between the two groups grow, the gang leader orders an attack on the home of Levi Jenkins, an ex-*Pecos Trader* crewman allied with Fort Box. The gang is narrowly defeated and withdraws to lick its wounds as a (very) temporary and uneasy peace ensues.

Meanwhile, Hughes reaches home in Texas to find chaos there as well. Local government has collapsed, and the area is ruled by escaped convicts masquerading as policemen. Vastly outnumbered, he avoids contact until a family rescue mission explodes into a running gun battle that leaves a dozen convicts dead. The stage is set for continuing struggle.

As events unfold in North Carolina and Texas, Congressman Tremble escapes from FEMA headquarters in Virginia, determined to get home to North Carolina and expose the President's perfidy. Tremble and his son are assisted in their escape by a chance meeting with Bill Wiggins and Shyla 'Tex' Texeira, two former *Pecos Trader* crewmen making their way home on the Appalachian Trail.

Shaken by Tremble's escape, the President launches an all-out manhunt for the escaped congressman and his son, as elsewhere FEMA attempts to crush rising resistance to governmental excesses and abuse.

The Trembles continue to avoid capture, hiding in the Virginia mountains while Wiggins and Tex make their way north towards home. The red herring in the mix is George Anderson, Simon Tremble's former FEMA guard, who Tremble has duped into becoming a diversion.

The chase is on.

CHAPTER ONE

APPALACHIAN TRAIL
MILE 1199.7 SOUTHBOUND
JUST NORTH OF US 50/17

DAY 20, 6:15 A.M.

Briers ripped George Anderson's clothes, and small branches lashed his face as he crashed downhill, leaving a trail through the dense undergrowth a blind man could follow. The dogs' excited baying in the distance left no doubt they were closing, and the outcome of the chase was a foregone conclusion unless he could think of something, and fast.

The brush thinned abruptly, and his right foot met thin air, plunging him on hands and knees into a small fast-moving stream. He cursed as his knees smashed into the hard slate of the creek bed and he barely managed to avoid sprawling face-first in the water. Then hope rose anew—would water confuse the dogs? He ignored aching knees and bolted downstream through calf-deep water in a limping run. He slipped and slid on the slick bottom, barely managing to stay upright, his pulse pounding and his breath coming in loud, ragged gasps.

He moved faster in the creek and even imagined the barking was fading, but minutes later a change in the timbre and volume of the baying told him the dogs had reached the stream. He held his breath to quiet his breathing in the desperate hope he'd hear some sign the water had defeated the dogs. The triumphant baying of the lead hound dashed that hope—the chase was on again.

Anderson pushed even harder, oblivious to the treacherous footing as he splashed downstream. He had even increased his lead a bit, when his left foot plunged into a shallow depression in the creek bed. He went down face-first, striking his head on a large rock.

He struggled to a sitting position, stunned, his vision obscured. Water swirled around him, tugging insistently, and when he wiped his eyes, his hand came away bloody. He bent his face to the creek and shoveled water over his head with his cupped hands until his vision cleared. The baying of the hounds grew louder. His left knee throbbed. Time for plan B, whatever the hell that was.

He'd read somewhere dogs followed scent through the air, and the failure of the stream to confuse them supported that theory. Could he use that?

He limped to the stream's edge to strip off his ragged backpack and shirt, setting them both on the bank to peel off his sweat-soaked tee shirt. The sodden fabric clung to him, the sour odor of stale sweat intense as he tugged it over his head. He grimaced as he held the tee in his teeth and rummaged in the backpack for his water jug, a gallon Clorox bottle. He dumped the water and recapped the bottle, then wrapped the stinking tee shirt tightly around it, securing it with a length of twine from his pocket. Satisfied, he tossed the reeking float in the middle of the creek and watched it zip downstream faster than any human—or leashed tracking dog—was ever likely to move. "Please don't hang up anywhere," Anderson murmured.

"Okay, Anderson, stay calm," he told himself as he slipped into his outer shirt without bothering to button it. "There's plenty of time, so don't screw this up." The baying was closer.

He fumbled in the pack again for an old plastic garbage bag then transferred the meager contents of the pack to the bag before tossing the empty backpack into the stream near the bank. It tumbled downstream, half-submerged in the rushing water, to fetch up on a tree limb dangling into the edge of the creek. Anderson nodded—it looked natural, not staged—but his self-congratulations were short-lived as something ran into his eyes and he looked down at a blood-soaked shirt front and blood spots dotting the rocks around him. Still bleeding!

The dogs were close now, their yelps increasingly excited and mixed with human shouts. Panic rising, he tore his shirttail into a makeshift bandage—then stopped. *Stay cool, Anderson, stay cool—lemonade from lemons.*

He limped into the creek and bent at the waist, his hand cupped to his head wound to collect the blood. When he had enough, he slung the collected blood downstream, dotting the rocks along the creek's edge before he tied the makeshift bandage around his head, praying it would staunch the blood flow long enough.

Heart pounding, he dunked bloody hands in the creek, then waded out, splashing the bank thoroughly as he came, both to wash away the blood drops and hide his wet footprints as he exited. On the bank, he pulled one last tool from his 'garbage bag of tricks,' his homemade water decontamination system, a half-liter plastic water bottle containing an inch of chlorine bleach. He slipped the bottle in his hip pocket, grabbed the garbage bag and moved away from the bank carefully, fighting an urge to crash through the brush.

Panic barely contained, he entered the thick brush carefully, gently bending tall grass and shrubs aside and stopping to disentangle himself from briers and thorns rather than bulling through, then making the extra effort of rearranging the foliage behind him as he backed into the brush. Every few feet he sprinkled bleach to mask his scent, careful not to leave enough for the humans to smell, but hopefully enough to irritate sensitive canine noses and divert the dogs to the far more interesting scent trail planted downstream. Thirty feet into the brush, he could clearly hear voices with the dogs. He eased to the ground.

He'd barely quieted his breathing when his pursuers arrived, two of the three breathing so hard noise from his own breathing was no longer a concern. The third man, probably the dog handler, wasn't winded at all. Anderson recognized two voices—Cooney and Maloney—it would be those assholes. The dogs' baying changed to confused and plaintive yelps.

"What the hell's wrong? Why are they running around in circles and yelping?" Cooney asked.

"He stopped here," the tracker said. "There must be a lot of scent and it'll take 'em a minute to process it before they pick up the trail. He might have—"

"Pick up the trail?" Maloney scoffed. 'The 'trail' is about twenty feet wide and has water flowing through it. Look! What's that? Get those mutts over there!"

Anderson heard splashing.

"He's tiring and shedding gear. And look, there's blood. He must be hurt," Cooney said. "We got him now! Let's get downstream."

Anderson heard Maloney laugh. "No hurry. I'll radio ahead to Renfro and Herndon and tell 'em to move up US 50 from the trail crossing to this hollow. The road's straight a mile in either direction from the bridge where this creek passes under the road. If they're on the bridge, they'll see him coming down the creek. Even if he gets out of the creek before the bridge, they'll spot him crossing the highway. We'll herd Tremble right to them."

"One thing bothers me, though," Cooney said. "If this is Tremble, where's his kid?"

"Who cares? That's a problem for our more 'specialized' co-workers back at Mount Weather. Our job is just to bring him in." Maloney spoke to the dog handler. "Get those mutts moving. If we keep him looking over his shoulder, he'll pay less attention to where he's going."

Their voices faded downstream. Son of a bitch! That bastard Tremble managed to use him as a diversion after all. He and the kid were laying up somewhere north, hoping Anderson would draw off pursuit—and he was. But why were the dogs following HIS scent? Surely they'd been given something of Tremble's to track?

Then it hit him. As Tremble's guard, he was constantly in and out of their apartment. His scent must be all over that place. And Simon Tremble escaped in Anderson's stolen uniform and his patrol vehicle, so depending on what FEMA gave the tracker, Anderson's scent was well mixed with Tremble's. The dogs were just following the best trail they found. Unfortunately that was his.

He briefly considered giving up, then dismissed the idea. He allowed Tremble to escape not once but twice and 'aided and abetted' the last time, even if it had been at gunpoint. That meant, at best, relocation to some squalid ''fugee' camp, but more likely a bullet in the head and a shallow grave.

The good news was this search wasn't about him. They probably thought Tremble left him in the woods somewhere with a bullet between the eyes. So if he DID get away, he was home free—assuming he kept his mouth shut and maintained a low profile.

Anderson considered his next move. The Appalachian Trail crossing at US 50/17 was now unguarded, at least for the moment, and he was sure his stinky decoy would sail under the highway long before Renfro and Herndon made it to the bridge. When his pursuers reunited at the bridge, they'd likely all conclude he'd just been faster than they figured, and start downstream after him.

He rummaged in his garbage bag for the dog-eared copy of *The AT Guide* he'd found at Bear's Den and flipped pages. The trail followed the ridgetop while the stream diverged at almost a right angle. He smiled as he traced the blue line to the Shenandoah River at Berry's Ferry—five miles west as the crow flew, but four or five times that via the stream's twisting route through rugged terrain. With luck a waterfall or two along the way might slow them down; it would be the better part of a day before they reached the Shenandoah, wondering where the hell he was. He'd bought precious time, now to spend it wisely.

They'd come back to the AT to pick up his trail—there was no help for that. But the roads were undoubtedly thick with FEMA agents, so the AT was still his only real option. He studied the trail guide. They'd watch trail crossings for sure. The pair Maloney so obligingly pulled off the nearest crossing was the primary containment, but Anderson had no doubt there was a second team where I-66 and Virginia 55 paralleled each other to the south at Manassas Gap. Would they set the net wider? Unlikely, for a fugitive on foot. If he could get south of I-66 undetected while they were looking the other way, he had a chance. He prayed the team at I-66 was listening to the radio traffic from the 'chase' now underway and had their guard down.

Another thought occurred to him. The average hiker under pack made twenty miles a day or less in this terrain. But the average hiker didn't have the motivation of a large group of heavily armed people trying to kill him. What if he made thirty or even thirty-five miles today, then rose at first light tomorrow to duplicate the effort? If he could just slip past I-66, chances were they would think he was hiding and focus the search—and the chopper coverage—where he'd BEEN instead of where he was.

Anderson fastened a better head bandage to avoid a blood trail, stuffed his meager belongings back into the garbage bag, and eased out of the brush, careful to leave no trail. He moved into the creek and glanced regretfully downstream—he had to leave the backpack undisturbed, as much as he wanted to reclaim it. Let them keep guessing as to when and how he eluded them.

He limped upstream in the creek, careful of his footing this time, to the point they'd all entered the water. The walk back uphill was easier in some regards, since his bull-like passage and that of his pursuers had blazed a trail. It was much more difficult in other ways, and his left knee throbbed as he walked uphill backward to avoid leaving a tell-tale footprint in the wrong direction.

At the point he'd originally left the AT, he diluted the remaining bleach with the contents of one of his smaller half-liter water bottles. The mixture wasn't strong, but there was more of it, and it would still be overpowering to the dogs' sensitive noses. He sprinkled the mixture behind him as he started south toward the US 50/17 crossing at a limping run, cursing the day he'd met Simon Tremble.

1 MILE OFF THE APPALACHIAN TRAIL
NEAR VIRGINIA-WEST VIRGINIA BORDER

DAY 24, 8:25 A.M.

Congressman Simon Tremble (NC), Speaker of the House of Representatives, looked down at his filthy stolen FEMA uniform and grubby hands and wished not for the first time they had managed to steal some soap during their escape. He sighed. Beggars can't be choosers, and he'd managed to get Keith to at least relative safety. Despite the circumstances, he smiled as he watched his eighteen-year-old move through the woods ahead of him, without the crutch now, but still with a noticeable limp.

"We got one!" cried Keith as he hurried forward in a limping run.

Tremble stifled a rebuke. They were in a densely wooded hollow and hadn't heard a chopper in days. He'd allow the boy what simple pleasures remained in this upside-down world, at least here in the deep woods. It would get a lot tougher when they left their sanctuary.

He followed carefully, head on a swivel and fully 'situationally aware,' employing all the skills learned as a US Army Ranger. He arrived at the snare to find Keith was already skinning the rabbit. His son grinned.

"That's two. We'll eat our fill today."

Tremble nodded. "More than we need. If there's anything in the last two snares, we'll smoke the meat. We won't have time to trap every day when we head south, not if we want to make any progress."

"When ARE we going? I'm sick of hiding."

"When you're ready, which isn't now. You've only been off the crutch two days, and it's not that tough to get around in this hollow, but it's a steep climb almost a mile just to get back up to the main trail."

"But, Dad, that asshole Gleason is lying to everyone and murdering people to cover it up and we're the only ones with proof. We HAVE to do something—"

"And it's BECAUSE we're the only ones with proof we have the responsibility to be cautious; if WE fail, there's no one else. We'll head south when we can, but that ankle's not near healed. We've got food, water, and shelter here and, most importantly, total invisibility. If they spot us when we start moving, we'll have to run for it, and you know what happened last time. If Wiggins and Tex hadn't come along, we'd both be dead. Have you forgotten that, or do you honestly feel you're up to running for it?"

Keith sighed and shook his head.

His father continued. "We have to give ourselves the best shot at success, and that's not starting across rugged terrain with you barely able to walk. Besides, we have to consider supplies."

"All right then," Keith said, "you're always telling me I need to have a plan. What's your plan for getting to Wilmington?"

Tremble nodded. "Now that you're off the crutch, you'll do exercises to strengthen your ankle. At the same time, we set as many snares and deadfalls as possible and dry or smoke jerky for provisions and gather up whatever else we can find—nuts, mushrooms, edible plants, whatever. I figure a week, but we'll reassess as we go along. When I think you're ready, I'll pick a steep slope on the side of the hollow as a dry run, and when you prove you can get up and down it without reinjuring your ankle, we're good to go. How's that sound?"

"Like it will take forever," Keith said.

"Take it or leave it," Tremble said. "I'm not putting you at risk without a fighting chance. Old and crafty trumps young and foolish, I'm afraid."

Keith sighed. "I'll take it." Then he muttered, "Like I have a choice."

Tremble suppressed a smile as his son turned back to the rabbit. *We'll all have to relearn old skills to survive*, thought Tremble as Keith finished and dropped the rabbit into the plastic garbage bag.

"Ready?" Keith asked, and Tremble nodded.

They walked through the woods, content in each other's company until Keith broke the silence.

"You think Tex and Wiggins will make it, Dad?"

"I hope so, son. I sure hope so."

SOUTH OF HARPERS FERRY, WEST VIRGINIA
INTERSECTION OF APPALACHIAN TRAIL AND CHESTNUT HILL ROAD

ONE DAY EARLIER
DAY 23, 9:35 A.M.

"You sure about this, Tex?" Bill Wiggins stared at the treeless gap where Chestnut Hill Road slashed through the woods in front of them. "I feel exposed anytime we come out of the trees now."

"So do I, but this is the best bet according to Levi's map," said Shyla 'Tex' Texeira. "It's less than a mile to a utility right-of-way that runs due east to US 340 and the bridge over the Potomac. Both this road and the right-of-way run through thick woods. We'll just walk the tree line and duck into cover if we hear anyone coming."

"How far before we get back on the AT?"

"Just on the other side of the bridge."

Wiggins sighed. "I'm not looking forward to that friggin' crossing."

Tex shrugged. "It's the best option. If we stay on the AT, we have to cross the Shenandoah bridge into Harpers Ferry and then cross the Potomac on the pedestrian walkway of the railroad bridge. It's ten miles longer and two bridges instead of one.

"Besides," she continued, "if those FEMA assholes are watching the southern approach from the AT, that's where they'll be looking. This way, if we're stopped on the eastern bridge, we say we're coming up 671. There's no way to connect us with the Trembles, and crossing via the eastern bridge fits our cover story. But no one walking north up 671 would go through Harpers Ferry unless that was their destination. Who the hell walks miles out of their way for no reason?"

"I know, I know. I'd just like to avoid bridges altogether."

Tex shook her head. "There are rapids and a lot of rocks, so even if we could find a boat, we might end up miles downstream. Or worse."

Wiggins sighed. "Yeah, I get that. Just wishful thinking. How are your feet?"

"They've been better, but I'll survive."

"When we get across this bridge, we need to find a secluded place to hole up and scout around the outskirts of Harpers Ferry to find you some better boots. You can't go much farther in those."

Tex nodded and looked up at the sky. "Then we need to get moving. It's two hours to the bridge, and we need to be across and well off the main roads before nightfall."

Wiggins nodded and started into the clearing.

SANDY HOOK BRIDGE—US 340
THREE MILES EAST OF HARPERS FERRY, WEST VIRGINIA
SOUTH BANK OF POTOMAC RIVER

SAME DAY, 11:55 A.M.

They crouched in the woods beside the highway and studied the bridge. "Not a soul moving," Tex said.

Wiggins nodded. "I'm not liking this. This is a main road; I expected at least local traffic. I was actually hoping we could mix in so we didn't stand out."

"I don't like it either," Tex said, "but maybe it's like Front Royal. Could be the locals banded together and barricaded the main roads further out. Loudoun Heights is due south, and there are other farming communities north of the river. Maybe they set up roadblocks to keep from being overrun? They wouldn't have blocked the AT, so we bypassed them."

"Or maybe those FEMA assholes did the same thing to make it easier to spot northbound AT traffic."

Tex shrugged. "Even if they did, what choice do we have? Besides, there are tons of secondary roads, so even with barricades, there'll be other people who make it this far. We're just two more lost souls trying to get home. They have no reason to detain us."

"We're armed. How will that go down?"

"How would I know?" Tex replied, temper flaring. "We just have to DO IT, all right? It's either that or turn back, and I'm going to get to my folks or die trying."

Silence grew between them until Tex spoke again.

"Look, I'm sorry I snapped, but my feet are killing me, and I don't see an option. If you do, I'm all ears."

Wiggins shook his head. "No, you're right. This is it. We'll play the hand we've been dealt." He gave her a nervous smile. "Let's cross the Potomac, partner."

Tex nodded at the Henry survival rifle. "Maybe you should break that down and stow it and move your Sig to the small of your back under your shirttail like my Glock. No point in showing our hand."

"Good point," Wiggins said as he shrugged off his pack and began to disassemble the little rifle. A minute later it was all stowed in the hollow plastic stock and he slipped it in his pack. He jammed the Sig into his belt at the small of his back and dropped his shirttail over it. He shouldered his pack and nodded at Tex, and they started across the weed-choked verge toward the highway.

"This is spooky as hell," Wiggins said as they stepped onto the long bridge.

"Tell me about it." Tex unconsciously moved closer.

"Uh, maybe we should separate," Wiggins said. "You know, just so they can't get us at the same time."

Tex grinned. "You want to run a zigzag pattern too? Anything else to make us look suspicious?"

Wiggins flushed. "Okay, dumb idea," he said, but they drifted a few feet farther apart anyway.

They walked in tense silence, eyes watering in the bright noonday sun reflecting off the water, and sweating profusely in the heat radiating from the hard pavement underfoot. It was an unwelcome change from the soft paths and comforting shade of the deep woods.

"I'll be glad to get back in the woods," Tex said, halfway across. "I feel like a bug waiting for a flyswatter."

"More like bugs on a friggin' griddle—"

He was interrupted by squealing tires as a black SUV swerved onto the bridge and roared toward them.

"FEMA!" Wiggins looked over his shoulder longingly at the sanctuary of the distant tree-lined south bank. "What are we gonna do?"

"Nod and smile a lot," Tex said out of the side of her mouth. The car swerved to a halt, blocking the bridge a hundred feet ahead of them. Two FEMA cops got out, male and female; both had their guns drawn but pointed down.

"Stop and place both hands on the top of your heads, NOW!" the man shouted.

"Doesn't look promising," Wiggins whispered as they complied.

"Walk forward slowly. Don't make any sudden moves," the man ordered.

They complied and he halted them twenty feet away. Both cops studied their faces as the man did the talking.

"Who are you and what's your business?" he asked.

"My name's Bill Wiggins, and this is Shyla Texeira. We're seamen who got stuck down south, trying to make it home to our families. We had a car until we ran out of gas. We've been afoot ever since."

"How'd you get past the south roadblock?"

Wiggins shrugged. "Didn't see it, but that's not surprising. There are bad people on the road, and we've been staying to the fields and woods as much as possible. We're only on the road now to get across the river."

The story seemed to be working, on the man anyway. His body language relaxed a bit and his gun moved a fraction lower. The woman was more wary. Tex saw her eyes narrow and followed the woman's gaze to Wiggin's boots. The boots he'd taken off the FEMA cop he'd killed to save the Trembles. Boots exactly like the two FEMA cops were wearing.

"FREEZE!" the woman yelled as she focused on Wiggins and raised her sidearm, but Tex's right hand was already going to the small of her back.

At over six feet and solidly built, Wiggins was the obvious threat, but appearances were deceiving. Tex aimed for center mass, but her shot went high and hit the woman in the throat. Too late, the man turned as Tex unloaded on him, hitting him twice center mass and multiple times in the legs. It was over in seconds, and Wiggins ran forward to kick the guns away from the fallen cops.

"Jesus, Tex! I think—"

He turned to find her trembling, staring at the female cop. The woman was face up, blood gushing from her throat as she made strangling sounds like a fish dying on a dock. Tex bent and vomited on the road.

The woman was beyond help, so Wiggins turned to the barely conscious man lying in a rapidly expanding pool of blood. A concealed vest caught Tex's rounds center mass, but from the blood pool, a round to his lower body struck a major artery. Wiggins knelt, fumbling with the man's belt. He tugged it free to make a tourniquet and twisted it tight, managing to slow but not stop the bleeding. He grabbed the man's hand and put it on the twisted belt.

"Hold this and you might have a chance. Do you understand?"

The cop nodded, unable to speak. Wiggins rose to find Tex still staring at the woman, now clearly dead.

"Tex! We have to go! Get in the car and start looking through your maps for a way out of here."

"I... I... killed cops—"

"Who would have killed us. Think about it later. We have to go!" Wiggins led her to the SUV and helped her out of her pack. He unzipped it and pulled the packet of maps out then tossed her pack in the backseat before shrugging out of his own pack and tossing it in behind hers.

"I'm okay. Give me the maps," Tex said as he slammed the back door.

He handed her the maps and she got in the passenger seat.

"Bill, the keys aren't here," Tex said.

"All right, I'll check the cops. You just concentrate on the maps."

The keys were in the dead woman's pocket. As an afterthought, he took the woman's boots and tossed them in the back of the SUV. He got behind the wheel to find Tex focused on *The AT Guide* and a local map.

"There are sure to be roadblocks on the main roads."

Wiggins nodded. "We can't be caught in this thing anyway. If we break contact, we'll have a shot at playing innocent if they catch us. There are two five-gallon gas cans in the back; let's find an empty car, gas it up, and get off road. With any luck we can find a four-wheel drive. Try to find us a nice secluded logging road that might keep us near the AT."

Tex nodded as Wiggins swung the car north and accelerated off the bridge. He floored it, and the trees flashed by on either side.

"How long do you think we have before someone comes looking?" asked Tex, eyes still on the map.

Wiggins shrugged. "Who knows? A half hour maybe?"

The radio squawked, "Unit 17, what is status of reported contact? Request immediate SITREP. Over."

"Or not," Tex said. "Should we try to fake it?"

Wiggins shook his head. "They didn't say anything about us moving, so either they aren't tracking this thing, or all the GPS birds are finally down. If we answer and they don't buy it, we're blown, but no response might just be a comms problem. That might buy us a few minutes of indecision. But there will be cars or a chopper coming our way soon, maybe both."

"So what's the plan?"

"We'll stick out like a sore thumb to a chopper no matter which way we run, so we have to ditch this thing and fast. Find a place to bury this beast in the woods." He sighed. "It was nice while it lasted, but we're afoot again."

Tex nodded and turned back to the map.

"Slow down," she said.

"SLOW DOWN? Are you serious? We have to get a little farther than this before we ditch—"

"Just slow down! I've got an idea, but I need a minute and I don't want to overshoot our turn," Tex said, turning back to the map.

Wiggins slowed and glanced over with a concerned look. "I sure hope you know what you're—"

"There! Right on Keep Tryst Road ahead."

Tires squealed as Wiggins powered the SUV around a long sweeping curve onto Keep Tryst Road and started to accelerate.

"SLOW DOWN," Tex said, "and get ready to turn onto Sandy Hook Road. It's a very sharp right just ahead."

Wiggins nodded and skidded around the turn onto Sandy Hook Road.

"Tex, this is taking us back—"

"Trust me. Watch for a dirt road to the left."

Wiggins' concern grew as they powered down the narrow road southwest, then swung due west and he saw US 340, the highway they'd just exited, loom above them in the near distance.

"WHERE THE HELL ARE YOU TAKING US, TEX?"

"There," she said, pointing to the left, "turn there. And put this sucker in low."

"WHERE?" Wiggins demanded; then he saw it, a dirt track through the trees. He braked hard to make the turn and dropped the SUV in low gear. He powered down the narrow track, dodging trees and mowing down scattered saplings as thick as his finger until they broke out of the trees and he slammed to a stop before a steep gravel-covered embankment rising across their path.

"What the hell—"

"Get us up on the railroad tracks," Tex said.

"What? Which way?"

"Either. We won't be there long," she said.

Wiggins cursed and started up the embankment at an angle, his heart in his mouth as the tires slipped in the loose gravel and the SUV rocked on its suspension, threatening to roll at any moment. He gained the top and they bounced due east along the tracks; Tex focused on the tree line down the embankment to their right.

"When do we get off this damn thing?" Wiggins asked, fighting the wheel, his speech unsteady as the vehicle slammed across the track ties at twenty miles an hour. "We may blow a tire any minute at this rate."

"As soon as I see a break in those trees," Tex replied, eyes glued on the tree line. "THERE!"

Wiggins whipped the wheel to the right, bouncing down the steep embankment toward a barely visible gap.

They lost the right-side mirror going in, and Wiggins was forced to a crawl, dodging larger trees and bulling his way over and through smaller saplings and brush.

"I give up," Wiggins said through clenched teeth as he held the wheel in a white-knuckled grip. "Where are you taking us?"

"In about fifty yards, we'll come to the old towpath for the Chesapeake and Ohio Canal, which runs concurrent with the AT here. Turn right and run due west along the river back to the bridge; then we'll hide in this same strip of woods that runs under the bridge. I figure the last place they'll look is the place we ran from. The woods should shield us from view, and the bridge will hide us from choppers. We don't have a chance of outrunning them, so we have to outsmart them."

They broke out of the trees as she finished, and a smile spread across Wiggins' face as he whipped the battered car right on to the towpath. "I'll be damned! Pretty smart, Tex."

She rolled down her window. "Save your admiration and step on it. I hear a chopper."

The chopper got louder as they raced for the bridge, but it was north of them, invisible below the tree line. They nosed their way into the wooded strip beneath the bridge with just seconds to spare. They heard the chopper circling as they cut brush and piled it around and on top of the SUV; it landed just as they crawled into their new hide.

"And now we wait," Wiggins said.

Tex nodded. "And hope like hell no one puts two and two together. We're sitting ducks if they figure this out."

CHAPTER TWO

DAY 24, 10:15 A.M.

The Honorable Theodore M. Gleason, President of the United States of America, glared at the two men seated across the desk, a study in contrast. One was balding and of late middle age, his receding chin clean-shaved. He wore an obviously expensive suit and sported a Mont Blanc pen in the pocket of his freshly pressed snow white shirt. A gold Rolex peeked from beneath the edge of a monogrammed sleeve bearing the initials OAC. Even given the man's current unease, he wore the uniform of the Washington power broker naturally, despite, or perhaps because of, the fact the world was going to Hell. But even wearing the external trappings of wealth and power, Secretary of Homeland Security Oliver Armstrong Crawford, or 'Ollie' to those who pretended to be his friends, was visibly uncomfortable. He was doing all he could to keep from squirming under the President's gaze.

The second man was the polar opposite. In his late thirties and the picture of composure, he wore the black uniform of the newly formed FEMA Special Reaction Force, with a tape above his breast pocket bearing the name RORKE, and a single star on each shoulder. His sandy hair was neatly trimmed, as was his goatee, and an otherwise handsome face was marred by a thin, ropelike welt of scar tissue emanating from the corner of his eye and running down his left cheek. In an odd way it seemed to enhance rather than detract from his appearance, and he looked for all the world like a movie version of a pirate or perhaps a Viking. Brigadier General Rorke returned Gleason's gaze evenly and without the slightest indication of concern.

Gleason focused his wrath where it was having the most impact. His voice was calm, but quiet menace dripped from every syllable.

"Four days, Ollie? Tremble gave you the slip four days ago and you're just now getting around to telling me?"

Crawford shifted uncomfortably in his chair. "Actually, Mr. President, it was a single fugitive, so it's unclear if it was really Tremble. I was attempting to ascertain—"

"Cut the crap, Ollie! Who the hell do you think you're talking to, some brain-dead group of congressmen on a fact-finding mission? The frigging dogs were following Tremble's scent, weren't they? The fact is, Tremble managed to give you the slip AGAIN, and you've been stalling for time trying to pick up his trail. You're in here now hat in hand because you've failed and you can't stall any longer. Tell me I'm wrong."

"We know which way he's headed, Mr. President, and we have a new strategy. it's only a matter of time before—"

Gleason pounded his fist on the desk. "ENOUGH BULLSHIT! Find the bastard. And if you can't pinpoint him, I want you sweeping up anyone moving in those woods along his path. Get him one way or another. Is that clear?"

"Yes, Mr. President," Crawford said.

"If I may, sir." Rorke spoke for the first time. "It's not quite as bad as it may seem. To date we've been pursuing Tremble and attempting to block his path and 'drive him into a net' so to speak. However, he's no fool and obviously can anticipate where we might have barriers and figure out a way to bypass them. In response, we've just implemented a two-prong strategy, keeping pressure up on his rear while simultaneously starting well south and sending search teams north up every even remotely viable route. Rather than stationary barriers and pursuit, he now faces active pursuit closing from all directions and must react to our actions rather than vice versa. As the Secretary said, it's only a matter of time, Mr. President."

Gleason stared at him a moment. "How far south?"

"Tremble is an ex-Ranger and stays in good shape," Rorke said, "but for all that, he's still in his fifties. He can't have much in the way of supplies either, so he's likely protein deprived. I doubt he can maintain twenty miles a day in that terrain at the outside, but we figured twenty-five to be on the safe side. This morning we started a unit north from Loft Mountain Campground, which is a hundred miles south of our last sighting. We're quite sure we're in front of him. We also put units in by chopper to start north on the few side trails in the area. We'll get him, Mr. President. You can count on it."

Gleason nodded, mollified. "Sounds sensible." He turned his gaze to Crawford. "And about damn time. Why didn't you think of that, Ollie?"

"With respect, Mr. President," Rorke lied, "this was Secretary Crawford's idea. He just hadn't had an... opportunity to inform you."

Crawford shot Rorke a grateful look and nodded.

Gleason nodded again. "All right, but catch the bastard. He's a loose end we can't afford, especially with this homegrown alternative to the Emergency Broadcast System. Now what are you doing to contain these damned HAMs? The information they're sharing about our FEMA operations is a direct contradiction to what we're putting out on the EBS."

"We got the HAM license database from the FCC, and General Rorke is preparing a coordinated operation to take all the operators and their families into custody and to destroy all of the equipment," Crawford said. "Our main concern is non-licensed operators, so we're waiting a few days to try to locate as many as possible via triangulation. Almost everyone is transmitting in the clear now, but as soon as we crack down, word will spread and any we miss will likely start evasive techniques. The more effective we can make the first raid, the more likely we are to stamp this out quickly."

"Okay, but don't take too long. And have your public affairs people gin up some sort of misinformation to cast doubt on the HAM operators. Say they're foreign infiltrators trying to spread discord and soften us up for an invasion at our time of weakness or something like that." Gleason paused. "Why didn't I think of that before? Let's run with that 'foreign invasion' thing. I can see all sorts of applications beyond smearing the HAMs."

"But, Mr. President," Crawford said, "we've already broadcast the situation is global and told people there wasn't an external threat. It was part of our strategy to keep the public calm. We can't—"

"We can do any frigging thing we want, Ollie, supposing you do your job and get those HAMs neutralized. We control the only means of mass communication and we'll employ it in the public good. See that it happens. Anything else?"

"Ahhh… there is one other thing, Mr. President. I'm having a problem out west. The Vice President inserted himself in the loop and countermanded some of my orders to the military there." Crawford paused. "I even have intelligence he's planning on leaving Cheyenne Mountain and returning to his home in Sacramento to, in his words, 'oversee recovery efforts.' I just heard about it this morning."

"That friggin' moron. He wouldn't even BE veep if I hadn't needed the support of all his moonbeam and granola Hollywood asshole buddies. When is this happening?" Gleason demanded.

"According to my sources, within the next few days," Crawford said. "Do you want me to—"

"I'll handle it," Gleason said, his tone leaving no doubt the topic was closed. "Now if that's all, you boys have work to do, so…"

"Yes, Mr. President," Crawford said. Rorke followed his lead and both men rose.

"And, General Rorke," Gleason added, stopping Rorke before he turned for the door.

"Yes, Mr. President?"

"I bumped you up on Crawford's suggestion, because you're one of the bright spots to date in his little shit show. A month ago you were a captain and now you're wearing a star. I don't think I need to remind you that sort of meteoric rise is unprecedented, so don't disappoint."

"It's appreciated, Mr. President," Rorke said, "but with respect, it's not totally unprecedented. Captain George Armstrong Custer was promoted directly from captain to brigadier general of the volunteers on the eve of the Battle of Gettysburg. He was only twenty-three at the time."

"I stand corrected, 'General,' but bear in mind what happened to him. Just don't start believing your own bullshit."

FEMA
EMERGENCY OPERATIONS CENTER
MOUNT WEATHER
NEAR BLUEMONT, VIRGINIA

SAME DAY, 2:20 P.M.

Ollie Crawford sat on his office sofa and sipped his ever-present bottle of water. He desperately wanted a drink, but knew the end of that road. He owed twenty years of sobriety solely to force of will. No twelve-step programs and, 'Hi, I'm Ollie and I'm an alcoholic,' for him. Power was his drug of choice now, and he mainlined it. The rush was almost sexual—better than sex, actually. Despite having to eat Gleason's crap, being the second most powerful man in the country was worth it—and he might not always be second.

He was relieved to be away from Camp David and back in his own luxurious office at Mount Weather, where he was the unquestioned king. He glanced at Rorke sitting across from him. He regretted his underling had witnessed this morning's humiliation, but it couldn't be helped. Gleason had insisted on a face-to-face with his newest 'general.'

"You did well," Crawford said to Rorke. "I didn't need your intercession. POTUS explodes at regular intervals, a bit like Old Faithful. But like Old Faithful, he can be anticipated and thus managed. He would have calmed down and listened eventually. However, I appreciate your effort, especially passing up credit for the strategy change. I value loyalty."

Rorke shrugged. "I succeed when you succeed. I figure it's my job to make the boss look good. But I thought you were going to bring up Harpers Ferry?"

Crawford snorted. "Yeah, well, given how spun up he got over Tremble, I didn't think an admission we also had a perimeter breach northbound was particularly relevant, especially since it appears unrelated. Did we get any more out of the wounded agent?"

Rorke shook his head. "I got a message a few minutes ago. He died without regaining consciousness. All he said to the guys on the chopper before he lost consciousness was something garbled about a woman shooter and shoes. The dead female agent was missing hers, so that fits. Nothing even remotely ties it to the Trembles."

"All right," Crawford said, "given the strong contact southbound, I think maintaining the northbound perimeter is a waste of manpower. Let's pull everyone off there and use them southbound."

"I'll see to it," Rorke said. "And speaking of manpower, we're still stretched. Any chance of more recruits from regular forces?"

Crawford shook his head. "I downplayed it with POTUS, but in truth those friggin' HAMs are having a bigger impact than I admitted. Some of your SRF deserters have spread the word about our ops, and the HAMs picked it up. The main source seems to be that group in Wilmington, but wherever it's coming from, word is reaching the regular forces, especially the fact that a 'temporary' transfer to SRF is actually a one-way trip. We haven't picked up a recruit in the last week."

Rorke sighed. "All right. I'll accelerate the timetable and put more teams on triangulation. We'll spot as many HAMs as we can and sweep up all we can identify within the next week, but that still leaves this Wilmington bunch and scattered groups like them. They have radios too, and they're forted up well. It's not like we can just waltz in and take over, at least without a fight."

Crawford was about to take a drink and he stared at Rorke over his water bottle. "Isn't that the point of the Special Reaction Force?"

Rorke shook his head. "With all due respect, sir, seriously? These mercenaries are occupation and intimidation troops. They're okay for attacks on soft targets or limited hit-and-run firefights, but I haven't had time to turn them into a fighting force. Hitting an enemy entrenched in a prepared defensive position with crew-served weapons is a nonstarter. If word spreads we're even considering that, at least half these guys will melt into the landscape."

"Your confidence in your troops is inspiring, General, but I expected a bit more of a can-do attitude," Crawford said, menace creeping into his voice.

Rorke shrugged. "I've been handling trash like this since I became a contractor, and it never pays to deceive yourself about the capabilities of your forces. It's far better to recognize their limitations and plan around them."

"So what's your plan?" Crawford asked. "We've been picking the low-hanging fruit and consolidating our position ever since the blackout, but you know the Brunswick Nuclear Plant is next on our short list. We can't afford to have this 'Fort Box' thumbing their nose at us just miles away, especially if they're linking up with other uncontrolled groups—defiance is contagious. Besides, they're sitting on a huge load of supplies and starting to waste them on the refugee population. We have to get a handle on this if we're ever going to get the lights back on."

Rorke stroked his goatee absently. "And there's absolutely no chance the regular military will take them out for us?"

Crawford shook his head. "Only as a last resort. I convinced POTUS to put the military under my command by executive order, but my interactions with the command structure so far haven't been exactly cordial. Frankly, I view them more as a potential threat than an asset. A growing threat actually, since there are more of them arriving from overseas daily. They're a wild card and I'd like to keep them out of the game as long as possible."

"Just how do you plan to do that?"

"By not poking the bear, at least for now," Crawford said. "POTUS's order and ingrained respect for civilian command authority will contain them a while. If we maintain isolation and don't force a choice between harming civilians or disobeying orders, they'll stay in line and execute whatever support tasks we assign. If we force a choice, we might not like the one they make."

"And longer term?"

Crawford sighed. "A work in progress, I'm afraid. Any thoughts?"

Rorke stared into space and lapsed into a long silence.

"Controlled decay," Rorke said at last, looking back at Crawford.

"What the hell do you mean by that?" Crawford asked.

"I mean the regular military is going to fall apart, that's inevitable. We can benefit if we manage the process."

Crawford looked skeptical. "Go on."

"Look, by orders they're concentrating at major bases with families and dependents. They have what, maybe another two months of resources?"

"If that," Crawford confirmed.

"And ships are arriving from overseas with MORE military and dependents, MORE government employees and families, and any expats who made it to foreign departure ports. What's going to happen to them? Is the military going to force them into the countryside at bayonet point?"

"Of course not," Crawford said, "they'll take them in…"

Rorke smiled. "That's right. They'll take them in, further straining resources. Our friends in uniform are going to have their own little private humanitarian aid crisis. They'll be well distracted."

"So. How does that help us?"

"Because you, kindhearted guy that you are, order them to focus on that humanitarian mission while we defang them. We'll sacrifice some of the provisions we strip out of the countryside to keeping them fed, and in return we gradually but steadily draw down their ammunition stocks. Not completely, mind you, but enough so they're no longer a threat. It will seem like a fair trade, since the SRF is now on the pointy end of the spear and needs ammo to keep order. I'm betting they'll just focus on their own problems and be glad not to have to deal with the civilians as a whole."

Crawford nodded. "I like it, Rorke."

Rorke's smile widened. "And when they're no longer a threat, we cut off the food. Not openly, mind you, we just never get around to delivering. Their operations will fall apart and start leaking people, and we'll scoop up those useful to us. Hunger is a great recruitment tool; you'd be amazed how quickly it erases moral qualms. I used it all the time in Africa."

Crawford shot Rorke an appraising look. "Why do I think you didn't just think of that?"

Rorke grinned and put his briefcase on the coffee table. He extracted a map of the Wilmington area and spread it before Crawford, pointing to a spot near the mouth of the Cape Fear River.

"Because I didn't, at least not the part about the ammunition," Rorke said. "I've been worried about ammo for a while. Until we can restore manufacturing, the only stocks available are those presently in hand or in storage, and the largest stocks in the country are right here."

Crawford followed Rorke's finger and nodded. "The Military Ocean Terminal at Sunny Point. Okay, that's not a secret, but so what? It's an Army facility, we'll just draw it down too."

"That's just it, I doubt we need to, and even if we did, we're talking a LOT of ammunition, much more than we'd be able to transport or store elsewhere. And the terminal is RUN by the Army, but there are less than half a dozen regular Army personnel in supervisory positions; everyone else, including security, is a civilian contractor. The place is run much more like a civilian terminal than a military installation, and I'm betting they used regular commercial means like phone and the Internet for comms, which means they're cut off. I suspect none of the civilians showed up for work, and any of the Army guys who tried have likely given up and melted away by now. You just give the order transferring the terminal to SRF command, and we'll control well over half the military ammo left in the country, maybe more. When we draw down the stocks elsewhere, we should have a lock on the remaining ammunition supply."

Crawford scowled. "Why didn't you say something earlier? It's probably been looted—"

Rorke was shaking his head. "Not a problem, Mr. Secretary, at least not a major one. It would probably take a thousand men with a hundred pickups a month to make a dent in this stockpile, even working full time and presuming they had gasoline for the trucks. The majority of it has to still be there, just because there's too much of it to move."

Crawford nodded. "All right. I'll issue the order. Get men there ASAP."

"I'm already on it," Rorke said. "The terminal is close to the Brunswick Nuclear Plant and I have a force going there in the morning. I'd anticipated your approval and have an advance team ready to deploy from there into the Military Ocean Terminal at the same time. We just need a small force to establish security and patrol the perimeter."

"Good," Crawford said, "but this puts us back where we started. We can't have opposition sitting a stone's throw from TWO key assets. We HAVE to neutralize those assholes in Wilmington. They're too close for comfort and they're getting stronger by the day."

"I've been thinking about that too. Maybe it's time to steal a page from the Special Forces playbook and utilize 'indigenous forces.'"

UNITED BLOOD NATIONS HQ
(FORMERLY NEW HANOVER COUNTY
DEPARTMENT OF SOCIAL SERVICES)
1650 GREENFIELD STREET
WILMINGTON, NORTH CAROLINA

DAY 26, 2:35 P.M.

Kwintell Banks, first superior of the SMM (Sex, Money, Murder) 'set' of the United Blood Nation, glared down the long conference table at Darren Mosley, his Minister of Information.

"And y'all just stood by and let one of these punk-ass soldier boys off a UBN brother and disrespect us without firin' a shot back, is that what I'm hearin'?" Banks demanded. "When did this happen, and how come I'm just hearin' 'bout it?"

Mosley shifted uncomfortably in his seat. "Late yesterday, but straight up, Kwintell, nobody could do nothin'. They was in one o' them tank things with a machine gun and—"

"How many soldiers were there?"

"I… I don't know. Four, maybe five, I guess. But the machine gun—"

"And how many UBN soldiers watched this? One? Two? Twenty?"

"I… I don't know for sure." Mosley slumped further in his chair in a posture of defeat. "A lot, I guess."

"So let's just guess and say a dozen," Banks said. "A dozen UBN soldiers stood by with their fingers up they asses, watching a brother get capped like they was being schooled." He turned his gaze to Keyshaun Jackson. "And this was some of your crew? How'd this happen? I thought I told y'all to just stay away from the soldier boys?"

"Straight up, Kwintell, wasn't nothin' they could do. We got intel some nigga was holdin' food in his crib, so we went to check it out and found him sittin' on a bunch of stuff. He tried to fight back, so they beat him down and held him so he could watch the boys having a little fun with his shorty in the front yard—you know, to make an example so the whole hood could see. Then the soldier boys showed up, sudden like. They held that big machine gun on the whole crew; then one of the soldiers got out the tank thing and capped the brother bangin' the shorty. Then they took the tom and his shorty off in the tank. I expect they took 'em to that camp they set up over by the golf course."

"What the hell they doin' in the hood?" Banks asked. "They been leavin' us alone long as we leave them alone."

"This was right off one of the streets they use to go back and forth to the new camp," Keyshaun said. "I figure they must have heard the ho screamin' and come to look."

Banks shook his head. "This ain't good. We can't have our brothers bein' disrespected. Else we gonna start having all sorts of shit."

"It… it's only happened once," Mosley ventured, "so I don't think—"

"You ain't supposed to think. I be doin' the thinkin' around here," Banks said. "But if you wanna think, think about this. First we had this nigga holdin' out food, and this ain't the first time. Ever since those soldier boys come out of their little box fort on the river and set up that feedin' station, we been seein' more disrespect. This the way it starts. We on top now and control most of the city and we spreadin' into the farms. I figured long as the soldier boys stayed near the river, that's cool. But they spreadin' out too, and that means trouble. First, we lost the crew we sent out with that fool Single-tary and the soldiers set up that machine-gun base on the river. Didn't mat-ter much 'cause we got the rest of the countryside, so we can let 'em have the river for now. But now they got this feedin' station with a little fort in it. It won't be long before the little fort is a bigger fort. Then they likely gonna set up ANOTHER feedin' station that turns into ANOTHER fort that pushes us out of more territory." Banks shook his head. "This can't stand. We gotta do something."

"But, Kwintell," Keyshaun protested, "they got—"

"SHUT UP, FOOL! I'm tired of all this 'they got this' and 'they got that' bullshit, you hear! They got OUR TERRITORY is what they got. Now be quiet, all of you. I gotta think about this a minute—"

He was interrupted by a knock on the door, followed by the squeak of neglected hinges as the door opened and one of his soldiers stuck his head in.

"Sorry, Kwintell, but there's some creepy-ass cracker in the parking lot with a white flag sayin' he want to talk to you."

"Tell him to make an appointment," Banks snarled.

"Ah, Desmond tol' me to tell you he think you wanna see this guy. He a general or somethin' like dat."

***

Banks stood in the doorway of his building and squinted out across the sunbaked parking lot at a sight he could scarcely credit. In the middle of the lot stood an armored Humvee with a white flag flying from a whip radio antenna. A machine gun graced a turret manned by a large man in a black uniform with full body armor. There were five other similarly clad and armored men, one visible through the windshield in the driver's seat and one standing at each corner of the vehicle, holding M4 assault rifles pointed down but obviously ready to use at a moment's notice. All six of the armored soldiers were African-American, but despite that, they eyed the mob of armed gangbangers surrounding them warily, obviously ready to engage at a moment's notice.

But Banks focused on the last man clad in the same black uniform but without a weapon, armor or helmet, leaning back nonchalantly against the front of the vehicle with his arms crossed over his chest and his legs crossed at the ankles. He had thick sandy hair and a matching goatee, the stub of a cigar clamped in his teeth, and an air of unconcern completely at odds with the tense posture of his escort. When he saw Banks, he flicked the cigar stub away and smiled, then uncrossed his ankles and stood, obviously intent on stepping away from the vehicle. Beside him, one of his men voiced a protest, but the leader motioned his underling to silence and strode purposefully toward Banks. He halved the distance between them, then stood still and erect, looking at Banks with an expectant smile.

Despite being on home ground, a chill ran down Bank's spine. *That cracker look like a pirate*, he thought, *and a mean one at that*. He really, really didn't want to walk across the parking lot, but knew failing to do so would lead to an irreparable loss of face. If you want to lead the badasses, you gotta be a badass, and a badass don't back down from no creepy-ass cracker, pirate or not. Banks assumed his most menacing look and swaggered across to meet the pirate, feigning a confidence he in no way felt.

The pirate's smile widened as Banks approached and stopped three feet away. "Mr. Banks, I presume?" the man asked, in a voice loud enough to be heard by the mob of gangbangers, who were keeping their distance.

"Who wanna know, fool?"

"General Quentin Rorke, FEMA Special Reaction Force, at your service."

"You one of them fools from the box fort?" Banks demanded loudly, determined not to be cowed before his followers.

The pirate's smile never wavered, but the look in his eyes made Banks' blood run cold.

"No, Mr. Banks," he said, his voice still carrying, "I'm not from Wilmington. However, I did come to discuss the operation there, and I believe we may have a common interest." He lost his smile and lowered his voice so only Banks could hear. "And now you've established your courage for the benefit of your troops, but before you go further than I'm prepared to tolerate, you should understand that there are three snipers with fifty-caliber Barrett sniper rifles aimed at your chest as we speak."

Banks glanced up at the surrounding buildings, but hid his terror. He lowered his voice to match Rorke's. "Anybody can say that, fool. You bluffin'."

"Be so kind as to glance down at your chest, Mr. Banks," Rorke said before touching his throat to activate a microphone. "Light him up. One second."

Banks struggled to keep his composure as three red dots flashed briefly on his chest.

"Now, Mr. Banks, we have business to discuss. I came to you in this manner as a show of respect so you didn't lose the respect of your men. However, I advise you once again not to try my patience. I'm going to summon a chopper and you and I are going for a little ride. You will come voluntarily and tell your followers you'll return shortly. You will also inform them to take no action against my men in the Humvee as they withdraw. Is that clear?"

"I ain't comin' with you, foo... Rorke. What if you just cap my ass?"

"If I wanted to 'cap your ass,' as you put it, I could have done so at any time in the past." Rorke paused for emphasis. "OR the future. As proof, I ask you to consider just how easily I got three trained snipers focused on your chest. I can take you out any time I please, Banks, but I don't really want to. You see, we can help each other. Now, tell your subordinates a chopper is inbound and you're coming with me."

"And if I don't?"

Rorke shrugged. "Then fifty-caliber rounds will shred you into hamburger, my man on the machine gun will open up on your surprised and disoriented followers while the rest of us get back to the safety of the Humvee, and chopper gunships will be over us in a heartbeat to shred anyone else who even remotely looks like one of your people. You die; we leave. Any more questions?"

Bank's mouth went dry. He said nothing for a long moment, then nodded, and Rorke touched his throat again to order in the chopper.

"Keyshaun," Banks yelled over his shoulder, "a chopper comin' in, and me and the general here gonna take a little ride. You let the rest of these soldier boys here leave when they want. You got dat?"

"But, Kwintell, you need security—"

"DO IT!" Banks yelled, the thump of chopper blades already growing in the distance.

***

Ten minutes later, Banks was aloft, apprehension over his abduction completely overcome by the novelty of his first ever ride in a helicopter. They circled above the Wilmington Container Terminal at a respectful distance, and Banks stared down at a beehive of activity, movement on the ground broken here and there as the tiny ant-like figures stopped to stare and point upward.

"There's a lot more of them than I thought," Banks said into his helmet microphone.

"More every day," came Rorke's reply in his ear. "Our intel is they're recruiting people with needed skills out of the refugee population."

"So why you wanna be helpin' us?" Banks asked as he looked over at Rorke. "Look like they doin' the same thing FEMA supposed to be doing, right?"

Rorke smiled. "There's an old saying, Mr. Banks. The enemy of my enemy is my friend. Or to speak in the vernacular, let's just say the folks in 'Fort Box,' as they call it, are getting a bit too 'uppity.'"

Banks had no idea what the hell 'vernacular' was, but he recognized a gang war when he saw one. "So why you need us?" he asked. "You got machine guns and Humvees. You even got choppers. Why not just cap the mofos yourself?"

"Because I'd prefer not to be seen as the force that wipes them out. They're in contact with other groups, and if it becomes known FEMA took action against them, it will be more difficult to deal with the others later."

"So lemme get this straight. You gonna give us Humvees and machine guns and stuff, so long as we finish these soldier boys off?"

Rorke laughed. "Not quite. I'm not fool enough to release control of weapons you might later decide to use against me, nor do I intend to provide vehicles which can be traced back to FEMA. I'm going to LOAN you certain weapons along with advisers to help you plan and execute an attack on Fort Box. We'll put together 'technicals,' mounting the automatic weapons on pickups and other regular vehicles, and my advisers will operate them. No one will know of our involvement."

"Better just let us have the stuff. These 'advisers' ain't gonna fool nobody. They gonna stick out."

"My men come in all colors, Mr. Banks. I'm confident we can assemble an adviser corps who will fit in well with your organization. Let's let me worry about that, shall we?"

Banks reflected a moment. "What about after?"

"After, Mr. Banks?"

"After we cap these mofos for you, what then? I ain't stupid. We get our asses shot up cappin' this bunch of soldier boys, then we be weak and you take us out, easy like. That why you want to use us, 'ight?"

Rorke shrugged. "The group in Fort Box has training, crew-served weapons, and undoubtedly, some sort of air defense strategy in place, perhaps with RPGs. They may expect an attack from us, but a sudden and massive assault from your group will be a complete surprise. It's simple logic. And as far as taking you out, don't flatter yourself. You're already weak, and we could take you out in an afternoon with chopper gunships and little risk; unlike Fort Box, you have no defense against an aerial assault.

"So you see, Mr. Banks," Rorke continued, "in this new world, no one can be neutral. There are only enemies and allies, and as long as you're a good and helpful ally, I have no reason to take you out. But if you're not, well, in that case, we'll crush you like bugs when it suits our purposes. Unlike our friends in Fort Box, you're not in radio contact with distant allies who might get upset when we take you out, nor are you sitting on nearly as large a stockpile of looted stores I don't want to see damaged." Rorke smiled. "So in your case, I have absolutely no problem burning down the house to kill all the rats, and I'm not the least concerned about collateral damage. Your very best option is to join my command as unacknowledged irregular forces, but of course, the choice is yours. However, you must decide now. If you accept, we'll return to my base and begin planning the op. If you refuse, I'll just take you back to your headquarters and drop you off."

Banks glanced around the chopper as his mind raced, parsing the options. No way he was gonna be this cracker's bitch. There was a pilot and copilot in the front of the chopper, and two more soldiers in the back with him and Rorke. Maybe when they landed, he could order his men to open up on the chopper as soon as he got clear. If they massed firepower, they could bring it down and he could cap this creepy cracker. With the head cut off, the snake would just flop around a while and let him come up with a plan to deal with this unexpected development. He looked at Rorke and nodded.

"Okay, that sound all right. I call the shots, but I gotta go back and consult my council, you know, just to be cool with the brothers. I have you an answer in maybe fifteen minutes after we land."

Rorke gave him a look of obviously feigned surprise. "Land, Mr. Banks? I just said we'd drop you off, I never said anything about landing."

Banks said nothing for almost a minute. "So when your people comin' with the machine guns?" he asked at last.

CHAPTER THREE

Fort Box
Wilmington Container Terminal
Wilmington, North Carolina

Day 26, 3:15 p.m.

Luke Kinsey, formerly first lieutenant, US Army; formerly captain (and currently deserter from), FEMA Special Reaction Force; and most recently major, Wilmington Defense Force, squinted into the bright afternoon sun and shaded his eyes with his hand as he stared up at the chopper circling Fort Box.

"Looks like they takin' a good long look, LT—I mean Major," said Joel Washington.

Luke looked at his former sergeant and nodded. "That they are, Lieutenant Washington. Let's just hope they see enough of our teeth to decide to leave us alone." He couldn't suppress a grin at the big man's obvious discomfort at being addressed by his new title.

"What's the problem, Washington? Overwhelmed by the awesome responsibilities of your new rank?"

Washington shook his head. "It's okay for you, L—Major, but I never wanted to be no officer. I'll do any job needin' doing, you know that, but sergeant suited me just fine, and I see no reason I had to change."

"Hunnicutt is right about that. We're growing fast, and folks with leadership experience are in short supply. We have to have some sort of defined structure and hierarchy, both military and civilian, but we can't necessarily be guided by the old rules. People get the tasks and responsibilities, and the rank to go with them, they can handle. New folks coming in are going to have a tough enough time adjusting without trying to figure out why a sergeant seems to have more authority than say a junior officer..." Luke trailed off as the look of skepticism on Washington's face morphed into a poorly concealed smirk.

"Seriously, Major?"

"Okay, bad example," Luke conceded, "but you know what I mean. Fact is, I'm having some qualms myself. One of the senior noncoms should have been promoted over me. I should have stayed a captain and Wright or Butler should have been bumped up to major; both have more experience."

"Not real combat experience," Washington said. "They're good people, but Wright is, or was, a National Guard sergeant, and Butler was a Coastie chief petty officer. They'll both get things done, but the only ones who have any real combat time are you and those of us you brought in with you, and I gotta feeling we're gonna need all the combat experience we can find." He sighed. "Anyway, Wright and Butler don't like bein' officers any more than I do, and none of us think it's really necessary. Folks always figure out who to turn to when they need something. Always have, always will."

"You might be right, but you're still a lieutenant, Lieutenant."

The look of dismay on Washington's face was so comical Luke had all he could do to keep a straight face. "And my orders, Lieutenant, are to set up a twenty-four-hour sky watch. That's the third chopper overflight in the last two days and I don't like it. Make sure they have NV and IR gear at night. Even if the choppers come in dark, we'll focus on the blade noise and know where to point the gear."

Washington nodded, his forlorn look fading as he contemplated his new task. "Yes, sir," he said. "I'll get right on it. Anything else?"

"Not at the moment," Luke said, "but I'm headed to the council meeting. Catch up with me in a couple of hours and I'll brief you on what we discuss."

"Better you than me, sir. I'll see you in two hours." He was grinning now. "Unless of course the council meeting runs long, but I'm sure that won't happen."

"Anyone ever mention you're a wiseass, Washington?"

Washington's grin widened. "Regularly, sir. Now if that will be all…"

Luke shook his head. "Go."

Washington moved away across the concrete, still smiling, and Luke turned back toward his original destination. The former terminal building was a squat, three-story structure of utilitarian appearance, now the headquarters for 'Fort Box,' a name initially used as a joke referencing their improvised defensive wall of empty shipping containers, but which quickly became a point of pride as their little community grew.

Luke stopped at the door to the terminal building and looked back over what had previously been the container yard, amazed by what his new comrades had accomplished in such a short time. The change was remarkable, even since he'd brought his little band of deserters into the walls of Fort Box a scant week earlier.

A stout defensive wall of steel shipping containers stacked two high formed three walls of the fort, topped with a barbed wire barrier along the outer edge and with fortified firing positions at regular intervals. Machine guns were mounted on armored platforms at each corner, extending outward to allow them to sweep the length of the wall in any direction. All of the firing points were connected with a three-foot-wide wooden scaffold hung below the inside edge of the top container and running the length of the wall, allowing defenders to quickly move from point to point without exposing themselves to enemy fire. The new walls were set well back from the original terminal fence, and the area between had been cleared of containers. No one could approach the walls now except by crossing fifty yards of asphalt or concrete, all under the guns of the defenders.

The fourth side of Fort Box was formed by the container berths on the river, currently occupied by a collection of container and grain ships. The ships were moored bow to stern, their high steel sides forming a fourth wall, also protected by machine-gun emplacements at both ends with fields of fire sweeping the river approaches. The river side was perhaps the least secure perimeter due to irregular-shaped gaps between the ships, which were impossible to seal, but the river was a strong ally. The open water offered much wider fields of fire than the land sides, and a coordinated waterborne attack was considered unlikely.

But it was the progress inside the walls that was most remarkable; a collection of travel trailers and RVs mixed with military tents were lined up in a bizarre but strangely orderly looking series of newly created 'streets' radiating like the spokes of a wheel from the terminal-building-turned-HQ. In the central area next to the HQ stood a series of large army tents serving as central kitchen, mess hall, and clinic, while on the dock next to one of the ships was a collection of covered aboveground swimming pools known as 'Wright's Waterworks' in honor of the man who'd solved their water storage problem. And everywhere there were containers, stacks and stacks of containers: large brightly colored steel boxes crammed with a cornucopia of canned food, packaged generators, and other goods, the full scope of which was still undetermined.

Luke marveled at the controlled chaos as men and women scurried in all directions. The faint smell of diesel exhaust filled the air, and the sounds of generators and heavy equipment assaulted his ears as the fortunate inhabitants of Fort Box labored to secure their future. Luke nodded and entered the building, smiling as cool air washed over him. Air-conditioning and ice were two things that made Southern summers bearable, and he was glad he'd have a little of both, at least as long as he stayed.

He glanced at his watch. He was five minutes early, but he'd quickly learned Major, now Colonel, Hunnicutt considered ten minutes early as 'on time.' By that standard he was five minutes late. He hurried down the hall toward the conference room and the sound of raised voices.

"I don't give a damn, Lieutenant Wright. You know—" Colonel Hunnicutt looked up as Luke entered. "Well, nice of you to join us, Major. I do hope it wasn't an inconvenience."

"Sorry, sir," Luke said, slipping into an unoccupied seat and nodding at the dozen people seated around the conference table. Hunnicutt gave him a curt nod and turned back to Wright.

"As I was saying, Lieutenant, you know the protocol and so should your men. We CANNOT police areas outside of our tasking and still hope to provide any relief to the bulk of the refugees. These criminals piss me off too, believe me, but we just don't have the manpower and resources to be diverted by a conflict with the gangs at this point. I thought I made that clear?"

"You did, sir. And I've reprimanded Corporal Miles for disobeying orders, but honestly, I don't believe he did so intentionally. Our mission is providing relief to the civilians, so when they heard a woman screaming for help, he used his own initiative. I can't fault him for that. So what exactly was he supposed to do when his patrol stumbled on a gang rape, say 'carry on' and drive away?"

Hunnicutt heaved a sigh and fell silent. "I suppose not," he said at last. "Where is the woman now?"

"Miles' patrol took her and her husband to the refugee camp. They didn't much want to go, but he couldn't leave them there," Wright said.

"And the bangers?"

Wright shrugged. "Too many to do anything with, even if we had facilities. They just told them to scatter, all except for the one they caught," he hesitated, "you know..."

"I get the picture," Hunnicutt said. "What did they do with him?"

Wright hesitated. "He was killed resisting arrest."

The room grew deadly quiet as the meeting participants awaited Hunnicutt's reaction.

"Boo fucking hoo," Hunnicutt said, and the room erupted in laughter.

"But seriously, folks," he said, "we can't afford to get entangled with these bastards. We just have too much to do. Any expectations this will escalate, Lieutenant Wright?"

Wright shook his head. "We have them outgunned and they know it. If anything, they might try to lure a patrol into an ambush as payback."

Hunnicutt nodded. "My thoughts exactly. Make sure not to answer ANY calls for distress, and double both the size and frequency of the patrols between here and the relief station until we're sure this isn't going to escalate."

"Already done, sir," Wright replied.

"All right," Hunnicutt said, "let's move on. Chief... I mean Lieutenant Butler, can you give us a quick SITREP on the facilities?"

Mike Butler, formerly chief boatswain's mate, USCG, now first lieutenant, Wilmington Defense Force, nodded. "Our defensive perimeter is complete, though I'd still like to improve on the gate arrangement. Our snipes, along with the engineers from the merchant ships, have nearly solved our water problem. Between all the ships, we have multiple water distillers, and they rigged up a way to triple process the river water and basically heat the hell out of it to kill any bugs." He looked over at Lieutenant Josh Wright and grinned. "They tell me by this time tomorrow, they'll be producing enough water to keep Wright's Waterworks topped up for the foreseeable future."

"Great news," Hunnicutt said, "but how'd they manage that?"

Butler shrugged. "They didn't say and I sure as hell didn't ask, sir. Else I'd have had to listen to a two-hour lecture explaining the process in great detail." He paused to let the laughter die down before continuing. "But it gets better. They plan to use Wright's swimming pools as reserve water storage for excess production, but they seem confident they can tie the shore facilities into the potable water system from *Maersk Tangier* and use her water pumps to pressurize it all. Her tanks are more than adequate to supply our needs on a day-to-day basis. They'll have to dig up and disconnect the old supply from the city system, but after that, we'll have running water in the terminal again. They said two or three days max."

"That's good news. We've been wasting a lot of manpower hauling water, and I for one will gladly give up the joy of flushing with a bucket." Hunnicutt grimaced. "As long as the sewage lines aren't plugged up, anyway."

"Actually, there's good news on that front, too," Butler said. "The treatment plant's only a mile or so downriver, and the snipes figure if we're the only ones with running water to flush, it will take a while before we top out the storage capacity, even if the plant's not running. And if we can get a generator and some fuel down there, they figure they might be able to restore the plant to at least limited operation. They think it will be more than enough to meet our needs."

Across the table from Butler, a petite, dark-haired woman sat up straighter in her chair. "So does that mean if we can get water restored at the country club, we can establish some basic sanitation for the refugee camp? It's horrific there. The port-a-potties you brought in were overflowing by the second day, and people are back to doing their business behind any bush. The stench is overpowering and it's only going to get worse."

The request caught Butler by surprise. "Maybe, Doc," he replied, "but I don't think there's any way we can get water pressure back there and—"

"We could use the toilets in the clubhouse and swimming club. I think there are even some toilets over by the tennis courts. You told me yourself you've got a container full of portable generators from China, and we could pump the flushing water out of the small lake there. It's fed by that little creek, so we should have plenty of water and—"

Butler held up both his hands in a stop gesture. "Whoa! Doc, slow down. I know you want to get things done, but you've been here less than a week, so I don't think you fully appreciate how stretched we are. We can't do everything at once and—"

The woman's eyes flashed. "And I don't think you fully appreciate what those people are going through, Lieutenant Butler. But I was in that hell for three weeks and I can't forget. Just because I was fortunate enough to be offered shelter here, I'm not going to turn my back—"

"We're not turning our backs on anyone, Dr. Jennings," Hunnicutt said, "and we recruited you from among the refugee population not only because we needed a doctor here, but to form a medical team to help the refugees as much as we can. But Butler's right. We have to use what resources we have wisely, or else we won't be able to help anyone." He turned back to Butler. "But the Doc's right too, Butler. The camp's already turning into a cesspool; can we get sewage service reestablished, and if so, how long?"

Butler rubbed his chin. "I expect the country club area is served by the same treatment plant since it's on this side of town, but I don't know how long it will support us here and thousands of refugees. The engineers figure there's probably enough room in the facility's holding ponds to last a while before we have to get the treatment plant running. But they weren't considering several thousand folks from the refugee camp. If we dump that output into the system, I think the plan goes out the window; they'll have to get the plant running sooner rather than later." He sighed. "And they have their hands full now. They were hoping to hold off on addressing the treatment plant for a couple of weeks."

Hunnicutt nodded. "Okay, let's think about this. If we flush everything in the system and don't get the plant running, the holding ponds overflow and things get nasty, am I right?"

Butler shrugged. "I guess so, sir. I hadn't really thought about it, to be honest."

"So that means if they CAN'T get the plant going in time, we have a stinking mess a mile or so downstream of us in the middle of an industrial area. It seems to me a stinking mess there where no one is around is much better than a disease-producing mess in the middle of several thousand refugees, wouldn't you agree?" Hunnicutt asked.

Butler nodded, and Jennings beamed as Hunnicutt continued, "Okay then, let's get the good doctor her flushing toilets, and tell the engineers to do the best they can on getting the treatment plant running, but not to let it override other priorities. This situation is going to throw new challenges at us every day, folks, and we just have to be flexible."

"Yes, sir," Butler said, and made a note on the pad in front of him.

"Thank you, Colonel," Jennings said, "but it's still going to be tough. We have toilets in the club house and the swimming club—"

Luke cleared his throat loudly, earning him a glare from Jennings. "I don't think we should allow the 'fugees—"

"DON'T CALL THEM THAT!" Jenning snapped.

Luke colored and nodded. "You're right, Doctor, I apologize. But as I was saying, I don't think we should allow the REFugees uncontrolled access to the swimming club facilities. We set up our container wall around the swimming club so we could clean the pool and cover it to use it as drinking water storage, and that whole facility is now our forward base and defensive strong point. We have absolutely no way to vet the refugees, and if we allow them free access in and out of our fortified area, we don't really know who might come in." He paused. "From a security standpoint, it's a very bad idea."

"Agreed," the colonel said, turning to Jennings. "You'll get your sewage system, Doctor, but the swim club facility remains off-limits to all but authorized personnel."

"But there are ten toilets there! Maybe we could reposition the wall between the clubhouse and the pool—"

"Jesus Christ," Butler muttered, unable to contain his irritation, and Jennings whirled on him, obviously intent on dressing him down.

"ENOUGH!" Hunnicutt said. "The issue is settled. Flushing water will be restored to all country club facilities, but the swimming club is off-limits to all but authorized personnel. We'll look at the possibility of finding portable toilets that can be tied into the fixed system. Now, next issue." He looked down at his notepad. "Mr. Van Horn, how are we coming with getting food to the refugees?"

A slender man with wire-rim glasses looked over at Hunnicutt and shrugged. "We're starting to provide some calories, Colonel, but I can't call it more than that."

Terry Van Horn, ex-chief steward on the *Maersk Tangier*, had been appointed 'food czar' by acclamation and over his own strong objections. When Hunnicutt scoured the skills inventory of his small but growing group within the confines of Fort Box, he hadn't neglected either the American or foreign merchant ships. Between the 'culinary specialists' (aka cooks) of his own National Guard unit and the steward's departments of the various ships, he had no shortage of people who could cook for large groups, with a 'large group' defined as twenty to a hundred or so. Feeding thousands of refugees was a different matter entirely, and when it came out that Van Horn had regularly volunteered for various Third World famine relief efforts, putting him in charge was a no-brainer.

Van Horn continued. "That many folks, all I can hope to do is get some calories down 'em. I pulled one cook and a couple of stewards from each of the ships to work with me, along with most of your culinary people. We stripped the ships of every big stew pot we could find, and we been using your field kitchen to boil corn from one of the grain ships into a gruel and throwing in some of the canned seafood and meat from the containers for protein. I got no seasonings to speak of, especially not for the volume of food we have to put out. Even at that and workin' almost round the clock, we can only manage to get out one meal a day. As more people come in, I'm not even sure we'll be able to maintain that." He shook his head. "It'll keep 'em alive, but quite frankly, it looks like crap and tastes the same. I'd be ashamed to serve it if it wasn't the best we could produce in bulk."

"We know it's tough and we appreciate the job you and your people are doing," Hunnicutt said, to nods around the table.

Van Horn shook his head. "Thank you, Colonel, but the truth is, this isn't gonna work much longer. We got plenty of grain, but as the population grows, we don't have the manpower, equipment, or time to cook it fast enough. Yesterday we started running low, but one of my guys spotted it in time, so they started cutting down on the portion size and just made it to the end of the line. The day the food runs out before the line runs out is the day we're likely to have a food riot. I've seen it before and it ain't pretty." He paused and said softly, "Never thought I'd see it here though."

The room grew quiet a long moment as the others considered the possibility.

Wright broke the silence. "This sucks! We have so much grain in the ships and grain terminal it's likely to rot before we can get it distributed, and we'll be starving people we likely won't be able to feed for lack of resources."

"We need more manpower," Hunnicutt agreed. "How's recruitment coming?"

"No shortage of people who want to join us," Butler said, "but vetting them to make sure they have the skills they claim is a full-time job. I mean, they're desperate, boss. Ask for crane operators and everyone raises their hand. Same with mechanics or forklift drivers. I doubt it would be any different if we asked for nuclear physicists."

Jennings sighed. "That's true, I'm afraid. Of the five 'nurses' we took in yesterday, I doubt half of them had so much as ever emptied a bedpan. They're all willing workers, but not knowing who I can trust makes it hard. Fortunately, we got two more docs yesterday, but—"

"Then there's your answer," Hunnicutt said. "If you didn't have the docs before, they're a bonus and won't be missed, so re-task one. Put him or her in charge of vetting all the incoming medical personnel. Either that or spread vetting duty over your qualified medical staff as it grows. Butler, you do the same in the other areas. If you need crane operators, put a crane operator in charge of finding them. The people doing the job are the most qualified to decide if the new recruits are blowing smoke, AND they'll be the most motivated to resist bringing in screwups, since they'll be working closely with the new folks."

Everyone nodded and Hunnicutt looked over at Van Horn. "And perhaps you could find some cooks to help you from among the refugees, Mr. Van Horn."

"What we're doing isn't exactly cooking, Colonel, so warm bodies to help shouldn't be a problem. But manpower isn't my real problem. What I need is big-ass pots and burners to put 'em on," Van Horn said.

Hunnicutt turned toward Butler, but the man was already scribbling on his notepad. "I'll have someone search the bills of lading to see if there's anything of use in the containers, and ask the engineers if they can figure out some way to expand your kitchen facilities," Butler said to Van Horn, who nodded his thanks.

Hunnicutt glanced at his watch and down at his notepad. "Anything else?"

When everyone shook their heads, he nodded. "Okay, folks, let's get back to work."

People started filing from the room, but Hunnicutt motioned for Luke, Wright, and Butler to keep their seats. Jennings was halfway to the door when she noticed the men still sitting and turned to Hunnicutt, her eyebrows raised.

"A private meeting, Colonel?" she asked.

"Security issues, Doctor. I'm sure they'd be a waste of your valuable time and bore you to tears besides. Would you please close the door on your way out?"

Her look communicated her disapproval more eloquently than any words, and when she left, the closing of the door was just short of a slam.

"I think you pissed the good doctor off," Butler said.

"So it appears, and I truly regret that. She's good people, and she'll make a big difference. She IS making a difference," Hunnicutt corrected himself, then shook his head. "The problem is she thinks we can save everyone, and we all know that's impossible."

The others nodded as Hunnicutt turned to Luke. "Was that a chopper I heard, Major?"

"Yes, sir. It's what held me up. That's the third overflight in as many days, so it appears the FEMA folks are taking an increasing interest. I had Lieutenant Washington set a round-the-clock sky watch," Luke said.

"Good," Hunnicutt said. "Given your recent 'association' with our FEMA friends, do you have any insights into how much of a threat they might be?"

Luke shook his head. "Just very generally. We were only with the Special Reaction Force a couple of weeks, but my gut feeling is they won't have the stomach for a stand-up fight. Intimidation and bullying the defenseless seems to be more their MO. They may make a lot of noise, but as long as we show our teeth, I think we can hold them at bay."

"Let's hope you're right, Major. We sure as hell don't need to add a combat mission to everything else we've got on our plates." Hunnicutt turned to Wright. "But if that comes to pass, how do we stand on readiness, Lieutenant?"

"Just over eighty combat effectives, sir, counting the Coasties and the men that came in with Major Kinsey here. I can up that a bit as we place civilian recruits in some of the support roles, like cooks, mechanics and so forth. They aren't line troops, but they've all had at least basic weapons training and we can put them on the wall with a rifle if we have to. But we'll max out at a hundred shooters." Wright paused. "That's as many as we can arm anyway, and ammo is a concern, especially for the crew-served weapons.

They're key to our defense, and if we have to hold off a sustained attack, those machine guns will burn through ammo like a house afire."

"We might be able to get some ammo from the Military Ocean Terminal downriver," Butler said. "The Coast Guard used to help them enforce an 'exclusion zone' around their wharfs, and I'm familiar with their facility, the part of it closest to the river, anyway. I was also pretty tight with a couple of NCOs that helped run the place."

Hunnicutt looked skeptical. "That's an Army facility, and I have no clue how the regular military is leaning. However, I doubt they're just going to hand out ammunition because we ask nicely."

"Maybe, maybe not, sir," Butler said. "It was actually kind of a hybrid operation and mostly civilian. The place is huge, much bigger than most people realize, and they used a lot of technology-based security to guard the place—CCTV, motion-detector-based alarms, stuff like that. None of that will be working now, and given how everything has gone to hell, we might just be able to slip in and grab some ammo at a five-fingered discount. With your permission, I'd like to do some recon and check it out."

Hunnicutt hesitated, then nodded. "Okay, go have a look, and JUST a look. We'll decide what to do based on what you find. And be careful, making an enemy of the Army is the last thing we need at this point. Put together a small team and go when you're ready."

"Yes, sir," Butler said and shot Luke a 'let's talk later' look.

"Now," Hunnicutt said, looking back and forth between Wright and Butler, "and before you two get your noses out of joint, you should know that I asked Major Kinsey here to have a look at our defenses. Given his much more recent deployment in the Sandbox, he's the only one with recent experience in setting up forward bases in hostile areas, and I figured we can benefit from a fresh set of eyes."

Wright grunted. "No problem here. I'd much prefer to be alive than admired for my work."

"Same here," Butler said, "I was a life saver, not a fort builder."

"Good," Hunnicutt said, nodding toward Luke. "You have the floor, Major."

"Okay," Luke said, "first let me say I'm blown away by what you guys have accomplished in such a short time. No one could have done a better job of establishing a defensive position with the materials at hand. I wouldn't have done a single thing differently as far as the defensive walls go. Establishing clear fields of fire between the walls and the original terminal fence was an especially good move. I only have one suggestion."

"Which is?" Hunnicutt asked.

"I think we have to take preemptive measures to keep the refugee population further away from the walls. You've set the relief station at the country club some distance away, which is a good thing, but it's still relatively close to us here. Despite your best efforts, the population will expand in this direction. They're desperate people, and they'll quickly figure out we're the source of the food and water, and they'll all want in. If we allow a lot of them to concentrate here, it could get ugly."

"So how exactly can we prevent that?" Wright asked.

"We need to set a perimeter much further out, as far out as we can without running into the gangbangers. We barricade all the roads in but Shipyard Boulevard with a container across the road, and put No Entry signage all around the perimeter to create an exclusion zone. We then enforce it with roving vehicle patrols on a random schedule so the bangers can't figure out a routine and try to ambush us."

Wright was shaking his head. "We can't possibly hope to stop people. That barrier will be porous as hell. They'll just walk around it."

"You're not expected to stop everyone," Luke said, "just discourage them from getting too near the fort. The signs and barriers will deter most of them, and a certain percentage of those who do slip through will be rounded up and politely but firmly returned to the camp. If we have repeat offenders, we can figure out some way to deal with them at the time."

"Extra patrols is extra manpower we don't have," Butler pointed out.

"Not extra," Luke said, "just task every third or fourth regular patrol headed out to patrol the route between here and the refugee camp with swinging through a portion of the exclusion zone. When we turn back a few people and return them to the camp, word will get out."

The room grew quiet as they considered Luke's plan.

"Worth a try," Wright said.

"Agreed," Butler added.

"That makes it unanimous. Set it up, gentlemen," Hunnicutt said, glancing down at his notepad again. "Which brings me to the last item on my agenda, the census; where do we stand, Lieutenant Butler."

Butler nodded. "As of this morning, counting military and dependents, the other civilians we brought in with us, all the merchant ship crews and the terminal personnel, and other folks we've recruited so far"—he glanced down at his pad—"eleven hundred and sixty-three, sir."

"And what's our capacity within the walls, best guess?" Hunnicutt asked.

"If we max out the living quarters we have now and start converting some of the empty containers to housing, we can probably shelter another two thousand people, maybe twenty-five hundred," Butler said. "We can push out the walls and accommodate more, but space isn't really the problem at that point, it's water. The engineers tell me they can probably make enough water to support three thousand total, at least until the diesel in their fuel tanks and the terminal starts to go off-spec in a year to two years. They're working on some solar-powered options for the longer term, but no way those will produce near enough water for that many folks. They're thinking maybe a stable long-term permanent population of fifteen hundred, with a bit of reserve for short-term increases."

"So we can survive here long term, but with a limited population, and in the short term we can accommodate extra people but have to find them some place to relocate, is that about the size of it?"

"Yes, sir, basically," Butler said.

"I've spoken to Levi Jenkins and Vern Gibson," Wright said, "they have pretty much all the farmers and landowners along the river out fifteen or twenty miles sold on the idea of a mutual protection network. I'm thinking we could build on that concept and turn the manned security stations we'd planned to establish along the river into small towns, each anchored around a fortified base. They could be mutually supporting and—"

"Whoa!" Hunnicutt said. "Towns and bases are a hell of a lot more intrusive than the security stations we were talking about, with much bigger footprints. How are the farmers going to feel about that?"

"I think they'll go for it, under the circumstances. We're talking fortified towns of up to two hundred people every mile or so on alternating sides of the river, each with maybe ten or twenty acres of land. A hell of a lot of that riverfront is undeveloped woodland anyway, sir, so it's not like they'd lose productive farmland," Wright said.

"So you figure everyone in these towns is going to live inside the fortified base." Hunnicutt shook his head. "That'll be a bit tight."

"Not nearly as tight as it will be here, sir."

Hunnicutt nodded. "Point taken. You think the farmers will go for it?"

"What's not to like," Wright said. "They'll have an employable labor pool without having to actually house folks on their own places. Each town can have a militia unit, and they can all be mutually supportive. We can house mechanics, medical facilities, and other needed services in the different towns, all accessible by water. We can—"

Hunnicutt held up his hands. "Okay, okay, I think I get the picture. Get with Levi and Vern and see if you can sell them on the plan, and if so, ask them to start scouting sites and working with their friends and neighbors to get buy in. Then I want you and Butler, in your spare time, of course, to start figuring out what skill sets we're going to need to start these towns from scratch. Grab anyone you need to help plan that, but make sure to include Levi and Vern. If we expect people along the river to buy in to us redesigning their world, it's only polite to get their input."

The pair nodded, and Hunnicutt muttered, almost to himself, "Then we just have to play God and decide which of these people get offered tickets to a decent existence and which ones we leave in Hell."

"It's going to be a tough call, sir," Luke said, sympathy in his voice.

"That it is, Major, that it is. Which brings me to contingency planning," Hunnicutt said. "We're hoping for the best, but we sure as hell need to be realistic and plan for the worst. I'm sure it hasn't escaped anyone's attention the odds are stacked against us."

Everyone nodded, and Hunnicutt continued.

"We're doing the best we can feeding and sheltering our growing refugee population, but we have to face facts. They're living in squalor in cardboard and canvas shacks, with minimal sanitation. We're essentially feeding them slop and providing them drinking water, and we'll do our best to improve that, but chances are pretty good that every advance we make is going to be offset by a population increase. And it's summer now; God knows how we'll cope when it gets cold."

Butler shrugged. "But what more can we do, sir? We're trying—"

"That's just the point," Hunnicutt said. "We're all flat out and working six-teen- and eighteen-hour days, seven days a week, and we're still falling behind. But I'm sure there's not a single person in that refugee camp who thinks we're doing enough. We wouldn't feel any different if we were there, because that's human nature. To those folks, we're the privileged ones with guns who eat good food, crap in real toilets, sleep in real beds out of the elements, and even get to take the occasional shower. Major Kinsey's suggestion to establish an exclusion zone, necessary though it is, will add to that resentment. I believe anyone in that camp who doesn't hate us already probably will within a week, or a month max."

Wright nodded. "Actually, you can already feel the resentment when you ride through the camp. But what can we do about it?"

Hunnicutt sighed. "There's nothing we can do except continue to do our best. But we can't ignore it either. That camp is becoming a powder keg of simmering resentment, subject to blowing up at any time. We need a contingency plan for rapid withdrawal of all our folks, including our civilian recruits like Dr. Jennings." He paused. "And we have to be prepared for the possibility safe withdrawal may require use of deadly force. I want you to pick out your most trustworthy NCOs and come up with rules of engagement if we have to activate the withdrawal plan. I want that strictly need to know, and God help anyone who lets any mention of the plan slip to ANYONE."

Wright hesitated. "Ah… what about the folks we have to evacuate? I mean Dr. Jennings—"

"Especially don't tell Jennings," Hunnicutt said. "She'll be appalled at the very idea, and advance notice won't make extracting her any easier. It will also likely mean endless arguments with her and guarantee everyone will know about the plan. If it comes to an emergency evacuation, just plan to hog-tie her and bring her along. In fact, make forced extraction of our civilians part of the plan if necessary. If things go to hell, we're not going to have a debate. After they're safely inside Fort Box, they can leave if they want, but at least they'll have an option at that point."

Hunnicutt's subordinates nodded in unison.

"Understood, sir," Wright said. "We'll get on it."

"Thank you, gentlemen," Hunnicutt said. "If there's nothing else, I think we're done."

The three nodded and began to rise.

"Oh, Major," Hunnicutt said to Luke, "a word, if you don't mind."

Luke settled back into his chair with a quizzical look and waited for the other two to file out. Hunnicutt waited for the door to close before speaking.

"Thank you, Luke. Have you given any more thought to your longer term plans?"

Luke shook his head. "I appreciate your confidence and the promotion, Colonel, and I'm not going to leave you while things are obviously as critical as they are, but I've always been up front with you. I want to join my dad and the rest of the family, which means they either come back here or I go down to Texas. Since there's only one of me, it makes more sense for me to go there. It would be near impossible for my dad to make it back up here with my sister and my aunt's family."

"You know my hope with the promotion was to make you second-in-command—"

"Yes, sir, and you know I declined. I'll stick around awhile and do anything you need me to do, but when the time comes, I'm leaving. That would be a great deal more difficult if I was in a leadership position." He paused and looked Hunnicutt in the eye. "And I think you know that, sir."

Hunnicutt smiled ruefully. "Busted. Okay then, any idea when that time will be?"

Luke hesitated. "I can give you six months, with the understanding if my dad needs me before then, I'm going."

Hunnicutt nodded. "Fair enough. I'll take what I can get. Thank you, Luke."

"You're welcome, sir. Now if that's all, I suspect Lieutenant Butler may want to talk to me about a little recon trip down to the Military Ocean Terminal."

CHAPTER FOUR

M/V PECOS TRADER
SUN LOWER ANCHORAGE
NECHES RIVER
NEAR NEDERLAND, TEXAS

DAY 26, 6:35 A.M.

Captain Jordan Hughes felt the heat of the rising sun on his neck as he stood bent at the waist, his forearms resting on the ship's rail, studying the curious operation unfolding on the water below. Some distance down the deck, Chief Mate Georgia Howell was also at the rail, her eyes glued on the river's surface and her right hand raised, signaling the bosun in the cab of the hose-handling crane as he lowered a strange-looking contraption to the water.

Hughes heard a slap and a curse and looked around to see Matt Kinsey, formerly chief petty officer, USCG, staring at a large blood spot in his open palm, a dark blob in the middle of it.

"I don't know whether this is a mosquito or a frigging bat," Kinsey said. "I may need a transfusion."

Hughes laughed. "Well, they'll be worse in bayou country. But I anticipated you." He reached in his pants pocket and pulled out a small bottle and held it out to Kinsey. "Polak has some insect repellent squirreled away somewhere, consider it our contribution to the mission."

Kinsey grinned. "Outstanding! Thank you, Captain," he said as he slipped the bottle in his pocket and stepped closer to the rail. His grin widened as he looked down.

"But not the only contribution. That chief engineer of yours is a pretty smart cookie. I'd been driving myself crazy trying to figure out how to get the boat around those locks. This is terrific!"

Hughes nodded. "Well, maybe. Presuming it doesn't fall apart on the way there. It's not exactly the sleekest craft in the fleet." He watched as Georgia Howell lowered the subject of their discussion the last few feet to settle on the river's surface. It was a sturdily built aluminum boat trailer outfitted on either side with two large and ungainly-looking pontoons, each constructed of four fifty-five-gallon oil drums held in rigid alignment by a skeletal structure of lightweight angle iron. A sheet metal cone was fitted at what was apparently the 'bow' of each pontoon.

Kinsey watched the makeshift craft bob on the water. "It floats well enough," Kinsey said, "and I watched Gowan and the boys put those pontoons together. They'll hold up just fine. I figured we had no more use for that trailer. It was a stroke of genius to make it water-mobile."

"Think it'll work?"

"Well, we won't know that until we try. If we're lucky, Calcasieu Lock at least will be open. It's only a salt water control gate to keep tidal water out of the agricultural area. There's no water height difference across the lock and they keep it open much of the time. If we luck out there, we won't have to use the trailer until the Bayou Sorrel Lock."

"How fast can you tow that thing?" Hughes asked.

Kinsey shrugged. "No clue. Those sheet metal fairwaters will help, but it'll still slow us way down. I'll start slow and see how she tows. I hope to tow her at ten or fifteen knots, but even at ten we'll make Calcasieu Lock before noon. God knows what we'll have to deal with there, but I'm hoping we can get clear of the lock and be well up the Intracoastal by nightfall."

Hughes nodded as he watched the Coast Guard patrol boat edging in to put a towing bridle on their new seagoing trailer. "I still don't like you going off shorthanded. Sure you don't want to find a car? It might take you a couple of days by boat, especially towing that thing. You could make it there in three or four hours by car, and we could send more people—"

Kinsey shook his head. "Pinch points are not our friend, Cap. We'd have to worry about the bridge at Lake Charles, to say nothing of twenty-plus miles of the Atchafalaya Basin Causeway with nowhere to run and nowhere to hide. And even if those places aren't compromised, I can almost guarantee you someone is sitting on the Mississippi River bridge into Baton Rouge. We couldn't send enough people to force a crossing in any of those places if someone is holding them, and if they decide to come after us, we likely couldn't outrun them long enough to break contact either." He nodded down at the Coast Guard boat. "But with that baby, we can outrun anyone on the water. We'll lose the tow if we have to."

Kinsey continued. "Besides, I don't want to leave YOU shorthanded. For sure those cons will be looking for some payback after the beat down we gave them last week. My family, my problem. Bollinger and I will be just fine."

"And my family was my problem, but y'all helped me get them on board. C'mon, Kinsey, at least take more of your own men. I know every one of them volunteered."

"They did, and I appreciate it," Kinsey said, "but everyone except Bollinger has dependents aboard, and I'm not going to let them leave their own families in possible danger to save mine. It was different when we went after your family; they were close by and we didn't fully appreciate how big a threat the escaped convicts were. Now we do, and we have to figure that into the equation."

Kinsey continued before Hughes could protest further. "Besides, as you may have noticed, our boat's on the small side. I have to pick up my daughter and my sister-in-law's family plus God knows who else." He sighed. "My wife has extended family all over Baton Rouge, and knowing Connie, they probably all went to her house. Which brings up another question, Captain Noah. Are you okay with me bringing everyone I find back to your rapidly filling ark?"

Hughes sighed. "How can I not be okay with it? We wouldn't be here if it wasn't for you and your guys. It's your ark as much as mine, so of course I'm okay with it. We'll make it work somehow." He hesitated. "I just hope... I just hope your trip is successful."

Kinsey cocked his head. "I hear a 'but' in there, Cap. If you have a concern, now is the time to voice it."

"Just thinking of the longer term. Everyone we take in has to pull their weight one way or another. We can't very well turn away immediate family members, but—"

"But we can't take in everyone without thinking how they can contribute to the survival of the group. Believe me, I get it." Kinsey grinned. "I figure having a small boat will be an advantage. I can be selective as to the passenger list."

Hughes nodded. "Good. We're on the same page, then. Now, about equipment. You sure you have everything you need?"

"Pretty much, but I'm still not sure about taking two sets of night-vision gear; you guys might need it. We can get by with one. I mainly figured to use it to run the canal in the dark if need be," Kinsey said.

"You might need it for more than that, and we'll still have two sets here, and some of the rifles have NV scopes. We'll be fine. And I wish you'd reconsider about taking one of the machine guns—"

"We've been all over that, Cap. If things DO go tits up, I'm not handing one of our three machine guns to the bad guys. The other boat can shadow us until we get to the Intracoastal. By the time the cons figure out what's up, we'll be well away from them. I'll try to contact you by VHF when we're in-bound, and you can send out the other boat to escort us in."

Hughes sighed. "All right, but I don't like it."

"I'm not wild about it myself, but you know it makes the most sense." Kinsey waited for Hughes' reluctant nod, then continued. "Okay, Torres is in charge of my guys, but he's clear he's to take orders from you. That said, I'm figuring you'll defer to his opinion when it comes to defense and security issues."

"Absolutely," Hughes said.

"READY TO SHOVE OFF, CHIEF?" came a shout from below. Both men looked down to see Bollinger standing in the patrol boat as it idled at the bottom of the accommodation ladder, the floating trailer secured to a tow-ing bridle behind it. Kinsey raised his hand in acknowledgment, turned to Hughes, and offered his hand.

Hughes shook Kinsey's hand. "Don't worry about us, Matt. Just get to Baton Rouge and bring your family back. And try checking in from the Calca-sieu Lock. Your antenna's not very high, so you may be beyond VHF range, but call if you can."

"Thank you, Jordan," Kinsey said. "I'll be back as soon as I can. Take good care of the Ark for us while we're gone."

Hughes nodded and Kinsey released his hand to rush down the accom-modation ladder to the waiting boat.

WARDEN'S OFFICE
FEDERAL CORRECTION COMPLEX
BEAUMONT, TEXAS

DAY 26, 10:45 A.M.

Darren 'Spike' McComb, formerly federal inmate number 26852-278, formerly recipient of a triple life sentence and currently captain of the Aryan Brotherhood of Texas, glared across the desk.

"So those idiots just let them cruise down the river liked they owned it? Is that what you're telling me, Snaggle?"

Across from McComb, Owen Fairchild, aka 'Snaggle' for his dental issues, squirmed in his seat. "They reported in soon as they saw it," he whined, "but you said no radios in case the ship had our frequency and was listening, and by the time they got word back here down the various lookout points along the river, the boats had already passed."

"And nobody thought it might be a good idea to, you know, SHOOT THE BASTARDS!"

"They had that damned machine gun, Spike. Can't blame the boys for not wantin' to tangle with that. Besides—"

"All right, all right," McComb said, "you say they split up?"

Snaggle nodded. "I had a couple of the boys on top of the big bridge. They said the Coast Guard boat with two guys on it turned up the canal toward Louisiana and our... the other boat with the machine gun hung around at the canal entrance for a while, like it was trying to make sure nobody followed the Coast Guard boat. Then they ran back to the ship at top speed."

McComb bit back his wrath at the mention of the Sheriff's Department patrol boat he'd lost in last week's fight with the ship's crew. He pondered the possibilities as the silence grew.

"Ahh... Spike?"

"Yeah, just thinking," McComb said. "So they put a machine gun on our boat, but what happened to the one on the Coast Guard boat?"

Snaggle shrugged. "The boys said it didn't have one. I guess that must be the one on our boat. Looks like they switched it over."

McComb rubbed his chin. "Which likely means they ain't got that many of them, maybe only the one. That's all we seen, anyway."

Snaggle shook his head. "I reckon one's enough when they got open water or marsh all around. Ain't no way to sneak up on 'em."

"You just let me worry about that, genius," McComb said. "Now what about this thing the Coast Guard boat was towing. What was it?"

"The boys said it looked like some sort of raft made out of oil drums. They never seen nothing like it."

"Well, whatever it is," McComb said, "I doubt it's a problem for us, and a boat and two shooters out of the way cuts down the odds a bit anyway. What sort of intel you been able to develop on that ship?"

"I been keepin' a lookout hidden at the terminal across the river, just like you said. Based on the uniforms and coveralls, we make it to be about a half dozen of those Coast Guard assholes, give or take counting the two that just left, and maybe twenty ship's crew. They also have a bunch of women and kids. Hard to tell for sure, we can only see who comes outside on deck, but for sure less than fifty all told."

"Shooters?" McComb asked.

Snaggle shrugged. "Best guess, I'd say max around twenty-five. We know the Coasties have M4s from our previous run-in, but we got no idea if the others are armed, and if so, how well. But it don't really matter, Spike. With all that open water and that machine gun—"

McComb silenced him with a look. "I swear, Snaggle, if you don't shut the hell up about that, I'm gonna cap your ass myself. It's hard enough to get these morons all movin' in the right direction without you wringing your hands like a pussy and moanin' about how tough it is. Keep it up and you WILL regret it. We clear on that?"

"S-sorry, Spike. It's just that—"

"How many troops we got?"

"Almost a thousand now," Snaggle said, "but that don't mean—"

"And how many shooters they got again? Maybe two dozen, if that? Now doesn't that seem like the situation is leaning our way pretty heavily? Maybe they shot the hell out of us when we weren't expecting it, but now we know the score, and we'll crush 'em like bugs."

"But that's just it, Spike. They're cut off on that ship, so they can't bother us. Why don't we just ignore 'em?"

"Because shit brain, they ain't a problem now, but they likely will be. They got guns, and they'll likely be lookin' to grow, 'cause they can't stay on that ship forever. Sooner or later, they'll be a problem, and I'd rather take 'em out while they're weak. They kicked our asses last week 'cause we didn't know who they were or understand what was happenin', but round two ain't gonna go like that at all." McComb paused. "I'll figure out some way to take 'em out. Leave that to me. Now, how's everything else going?"

"Damn good, actually. With the National Guard units tied up in Houston and Dallas and those FEMA assholes all clustered around the nuke plant in Bay City, we're golden. And pretending to be cops is the icing on the cake. The nigger and beaner gangs have been runnin' wild, and everybody was happy to see uniforms." He smiled. "At first anyway. Course, they feel a bit different after we mostly cleaned out the bangers and started collectin' taxes. But there's still a lot of guns out there, and people are startin' to get pissed, but we can handle it 'cause we're the only ones with any organization."

"Which is just my point. We don't want this friggin' ship to become the center of any organized push back. We need to take care of them now."

M/V *Pecos Trader*
Sun Lower Anchorage
Neches River
Near Nederland, Texas

Day 26, 1:35 p.m.

Hughes stood on the flying bridge, struggling to hide his skepticism as he watched the two engineers put the finishing touches on what he'd secretly christened 'Gowan's Folly.' He cleared his throat loudly, and Dan Gowan, the chief engineer, turned from what he was doing, his irritation obvious, if unstated.

"You need something, Cap?"

"Uhh… are you sure this is completely safe, Dan. I mean, the starting air pressure is, what, three hundred pounds?"

"Four hundred and fifty pounds," Gowan corrected, nodding to the first engineer who was working beside him, "but Rich used extra-heavy pipe for it all and ran the new line straight up from the starting air tanks in the engine room. We hydrostatically tested it to over seven hundred pounds; she's safe. Whether it works is another question."

Hughes studied the arrangement. It was simple enough, a two-inch pipe running up the outside of the deckhouse and terminating in a high-pressure ball valve mounted on the top handrail at the edge of the flying bridge. The valve was connected via a short section of hydraulic hose to the closed end of a six-foot-long section of three-inch pipe, with the open end of the pipe pointed at the riverbank in the distance. The three-inch pipe was fastened to the top handrail via a ball joint that allowed the 'muzzle' of the little makeshift cannon to be pointed in any direction, and the flexible hydraulic hose accommodated that freedom of movement. Two handles welded on the back end of the pipe could be grasped like a steering wheel and used to aim the crude device.

"We'll need some sort of sight, but before we invest time in that, I figure we need to see if it even works. Ready, Rich?" Gowan asked the first engineer.

"Ready as I'll ever be, I guess," Rich Martin replied. He reached over and swiveled the muzzle of the cannon inboard, then dipped into a canvas bag at his feet and pulled out a Coke can. He held it with a rag and smeared it with a thick coating of grease from an open pail on the deck, then eased the greasy mess into the muzzle of the makeshift gun. It was a snug fit and the muscles in Martin's arms flexed as he pushed the can down the pipe with a broomstick handle.

Martin looked puzzled, then glanced over at Gowan. "It's getting harder. We forgot to open the vent, Chief."

Gowan nodded and opened a small vent valve at the rear of the crude cannon, rewarded by a hiss as trapped air escaped and Martin pushed the can all the way down the pipe with ease. Gowan grinned and closed the valve.

"Now that's a tight fit," he said.

Hughes gasped. "We're shooting COKES!"

"Just the cans," Gowan said. "Polak had a bunch of empties and I stopped him before he crushed 'em so we could use them as molds. We cut the top off and filled 'em with Quikrete. But this is just an experiment; we should be able to shoot anything that's a relatively snug fit. We're smearing grease all over 'em to make a tighter seal and speed the exit. Also if we have to point it down at something close, there's a vacuum behind the can now, which will keep the round from sliding out the barrel. That was Rich's idea."

Hughes was shaking his head in disbelief, but beside him, Manuel Torres, formerly petty officer first class, United States Coast Guard, was grinning. "First class, Chief," he said to Gowan. "So what's the range?"

Gowan shrugged. "We're about to find out." He turned to Martin. "You want to aim or work the valve, Rich?"

"The honor's all yours, Chief. You take the shot and I'll work the valve. What's your target?"

"I'm just gonna aim her up over the refinery docks so we see how far she'll throw a round."

"Sounds like a plan," Martin said, moving to the valve. "Just say when."

Gowan grabbed the handles with both hands and turned the pipe toward the refinery docks on the far bank, elevating the muzzle at approximately forty-five degrees.

"Ready. Aim. Fire!"

Hughes flinched as Rich Martin moved the valve handle a quarter of a turn and back, cycling the valve open and closed, and a roar momentarily filled the air. Then Torres shouted, "There," and Hughes followed his pointing finger to be rewarded by a flash of bright red as the sun reflected off the can already across the river and high above the refinery docks. It flew out of sight, and scant seconds later, a loud metallic CLANG was heard in the distance.

Rich Martin grinned over at Gowan. "Sounds like you killed a tank in the tank farm, Chief."

Gowan's grin was equally wide. "Well, I'll be damned. It actually worked."

Hughes was grinning too now, but he looked over to see Torres staring at the Sun Terminal docks across the river.

"What's up, Mr. Torres?" he asked.

"Watch the docks over there a minute. You'll see it."

Hughes turned his attention to the far terminal, and soon he did see it, the flash of sun reflecting off a binoculars' lenses.

"Dan, do you see—"

"I got it," Gowan said. "Right below the loading arms."

"Well, you got your range test," Hughes said. "You want to try for accuracy?"

Gowan grinned at Hughes. "Why the hell not. Let's see if we can treat our curious friend to a Coke, Rich."

Martin reloaded, and Gowan pointed directly at the target, but the shot splashed into the river just short of the terminal dock. They reloaded again and Gowan elevated the muzzle a bit, and the shot flew over the top of the loading arms to land out of sight in the open field behind the terminal. On the next reload, Gowan aimed lower and was rewarded by the ringing sound of a rock on steel as the fourth shot slammed into the top of the loading arms.

"Movement on the dock," Torres said, binoculars clamped to his eyes. Moments later they heard the roar of a distant engine and saw a plume of dust rising from the gravel road hidden from their view by the terminal dock.

"I do believe our peeping tom decided to leave," Hughes said, and the others laughed.

Hughes grew serious. "This is great, Dan. Can you rig up any more?"

Gowan stroked his chin. "I think we can probably scrounge up enough material to rig up a few more. But it needs work. We need to come up with a better sight for close shots and some sort of graduated angle marker so we can make sure we get it back on target after each reload when we have the muzzle elevated. Then we need to—"

Hughes held up both hands, palms outward. "Spare me the details. Let's just say you're going to improve it, right?"

"Well, of course," Gowan said.

Hughes' grin returned. "Good, because your new title is chief of engineering and artillery."

Gowan was about to protest when they heard the ring of footsteps on steel treads and turned in time to see Georgia Howell at the top of the stairway to the flying bridge.

"Captain," she said, "Matt Kinsey's on the VHF. They made it to Calcasieu Lock and he wants to talk to you."

CHAPTER FIVE

Day 26, 11:55 a.m.

Kinsey shook his head as he returned the VHF handset to its rack. "Nothing. I guess we're out of range. I figured it might be a stretch."

"Too bad," Bollinger said as he steered the boat toward the sharp bend in the river. "I gotta admit, knowing the cavalry was on the other end of the radio was reassuring. But we knew it wouldn't last."

"Yeah, but it sure makes it all real, doesn't it," Kinsey said, adding, "And I thank you for coming along, Bollinger. You know you didn't have to."

"Wouldn't have it any other way, boss. Besides—" Bollinger grinned "—Torres said it was my turn to watch you."

Kinsey chuckled, and Bollinger focused on the river ahead.

"Crap!" Bollinger said as he eased the boat around the bend in the short section where the Intracoastal Waterway followed the existing river channel. "I guess that settles whether or not the lock's open, Chief."

Ahead in the distance, where the Intracoastal left the winding river to continue southeast as a man-made gash through the marsh, both sides of the entrance to Calcasieu Lock were lined with push boats, their barges grounded in the soft mud of the banks to hold them in place. Like the rest of the idle tows they'd seen so far, there were no signs of life. Anyone aboard was either staying out of sight or the crews had abandoned the boats to strike off for their homes.

"Half a dozen tows," Bollinger said. "Actually, I'd have expected more with the lock closed all this time."

"Me too, now that you mention it." Kinsey stifled a curse. "I'd hoped we wouldn't have to try the trailer until the locks further on. And I hadn't figured on all these tows jamming access to the bank. I'm not sure we can get close enough to pull her out."

"What are we going to do?" Bollinger asked.

Kinsey turned the VHF selector to channel 14. "Well, I doubt it does any good, but I guess I'll hail the lock and see if anyone's still there."

He keyed the mic. "Calcasieu Locks, Calcasieu Locks. This is the US Coast Guard. Do you copy? Over."

He repeated the call with no response. He was about to hail a third time when his radio crackled.

"'Bout time y'all showed up, Coast Guard. Ain't nobody home at the lock. Y'all come on over and have some coffee."

Movement caught Kinsey's eye and he saw a man waving from the wheel-house door of one of the towboats.

"That you waving at me?" Kinsey asked into the mic.

"That would be me," came the reply.

"Take us alongside, Bollinger," Kinsey said. "But lay off a ways until we get a better feel for the situation."

Bollinger nodded, then glanced back to see how their own tow was riding before edging alongside the towboat. Kinsey studied the vessel as they approached. It was an older boat, but well maintained. Even under the present conditions, the blue and white paint looked fresh, the brass was bright, and the decks were clean, obviously freshly washed. The name JUDY ANN was neatly lettered across her stern and on a name board attached to the pilot-house. Under her name on the stern was her hailing port, Greenville, Mississippi.

Kinsey's study of the boat was interrupted as someone came out of the deckhouse to stand at the rail. He recognized the man who'd waved to him and let Bollinger bring their boat to within twenty feet of the towboat.

"Hold her right here, Bollinger. And be ready to jet if I give you the word."

"Got it, Chief," Bollinger replied. Kinsey exited the small cabin, his hand resting casually on his sidearm.

"Mornin'," he called across the gap.

The man's smile faded as he noticed Kinsey's hand. He nodded. "Mornin' back. You plannin' on shootin' somebody?"

Kinsey flashed an uneasy smile. "You can't be too careful these days."

The man nodded. "That's a fact. So why don't you take that hand away from your gun nice and slow."

"And why would I do that?" Kinsey asked.

"Because there's a feller in that boat just ahead of us who has your head in the crosshairs of a thirty ought six, and another one with a bead on your boat driver there. One signal from me and you're both dead meat."

Crap, Kinsey thought, *how could I be so friggin' dumb?* He started to glance back toward Bollinger.

"I wouldn't do it," the man said. "I don't want to blow y'all away, but I will, you force my hand. Now do us both a favor and take your hand away from your gun, slow like."

Kinsey hesitated, wondering whether the guy was bluffing, then did as ordered.

"Look," he said, "You don't want to—"

"Now," the man said, "unzip them coveralls and drop them to your waist. I want to see your arms."

"What the hell—"

"I'm lookin' for tattoos. Just do what I say and don't make a move for that gun, and everything will be fine," the man said.

Suddenly, Kinsey understood. He shucked his Coast Guard coveralls to his waist, exposing his tee-shirt-clad upper body and bare arms. On his right upper arm, a small tattoo read US Coast Guard and, below that in script, *Semper Paratus*.

The man smiled. "Now that there's about the most welcome sight I've seen in almost a month."

"A youthful mistake," Kinsey said, 'but one I'm glad I made now. Can I pull my coveralls back up?"

"Oh yeah, sorry," the man said, "but like you said, you can't be too careful these days."

Kinsey nodded and struggled back into his coveralls. "I understand," he said, glancing at the boat ahead. "Now about those rifles…"

The man grinned again. "You might say that was a little creative exaggeration."

Kinsey felt a flash of irritation, but it passed quickly. Things had worked out well, considering the alternatives. He returned the man's grin. "Play much poker?"

"Now and again," the man replied. "By the way, I'm Lucius Wellesley. The *Judy Ann* is my boat." There was obvious pride in his voice when he mentioned the boat.

"Matt Kinsey," Kinsey replied as he zipped his coveralls and nodded toward the small cabin of his own boat. "And that's Dave Bollinger at the wheel. So you were looking for prison tattoos, right? How'd you know about that?"

"It's a long story," Wellesley replied. "Why don't y'all come aboard and I'll tell you all about it. And the offer of the coffee stands. I just made a fresh pot."

Kinsey nodded and instructed Bollinger to bring them alongside the *Judy Ann*, then moved to pass lines to Wellesley. Minutes later with their own boat secure alongside, the Coasties boarded the push boat and followed Wellesley into the mess room, where other men waited. Wellesley made introductions, going down the line of men, who each nodded as they were introduced.

"This here's Dave Hitchcock, captain of the *Rambling Ace* tied up just ahead of us. Then we got Jerry Arnold, Sam Davis, Bud Spencer, and Tom Winfield; they're all from boats that left." Wellesley grinned. "And that greasy-looking customer on the end is Jimmy Kahla, chief engineer of the *Judy Ann*."

Kinsey introduced himself and Bollinger, and Wellesley waved them to a table as the other men took other available seats in the galley and Wellesley excused himself and moved into the small galley. He returned with three steaming white china mugs of coffee on a tray and set it down on the table before them.

"The rest of you jokers can serve yourselves," Wellesley said, "I'm only waitin' on the guests." There was good-natured laughter as the others got up and headed into the galley. "There's sugar and creamer there on the table if you need it," Wellesley said to Kinsey and Bollinger.

The Coasties nodded and took a cup, both preferring it black. Kinsey sipped his and set it down on the table as the other men drifted back into the mess room to take seats.

"So, back to my original question, Captain Welles—"

"Call me Lucius," Wellesley said. "You mean about the tattoos?"

Kinsey nodded, and Wellesley continued. "Well, some of the boys that left ran into some trouble west of here—"

"The boys that left?" Kinsey asked, obviously confused.

Wellesley sighed. "It would probably be better if I just started at the beginning."

Kinsey nodded.

"Well, there were already tows stacked up on either side of the lock, waiting transit, when the lights went out. We was all just sitting here the night before, watching all the pretty lights in the sky; then come daylight, the power went down ashore. At first we just thought it was some sort of routine problem, and we didn't hear much else because VHF reception was horrible and nobody had cell reception. Then after a couple of days, more tows were stacking up, and nobody showed up to work on the lock. VHF reception started to gradually improve, and we started hearing bits and pieces of news from Lake Charles all about this solar storm thing. There wasn't much we could do but sit here, because even when the radios started working better, cell reception was out, and none of the boats could call their company offices to find out what we were supposed to do. What we were hearing on the radio didn't sound too good, and of course, everyone started worrying about their families."

"Understandable," Kinsey said. "What happened?"

Wellesley smiled wanly. "You might say we had a little imbalance. Most everyone on the stranded tows lives somewhere along the waterway system, but way more of 'em live east of here, either along the coast near the Intracoastal or up the Mississippi system. Thing is, it's not divided evenly by boat; most crews are a mixed bag with crewmen from all over. Well, naturally, everyone wanted to head home, or at least in the general direction, and based on what we were hearing on the VHF, we all figured sticking to the water was way safer. Headin' home in the boats seemed the natural choice, but the problem was, only the tows on this side had anywhere to go."

Kinsey nodded. "The locks."

"That's right," Wellesley said. "All the boats on the east side are trapped between locks. They can't get north to the Mississippi from Morgan City because of the locks at Bayou Sorrel and Port Allen. And likewise, they can't get east to New Orleans because the Bayou Boeuf Lock is closed at Morgan City, and even if they could, they couldn't lock up into the Mississippi, 'cause both the Harvey and Algiers locks are abandoned, just like everything else." He shook his head. "Not that anybody in their right mind would head for New Orleans. It's a war zone, last we heard."

"You have contact?"

"Had. Just a VHF relay passin' news from boats spread along the waterway as far east as New Orleans and north to Memphis. But we ain't heard nothin' from those guys for a week now. It appears like anyone who could leave the cities did, and the gangs are running wild. From what we hear, those FEMA assholes ain't doin' nothing to help the situation. They seem more focused on looting the civilians."

Kinsey stiffened. "Baton Rouge?"

"Not quite as bad, I hear. The governor and the state government are there, so I imagine they kept some National Guard troops there to try to keep a lid on it." Wellesley sneered. "Politicians are right good at lookin' out for number one."

Kinsey gave a relieved nod, then refocused on the topic at hand. "You said something about an imbalance...?"

"Oh yeah. Like I said, the crews were mostly a mixture, so we all congregated up there on the lock wall to try to hash it out. As you can probably imagine, there was a lot of arguing back and forth. Finally, everybody who lived on the west side of the lock, which means this part of Louisiana and Texas down as far as the Mexican border, came over to boats on this side. The problem was, there weren't near enough people left on this side to crew all the boats, so there was a lot more arguing. They finally decided on six boats, and each one of them took a barge of diesel and loaded up on groceries and water from the abandoned boats and headed west. That's how we knew about convicts pretending to be the law."

"They warned you?" Kinsey asked.

"Not directly," Wellesley said. "They separated and one of 'em stopped in Port Arthur to let some guys look for their families, and had a run-in with the fake cops. They were at the edge of VHF range and breaking up pretty bad, but we heard 'em warning the other westbound boats about the cons on the radio; then we lost 'em. They mentioned prison tattoos. That's why when you showed up from that direction, I wasn't sure if you were legit or not. I didn't know what to do, which is why I bluffed you into the little striptease."

Kinsey laughed. "And quite well, I have to admit. But what about the boats on the other side of the lock?"

"Still there, of course," Wellesley said. "The tows anyway. Lots of the guys took the towboats' aluminum skiffs and took off to see how far they could get, and a few lit out up the road, luggin' gas cans and hopin' to find an abandoned car. There are a lot of single guys in this life, though; those of us with no close family figured with everything going to hell, this didn't seem to be a bad place to ride things out. We're at the dead end of a road in the middle of nowhere with marsh and river all around us, so I doubt we'll attract much unwanted attention. The boats that left loaded up supplies, but that still left plenty of groceries on the abandoned boats. We got power and showers and air-conditioning. Our biggest worry is fresh water, but between the tanks on the abandoned boats and the few of us, we'll be okay until things get better." He paused. "Which I think makes it your turn to share. I'm hoping the US Coast Guard showing up means things ARE getting better."

Kinsey shook his head. "I'm afraid I have to disappoint you there, Cap—Lucius. I'm actually trying to get to Baton Rouge to find my own family. This isn't in any way an official Coast Guard operation."

"So is the government doing anything?"

"Nothing I want to be a part of," Kinsey said, and beside him Bollinger nodded.

Wellesley's face fell; then he looked resigned. "Yeah, actually that's kind of what I'd figured from the VHF traffic. It's kind of a shock to hear it 'official like' though."

"How many of you are left?" Kinsey asked.

"Seven on this side, and around thirty on the other side of the lock, grouped together on four boats. Staying close to where the stores are made more sense than trying to drag everything to a few boats." He grinned. "Besides, I kind of like being on this side where I can take off if the need arises."

"So thirty-seven all told?"

He shrugged. "Last time I heard. We don't keep a muster or anything. Could be some of those boys took off. Why?" Wellesley asked, suspicion rising in his voice.

"Just curious," Kinsey said.

Wellesley gave him a long look, then nodded. "All right, but like I said, it's your turn to share. How exactly do you plan on getting to Baton Rouge? Small boat or not, you're not getting through that lock or the ones after that."

"We brought a trailer and we figured—"

"Is that what you're towin'?"

"Yeah," Kinsey said. "We got a winch we can mount on the front of the trailer, and long leads to run from the winch to an extra battery in the boat. I figure if we can find someplace with a reasonable slope, we can hook on to something ashore and drag the boat out of the water on the trailer, then push it around the locks by hand and relaunch on the other side of each lock."

Wellesley looked skeptical. "You better have a look at the canal bank before you go settin' your hopes on that."

"Excuse me, Chief," Bollinger said, "but if the *Judy Ann*'s higher antennas give her VHF coverage as far as Port Arthur, we could probably give Captain Hughes an update."

Kinsey looked at Wellesley, who shrugged. "Help yourself. If there's friendly folks within VHF range, I'd like to connect with them anyway."

Kinsey nodded. "We'll take you up on that, but first I think we ought to have a look at the situation so we can let our people know what we plan to do."

Wellesley nodded. "Leave your rig tied off to us. The boys will keep an eye on it, and I'll run you up to the lock wall in our skiff. That'll be a lot easier than crawling across all these tows. Matter of fact, I probably need to go on over with you, just so the boys on the other side don't get antsy."

***

Fifteen minutes later, Kinsey and Bollinger stood beside Wellesley on the steel and concrete bulkhead leading into the lock, staring across a narrow backwater at the canal bank. Kinsey studied the sloping bank covered with a jumble of rough-cut granite blocks the size of washing machines.

"See what I mean?" Wellesley asked.

Kinsey nodded. "Even if we can get you to shuffle the barges so we can access the bank, that riprap stone is pretty rough. I don't see us dragging the boat and trailer over that."

"I was hoping there might be a boat launch ramp, but I guess that was wishful thinking," Bollinger said.

"Nothing solid to hook the winch cable to either, and no way we'll be able to manhandle her out of the water without a mechanical assist." Kinsey sighed. "All right. Let's look the whole situation over and start working on a plan B."

Bollinger nodded and the Coasties followed Wellesley along the top of the narrow bulkhead until they got to the wall of the lock proper and walked across a grassy verge to step into a large square asphalt parking lot flanked by a metal storage building. Across the expansive square the asphalt narrowed to a road running the length of the lock, with what were obviously the administrative offices and workshops at the far end.

Bollinger cast an appraising eye down the long straight road. "This is good surface. It shouldn't be too hard to roll her past the lock, presuming we can just figure a way to get her up the bank to start with."

"Let's go see what we're up against on the other side," Kinsey said, and they started walking down the quarter-mile length of the lock.

"Whoa. Slow down there," Wellesley said, and led them around the storage building to a bicycle rack holding a dozen battered bicycles. "No use walking when we can ride. The lock workers used these to get back and forth. There's another rack at the opposite end of the lock."

Kinsey grinned. "No argument here, Lucius."

They pedaled to the opposite end of the lock, only to find more problems. Even more tows jammed both banks of the canal. The bank sloped steeply to the water's edge, and the jumbled riprap stones protecting the bank from erosion were even larger here, sharp corners pointing skyward at odd angles. Kinsey's heart sank at the sight of it.

"Even if we manage to get the boat out, there's no way we're getting the trailer back down over that crap, even with the planks," Bollinger said. "What are we gonna do, Chief?"

Kinsey said nothing for a long moment. The access road ran straight and true beside the canal another quarter mile, then turned sharply to the left, away from the water. A tall bridge loomed over the waterway in the near distance.

"Okay," he said. "This whole area is marsh, with inlets and bayous all over the place. We only draw three feet or so of water, so we can likely get up most of them. We just need to find one that gets us close enough to the canal on the east side of the lock for us to use the trailer to get the boat across and back into the canal."

"But how, Chief? There's probably a dozen inlets like that, and the marsh grass and cane is six or eight feet high. It'll be like a maze. We won't know which one to go into, and even if we get close to the canal, we likely won't know it. We can't see anything from water level."

"Which is why we're gonna have a look from up there." Kinsey said, pointing to the top of the highway bridge arching high above the canal and the flat land it ran through.

Wellesley cleared his throat, and Kinsey turned his attention from the bridge to one of the boats about halfway down the road. A group of men was starting to form at the rail of one of them, obviously in expectation of a visit.

"I figure y'all are eager to have a look at that bridge," Wellesley said, "so let's ride down together. I'll stop and fill the boys in and y'all can head on up the bridge. These fellas haven't had anyone new to talk to in a while. Stop now and I doubt y'all will get away before nightfall.

***

Accessing the bridge proved easy. The lock road turned left and intersected State Route 384 a half mile north of the bridge; then it was a straight shot back south. They ate up the distance quickly, and minutes later they hopped off to push their bikes up the bridge, the old single-gear, fat-tire conveyances no match for the steep incline. Soon they stood atop the bridge, surveying the flat land spread before them, the sun glistening off channels crisscrossing the half-submerged terrain.

"I'll be damned," Bollinger said.

A wide channel roughly paralleled the south bank of the canal, punctuated at intervals with side channels that extended northward toward the canal like crooked, arthritic fingers. One of those fingers ended at the southern abutment of the bridge they stood on, the 'fingertip' separated from the canal itself by a narrow strip of land. At the bridge abutment there was a gravel parking lot, and Kinsey grinned as he pointed down at it.

"You see what I see, Bollinger?"

"Well, I'll be double-damned. A boat ramp!"

Kinsey nodded. "That takes care of the hard part, and there's not any riprap on the canal side down this far, so we should be able to get her back in without any problem."

"And getting there's a piece of cake," Bollinger said. "We just go back out into the river and turn into the first wide channel south of the lock."

Kinsey grinned. "Well, let's get to it. If we can talk the towboat guys into helping, we may be able to get around the lock and well down the canal before dark. But first, we need to have a long talk with our new friends. I've got an idea."

***

Matt Kinsey stood on the lock wall in front of the assembled group, glancing at his watch. This was taking far longer than he'd anticipated and he was eager to get away. He'd had Wellesley assemble the towboat men so he could present them with his proposal, but it had ignited a much more spirited debate than expected. Finally, Kinsey put two fingers in his mouth and whistled loudly. When he had the group's attention, he held up both his hands in a stop gesture and raised his voice.

"Okay, fellas, I understand this is a big decision, but I can't give you any more time. I have to call *Pecos Trader* and put the proposal to Captain Hughes, and I'm not even sure he'll go for it himself. But first I need to know how many of you are in. It's entirely your call, and not everyone has to agree. But if you'd like to give it a shot, I need to know now, because Bollinger and I need to get out of here."

No one said anything for a long moment; then Lucius Wellesley shook his head. "I don't know, Kinsey. We've got a pretty good setup here, and it sounds like those folks over in Texas have already attracted some unwanted attention. I mean, I sympathize, but I'm not sure puttin' ourselves in the middle of that is very smart. I think it might be best if we just stay here and lie low until things get back to normal."

Some of the others nodded their agreement.

Kinsey sighed. "You might be right, Lucius, assuming things do get back to normal, but from the way I understand it, the time frame for that happening, if ever, is years not months. How long you figure you can stay here?"

"We've got food and water for maybe six months, a bit longer if we ration it," Wellesley said, "and enough diesel, gasoline, and lube oil in all these barges for years. I figure when push comes to shove, we can trade for what we need."

"And trading means letting people know you're here with fuel to trade," Kinsey said, "so you'll be sitting on a goldmine with no means to defend it. Just how long you think that's going to last before either gangs out of Lake Charles or FEMA shows up to take your boats and cargo? You got what, three or four handguns between you all?"

Wellesley said nothing for a long moment, then glanced at the other towboat men before turning back to Kinsey. "Would you and Bollinger mind taking a walk down to the other end of the lock for a bit. I'm not the king here, and I don't speak for these other fellas. We really need to discuss this among ourselves in private."

"Understood," Kinsey said as he and Bollinger walked toward the far end of the lock. When they were well away from the group, Bollinger shot Kinsey a questioning look.

"Ah, you sure about this, boss? How do you think Captain Hughes is going to feel about us 'recruiting' extra people? Shouldn't we have checked with him first?"

Kinsey shook his head. "I thought about it, but I figure Wellesley's gonna be standing right beside us when we use the VHF, so I didn't figure he should hear my idea for the first time while we're on the radio. And we don't have time to engage in a lengthy debate and negotiation. They either want to go or they don't. As far as Hughes goes, he can always say no, but I don't think he will. If even a few of them take the deal, it will add guys with needed skills, and from the looks of 'em, I'm thinking at least half of them have some military service, and I'm betting the others are probably at least hunters. We start increasing our dependent population, we're gonna need more shooters to protect them. Besides, that's not the only thing they bring to the table, there's also—"

Kinsey turned at a shout from down the lock wall, to see Wellesley waving them back. They turned and walked back to the group.

"Well," Wellesley said when they reached the group, "it appears we should get on the VHF to your Captain Hughes."

"How many?" Kinsey asked.

"All of us," Wellesley said.

Crap, thought Kinsey.

CHAPTER SIX

M/V *Judy Ann*
INTRACOASTAL WATERWAY
WEST END OF CALCASIEU LOCK
LAKE CHARLES, LOUISIANA

DAY 26, 2:40 P.M.

The relief in Hughes' voice changed to irritation when he learned of Kinsey's freelance recruitment efforts.

"You did what? Thirty-seven guys? Dammit, Matt! You know—"

"They've got their own food, at least for six months or so. Water too. And they're bringing their own housing with them. Over," Kinsey said. Beside him, Wellesley nodded, suddenly concerned Hughes might reject the deal.

But news the recruits wouldn't strain existing resources mollified Hughes to some extent, and as Kinsey presented the merits of his case a bit more fully, he sensed Hughes' resistance weakening. Kinsey sealed the deal.

"Is the chief engineer with you, Captain Hughes? Over," Kinsey asked.

"Yes, Dan's standing right beside me. Over," Hughes replied.

"Well, ask him how he'd like a couple of twenty-thousand-barrel barges full of lube oil of various grades. It seems like I recall hearing him moaning about how hard it was going to be to find any. Over," Kinsey said.

There was a long pause until the radio crackled again. "This may be the only time I've ever seen Dan Gowan speechless," Hughes said. "He's nodding his head so hard I'm afraid it might fly off his shoulders." Kinsey heard Hughes sigh into the radio. "Put Captain Wellesley on and we'll work out the details. If he gives me an ETA at the Neches intersection, we'll send the patrol boat out to escort his little convoy in and keep the cons off him. And, Matt," Hughes added, "this will likely be the last we hear from you before you return, so Godspeed in finding your family. Over."

"Thanks, Cap," Kinsey replied. "Here's Captain Wellesley. Over."

***

Kinsey and Bollinger sat at a table in the galley of the *Lacy J*, one of the towboats trapped east of the lock. They had a chart booklet open on the table between them, and Wellesley was hunched over them, studying a chart.

"We appreciate this, Lucius," Kinsey said. "Obviously, *Pecos Trader* didn't carry inland charts."

Wellesley laughed. "Well, it ain't like these boats are likely to need them anytime soon."

"Still, we appreciate it," Kinsey said. "I knew the route, but operating with a Louisiana road map and a general idea leaves a lot to be desired."

Wellesley waved away their thanks. "No problem. Y'all about ready to shove off?"

"Yeah," Bollinger said, "thanks again to you fellas."

As hoped, their new shipmates had readily agreed to help get the Coasties' boat over the narrow strip of land and back into the canal. If many hands hadn't made 'light work,' they had at least made it much faster and possible without necessitating the use of the electric winch.

A dozen towboat men had taken their flat-bottom aluminum skiffs and motored over to come ashore by the bridge abutment and meet the Coasties at the boat ramp they'd discovered earlier. The patrol boat nosed into the ramp and Kinsey untied the trailer tow rope and tossed it to the men ashore before Bollinger backed the boat back out into the bayou. Their new helpers pulled the trailer toward shore until the wheels engaged the sloping concrete ramp and then held it there until Bollinger drove the boat onto the trailer, and Kinsey splashed down to hook the securing cable into the pad eye on the front of the boat and used the hand winch to pull the boat the rest of the way on to the trailer. Bollinger hopped out of the boat as well, and the mass of men clustered around the trailer, straining and grunting, to roll it up the boat ramp.

Even with a dozen extra men, the task had been difficult, with the combined weight of the boat and trailer increased by Dan Gowan's improvised flotation pontoons. They worked the trailer up the ramp in increments, all of them heaving on a count of three. It took two dozen heaves to get the trailer to level ground, but after that, rolling it over to the canal had been relatively easy.

They reversed the process to relaunch the boat into the canal, the challenge here being the muddy slope of the canal bank. They countered that with wide wooden planks the Coasties had brought along, lashed to the trailer in anticipation of just such a situation. They laid the planks end to end behind each wheel, providing a firm path for the trailer to roll into the water until the boat and trailer were both afloat. The boat had separated from the trailer easily and was now tied alongside the *Lacy J*, the floating trailer in tow behind her, with the planks lashed down securely.

"About that," Wellesley said. "That was a bear even with a bunch of folks to help. And I ain't so sure you're gonna find convenient shortcuts at the Bayou Sorrel and Port Allen locks. I'm thinkin' you and Bollinger here are gonna have a tough time gettin' around those locks. I mean, you really think that electric winch is gonna work?"

Kinsey's nod was less than confident. "I think it will if we can find some sort of reasonable slope to pull the trailer up and something heavy and stationary to hook the winch cable to. For that matter, we got plenty of spare gas in the boat; if we can find an abandoned car or truck, we can use that. Don't worry, Lucius. We'll make it work."

Wellesley nodded and held out his hand. "All right then. I best get to work before the rest of the fellas think I'm goofin' off. Y'all have a safe trip, and I hope to be meetin' that family of yours one of these days before long."

Kinsey stood and took the outstretched hand as Bollinger rose to follow suit.

"Thank you, Lucius," Kinsey said. "When are you leaving for Beaumont?"

"It'll be a few days, at least. We got enough folks to take all six tows on the west side of the lock. I mean, I can't see leavin' all that fuel here. Even if we can't use it, it'll sure come in handy for trading. And besides, the boats will give us some extra beds when we get to Texas. Likewise, we're stripping all the tows on this side right down to parade rest. Not just the food, but mooring lines, spare parts, basically everything." He smiled. "I got a feeling we ain't gonna be sendin' in any purchase orders any time soon."

"That's a fact," Kinsey said. "Sounds like you have your work cut out for you."

"You know, it feels good for a change. We been sittin' on our asses for weeks, gettin' on each other's last nerve, but now we got a plan and it just feels good to have a purpose." He smiled again. "Even if we don't really know what the hell we're doing." He grew serious. "But the problem is gettin' it all to the other boats. Some of that stuff is heavy and gettin' it up on the lock, all the way down to the other end, and back down on to the boats is gonna take some time."

"Something tells me you'll make it work," Kinsey said.

"You can count on it," Wellesley said.

Day 26, 6:45 p.m.

"So how long before these towboats get here?" Gowan asked.

Hughes grinned across the coffee table. "You mean how long before you get your hands on that lube oil, don't you?"

Gowan shrugged. "I can't deny it was welcome news. We got diesel coming out of our ears, but lubes are gonna be hard to come by, especially in the quantities we need. It's not like we can raid an AutoZone for a thousand gallons of lube oil. Two barges full is about a gazillion times overkill, but it means we'll have enough for anything we do in the future, to say nothing about its trade value. Everyone's worried about fuel, but machinery won't run very long without lubrication."

Hughes nodded and looked at the group assembled in the sitting area of his office, his ad hoc advisory council, for want of a better term. There was no doubt he was in charge (whether he wanted to be or not), but it wasn't the military, and the situation on the 'Ark,' as everyone had begun to jokingly refer to *Pecos Trader*, was outside anyone's experience. He needed all the help he could get and had no problem whatsoever listening to the advice of subordinates.

His three senior officers sat across the low coffee table from him on the sofa, Dan Gowan in the center flanked on either side by Georgia Howell and Rich Martin. Torres sat to his right in an armchair, filling in for the absent Kinsey as security chief. But perhaps the most surprising member of the informal advisory council sat beside him on the love seat. He glanced at his wife and silently marveled at how quickly she'd adapted over the last week.

Laura Hughes had rebounded quickly from the harrowing ordeal of her family's rescue. With their twin daughters safely aboard *Pecos Trader* and with neither the obligations of the farm at Pecan Grove nor her large animal veterinary practice to occupy her, she'd quickly become bored. She first attempted to 'help' in the galley, where her suggestions to make things 'more efficient' did nothing to endear her to Chief Cook Jake 'Polak' Kadowski. Rebuffed there, she'd found a perfect outlet in seeing to the needs of the Coast Guard dependents who'd joined *Pecos Trader* in Wilmington.

Essentially passengers, the five Coast Guard wives made themselves as unobtrusive as possible and tried to keep their nine kids out of the way. The officers and crew of *Pecos Trader* were kind, but there were neither facilities nor activities for dependents on a working ship, and no one really knew what to do with the non-sailors. For their part, the women never complained, as they understood they represented a disruption to the normal rhythm of shipboard life, but they were nearing their wits' ends. As one woman confided to Laura soon after she arrived, they were all going 'totally frigging Loony Tunes.'

But if the Coastie wives had been hesitant to address the situation with the captain, Laura was anything but. He wasn't the 'captain' to her, but 'Jordan,' and she quickly pointed out that unless accommodation was made for the children and if the women weren't somehow blended into shipboard life, things would go downhill in a hurry, especially since they expected even more passengers as the families of other crewmen were rescued.

Hughes had conceded the point and placed her in charge of organizing the dependents. Delighted to have a representative with 'the captain's ear,' the wives responded enthusiastically, and Laura was presently engaged in planning classes for the children as well as learning as much as she could about shipboard routine to see where the women's skill sets might be most useful.

As a veterinarian, she was also the closest thing they had to a doctor and was already treating minor injuries, earning her the nickname of 'Doc' from both the Coasties and the *Pecos Trader* crewmen. Hughes was proud of Laura, but a bit uneasy. This was a dynamic they'd never before experienced in their twenty years of marriage, and he wasn't completely sure he liked it.

He turned his attention back to the group and cleared his throat.

"I talked with Captain Wellesley on the VHF a couple of hours ago," Hughes said. "They're stripping all the trapped tows of everything that might possibly be of use. He figures three days minimum before they head this way. He's gonna check in with us every day with a progress report."

"Which gives us some time to try to gather in some of our folks," Gowan said. "The crew is getting restless, Cap." Both Howell and Martin nodded agreement.

Hughes sighed and sat back in his chair. Things had been tense since the rescue of his own family and the unexpected skirmish with the escaped convicts ashore. They'd all been on high alert since then, as well as helping Kinsey prepare for his mission to Baton Rouge. He knew his crew was anxious about their own families, and rightfully so, but he just couldn't figure out how to send out shore parties and protect the ship simultaneously.

"The problem is intel," Torres said. "They got it; we don't. We got no idea how many people they have and how they're spread out, but they can watch us easy enough. We scared 'em away this morning with the air cannon, but they're probably back by now, and there's a hundred places to hide across the river. They'll just be more careful."

"That's my concern," Hughes said. "They already saw Kinsey leave, so they know we're down a boat and two shooters. If they see the police boat leave, loaded with a shore party, I'm afraid they might be tempted to hit us when we're the weakest."

"Well, we can't just SIT here," Gowan said. "Most everyone's got family out there, and with these assholes pretending to be the law, who knows what's happening."

Hughes started to respond, but Torres spoke first. "Maybe we can send out a party without them seeing it."

"How?" Hughes asked. "At night? Y'all have night-vision glasses, so what makes you think the cons haven't looted police and sheriff's armories. They might have it too."

Torres shook his head. "Nope. I'm talking broad daylight. We're anchored with the bow upstream, so they can't see the starboard side from the opposite bank. What if we launch the starboard lifeboat and go around the island, keeping the ship between the shore party and any observers on the opposite side of the river? If we're slick enough, they won't even know anyone left."

Hughes stroked his chin. They were anchored in what was known locally as the Sun Lower Anchorage, directly across from the Sun Oil Company docks. An inlet off the main channel of the river, the secondary 'oxbow' channel continued inland perhaps a mile and then made a U-turn, rejoining the main channel of the Neches about a half mile upstream of their present location. The mouth of the downstream inlet had been dredged to the same depth as the main river channel, both to give loaded tankers a place to turn around in the narrow river and to anchor when fogbound or awaiting a berth. Nestled between the hairpin turn of the secondary channel and the main channel was a low marshy island and, at the slightly higher third of the island nearest the main channel, a thick stand of Chinese tallow trees and brush.

Hughes shook his head. "They'll hear the engine and see the boat when it comes out the upper inlet. It's only a half mile away and the boat's bright orange, for God's sake."

"It's bright orange now," Torres said, "but it doesn't HAVE to be. And as far as the noise, I think we can mask the noise of the lifeboat engine as well as giving any peeping toms something to worry about. With any luck, they won't even know anyone left."

"That might work once," Georgia Howell said, "but we have over a dozen crewmen with families in the area. No way we're gonna find everyone and get them back with one shore party, so how are we going to handle that?"

"How about a collection point?" Gowan suggested. "We take enough food and water to feed people a few days, then head upstream and find a place to hole up. That way we can just leave a few guys up there to find and collect folks, then bring 'em back as a group, or maybe groups. In fact, we could probably use the yacht club just north of the I-10 bridge. It might take a couple of trips, but that's better and a whole lot less obvious than sending out parties every day."

Hughes nodded. "Might work. In fact, it sounds like our best bet."

"I'll do it," Gowan said. "Me and—"

"No way," Hughes said, "we need you here."

Gowan reddened. "Dammit, Jordan, it was my idea."

"And it's a good one, but you and Rich have a hundred things working no one else can handle, at least easily. I'm sending Georgia and whoever she wants along, along with some of the Coasties for security." Hughes turned to Torres. "That is, if you agree."

Torres shrugged. "It's not perfect, but it's probably the best option. We'll make it work, but I sure wouldn't send less than two."

"I still think I should go. I know where the yacht club is," Gowan said lamely.

Georgia Howell grinned. "Let's see. It's on the river just upstream of the I-10 bridge. I think I can find it, Dan. I did pass the navigation part of my license exam you know."

"I know you're worried about Trixie, Dan," Hughes said, "but sending Georgia is the right choice. It's not like we're standing navigation watches or handling cargo. The second mate and I can handle any deck-related stuff in her absence, but I need you here to help me figure out how we're going to make a ship built to accommodate twenty-five people house four times that many."

Gowan nodded sullen acceptance, and Hughes looked around. "Well, if that's it, let's make it happen."

Howell was the first to stand. "I'll head down to the paint locker and see what we have to redecorate the lifeboat."

M/V *PECOS TRADER*
SUN LOWER ANCHORAGE
NECHES RIVER
NEAR NEDERLAND, TEXAS

DAY 28, 5:45 P.M.

Chief Mate Georgia Howell looked at the starboard lifeboat and raised her voice to be heard over the racket of the power saw. "That looks like crap."

Beside her, Hughes nodded agreement. "That it does, but Torres is right. It will be much harder to spot."

The previously bright orange enclosed lifeboat was now a collage of dull greens, grays, and browns of differing shades, some original from the can, and others mixed to yield over a dozen different hues. The paint was applied randomly in irregular splotches to help break up the outline of the boat. In the middle of the river, it would still be quite visibly a boat, but if Howell hugged the far bank, the boat would be considerably harder to spot against the brush, marsh grass, and mud flats bordering the riverbank in this area.

"You all set?" Hughes asked.

"We are from my side. We're just waiting on Dan."

She nodded to the boat, where the end of a reciprocating saw blade poked out of the fiberglass canopy, doing a jittering dance in time to the raucous roar as a cut line appeared behind it. They watched as the line traced a narrow rectangle, then the noise stopped and the saw blade disappeared back inside the canopy. There was a dull thud as something struck the inside of the canopy and the rectangle of fiberglass popped out and landed on the deck at their feet. A neat hole framed Gowan's sweaty face.

"Whadda ya think, Georgia?" Gowan asked. "Maybe four firing ports like this on each side?"

Howell nodded. "That should do it, just so we're not completely blind."

"Rich is down in the engine room, cutting up some steel plate," Gowan said. "We'll manhandle it through the lifeboat door in sections and rig it to the inside of the canopy. We can do the same around the conning position. It might not stop everything, but it should offer considerably more protection than fiberglass."

"Thanks, Dan," Howell said.

"Think nothing of it." Gowan grinned. "Besides we don't have time to train a new mate." He laughed as she grinned back and shot him the finger.

"How long, Dan?" Hughes asked.

"An hour, two max," Gowan said.

Hughes nodded and turned back to Georgia Howell. "You and Torres all squared away?"

"Yeah. Twilight's at 8:20, and he'll start raising hell at eight. That'll cover our engine noise and give us twenty minutes to get around the island and ready to scoot out the upstream mouth of the inlet. He'll lay it on heavy again right at 8:20 and we'll make our run for it then. Between him distracting any watchers, fading light, and our new paint job, I don't think we'll have any problem. We'll slip around the bend into the McFadden Cutoff and hide among the reserve fleet ships overnight, then head upriver at first light. At that point, even if our engine noise carries, it'll be coming from well upriver and they won't connect it with *Pecos Trader*."

Hughes nodded again. It was the best plan possible under the circumstances, allowing the boat the chance of escaping unnoticed while there was still enough light to make it to a safe haven for the night. He marveled again at just how dark a moonless night was in this new blacked-out world. There would be absolutely no references for Howell to use to navigate through the darkness, and if her own boat tried to use a searchlight, it would be a beacon to any watchers. He said a silent prayer of thanks that the mothballed ships of the US Maritime Administration Ready Reserve Fleet were clustered together at anchor just around a bend in the river.

"I wish we had enough night-vision equipment to give you a set," Hughes said.

Howell shrugged. "Me too, but we don't, and you'll need it more here if you're attacked, because you know they may come at night. They're likely terrified of those machine guns. Anyway, it's like Torres said, our best protection is invisibility. If we have to fight it out with anyone, we're screwed, and if they have a boat, it's not like we can outrun them in a six-knot lifeboat."

Hughes hesitated. "Maybe we should rethink this. We could delay a day and set up the collection point with the fast rescue boat and then send the lifeboat to pick up people after you've rounded them up."

"You know that won't work, Cap. The rescue boat can't carry enough supplies, and besides, the cons have seen it. If it disappears, they'll put two and two together and start looking for it. You made the right decision."

"It's hard to know what the right decision is when all of the options suck and any one of them might get people killed," Hughes said, almost to himself, then louder, "But be that as it may, we have to get it done. You need anything else we CAN provide?"

"I don't think so. The boat's loaded with food and water, and I'm all set crew wise. Everybody volunteered, so I had 'em draw straws. I'm taking

Jimmy and Pete, and I have a list of addresses and directions for all the families within a twenty-mile radius and a map with the locations marked. That's seven families, including Jimmy's and Pete's."

"Any heartburn about that?"

"Some, but everyone understands we're doing the best we can. Truthfully, I'm not quite sure how successful we're going to be with the twenty-mile radius, but I figure we'll play that by ear. I'm bringing as much gasoline as we can find containers for and figure we'll have to find transportation ashore. I'll hit the closest families first. If they have wheels, we'll give 'em some gas and let 'em make their own way to the collection point while we continue to the other addresses. And if they have more than one set of wheels and someone willing to help, we'll enlist them to help spread the word and contact as many crew families as possible." She shrugged. "So I guess we're as ready as we can be."

Hughes nodded. "Good plan. Did Dan talk to you?"

Howell made a face. "Yeah, Trixie's on the list, though I didn't really count her as one of the families. I mean, I thought the divorce was final." She shook her head. "Though with Trixie, I guess that didn't make much difference one way or another. How a smart guy like Dan can be so stupid about a woman, God only knows."

Hughes shrugged. "Like they say, love is blind. And listen, bring her along if you find her and she wants to come. We owe that to Dan, but if she's not right where she's supposed to be—"

Howell snorted. "Not something you have to worry about, Cap. And if we don't find her, it's on me, not you. I know you and Dan go back a long way."

"Fifteen years, give or take," Hughes said, then changed the subject. "How about the Coasties?"

"I'm taking Jones and Alvarez. They volunteered, and Jones at least has some experience with the cons from when you rescued Laura and the girls." She added, "And Torres says Alvarez is a good shot."

"High praise, coming from Torres," Hughes said.

Howell laughed. "Actually, what he said was 'Alvarez is almost as good as me.'"

***

Hughes stood at the rail on the starboard side of the deckhouse, staring down to where the newly camouflaged lifeboat floated beside the ship. Behind him on the port side of the ship, he heard the roar of powerful outboards as Torres sped away from the ship at full throttle, in full view of any possible watchers. Georgia Howell heard it as well, and she looked up and waved to Hughes before stepping through the door in the rear of the enclosed lifeboat. He heard the growl of the starter then the more subdued sputter of the lifeboat engine, and watched Howell move the boat away from the ship and up the inlet, hugging the grassy shore and keeping the bulk of *Pecos Trader* between her boat and any watchers on the far bank. He murmured a prayer for his crew's safety and moved across the ship to watch Torres' show.

Hughes got to the port side to find the former sheriff's patrol boat in midstream, blasting upriver at full throttle, already a quarter mile away. As he watched in the fading light, the boat turned toward the opposite bank and then downstream before throttling back to idle noisily along the far bank, as if in search of something. He smiled as the Coastie manning the M240 sent a short burst of automatic fire into the opposite bank.

***

Bolton lay prone on the concrete dock, peeping upriver over the twelve-inch-square creosoted timber that bordered the dock's edge. "What the hell is he doin'?"

"Lookin' for us, I suspect," his partner said, then laughed. "But it looks like he ain't got a clue."

Both men flinched and ducked down behind the timber as the heavy machine gun fired.

"Looks like he's just shootin' at any place he thinks we might be," Bolton said.

The other man was pressing himself into the concrete so hard his cheek was turning red. "Should we haul ass?"

Bolton shook his head. "He ain't that far away, and this is a long dock. If he sees us and cranks that boat up, he'd be even with us before we could get away, and that machine gun will chew us up. He's just guessin' where to shoot, so our best bet is to keep our heads down until he leaves."

***

Hughes watched as Torres cruised down the far riverbank, punctuating his progress with bursts of machine-gun fire at random targets. At 8:20 p.m. on the dot, he reversed course and roared full throttle back to where he'd started, then retraced his previous route downriver, his gunner firing sustained bursts at more regular intervals. *That should keep their heads down if anything will*, Hughes thought.

Light was fading fast, and in ten minutes, the opposite bank was almost invisible. Hughes heard the engine noise increase and grow nearer, then decrease as Torres throttled back and edged up to the boat's mooring point at the bottom of *Pecos Trader*'s port accommodation ladder. Hughes watched the Coasties secure the boat and scramble up the ladder to the main deck.

"Hear anything from Georgia yet?" Torres asked.

"Not yet," Hughes said. "It may take a while to—"

His radio crackled. "Mate to Captain Hughes. Do you copy? Over."

Hughes keyed the mic. "Go ahead, Mate. I copy."

"Captain, I'm on the bow and I checked the anchor chain like you asked. Everything is fine," Howell said, using the prearranged code to let Hughes know they were safely sheltered behind a cluster of mothballed vessels and tied off to one of the big ships' anchor chains.

"Thank you, Mate. Now get some rest. You have a busy day tomorrow. Over," Hughes said.

"Roger that. Mate out."

CHAPTER SEVEN

INTRACOASTAL WATERWAY
8 MILES WEST OF MORGAN CITY, LOUISIANA

DAY 26, 4:25 P.M.

Kinsey flipped a page in the chart booklet and nodded to himself before speaking to Bollinger over the muted roar of the twin outboards.

"Shut her down a minute, Bollinger. We need to strategize a bit."

Bollinger pulled back on the throttles, careful not to cut speed too fast so the trailer didn't plow into them. As they drifted in mid-channel, the outboards idling, Kinsey laid the chart booklet on the console.

"That channel we just intersected goes north to Calumet and south straight to the Gulf, so I figure we're here," he pointed at the chart, "less than ten miles west of Morgan City, way ahead of schedule. I think we need to adjust our plan. We're getting into a more populated area, and the natives we've seen so far didn't look too friendly. I'd just as soon not run into a large group of them."

Bollinger nodded. They'd encountered three boats since they left Calcasieu Lock; the first two fled up side channels as soon as they spotted the Coasties' boat. The third they'd met less than an hour before, coming toward them westbound, a large center console boat carrying four armed men. That boat cut speed and hugged the north bank, not fleeing but obviously intent on keeping their distance. When Kinsey and Bollinger motored past, the occupants glared at the Coasties and held their guns at the ready, not returning or even acknowledging the Coasties' waves. A far cry from the friendly greetings almost universally directed at Coasties in times past.

"It won't be full dark for at least four hours," Kinsey said, "and we're going right through the middle of Morgan City. We need to find a place to hole up a while, then travel at night with the NV goggles, at least through the populated areas. It'll slow us down, but I'd like to be as low profile as possible."

"Roger that, boss," Bollinger said. "I didn't like the way those guys were looking at us either."

"All right," Kinsey said. "Pull into the next side channel. The grass is high enough we should be able to get out of sight in the marsh while we're waiting."

"Maybe I can find one with a shade tree," Bollinger joked. "Damn, I thought it was hot when we were moving, but stopped with no breeze blowing through the windows, this friggin' cabin is like an oven."

Kinsey looked out over the featureless marsh. "Well, good luck finding a shade tree."

Bollinger grinned. "A guy can dream, boss." He pushed the throttles forward and the boat roared to life.

A mile east, they rounded a slight curve in the channel and spotted an inlet entering the south bank at a sharp angle, an empty tank barge, riding high, grounded in the inlet mouth.

"Let's check that out," Kinsey said, but Bollinger was already changing course.

They moved into the inlet slowly, eyes on the depth finder to ensure they had enough water as they maneuvered around the stern of the barge and into the narrow width of the inlet not occupied by the barge. Bollinger grinned.

"Well, my, my. There's our shade tree," he said, staring down the length of the barge.

Kinsey nodded. It was late afternoon, and the high-sided barge cast a shadow over the narrow sliver of water next to it, a shady oasis in the flat, sunbaked marsh.

"We can slip right up in that shady spot. And what's even better," Bollinger said, swiveling his head to look behind him, "if it's deep enough to pull up a bit, we'll be completely out of sight from the main channel."

"But then we can't see the channel either."

Bollinger shrugged. "I doubt anyone is going to sneak up on us in a canoe, especially since they won't even know we're here, and we can hear an outboard or engine a mile away. This looks like a winner to me, boss."

Kinsey thought a minute. "Okay, but we have to get far enough behind the barge to hide the trailer, and I don't want to pull in bow first with the trailer behind us. I want to be pointed out in case we have to leave in a hurry. Take us back out into the channel a bit. I'll untie the trailer and you circle around and nose up to it. I'll get in the bow and hold it and you push it up behind the barge. When it's in place, we'll back out, turn around and back into the gap. Then we can make up the tow again."

"Roger that," Bollinger said, and eased the boat back into the main channel.

Fifteen minutes later, the maneuver complete, Kinsey was reattaching the tow rope. Bollinger killed the outboards and stepped out of the oven-like little cabin just as a faint breeze stirred the tops of the nearby marsh grass and moved through their shady hiding spot.

"Feels better already... DAMN!" Bollinger slapped a mosquito on his forearm.

Kinsey laughed and dug the bottle of repellent from his pants pocket and tossed it to Bollinger. "I suggest a liberal application. Now that we're stationary, I expect every mosquito in ten miles will be looking for a meal."

Bollinger began rubbing the clear liquid over his exposed skin. "What now, boss?" he asked as he rubbed.

"We'll be up all night, so let's get some sleep. I'll take first watch and wake you in a couple of hours."

Bollinger nodded and tossed the bottle back to Kinsey, then stretched out full length on the deck in the narrow walkway beside the little cabin. Kinsey checked his watch and sat down on the deck forward of the cabin, his back against the side of the hull. Soon Bollinger was snoring softly and Kinsey rechecked his watch. Five minutes. Not bad.

The untroubled sleep of a man with only himself to worry about, Kinsey thought, with a transient flash of envy. Worry had been his constant companion since this whole mess started, first for his men and their families, the focus on that immediate problem masking the deeper concern for his own family. Worry came with the title of parent, no matter how old your kids were. A 'good night's sleep' for Kinsey these days was two to three fitful hours, punctuated by the occasional period of five or six hours when exhaustion led him to the edge of collapse. Only on *Pecos Trader* at sea had he felt a temporary respite, and that was over a week ago.

He was running on adrenaline and, thanks to several cups of strong coffee on the *Judy Ann*, caffeine. He thought about the thermos Wellesley had pressed on them and considered having another cup now, then dismissed the idea. They'd be up all night; better to save it until he really needed it. Besides, if he chugged coffee now, he'd have no chance of even a catnap when it was his turn.

He knew he should probably stand and pace, but the cramped confines of the boat allowed little room for movement without disturbing Bollinger. So he sat, parsing the possible outcomes of the coming mission, but focused on the positive. Things were looking up, really. His son, Luke, was safe in North Carolina. With any luck, by tomorrow he'd be with his daughter, Kelly, and his extended family, preparing to return to *Pecos Trader*. He smiled as he imagined their reunion and let his thoughts drift to happier times.

***

Kinsey awoke with a start, heart pounding, confused and disoriented until he saw Bollinger snoring away. He silently cursed himself for falling asleep and checked his watch. An hour. But what woke him? He listened. No noise coming from the main channel. A voice above him chilled him to the bone.

"*Bonne après-midi.*"

He looked up into the barrel of a shotgun ten feet above him. Three shotguns, actually, in the hands of decidedly hostile-looking bearded men staring down from the deck of the tank barge.

"Now," the man in the middle said, his Cajun accent distinct, "wake up your friend. I could do it, but he might react badly and we would have to shoot him. It would be a shame if a slug went through him and damaged the nice boat you have been so kind to bring us, eh?"

Kinsey looked over to see Bollinger on his side, still snoring with his hands folded beneath his head. His snoring eased and he began restless movements indicating he was on the edge of wakefulness. Kinsey's eyes darted to his own M4. The man above him spoke again.

"And do not move anything but your lips," he said, "because if you try for that gun beside you, you will soon have a large hole in your chest, even if it means damaging my new boat. *Comprenez vous*?"

Kinsey nodded. "BOLLINGER! BOLLINGER, WAKE UP," he called.

Bollinger's eyes fluttered open and he lay unmoving for a moment before raising his head and giving Kinsey a sheepish grin. "I was having a dynamite dream—"

"Don't move, Bollinger. We've got company and they have the drop on us."

Bollinger followed Kinsey's gaze to the three men standing above them.

"Motherfucker," Bollinger said.

The spokesman shrugged. "It is possible. Did your mother hang around the honky-tonks in Lafayette thirty or thirty-five years ago?"

The other two men chuckled, but when their leader spoke again, his voice was hard. "Now both of you turn—"

"You're making a big mistake here, friend," Kinsey said. "We're US Coast Guard and we're—"

"First, I am not your *ami*, and a blind man could tell you are Coast Guard, or at least pretending to be Coast Guard." He shrugged. "For me it makes no difference. And the mistake was not mine, but yours."

"Look, we mean you no harm. We're just—"

"Let me guess, eh? You're from the government and you're here to help? And how do you intend to help, eh? Perhaps by shooting my son, raping my daughter-in-law and killing my wife? Well, you are too late, as we already got that 'help' from your government friends. *Mais*, it is nice of you to come back. I thought I would have to leave the bayou to start killing you bastards." He smiled, but there was no humor in it. "But now me and the boys gonna pass a good time, eh?"

Kinsey's blood ran cold. "Look, I don't know who you think we are, but shooting us won't—"

"Shoot you? Only if you make me. *Mais*, I think in a few days you gonna be begging me to put a bullet in your head."

APPALACHIAN TRAIL
MILE 1379.9 SOUTHBOUND
10 MILES EAST OF BUENA VISTA, VIRGINIA

DAY 29, 11:20 P.M.

Anderson staggered the last few steps up to the crest of Bald Knob and stared out over the sea of green spread before him in all directions. A few miles away, a break in the treetops formed a line roughly north to south, indicating a road through the woodland—Lexington Turnpike according to his battered trail guide. Another highway to cross, another chance to be killed or captured.

He was almost beyond caring, a hunted animal driven by survival instinct. His initial goal of making thirty-five miles a day proved far too ambitious, but the effort had been sufficient, barely. He made over a hundred miles in four days and had just passed Loft Mountain Campground when he'd heard the choppers. Terror mounted as they set down at the campground three miles behind him to the north, followed by a relief bordering on elation as the sounds faded. They were searching back to the north. He'd cleared their cordon and bought more time, but how much?

He lived on adrenaline the next five days, using every moment of daylight to force himself over rugged terrain. He made another twenty-five miles the first day after escaping the cordon, then twenty-two the next, but rapidly reached the limits of his endurance as fatigue and hunger took their toll.

His stale protein bars gone, he stopped before dark on the third day to hunt. Supper was a handful of darting minnows chased through a shallow creek and flipped out on the bank with one of the plastic bags from his makeshift pack. Two crawfish supplemented his catch, and afraid to start a fire, he wolfed it all down raw then filled his still-near-empty stomach with water from a nearby spring. His bleach was long gone, used to kill his scent, and he hoped like hell the water didn't give him the runs.

He was burning through calories at an insane rate, and the fourth day 'post-cordon' he made barely fifteen miles as his malnourished body rebelled. He stopped early again near another spring, where he managed to kill a fat squirrel with his homemade slingshot. Unable to stomach it raw, he risked a small fire. He seasoned the animal with the salt and pepper he'd scrounged from Bear's Den, then smeared it with the contents of his last two ketchup packets. It was charred on the outside and semi-cooked on the inside. It was delicious.

But that was yesterday, and hunger pains once again competed with blistered feet and his left knee, now swollen to almost twice normal size. The injury from the spill in the creek hadn't benefited from nine days of pounding, and Anderson knew he couldn't go on. He needed food, real food, and a place to rest for at least a day or two.

He looked out over the green canopy again and spotted the faintest wisp of smoke rising above the trees in a place where no road or habitation should be, well off the beaten track. Would they be hospitable? Yeah, right. Who was hospitable these days? He laid his hand on the Glock. *Well, like it or not, folks, you're about to have a houseguest.*

Anderson started the steep descent down Bald Knob, pain shooting through his left knee at every jarring step.

***

He sat on the slope behind a large oak, well back in the trees as he watched the house in the little clearing. He'd left the trail a quarter mile from the Lexington Turnpike crossing and made his way carefully down the steep wooded slope, clinging to saplings to keep his balance. He'd have missed the old logging road if he hadn't been looking for it. It was an overgrown slash through the trees, probably originating down on the turnpike and disappearing north into the thick woods to his right. He followed it deeper into the woods in the direction he'd seen the wisp of smoke.

The house was over a mile up the rough track, set on a level shelf about a half-acre wide at the base of Bald Knob. As soon as he'd spotted it, he moved back in the woods and circled around, struggling back up the steep slope with difficulty to his current vantage point. It was more a glorified garden shed than a house, like the largest models of the kit-built storage buildings found at Lowe's or Home Depot. For all that, it was neatly built. No smoke came from the metal stovepipe now; he'd probably spotted them cooking a meal.

A white PVC pipe led down the slope beside him and disappeared into the house; from a spring, he figured. There were both front and back doors and windows on both sides of the house, and a lean-to-like back porch with a small generator, silent at the moment. There was what appeared to be a side-by-side UTV under a black cover in the front of the house and a small structure in the rear; a chicken coop, he realized, as he spotted a few rust-colored birds pecking at the ground in the shade under the house. He salivated at a sudden vision of golden fried chicken.

A wire stretched from under the eaves of the house just below the center ridge of the roof and up through the branches of a large oak tree nearby. A friggin' antenna, probably for a HAM set. So much for being isolated. Maybe he should move on.

He was cursing his luck when the back door opened. A man moved across the small porch and down into the dirt patch that served as a backyard. He was short, with close-cropped dark hair, and appeared to be solidly built. He wore jeans and a white tee shirt and he had a tin can in his hand.

"Here, chick! Here, chick, chick, chick!" the man called, spreading the contents of the can on the ground. A dozen chickens exploded from under the house to peck the ground furiously at the man's feet. Thoughts of a chicken dinner rose unbidden once again, and Anderson contemplated taking a couple of those chickens with him, even if he did move on. They'd roost for the night in the chicken coop. If he waited until the people in the house were asleep, he could grab a couple and take off. He could likely make it down the old logging road and across Lexington Turnpike with his small flashlight. It was only a couple of miles, maybe three miles tops, and it would be better to cross the road under cover of darkness anyway.

He was laying his plans when the back screen door opened again and a woman stepped out, also in jeans and a tee shirt, though she filled it out considerably more attractively. She was petite, a bit over five feet, he guessed, and looked to be in her thirties. She had dark hair like the man's, but hers was pulled back in a ponytail.

"Jeremy, please bring in some wood when you finish there, and then get on your homework. This is the third time I've reminded you and I'm not going to do it again. Just because things aren't normal doesn't mean you get to ditch your lessons. No homework, no dessert tonight."

"What does it matter now, Mom? I know everything I need to know to keep up the place. Ain't nobody else going to school anyway."

"No one else is going to school," she corrected, "not 'ain't nobody.' And it matters to me. You've got a year of home schooling left and you're gonna finish it, even if I have to stand over you eight hours a day. Is that clear?"

"Yes, ma'am," the man answered with a put-upon sigh as old as the concept of homework itself.

Anderson reevaluated. The man-boy's age was indeterminate. Though physically mature, perhaps in his late teens or early twenties, his deference to his mother and mannerisms seemed much younger. His round face was animated and expressive, but seemed somehow innocent. Down syndrome. Anderson shook his head; this brave new world was tough enough without being handed that challenge. He sighed. Maybe he wouldn't steal their chickens.

His head snapped up at the growl of an engine, and he edged further behind the tree trunk. The boy heard it too and turned, then moved toward the logging road.

"Jeremy! Come in the house, now," the woman called from the porch.

Excited, the boy ignored her. "Maybe it's Uncle Tony! We haven't—"

The woman cursed and flew down the steps toward the boy. "Jeremy! Get inside—"

A Humvee burst into the clearing, a black-clad figure manning the machine gun on top, and a loudspeaker blaring.

"GET ON YOUR KNEES NOW, AND PLACE YOUR HANDS ON YOUR HEAD. COMPLY IMMEDIATELY OR WE WILL SHOOT!"

Anderson ducked completely behind the tree trunk. Special Reaction Force! He didn't think much of his former colleagues in the regular FEMA police, but these SRF thugs were in a class by themselves. But how did the assholes find him? Guilt washed over him at the thought of having drawn the bastards down on these people. He shook it off. If he could escape, they'd be all right; he'd had no interaction with them. That should be obvious to even these SRF morons. He glanced uphill, searching for a large tree he could fall back behind.

But despite himself, he couldn't ignore the drama playing out below him. "Is there anyone in the house?" he heard and peeked around the tree trunk.

There were three troopers, all in the black uniforms of the SRF and in tactical vests but wearing boonie hats instead of helmets—obviously they weren't anticipating much resistance, he thought. They were all out of the vehicle now and holding the boy and the woman at gunpoint. The pair were on their knees in the dirt about ten feet apart, both with their hands on their heads.

"N-no. There's just us," the woman said.

"If you're lying, you're dying," the SRF trooper said.

"It's the truth. I swear," she said.

"Carr, check it out," the spokesman said, and one of the men trotted to the house, his gun up and ready as he mounted the back porch and burst through the back door.

He emerged. "Clear, Sarge," he called. "It's all one big room and a bathroom. And I found the radio."

The sergeant waved his man back then turned to the woman. "You're both under arrest for unlawful possession of a radio transmitting device, spreading false information prejudicial to public order, treason, and sedition."

"But I didn't mean any harm. J-just take the radio if you want—"

"No need. It'll be destroyed when we burn down the house." The sergeant smiled. "After we take anything of use, of course. A traitor's property is subject to forfeiture."

All the men were laughing now.

Anderson looked back at the Humvee. There had been rumors of an operation to take out the HAMs when he was at Mount Weather, but this didn't look anything like he'd have expected. They would certainly hit targets simultaneously, but where were the transport vans? Unless they didn't intend to transport anyone.

"Can I have her second, Sarge?" the man called Carr asked. "Dwyer got seconds yesterday."

The third trooper bristled. "Screw you, Carr—"

"Flip a frigging coin," the sergeant said, stepping over to grab the woman by her wrist and pull her to her feet. She tried to twist away and, when unable to, spit in his face. He twisted her arm behind her back savagely. She screamed.

The boy was on his feet in a single motion, surprising them all with his speed. He buried his shoulder in the sergeant's gut, driving the bigger man to the ground. He was clawing his way on top of the surprised mercenary when Dwyer clubbed him down with a vicious rifle butt stroke to the side of the head.

"Jeremy!" the woman screamed, starting toward the fallen boy, but Carr slapped her to the ground just as the sergeant regained his feet.

The sergeant leveled his gun at the fallen boy's head. "YOU FRIGGING LITTLE RETARD. I'LL SHOW—"

"STOP! D-don't hurt him. I-I'll do whatever you want. Just please don't hurt him," the woman said.

The sergeant leered at the woman, renewed lust replacing anger. A slow smile spread across his face. "Well, that's more like it. Let's me and you head on into the cabin and get to know each other a little better."

He looked down at the boy lying still with blood flowing from a two-inch gash in the side of his head. "Carr," he said, "you and Dwyer zip-tie the retard."

As Anderson watched, the sergeant stepped over the boy and dragged the woman to her feet by her ponytail, then shoved her toward the cabin.

Not your fault, Anderson, he told himself. *It was the radio, nothing to do with you. This is happening a hundred times a day out here, and there's nothing you can do about it. NOTHING! Not your problem. Just slip away while the assholes are preoccupied. You're outnumbered and outgunned, and getting yourself killed or captured won't help anyone. Walk away, Anderson. Walk. Away.*

He eased back up the slope, then moved to his left slowly to a large maple tree. When he was totally out of sight of the clearing, he moved more quickly, reaching the logging road in less than three minutes. He started toward Lexington Turnpike and walked twenty feet before he stopped.

He looked back north at the road disappearing through the woods toward the cabin. He shook his head and turned back south. He walked ten feet this time before he stopped again.

"You're a damn fool, Anderson," he said to himself. He unholstered his Glock and turned back toward the house.

CHAPTER EIGHT

The Cabin
9 MILES EAST OF BUENA VISTA, VIRGINIA

DAY 29, 12:45 P.M.

Anderson stayed off the road and crept to the edge of the woods. Sun washed over the little clearing and the house, but the Humvee was parked just beyond the tree line, still in the shadows. The boy lay facedown in the sun, his wrists and ankles zip-tied, but there was no sign of his captors. Anderson panicked, then calmed when he heard voices on the far side of the vehicle. Of course. They were staying out of the sun.

He eased his makeshift pack to the ground and stooped. He looked under the vehicle and spotted both pairs of feet. The men were leaning back against the other side of the Humvee, facing the house. He belly-crawled to the vehicle, keeping their feet in sight.

Anderson lay on the ground and considered his options. He could shoot them both in the ankles then finish them when they hit the ground. But what then? The other bastard would hear the shots and hold the woman hostage—or just kill her. He had to take them silently, and he was no commando.

"It ain't right, even if you won the toss," a voice said. "You got seconds last time, and you bastards take so long I won't have any time at all. We got two more places to hit before we head back, and when Sarge finishes, he's gonna be in a lather to finish these two off and head out."

Laughter. "Tough shit, Carr. Luck of the draw, dude. Besides, take it up with Sarge. He's the one who strings it out, especially when we get a hot one. I guarantee he's in there making her put on a little show. He's into that."

"Whatever. I'm hungry. What did you do with that chili we got from the last place?" Carr asked.

"It's in the back, but Sarge will be pissed if you get into that stuff before he's had his pick," Dwyer said.

"Well, screw him. Anyway, he's kind of busy right now and he won't know unless you open your big mouth, now will he? Want some?"

"No. I gotta piss," Dwyer said.

"Well, move off a ways, you lazy turd!" Carr said. "You're always doin' that; then everybody gets your piss on their boots and it starts stinkin'."

"Maybe I'll go piss on the retard," Dwyer said.

"You're a sick bastard. You know that?"

Laughter. "Ain't we all?" Dwyer said.

Panic shot through Anderson as the boots moved out of view, and indecision cost him his shot. He scrambled to his feet and crouched behind the vehicle. He stuffed the Glock in his waistband for quick access and pulled a large knife from his pocket and unfolded it as he stayed low and moved to the back of the vehicle.

Anderson peeked around the back of the Humvee to see Dwyer with his back to him, walking toward the boy. He crept further around to find Carr standing in the open rear door of the vehicle, oblivious as he rummaged in a cardboard box, looking at cans. Anderson covered the distance to Carr in three steps. The man sensed his presence and turned, no doubt expecting to see Dwyer. His surprised cry never reached his lips as the blade penetrated his throat to the hilt, ravaging his vocal cords then severing his carotid artery as Anderson sawed sideways with the sharp edge of the blade as he withdrew it. Bright red arterial spray soaked the front of Anderson's shirt as he held Carr upright until he was sure the fight was out of him, then lowered him to the ground. The seconds seemed like hours.

He spun to find Dwyer oblivious, standing over the boy perhaps fifty feet away, intent on unzipping. Anderson drew his Glock and closed the distance, adrenaline erasing all pain from his battered knee. He was within ten feet before Dwyer realized he was there, and five by the time the man turned, right hand holding his penis. Anderson had the Glock pointed between the man's eyes, his hand steady as a rock.

"Put both hands on the top of your head, turn toward the house, then get on your knees," Anderson said.

"You're screwed, friend," Dwyer said.

"Do it!"

"Can I put my dick back—"

"NO! Do it!" Anderson said.

Dwyer grinned. "So what if I don't? You shoot me and you'll have company."

"And you'll be dead and the odds are even. I can handle that as a worst-case scenario."

"But you don't have a hostage."

Anderson laughed. "Who cares about them. I'm after your gear. Soon as I got you out of the way, I'll give your buddy a chance to give up. If he doesn't, I'll just shred the house with the Ma Deuce on your Hummer and haul ass. Collateral damage, dude. I'm sure you're familiar with the concept. Cooperate and I'll leave you alive for your buddies to find. Or I can waste you. Your call."

Dwyer looked at Anderson's blood-soaked FEMA uniform and his smile faded.

"Now! Turn. Around," Anderson repeated. "I'm not gonna tell you again."

Dwyer complied, dropping to his knees as he did so.

"Zip ties?" Anderson asked.

"The left side pocket of my vest." Anderson bent down behind Dwyer and fished out several with his left hand as he pressed the Glock to the back of the man's head with his right.

He straightened and considered the situation. Dwyer was a head taller than him and powerfully built. If he put down the Glock to zip-tie him, the man might jump him. Anderson quietly backed up two steps then sprang forward, planting his right foot in the middle of Dwyer's back and driving him face-first into the stony dirt, all his weight behind the blow. Air rushed from Dwyer's lungs with an audible *WHUMP* as his chest hit the ground. Anderson stuffed the Glock in his waistband and jerked the stunned man's hands behind his back. He had Dwyer bound wrist and ankle before the man could manage even a strangled gasp. He gagged him with his own boonie hat, using the drawstring to secure it behind his neck, then took Dwyer's sidearm and shoved it in his pants pocket before relieving him of the two spare M4 magazines in the tactical vest. The M4 itself was leaning up against the Hummer with Carr's, and on the way back to collect one of them, Anderson knelt and checked the boy.

He was still unconscious and covered in blood, though the bleeding had stopped. He seemed to be breathing all right, and Anderson felt his neck and found his pulse strong. Possible concussion, but no time to deal with it now. He glanced at his watch and started across the clearing, scarcely crediting it had been only seven minutes since he left his hiding place up the steep slope.

He circled wide to approach the house from a windowless end wall, then stayed pressed up against the house as he moved around to the back wall and climbed up over the porch railing, hoping against hope none of the porch boards creaked. Pain shot through his swollen left knee as he knelt on the rough boards, spiking with each contact as he crawled awkwardly along the porch with his side pressed to the wall of the house, trying to keep the M4 from rattling over the boards. He was almost under the window when he froze.

"You can do better than that! Dance, you bitch! Make me want you! Or do you want me to bring the retard in and let him watch?" The words were followed by a muffled sob some distance away from the speaker.

The man was close to the open window. Very close, maybe just on the other side of the screen. Anderson carefully laid the M4 on the porch and eased out the Glock. He'd determine the man's position, then shoot him through the screen. Chances were the asshole wasn't looking out the window. He eased forward.

SQUEEEEAK!

Anderson froze at the sound of cursing on the other side of the screen.

"Dwyer, you friggin' pervert, get the hell out of here. I'll call you when it's your turn."

Anderson kept stock-still for a long moment, then began to ease back.

SQUEEEEAK!

"All right, that does it! I'm comin' out there to kick your ass!" There was the sound of squeaking bedsprings and heavy footsteps.

Well, how about that? Anderson thought as he braced himself against the cabin wall and leveled his Glock at the back door. The man charged onto the porch naked and turned toward the open window, stopping short at the sight of Anderson. His face registered surprise, then understanding, seconds before two nine-millimeter hollow points penetrated the center of his chest.

Anderson deflated like a balloon as the adrenaline ebbed. His hands were shaking and his left knee hurt so badly he wanted to cut the thing off. He leaned against the cabin wall and struggled to get his shakes under control, then attempted to stand up; it took three tries. No time for this. He had to come up with plan B. He scooped up the M4. He'd help the woman and kid as much as possible and get the hell out of here.

"IT'S ALL RIGHT! YOU'RE SAFE NOW," he called as he opened the screen door and moved into the house.

The woman was nowhere to be seen. He took another step into the room.

"I'M A FRIEND—"

BLAM! A two-inch-diameter section of the door jamb exploded at head height just behind him, driving splinters into the back of his neck as he dove for cover. He heard the racking sound of a pump shotgun.

"DON'T SHOOT! I'M A—"

BLAM! The back of the recliner he was hiding behind exploded in a shower of Naugahyde fragments and furniture stuffing. A buckshot pellet stung the top of his right ear.

Well, this obviously wasn't working. Anderson played his ace.

"LOOK, JEREMY'S HURT BADLY, AND WE CAN'T HELP HIM IF WE'RE SHOOTING AT ONE ANOTHER."

Silence.

"H-he's still alive?" Quieter now. "I figured..." She trailed off, unable to finish the question. It was replaced by another—a demand. "How do you know his name?"

"I... ah... I was watching you from the woods when these guys showed up. I heard you talking to him."

"Well, that's not too creepy, is it? Watching us why?"

He hesitated. "I'm starving, okay? I was gonna steal some chickens?"

More silence. The woman's voice hardened. "I know that uniform. You're FEMA, just like these other assholes. Why should I trust you?"

"I'm not. I mean I WAS with FEMA, but I was a cop. Never like these guys." Or not quite anyway, Anderson thought. "Besides, you don't exactly have a lot of options here, lady. Or much time."

"So you just grew a conscience and decided to leave FEMA? Yeah, right." He heard uncertainty in her voice despite the dismissive words.

"It's a long story, but let's just say I'm not very popular with FEMA these days. They're doing their best to kill me." He paused. "Look, how about this? We lower our weapons; then we both stand up nice and slow and try not to shoot each other."

A long pause. "All right. You first."

Anderson cursed under his breath. Why the hell hadn't he just kept going? He sighed. In for a penny, in for a pound; if they didn't get moving soon, he was likely dead anyway. He rose slowly, half-expecting a blast of double-ought buckshot to rip into his chest.

He stood there a long moment until the woman rose from behind a center island near the kitchen sink, her shotgun held tightly, but with the muzzle pointed toward the floor. She was stark naked, with the tight, sculpted body of a dancer. She seemed totally unselfconscious and in control, a far cry from the sobbing woman he'd seen dragged into the cabin. She saw him ogling her body and sneered.

"So much for 'I'm not like the others.' Go ahead, get an eyeful, pig," she said.

"Ahh… sorry," Anderson said. "Uhh… you wanna get some clothes on?"

"So you can get the drop on me while I do? No, thanks, I'm good," the woman said. She walked backward as she spoke, feeling around on the floor with her feet. She found a pair of well-worn moccasins and slipped her feet into them, her eyes never leaving Anderson.

"I'm George."

She sneered again. "Great. Nice to meet you. I'm none-of-your-damn-business. You can call me 'none' for short. Now grab that first-aid kit off the shelf behind you and let's go look at Jeremy. You first."

Anderson did as ordered and led the way outside and down the short steps. When the woman saw her son on the ground, concern overcame control and she rushed across the bare clearing. Dwyer had recovered somewhat and was sitting up, the boonie hat protruding from his mouth looking almost comical. His eyes widened at the sight of the naked woman. She ignored him to squat beside her son and place her left hand to his neck, keeping a firm grip on the shotgun with her right.

"I think he might have a concussion," Anderson said as he walked up.

The woman bobbed her head in agreement, then looked momentarily pensive, as if making a decision. She laid down the shotgun and held out her hand.

"Give me the first-aid kit. I suppose if you meant to kill us, we'd already be dead," she said.

He handed her the kit. "Yeah, well, thanks for the vote of trust, None."

"It's Cindy," she said as she opened the kit and extracted a small bottle of alcohol and some sterile gauze pads.

Anderson nodded and then squatted beside her and watched silently as she gently but expertly cleaned the blood off her son. The boy groaned and stirred. The woman laid a hand on his cheek.

"Jeremy? Are you all right, honey?" she asked softly.

His eyes fluttered open and he immediately squeezed them shut. "My head hurts, and why is the light so bright?"

"You'll be fine, honey. Just keep your eyes closed if it hurts. I'm going to bandage the cut on your head; then we'll get you into bed. Okay?"

The boy groaned and nodded. Cindy looked over at Anderson, the hard set of her features replaced by a mother's concern. "We need to get him into the house. I'll have to watch him for at least—"

"Negative," Anderson said. "We can't stay here. We're bound to have company sooner or later. Probably sooner."

"He needs to rest!"

"Agreed," he said, "but not here."

"Then where? If these assholes are coming after us, we sure as hell can't outrun them."

WE can't, but I sure as hell can, Anderson thought. *I've been doing it for nine days now.* He looked wistfully at the logging road, and the woman followed his gaze. Her face hardened.

"Go ahead and take off," she said. "Thanks for your help, but I got this now."

Anderson looked back at the pair on the ground, shook his head and sighed. In for a penny, in for a pound. "It's too late for that now. I'm in this up to my neck whether I want to be or not. I've given them the slip twice, but if they pick up my trail again, I won't escape them a third time. And if they catch y'all, they'll figure out—"

"We won't give you up, if that's what you're thinking—"

He laughed mirthlessly. "Oh yeah you will, regardless of what you think now. When they start cutting pieces off Jeremy here, you'll sing like a bird. That's just the way it is, and we both know it." Anderson nodded toward Dwyer. "And then there's Mr. Loose End over there."

She looked at Dwyer and narrowed her eyes. "That the asshole that hit Jeremy?"

Anderson nodded and she stared at the man. He was ogling her naked body despite his circumstances. She broke eye contact with Dwyer and turned back to Anderson.

"All right. I know a place that might work. I'll finish dressing Jeremy's wound while you pull their vehicle over here to give him some shade. We'll make him as comfortable as possible while we work things out. Then maybe you can have a little chat with our friend over there to see if you can figure out how much time we have, while I go put some clothes on."

Anderson nodded. "I have to admit the view is a bit distracting."

"Yeah well, that was the idea. I figured if you were watching my ass, it would be a lot easier to get the drop on you."

***

"He says they were supposed to hit two more places and return to their base, which is in Buena Vista," Anderson said. "And I'd say their radio protocol is pretty lax, else someone would have been calling on the Hummer radio by now."

"You trust him?" Cindy asked, now fully clothed in jeans and a tee shirt.

"Hell no," Anderson said, "but that concurs with what I overheard him and the other one say when they didn't know I was listening, so I think he's telling the truth. We may have two or three hours. Maybe more if we can create a diversion. How far did you say this cave was?"

"Six or seven miles, but rough miles. We can follow a creek bed maybe five miles in the UTV, but the last leg is too steep for the vehicle. I'm worried about bouncing Jeremy around on the ride up, so we need to go slow, and I have no clue how long it will take us to get him up to the cave. We'll need all the time we can get."

Anderson looked down at the boy. He'd started opening his eyes for short periods and made a halfhearted attempt to sit up a bit earlier, but his mother chided him and pushed him back down gently but firmly.

"Looks like he may be feeling a bit better," Anderson said.

"I hope so, but we still need that time. What's your diversion?"

"This Hummer will have a GPS tracking device on it. I don't know if the satellites are still working, but if they are and FEMA pings the Hummer, they'll know it's sitting right here. I doubt they will as long as these guys don't call in any problems. However, I'm sure they check in at least sporadically, and if someone at their base can't raise them, they'll start pinging the tracker to locate the Hummer. When they do, we don't want them to send the cavalry here. Is there a gorge or steep drop-off near here on the turnpike?"

"Take your pick," she said. "There are a dozen places on the turnpike within a mile in either direction."

Anderson nodded. "The nearest one to the south then, since that's the direction of the assholes' next stop."

She shot him a questioning look and he told her his plan.

***

Anderson had just finished stripping the Humvee when Cindy drove up in the UTV. She looked at the pile and the two five-gallon fuel cans sitting beside it.

"That's diesel, right? What good will it do us?"

"We'll need a couple of cans here, for... you know."

Cindy sighed. "You sure we have to?"

He nodded. "Yeah. I'm sure. That seems to be their standard operating procedure. Otherwise they may start searching for us."

"All right." She glanced at the bound Dwyer and let out a slow, ragged breath. "I… I'll take care of him then help you load the bodies."

"I got the bodies. I'm already covered with blood anyway." He paused. "You sure you don't want me to take care of this asshole?"

She shook her head. "It was Jeremy and me he was going to murder. If we had a trial, I have no doubt how it would turn out. It's just quicker now is all. Besides, you said it yourself, leaving him alive guarantees they'll be on us. He has to die. You did your share taking out the other two. This one's on me."

Anderson nodded, then changed the subject. "What about Jeremy?"

"I think he'll be okay here. We shouldn't be gone over twenty minutes tops, and I'd just as soon bounce him around as little as possible."

Anderson nodded, then reached down to lift Carr's body and wrestle it into the Hummer. He finished and drove the short distance to the house and dragged the sergeant's naked body off the back porch. He noticed the man was his size and had conveniently left his uniform in the house. He filed that for future notice. He'd just heaved the body into the Hummer when he heard the Glock bark twice. He looked back toward the logging road and saw Cindy standing over Dwyer's body, the gun in her hand. *That's one tough woman*, he thought.

***

Fifteen minutes later, the Humvee was burning at the bottom of a steep embankment half a mile south of the logging road intersection with Lexington Turnpike. They drove the UTV back to the cabin to find Jeremy as they left him, no better, but no worse. Anderson went into the cabin and stripped off his bloody clothes to put on the dead sergeant's uniform, but the rank stench of his own unwashed body overwhelmed him. He looked longingly toward the small bathroom. Screw it! He finished stripping and stepped into the small bathroom to wash.

He emerged from the cabin feeling ill at ease in the SPF uniform, but almost human after cleaning up. The woman was loading the UTV.

"Sorry, I took some time to clean up," he said.

She nodded. "And we're all glad you did. No offense, but you smelled like a dead skunk rotting in the sun. I wasn't looking forward to being cooped up in a cave with you."

"Hey, it wasn't that bad."

"Oh yeah, it was." She sniffed the air. "But it's much better now."

Anderson looked at the rig. It was a Kawasaki Mule, the big crew cab model. She had the rear seat folded down to extend the bed, and a small trailer attached behind.

"Where did the trailer come from?" he asked.

"Behind the chicken coop. I'm not sure it will make it, but if we have to ditch it, we'll at least have a cache closer to the cave."

He looked skeptically at the piles of gear beside the Mule. "Are you leaving ANYTHING here?"

"Not if I can help it. If it won't all fit, we'll toss it back in the house and torch it, but I can't see leaving it for those assholes. And like I said, if we can't get it to the cave, we'll cache it somewhere in the woods."

He nodded. "Point taken. How can I help?"

"I want to check on Jeremy. You keep loading."

Anderson nodded and set to work as Cindy moved to where Jeremy still lay on the ground, a pillow from the cabin under his head. He focused on the task at hand and looked up twenty minutes later when Cindy returned leading a slow-moving and still befuddled Jeremy by the arm. She guided her son gently to a seat on the front steps of the cabin and turned to Anderson.

"Wow. That's progress," she said, looking at the Mule and trailer.

"I think we'll be able to load it all," he said. "Assuming you don't have another pile somewhere."

"Just the chickens."

"Seriously? How the hell we gonna carry chickens?"

"We tie them in pairs by their feet and throw them over the crossbar above the seats. And you'll be happy to have them if we have to hole up in that cave. Chickens and eggs are protein we don't have to hunt."

Anderson shook his head and looked at his watch. "All right, but we've burned almost an hour of our grace period. We have to get out of here soon."

∗∗∗

Thirty minutes later, Cindy pulled the fully loaded and chicken-festooned Mule well away from the cabin. She left Jeremy resting comfortably on top of a pile of softer items in the bed of the UTV and walked back to where Anderson stood in front of the cabin. He looked up as she approached.

"I spread the diesel from the Humvee all over the place inside and spread piles of easily flammable stuff like curtains and books around. It should go up fairly quickly."

Tears glistened in Cindy's eyes. She nodded.

"You okay?" Anderson asked.

"Yeah. It's just hard. Jeremy and I built this place ourselves from one of those kits, then insulated it and turned it into a real little house. It might not look like much to you, but we were happy here. It... it's just hard, that's all."

Anderson nodded. "It looks fine. Better than fine the way things are now, but we have to do it. They'll find the burned house and think the SRF thugs torched it with you inside. Then hopefully, they'll figure the patrol left the scene and was ambushed by forces unknown." He paused. "It's the only way, Cindy."

Her face hardened. "Okay. Do it, and let's get the hell out of here."

***

They pulled out of the clearing five minutes later, Anderson at the wheel, and Cindy riding in the bed with Jeremy's head on a pillow in her lap. The cabin blazed behind them as they headed north, deeper into the woods.

"How far to the creek?" Anderson asked.

"About a quarter of a mile," Cindy said. "Then just turn right up the creek bed and we'll go as far as we can."

Anderson did as instructed, and soon they were bumping north in four-wheel drive along the slate-bottomed creek. He drove up the middle of the shallow creek, leaving no tire tracks on the hard rock of the creek bed. He drove slowly, trying to minimize the jarring, but the creek descended the slope in terraced steps, and it was like driving up a staircase in places. He kept glancing back to see Cindy riding tight-lipped, holding on to a crossbar above her with one hand while she steadied Jeremy's head with the other.

The fast-running water was only an inch or two deep in most places, though it collected in scattered tranquil pools. He rolled through each with a silent prayer none hid a hole deep enough to swallow a tire or break an axle. At spots the stair-stepped slate bottom was covered with slick green slime, and the wheels slipped as the Mule slid from side to side. He powered through each spot, voicing apologies over his right shoulder for the rougher ride, and with a nagging worry they were leaving tracks in the slime.

The creek bed followed a meandering path, almost doubling back on itself in places. He found it all but impossible to judge how far they'd come. When they'd been traveling a little over an hour, he shot a worried glance up at a darkening sky and the steep, rocky sides of the stream. The creek was narrowing and the banks were getting even steeper as the creek disappeared around a bend. He stopped the Mule and set the brake before he turned back to Cindy.

"How's he doing?" he asked.

Cindy shrugged. "Okay, I think. Why are we stopping?"

"The banks are getting really steep. We couldn't get the Mule out here if we tried, and it looks like this thing is turning into a gorge. Are we going to be able to get out when we get where we're going? And how much farther is it anyhow?"

"Another mile, more or less. Look for three big oak trees on the left bank. And the creek does narrow between high rock walls for most of the way, but then the banks drop down again. We should be able to drive out just past Three Oaks, if not before."

"SHOULD? Aren't you sure—"

"Look, I've never been here in the Mule, so I'm not SURE of anything, all right? Except my kid's hurt and I just killed someone and burned down my friggin' house and—"

Anderson was raising his hand in a 'calm down' gesture when he heard something over the Mule's engine. He reached down and switched it off.

Cindy stopped mid-rant. "Why did you—"

She was silenced by a low distant rumble echoing down the little hollow.

"Thunder," Anderson said, "and this is absolutely the last place we want to be in a thunderstorm. It looks like this creek drains the whole hollow."

He swiveled all the way around and looked back downstream. He had no room to turn around without unhitching the trailer, and even then, it would be blocking the way downstream. He contemplated trying to back the trailer down the windy, bumpy stream bed until he could find a place to get out of the creek. How far? A half-mile at least with a dozen hairpin turns to back around. He envisioned missing a turn and the Mule and trailer jamming between the steep banks of the creek.

"Crap!"

He faced back upstream and felt a freshening breeze and the smell of ozone as the sky got darker. He started the Mule and released the brake.

"I'm sorry, but this is gonna be bumpy. We have to try to make it through that gorge before the creek floods. Hang on!"

"DO IT!" she shouted over the engine and a sudden crash of thunder.

CHAPTER NINE

Day 29, 4:45 p.m.

Anderson picked up speed, and the Mule bounced over the rough creek bed, the hitch shrieking as the trailer bounced over its own rocks out of sync with the Mule. Fat raindrops exploded against the Plexiglas windshield, mixing with the film of dust and running down in muddy streams. It hardly mattered—within two minutes the rain was hitting them in sheets and the windshield was both washed clean and totally opaque as the rain washed over it in buckets. Anderson hung his head out to the left around the windshield, squinting as the driving rain lashed his face. The chickens, quiet up to now, all began to cluck plaintively.

He was driving by guess, using the left bank as reference and hoping like hell he didn't hit anything on the right. But hope failed him regularly, and both the Mule and the trailer sideswiped the right bank frequently as he swerved around blind turns. On a particularly sharp turn to the left, a protruding tree root lashed his shoulder, narrowly missing his head. He cried out in pain and surprise, jerking the wheel and almost running the Mule directly into the right bank before he recovered.

They were well into the gorge, the sheer stone of the banks towering fifteen or twenty feet on both sides, the water rising higher as it rushed beneath them. He leaned out and looked—six inches up the front tire and beginning to offer resistance. He mashed the accelerator harder in an effort to maintain headway and risked a glance back over his shoulder. His passengers were wet to the skin, with Cindy hunched over Jeremy, holding him tight. The boy was fully awake now, his eyes wide with terror.

Anderson turned back just in time to dodge another tree root protruding from the rock wall, then leaned out again. It was almost dark as night now, and he turned on the Mule's headlights, which did little but illuminate the driving rain. He had no idea how far they'd come, but it seemed like miles, and still the banks towered above them, sheer and unforgiving. The water was rising insanely fast. It was over halfway up the wheels now, the wake from the front tires rebounding off the creek sides and sloshing into the Mule. He had the accelerator to the floor, but he could feel the Mule slow with each passing second.

He hunched over the wheel, the water sloshing up to the headlights now and the motor straining to inch them forward. He was desperately searching for plan B when he noticed the left bank was not nearly as high, barely above the top of the Mule. Three vertical shapes flashed white in the headlights—Three Oaks!

"ALMOST THERE!" he yelled back over his shoulder and mashed the accelerator so hard his foot hurt, even though he'd floored it long ago.

The Mule was almost stopped, and he willed it forward. The rain was slackening a bit, the sky slightly lighter, and he felt a rush of adrenaline as he saw the left bank ahead was fairly steep but climbable. Inch by inch, the Mule gained ground and he felt the front end rising out of the water; then the wheels started spinning, and forward progress halted. He set the brake and turned to Cindy.

"WE'RE TOO HEAVY TO GET UP THE BANK. I'M GONNA TRY TO RUN THE WINCH CABLE UP AROUND ONE OF THOSE TREES TO HELP GET US OUT. I NEED YOU AT THE WHEEL IN CASE WE START SLIDING BACK!"

Cindy wiped a wet strand of hair out of her face and nodded. She gently disentangled herself from her frightened son and splashed down in the creek on the driver's side and slid into the driver's seat as soon as Anderson exited.

"WE COULD SLIDE BACK AT ANY TIME. KEEP A CLOSE EYE ON IT AND FLOOR IT THEN RELEASE THE BRAKE IF IT LOOKS LIKE YOU'RE LOSING IT. IF I CAN GET THE CABLE AROUND ONE OF THOSE TREES, I THINK WE'LL BE OKAY."

She nodded as he moved to the front of the Mule and hit the cable release on the winch; then she watched as, hook in hand, Anderson pulled out the cable and scrambled and limped up the slippery slope. He hooked the cable around one of the big oaks and started back down, almost falling several times.

"HIT THE WINCH AND TRY TO DRIVE OUT! I'LL STAY OUT TO TAKE THE WEIGHT OFF."

She nodded again, and Anderson stepped back and gave her a thumbs-up. She hit the gas and the winch simultaneously, and the Mule shuddered and began an agonizingly slow crawl up the steep bank. Anderson grinned like an idiot; a bit prematurely, as it turned out. The Mule ground to a halt and Cindy yelled over the pounding rain and roaring creek, the Mule, and the shrieking chickens.

"IT'S STILL TOO HEAVY. MAYBE IF WE HELP JEREMY OUT—"

Anderson looked back at the fast-rising creek, well up his calves even close to the bank. He shook his head.

"I DON'T THINK THAT'LL BE ENOUGH, AND WE'VE ONLY GOT ONE SHOT AT THIS. IT'S THE TRAILER. IT'S JUST TOO HEAVY. WE HAVE TO DITCH IT NOW, OR WE LOSE EVERYTHING."

Cindy gave a hesitant nod, and the chickens shrieked agreement as Anderson splashed to the back of the Mule. He felt for the hitch in the dim light, operating as much by touch as sight. The safety retainer clip came off easily, and he popped up the lever on the coupler, but there progress stopped. The overloaded trailer was sitting cockeyed, with one wheel halfway up one of the stair-step ledges in the slate creek bottom, with all of the weight pulling backward on the ball of the trailer hitch. No amount of lifting or bouncing would free it. And the water was rising.

Anderson's panic was rising as fast as the water and he forced himself calm. If he couldn't unhitch the trailer, then he'd unhitch the hitch. He'd pull the receiver tube retaining pin and let the ball mount go with the trailer. He squatted and felt for the receiver tube then pulled the cotter key on the retainer pin, cursing when it slipped from his hand into the water. He tugged at the retainer pin. CRAP! Jammed in place just like the ball hitch by the weight of the trailer. But it was a straight pin, and he might be able to knock it out from the opposite side. Desperate, he patted the creek bottom for a rock, then rose and stepped over the trailer tongue to squat on the opposite side, waist deep in the rushing water. It was up to the trailer hitch now, boiling over the pin and obstructing his already poor view. He adjusted his squat, gripped the back of the Mule with one hand for balance and hammered blindly at the pin with the other. Hindered by the rising water and unable to see his target, he smashed his knuckles on the steel, but held on to the rock and bit down the pain. It took a dozen blows before he connected solidly enough to free the pin, and the result was both immediate and unexpected.

Free from constraint, the trailer tongue whipped to the right as the trailer sought equilibrium and rushed backward into the torrent. A glancing blow from the swinging tongue knocked Anderson back. He shot upright and took a step backward in a futile attempt to maintain his balance, but stepped into a shallow depression in the creek bottom, unbalancing him further. He stretched out full length in the raging water, sucking water up his nose as his head went under. The flood rolled him along the creek bottom underwater, strangling and gasping for air, as he clawed for something, anything, to keep from being swept away. His hand closed on a tree root and his legs swung downstream. He felt his hand slipping and scrambled futilely to get a purchase with his feet so he could stand.

He felt something snag the back of his collar, then a tug under his armpit, strong hands helping him to his feet. His head broke the water and he gasped and coughed before wiping the water from his eyes to see—Jeremy. The boy was hip-deep in the edge of the flood, his lower body braced against a thicker section of the same tree root that saved Anderson. The fear in the boy's eyes was mixed with something else—determination.

"JEREMY!"

Cindy was in the creek, splashing toward them.

"STAY THERE," Anderson shouted. "WE'RE OKAY."

She did as ordered, though with visible reluctance, and Anderson surveyed the left bank. There were scattered handholds, and with Jeremy's help, Anderson pulled himself to the edge of the creek and made his way upstream to the nearest one, then reached back and gave Jeremy a hand forward. They alternated, leap-frogging back to the half-submerged Mule. Water was over all four tires now and running over the floorboard. Steam rose from the rear of the Mule where the water was flashing against the hot muffler. They had minutes to get the Mule up the bank.

"GET IN AND DRIVE. JUST LIKE BEFORE. ENGINE AND WINCH TOGETHER. JEREMY AND I WILL PUSH."

Cindy nodded and jumped behind the wheel, and Anderson turned, putting his back against the tailgate and then squatting to push with his legs. Jeremy copied him and they both pushed for all they were worth when the engine pitch changed and the Mule began to move. It was slow at first and then faster, and they walked backward, pushing as they went. Then the Mule was free of the water and it raced away from them up the bank, dumping them both on their butts on the sodden creek bank.

Anderson looked over at Jeremy as they lay in the mud, soaked to the skin with hair plastered to his scalp framing his mud-spattered face. "YOU OKAY, JEREMY?"

The boy nodded, wide-eyed and serious. "Did I do good?" he asked, barely audible above the ambient noise.

"YOU DID GREAT, BUDDY! YOU SAVED MY LIFE," Anderson said.

The smile that split Jeremy's face was like the sun itself.

NEAR THE CAVE
15 MILES NORTHEAST OF BUENA VISTA, VIRGINIA

DAY 30, 6:15 A.M.

The rain didn't stop until well after midnight, continuing to swell the creek. They spent the night well up the rocky creek bank, huddled together under the shelter of a tarp pulled from the back of the Mule. At some point, exhaustion had overcome him, and Anderson fell asleep. He awoke stiff and sore from his night on the hard ground, his multiple injuries competing for his attention. Jeremy snored softly beside him, but Cindy was already up, inventorying the contents of the Mule. He slipped from beneath the tarp and walked stiffly over to the UTV.

"How's it looking?" he asked.

Cindy shook her head. "Most of the food was in the trailer. That's gonna be a problem."

"After we get settled in the cave, maybe I can scout downstream. I might be able to find some of the stuff."

She looked skeptical. "You might want to check out the route up to the cave before you volunteer for that. It's a pretty tough climb and I saw you favoring that leg."

Anderson shrugged. "It is what it is. But I suspect you're right, and if it's as steep as you say, the rain won't have helped. You think we'll be able to get up there today?"

"Shouldn't be a problem," she said. "Most of the path is rocky, and it looks like it's going to be a sunny day. Any patches of mud will dry quickly. We'll start as soon as we break this gear up into loads."

At the mention of the upcoming climb, hunger won the competition as Anderson's most pressing problem. "Ahh, I know we don't have much food, but is there anything at all for breakfast? I'm freaking starving."

Cindy reached in the back of the Mule and tossed him a gallon-size Ziploc bag stuffed with something nasty looking. "Venison jerky. Knock yourself out. You'll need the calories, trust me."

He ripped the bag open and stuffed his mouth full, chewing happily.

Cindy laughed. "I never saw anyone quite so enthusiastic about that stuff. You better take it easy, or you're gonna choke."

Anderson nodded and swallowed a half-chewed lump. "I told you. I haven't had anything to eat in two days." He looked over to where the chickens were hanging quietly. Here and there one stared at him, but most were unmoving. "And I'm looking forward to a chicken dinner. How many of them bought it?"

"You're out of luck there, I'm afraid. They're all hale and hearty, so no fried chicken. However, we might have eggs in a day or two, provided they weren't too traumatized."

She smiled at his crestfallen look. "I'm going to wake Jeremy up. We need to get this show on the road."

***

With Jeremy's apparent full recovery and their reduced inventory of supplies, load distribution proved less difficult than anticipated. Cindy had backpacks for herself and Jeremy, and they jury-rigged one for Anderson out of a small tarp. Cindy divided the loads efficiently and equally, snorting at Anderson's not-so-subtle inference she was making her own pack too heavy for 'a person her size,' and suggesting she divide the heavier ammo between his pack and Jeremy's.

"You mean a 'woman' my size?" she asked, looking pointedly at his swollen left knee. He shut up.

Other than a few days' supply of food, Anderson's bag of scrounged and improvised equipment, and an assortment of gear and tools, there were, of course, the chickens. They each tied four clucking birds to their packs, Cindy watching Anderson carefully to ensure he didn't 'accidentally' kill one.

Cindy carried her shotgun, and Anderson took one of the M4s, giving a second to Jeremy and hiding the third in the Mule. They pulled the UTV into a thick stand of trees and piled brush around it, then set out for the cave. Cindy led up the steep slope with Anderson bringing up the rear, his left knee already throbbing with every tortured step. Jeremy was in the middle, visibly proud of being trusted with the M4.

The trail was as challenging as Cindy said, and sweat poured off Anderson as he struggled upward. They walked with their long guns slung, leaving both hands to grab brush and saplings as they scrambled up the slope. At particularly steep points, Jeremy gripped a sapling with one hand and extended his free hand back to Anderson. The first time Anderson was annoyed, but quickly got over himself. So this was the kid they were worried about helping up the slope?

Anderson's knee throbbed, and Cindy was a hard taskmaster. Despite her diminutive frame, she handled the heavy pack with ease, and she was obviously no stranger to hard physical effort. Each time he noticed her looking, judging how he was doing, he nodded and motioned her onward. The quicker they got to this cave, the quicker he could get off his knee.

Well over an hour later, he limped over the lip of a rocky ledge to stand by Cindy and Jeremy as they stared into the cave. He was bitterly disappointed.

It was big all right, maybe fifty feet wide and twenty feet high. But it was just a shallow depression in the rock face no more than twenty feet deep, with the low morning sun shining all the way to the back of the 'cave.' It was little more than an overhang really, something to keep the rain off if the wind wasn't blowing, nothing he would dignify with the term cave.

Cindy looked at him expectantly. "So what do you think?"

"Ahh... it's great," he said.

Jeremy was grinning, and Cindy managed a straight face for only a second before she too burst out laughing.

"Follow me," she said, walking toward the back of the depression.

Anderson limped after her, Jeremy at his side. The boy burst out laughing again, and Anderson looked over at him, then turned back to Cindy. She was... gone.

Then he saw it, a vertical fissure in the back wall of the cave, just a fine line from his present vantage point. As he approached, he saw it cut into the rock face at an angle and was perhaps eight feet high and two feet wide, running straight back, a black vertical gash in the rock face, narrowing to a point at the top. Cindy's pack with her clucking chickens lay on the ground by the opening, and a bright light flashed out of the blackness.

"Just drop your pack and come on in," Cindy said, and he did as ordered, turning sideways and ducking slightly to squeeze in, with Jeremy close behind.

In twenty feet the passageway widened, and soon he could neither touch nor sense the walls. She ordered him to stop, and he complied as she bent down, her flashlight illuminating a stack of what looked like sticks on the rock floor. There was the snap of a butane lighter and flame flared. She was lighting a torch, and as it caught, the growing circle of light illuminated only the single wall next to them with blackness on the other sides. She handed him the burning torch then reached down and picked up two more, keeping one and handing the other to Jeremy.

"Might as well save batteries," she said as they lit their torches off Anderson's. His eyes widened as the circle of light grew. Even with all three torches going, he couldn't see any other walls.

"How big is this thing?"

Cindy shrugged. "Don't know. We've only explored this part. This room is about a hundred feet wide by two hundred feet long, but after that it gets dangerous. The floor drops straight off into a hole. You can't see the bottom even with a real strong flashlight, but there's water. If you throw a rock in, it takes a long time to fall and then you hear a splash."

"This is amazing," Anderson said.

"That's not all," Cindy said. "Watch the smoke from the torches."

Anderson did, unsure what he was supposed to see. Then he noticed it, the smoke was moving away from them toward the back of the cave.

"We figure there's some sort of crack all the way to the surface further up on the mountain. It must make a kind of natural chimney. We've had some pretty good size fires in here and never had to worry about the smoke."

Anderson laughed. "Next you're going to tell me you have running water and a bathroom."

"Not quite. But there are a couple of springs in the back of the cave. Just trickles running into the hole I was talking about, but it's good water."

"How the hell did you find this place?" Anderson asked.

"We didn't, our grandpa did. Or maybe his father, I was never quite sure about that. This all used to be Grissom land, back before they had to sell to the timber companies during the Depression."

"Grissom land?"

"That's our last name, Grissom," Cindy said. "But we can talk later. You need to get off that knee, and Jeremy and I need to get in some firewood and more torch material."

***

Anderson sat by the fire, perched on a short, round log Cindy had rolled from somewhere in the back of the cave and upended as a stool for him. His left leg was stretched out in front of him, the knee pain dulled by the Extra-Strength Tylenol Cindy had dug from her pack. At the edge of the flickering circle of light, Jeremy snored softly on a bed of evergreen boughs brought in to cushion the hard rock. Across from him, Cindy sat on an identical makeshift stool and poked the fire with a stick.

Dinner had been more venison jerky, chopped fine and boiled with most of their remaining noodles in a battered, blackened, and disreputable-looking iron pot also fetched from somewhere in the cave. He figured boiling water killed any pathogens, and the salty jerky flavored the noodles. It was surprisingly good.

"This is a pretty good setup," Anderson said. "Y'all been using it a long time?"

Cindy looked up. "Not lately, but we used to come all the time with my grandpa."

"You and Jeremy?"

She shook her head. "No. I meant my brother, Tony, and I when we were kids. Then things got... complicated. Anyway, Jeremy's only been here once, but he's always bugging me to come back." She looked over at her snoring son, her face softening. "I expect he'll get his fill of the place now."

"He's a good kid. How old is he? He seems pretty capable."

Cindy's head snapped around. She scowled. "For a 'retard' you mean?"

"Whoa! Time out! I didn't mean it that way."

She sighed. "Yeah, you did, whether you realize it or not. But I'm probably a bit hypersensitive too. Anyway, he'll be twenty-one next month."

"You don't look old enough."

She laughed. "Thanks, I think. I started early. I was fifteen when I had him. Same sad old story, I guess, local teen gets knocked up by older boyfriend. He was seventeen."

Anderson just nodded. It was none of his business, really, but Cindy looked over to make sure Jeremy was fast asleep and lowered her voice.

"Our parents were super religious, and we got married and moved in with my folks. I'd embarrassed them terribly, and despite being outwardly supportive, it was pretty obvious they considered Jeremy 'God's punishment.' They made excuses not to be with me in public, and I soon understood without them saying it that it might be better if I didn't take Jeremy out at all."

"How about your husband and your in-laws? Were they supportive?"

She laughed mirthlessly. "Not hardly. Jimmy's dad was a deacon in our church and even more ashamed than mine. And Jimmy? Well, Jimmy was a hotshot high school jock not at all thrilled with marriage, much less having a Down syndrome son. On graduation day he joined the navy and never came back. It took several years, but we divorced, yet another cause for family embarrassment."

"So how did y'all end up in the cabin in the woods?" Anderson asked.

She sighed. "That's a long story."

Anderson shrugged in the flickering light. "I got nothing but time."

"I didn't go back to high school after Jeremy was born. I just studied at home and got my GED. Then I got a job as a nurse's aide in the local nursing home. There aren't that many jobs available in a small town. I knew that wasn't going to work. Jeremy had no chance for any sort of life unless I got him out of the house where he was considered a burden. I left him with my folks and took the bus to Richmond to find a better job."

Anderson looked puzzled. "But how was that better? Even if you got a job that paid more than minimum wage, you would've still had living expenses. And Jeremy was with your folks, so how did that get him out of the house?"

Cindy didn't say anything for a long moment. "Because I had no intention of looking for a minimum-wage job. I... I took a job dancing in a club. The tips were good and it was all cash. It was the only way I knew for Jeremy and me to be independent. I told my folks I was in business college on a government grant and came home once a week to see Jeremy. It didn't take long to save enough to get a decent apartment and afford a babysitter for Jeremy. We only came home for the holidays, and things actually improved with my folks. At least until they found out."

"But how—"

"I'd been dancing about three years. I stayed away from drugs and resisted the considerable pressure to do... other things, and I was saving a lot of money. My folks believed I was working as an administrative assistant. Then one day one of the local good old boys from Buena Vista came into the club and recognized me. I suspect he couldn't get home fast enough to spread the news, and needless to say, my folks didn't take it very well. In fact, the entire family disowned me except for Tony, and he took a lot of crap from everyone for still talking to me."

She sighed. "So then I pretty much had to make it work, because I sure wasn't getting any help from anyone else. Dancing isn't the sort of thing you can do forever, and besides, when Jeremy got older, I didn't want him asking what I did for a living. So I danced five more years, socking money away and learning about investments. When my grandparents died, Tony inherited some of this land. As the disowned family slut, I wasn't in the will, but when the dust settled, Tony quietly gave me half of what he'd inherited. That's the ten acres our cabin is... was on. By that time I had enough investment income to live modestly, presuming we kept our expenses minimal. Jeremy loves the woods, so I decided to build a cabin and live a simple lifestyle. So that's my whole sad story."

Anderson nodded in sudden realization. "The dancing. That's why you weren't self-conscious back at the cabin. When—"

Her face hardened, and she nodded. "You learn to make yourself numb and ignore being stared at like a piece of meat. If you're smart, you even learn how to use it. I had a plan even before you made your grand entrance. The shotgun was under the bed and there was a knife along with it. I knew they were going to kill us regardless of what I did. I planned to take out the sergeant with the knife and just play it by ear with the other two."

She'd tensed visibly at the mention of the previous day's ordeal, and Anderson tried to change the subject.

"Tony sounds like a stand-up guy," Anderson said.

Cindy grew very quiet, but no less tense. "He is," she said at last. Her eyes glistened in the flickering firelight and she wiped them with the back of her hand.

"What's the matter?"

She glanced over to confirm Jeremy was still sleeping. "Tony and his family live in Staunton. We've been talking on the HAM set every day since the blackout, and there was a lot of FEMA activity in his area lately. I haven't been able to raise him in two days, and given what happened to us yesterday, I figure FEMA probably hit them too. Otherwise I would've heard from him."

He nodded and they drifted into silence again. After a long pause, Cindy changed the subject.

"Okay, I spilled my guts, so what's your story?"

Anderson smiled. "Not nearly as interesting as yours, I'm afraid. I graduated from high school, tried college, but it didn't work out, then ended up in the Army just in time to be sent to the Sandbox and shot at. I got out and was a deputy sheriff for a while down in Georgia; then I got on with FEMA as a law enforcement officer—"

"And FEMA is now trying to kill you. That sounds fairly interesting."

He shook his head. "It's probably better for both you and Jeremy if you don't know about that. Sometimes knowledge is a liability."

Cindy looked skeptical. "Aren't you the frigging man of mystery," she said. "All right then, what about family. Married?"

"Once. Quite happily," he said. "But now divorced."

"Care to elaborate?" she asked.

"Infidelity," Anderson said.

"Yours or hers?"

"Mine," Anderson conceded.

"I thought you were happily married?"

Anderson grinned. "Well, I wasn't a fanatic about it."

She shook her head. "Pigs. You're all pigs."

"Hey, at least I'm an honest pig," Anderson said.

Cindy laughed. "Yeah, I guess you are at that."

CHAPTER TEN

Delaware River Viaduct (Abandoned)
South Bank of Delaware River
Mount Bethel, Pennsylvania

Day 30, 5:55 a.m.

Shyla Texeira stared across the weed-choked length of the abandoned bridge to the New Jersey shore beyond and thought of home, less than twenty miles away. A few minutes' drive in normal times, but times were anything but normal. Still she shouldn't bitch. They'd made much better time than she dreamed possible when they sat trapped under the bridge at Harpers Ferry a scant week before.

Their elation at having eluded their pursuers by ducking under the bridge was short-lived when they realized escape was near impossible. They heard traffic overhead on the bridge regularly and choppers beat the air at all hours as the search for them intensified. They had a ringside seat to the search, because through negligence or indifference, FEMA failed to change radio frequencies. They pieced together what was happening from reports on the radio in the stolen SUV.

It was hot in the car, but the shade of the bridge overhead helped. There was the added discovery of a supply of both bottled water and MREs in the vehicle, allowing conservation of their own meager supplies, along with two M4s and ammunition. Activity on the bridge above and radio traffic was frantic that first day and most of the next, but the third day brought a reprieve. They could hardly believe it when radio calls went out for all units to stand down. The 'suspects' had been spotted southbound, and all resources were being reallocated in that direction.

They assumed the suspects were Simon and Keith and felt a twinge of guilt their deliverance resulted from the Trembles' misfortune, but they could neither help that nor afford to dwell on it. They focused instead on their big decision: whether or not to use the stolen car. It had almost a full tank of gas and two extra five-gallon jerry cans in the rear. Tex and Wiggins

were already exhausted, and both nursed badly blistered feet. The tempta-
tion to ride proved to be too great. At first light on the fourth day they
dragged the brush from the vehicle and drove east on the AT where it ran
concurrent with the Chesapeake and Ohio Canal towpath.

They had no illusion as to the danger. Having observed radio traffic and
FEMA activity seemed lightest during early mornings, they started each day
at first light and drove no longer than two or three hours before finding a
hiding place. Firm believers in Levi's plan now, they stayed as close as possible to the Appalachian Trail and always knew the direction and distance to
the nearest access. They used secondary roads, logging roads and power line
right-of-ways—any route the SUV could handle that kept them close to the
AT and away from people. It was a disciplined progress, darting between
hiding places for forty or fifty miles at a stretch, resisting the siren song of
the open road, which might get them home—or dead—in a matter of hours.
It was agonizingly slow, but orders of magnitude faster than traveling by
foot.

The challenges were the rivers and streams: the Delaware and the Lehigh,
the Schuylkill and the Susquehanna, and a half dozen major creeks in between. They planned each crossing like a military campaign, poring over
their inventory of local maps for the least traveled bridge, and saying a silent
thanks to Levi Jenkins each time they did so. At times they went miles out of
their way to access seldom used and hopefully unguarded crossings. They
bumped across rivers on railroad bridges, and twice crossed creeks on pedestrian bridges barely wide enough to accommodate the SUV, holding
their breath and gambling the bridge would take the weight.

Twice they were fired on by civilians who no doubt mistook them for
FEMA, but they escaped both encounters with only a bullet hole in the SUV.
At one point they rolled into a concealed checkpoint when they attempted
to cross a little-used bridge across the Lehigh River. Fortunately the new
toll-keeper was a semi-honest former sheriff's deputy now in business for
himself. Negotiation rather than gunfire ensued, and three MREs turned out
to be the toll. A man had to feed his family, after all.

And now they were here, the last bridge between Tex and home.

"What the hell is this?" Wiggins asked. "I never saw a bridge with bushes
and trees growing on it."

Tex laughed. "It's structurally unsound. They condemned it years ago, but
never tore it down because some group or another was always coming up
with a plan to fix it. After a while, it turned into kind of a local landmark.
The kids crawl around up underneath and inside it and paint all sorts of
graffiti; some of it's actually pretty good. And it's sort of an unofficial walking path too. There's… well, there used to be… a really good ice cream place

here on the Pennsylvania side. We'd come here when I was a kid and walk across to get ice cream."

"Well, they sure as hell don't want anybody driving on it," Wiggins said. "I didn't think I was going to make it around that barrier. And for that matter, I don't know if I WANT to drive on this thing. Are you sure it's not gonna fall down?"

Tex shrugged. "No, but I think it will be all right. Besides, it's a minor risk given what we been facing lately."

"Yeah, you got that right," Wiggins said. "How far to your folks' place?"

"Twenty miles more or less. How's the gas?"

Wiggins shook his head. "Running on fumes, but I'll try to get us there, or as close as I can, anyway."

***

Reynoldsville, New Jersey, looked like a typical American town. Or more accurately it looked like it at one time HAD been a typical American town. As Wiggins followed Tex's directions through the deserted streets, he saw the flash of a face in a window or a curtain quickly drop back in place. In the small-business district, two fast-food restaurants stood empty, their windows smashed, and trash blew through the empty parking lot of the looted supermarket.

Wiggins glanced over at Tex. She was visibly upset, and he tried to take her mind off what she was seeing.

"So how's a Portuguese girl end up in western Jersey?"

She glanced over. "Make that Portuguese-American. My folks came here from Newark, where there's a very big Portuguese community. My dad is actually kind of a big deal here. He and Mom came here first, long before I was born. They liked it, and Dad saw an opportunity. Land was relatively cheap, and he was a contractor. A lot of people in Newark were really sick of the inner-city blight and many had the money to move. The only thing holding them back was reluctance to leave the established Portuguese community. Dad figured if they were able to move in groups, they might be willing, so he got a loan and built six houses and marketed them in Newark. He sold them right away and plowed the profits back into twelve more houses. In a few years, Reynoldsville had the biggest Portuguese population in New Jersey outside of Newark, and Dad became sort of the unofficial patriarch."

Wiggins grinned. "So does that make you, like, first daughter?"

Tex laughed. "Maybe first daughter to run away to sea."

"Yeah, so how did that go over—"

"Turn here." Tex pointed. Wiggins turned right, and they moved down the tree-lined street into an upscale area of nice homes. Very nice homes.

"So you really are a princess," Wiggins joked, but Tex ignored him, intent on studying the silent street ahead.

"It's the third house on the left, just past the next cross street," Tex said. "But where the hell is everyone? I expected at least a little activity."

Wiggins had no answer, so he just followed Tex's instructions and turned into the driveway of an impressive stone house. It looked abandoned, curtains fluttering in the wind from an open upstairs window. They got out and Tex ran to the door. It hung open on one hinge, the door frame around the deadbolt splintered.

***

Tex stopped and stared as Wiggins moved up beside her. Wiggins drew his Sig. "Uh... Tex, maybe I should go first."

She shook her head and moved through the open door, Wiggins close behind her. The overpowering stench stopped them.

"Stay here," Wiggins said, and slipped past Tex with his Sig in a two-handed grip.

Even breathing through his mouth, he had difficulty forcing himself forward. Had it not been for Tex, he had little doubt he would've turned and left. He found them in the living room and, from the state of decomposition, figured they'd been lying in the heat quite a while. They were facedown on the floor, a pool of long-dried and stinking blood spread around them on the hardwood floor. He disturbed a cloud of flies, who buzzed their annoyance before settling back down to their meal. Both the corpses had their hands zip-tied behind their backs.

Wiggins heard a strangled sob behind him and turned to find Tex staring down at the bodies. He took her arm and gently led her back outside, into the yard and away from the house. He took a deep breath, but the fetid stench of death clung to him like it had soaked into his clothes. Tex was almost catatonic.

"Was it—"

She nodded. "I... I recognize Dad's slippers, and that was Mom's favorite housedress."

The silence grew, and after a long moment, Tex spoke. "We... we have to bury them."

Wiggins shook his head. "Not you. Me. That... that's just too much to expect anyone to deal with."

Tex looked as if she was going to object, then closed her mouth and nodded.

***

Tex seemed still in shock, and Wiggins rethought things. His grisly task was going to take a while and she needed something to keep her mind occupied. They found two shovels in the garage and he gave her one and suggested she find an appropriate resting place in the expansive backyard. Tex nodded and disappeared out the back garage door with the shovels while Wiggins mentally steeled himself. This was easily the most difficult thing he had ever done.

He protected himself as well as possible, donning a pair of coveralls and some rubber gloves he found in the house; but he could do nothing about the smell but breathe through his mouth. He found heavy-duty black garbage bags in the garage and made his way reluctantly into the living room. Over an hour later he stepped back and surveyed his work critically, looking at two bundles neatly wrapped in colorful quilts he found in the upstairs bedrooms, the blankets held tight by duct tape. He nodded, satisfied. He hadn't wanted Tex to have a final memory of her parents wrapped in the black bags like so much garbage; no trace of the black plastic was visible.

One by one he carried the bodies out and laid them on the large patio, then walked to the back of the yard where Tex was working. She'd gone back into the garage and gotten a pickax, the better to break the ground, and she was working with a will, slamming the heavy implement into the ground with a ferocity bordering on savagery. He watched as, oblivious to his presence, she buried the blade so deep it took all of her strength to pry it free. She punished the ground as if it were the murderer, and tears streamed down her cheeks. Wiggins cleared his throat and spoke.

"Tex?"

She looked up. "Oh. Sorry," she said, climbing out of the hole.

She looked over and saw the bodies and her chin began to quiver. "Those were Mom's favorite quilts."

Oh no, thought Wiggins. "Tex, I'm so sorry—"

She shook her head. "No, it's all right. Actually it's perfect. She would have loved that. Thank you, Bill."

Wiggins nodded, relieved, and picked up one of the shovels to begin removing loosened dirt from the grave.

They buried them in a common grave, together in death as they had been in life. Tex and Wiggins worked wordlessly, as if idle chatter would profane the task. It took two hours, and when they finished, Tex dropped to one knee and bowed her head over the graves and Wiggins followed suit respectfully. Her lips moved in a silent prayer; then she crossed herself and rose, wiping a tear from her eye.

She looked over at Wiggins as he stood. "What now?"

Wiggins reached over and squeezed her arm. "We'll figure it out, Tex."

***

Wiggins had covered the spot on the living room floor with plastic, then covered that with blankets. The stench still lingered in the house, but it was far less pervasive. They found the motive for murder in the walk-in closet in the master bedroom. The large floor safe was open and empty.

"They got what they wanted. Why did they have to kill them?"

"Because some people are just murdering scum," Wiggins said. "And with no law enforcement around, those assholes all crawl out from under their rocks."

Tex nodded. "I saw other broken doors up and down the street as we rolled in. I'm betting whoever did this probably hit the entire neighborhood. Maybe even the whole town. That's why there's no one on the streets. They've likely run away, or they're dead or in hiding."

Wiggins nodded. "So what do you want to do, Tex? You want to stay here?"

She shook her head. "Definitely not here. Not after what... what happened."

"How about other family? Anyone nearby?"

She shook her head again. "We weren't the stereotypical big Portuguese family. Mom had a tough time getting pregnant, and I'm an only child. They had me late in life, and all of my grandparents died when I was a kid. I've got a lot of relatives in Newark, but no way in hell I'm going into a city right now."

"Well then," Wiggins said, "I guess you're going to Maine."

"You... you don't mind?" Tex asked.

"Mind? Like I WANTED to travel all that way alone? You think I'm nuts?"

Tex smiled wanly. "Well, now that you mention it—"

"Very funny. Ha-ha," Wiggins said. "Do you want to stay here until morning? Is there anything we can use?"

She considered it. "The place is ransacked, but I doubt they hit the attic. There may be some camping gear and other stuff up there we might be able

124

to use, and it didn't look like they hit the garden shed either; there might be something there." She shook her head. "But I don't want to stay in here. Not… not in the house anyway. Let's just pull the SUV into the garage and close the door."

"Understood. Let's see what we can find, then make a plan," Wiggins said.

***

The attic yielded a pair of old but serviceable hiking boots Tex had put away years before, and they found a pair of Tex's dad's boots that fit Wiggins well. They threw those in the SUV to replace their own rapidly deteriorating footwear. There were also a few odds and ends of camping gear. But the real find was in the garden shed, a nearly full five-gallon can of gasoline for the riding lawn mower, with another half-gallon or so in the mower itself. Wiggins drained the gas from the mower into the can and was about to pour it all into the near-empty SUV when he stopped.

"We should change cars," he said. "We've been hiding way off the beaten path most of the time, but surely we can find another ride here. If we get stopped, a stolen FEMA vehicle previously driven by two dead people might be kind of tough to explain."

Tex nodded. "Gas is more valuable than cars these days. I'm thinking we need to scour all the garden sheds and garages anyway to scavenge as much overlooked gas as we can find, so we might as well look for a car while we're at it."

They found one several houses down the street, a ten- or twelve-year-old Honda SUV sitting in a driveway. The hood was down, but not latched, and Wiggins opened it to find the battery gone.

"It figures," he said, "but I can just swap the battery out of our car. I'm sure the gas has been siphoned as well. I guess we need to see if we can find the keys."

Tex pointed to where the front door of the house stood open, and they started in that direction. A now familiar smell washed over them as soon as they stepped inside, and Tex's face turned white.

Wiggins gently led her outside. "Stay here."

He ignored the smell and moved through the house, hoping to find the keys before he found the source of the smell. He found a high-end kitchen, all natural wood and granite and stainless steel. A door led to a spacious mudroom and what he presumed was the garage beyond. On the wall by the garage door was a keyboard with multiple hooks, but only one set of keys. He confirmed they were Honda keys and then grabbed them and fled the house. Tex was still where he left her, staring at the open door.

He held up the keys. "Got 'em."

Tex nodded and turned, almost running in her haste to get away from the open door.

They moved their car over, and Tex transferred gear while Wiggins swapped the battery. He sloshed a little gas into the Honda to confirm it started and ran, then grinned at Tex and dumped the rest of their newly discovered fuel into the tank.

Wiggins drove the Honda back to Tex's house and parked it in the garage; then they grabbed the empty gas can and siphon hose and went scavenging. They pilfered garden sheds and garages and found enough gasoline in dribs and drabs to almost fill the tank of the Honda. Toward sundown they celebrated their good fortune by sharing the last of their MREs and leaned the front seats of the Honda back to settle in for the night. But sleep wouldn't come, and they talked until well after sundown.

"How far back to the AT?" Tex asked.

"About twenty-five miles if we head due west," Wiggins said. "But I still think heading north and angling back toward it is a better idea. We'll pick up a full day at least, and this whole side of New Jersey seems pretty rural."

Tex put her hand on Wiggin's forearm. "And it will also put us a hard day's walk from the trail and exposed, with no exit strategy for a full three days if we have to abandon the car and run for it. I know you want to get home, Bill, but there are still plenty of bad guys around. Levi was right; we need to stick close to the trail, even if it is longer."

Wiggins sighed and nodded in the growing gloom. Nine hundred more friggin' miles at fifty miles a day. He did the mental calculation and stifled a curse.

BRUNSWICK NUCLEAR POWER PLANT
CAPE FEAR RIVER
NEAR WILMINGTON, NORTH CAROLINA

TWO DAYS EARLIER
DAY 28, 10:00 A.M.

Rorke sat behind the plant manager's desk and looked around the spacious office. It was a far cry from his luxurious new office at Mount Weather, but it would do for those occasions when he had to be 'in the field.' The uniformed man across the desk from him shifted nervously in his chair, focusing Rorke once again on the task at hand.

"We need to get this plant up and running as soon as possible, Saunders. Give me a SITREP, just the high spots," Rorke said.

The man nodded. "Everything is going according to plan, sir. We've got the area fenced off for the family residence camp, and the communal tents are going up today. The barracks tents for the workers are already finished. We should have everyone at work in two days, four at the outside."

"How did they take the separation?"

The man shook his head. "About like you'd expect, sir. But a few beat downs and a little armed intimidation took care of it."

"They'll fall in line," Rorke said. "Allow them all daily family visits at first until they get used to it. Then we'll make the standard weekly visits as long as they're on good behavior. Daily visits will be conditioned upon how much progress we make getting the lights back on. Make it quite clear to them those visits must be earned, and their families' well-being depends upon their full and enthusiastic cooperation."

"Yes, sir…" The man looked hesitant. "But about the single guys—"

"What about them?"

"A few of them are getting mouthy. You know, making noises about this 'not being what they signed up for.' That kind of stuff. And they have no families we can use as leverage. Should I pick one or two and make examples of them?" the man asked.

Rorke fell silent, considering the problem. He shook his head. "Only as a last resort. There aren't that many of them, so let's try a more positive approach. Let them know in no uncertain terms their behavior won't be tolerated, but couple that with inducements. Better food perhaps, and set up a few small 'recreation tents' and round up some local women to staff them." Rorke smiled. "Food and sex are the best inducements we have in our brave new world."

The underling nodded, and Rorke changed the subject. "What about the terminal, is everything in hand?"

"Yes, sir. I sent a ten-man force in by chopper yesterday, carrying a copy of secretary Crawford's order. There were only three guys there, a major and two sergeants. The major gave our boys some lip, so I had them arrest him and one of the sergeants. We're holding them here, but we had to leave one of them back at the terminal to show us around."

"How about security? Can we spare ten men?" Rorke asked.

"Possibly, sir, but we can always use them elsewhere, and truthfully, it's a waste of manpower. The place is huge, and we couldn't guard the perimeter adequately with a hundred men. They relied heavily on electronic surveillance, which obviously isn't working now. Realistically, I think we should leave a small force in radio contact, just to establish our control and begin an inventory. That's all we really need at present. The terminal's only a couple of miles away, and we can have additional boots on the ground there in less than five minutes by chopper. I took the liberty of establishing a four-man force there and pulling everyone else back here. Subject to your approval, of course."

Rorke nodded, satisfied. He sensed an unasked question. "Something else, Saunders?"

"What about those people upriver, sir?"

The general smiled. "Oh, I don't think we'll have to worry about them much longer. Our friends at Fort Box will soon have their hands full."

CHAPTER ELEVEN

Day 29, 1:35 p.m.

Mike Butler stood at the wheel and idled the Coast Guard patrol boat in the current, just north of the Military Ocean Terminal Sunny Point, the world's largest military terminal. Luke Kinsey stood beside him in the cabin, and Washington, Long, and Abrams from Luke's old unit stood on the small deck outside. With possible hostile contact in the offing, Butler and Luke agreed the mission should be long on combat experience. Like Butler, they all wore Coast Guard overalls. If they encountered Special Reaction Force troops, there was no point advertising they were SRF deserters.

Butler studied the empty wharf through the windshield. "About what I figured," he said. "Deserted. Most of the workforce is civilian. I figured if anyone came to work to start with, they would have stopped coming by now. There may be a few Army types around, but even that's doubtful."

Luke looked skeptical. "So we just tie up and look around?"

Butler shrugged. "What the hell else are we gonna do? The place is huge. I guess we could come up an inlet and approach from the far side, but to be honest, I wouldn't have a clue where we were. We'd just end up tramping around in the woods."

Luke sighed. "I guess you're right, but it still feels hinky."

Butler chuckled and eased the throttle forward, moving their boat down the length of the northernmost of three long concrete wharves. At the downstream end of the high wharf, a ramp led down to a floating dock that accommodated a number of service boats. Butler eased up to an unoccupied stretch of dock, and Long and Abrams jumped out to tie up. Butler studied the little marina, eyes resting on a pair of small patrol boats.

"Hmmm. A lot of good stealin' material here," he said. "We might go home with more than we figured."

Luke nodded absently, eyes on the wharf looming above them. "Tell me again how this is gonna work?"

"We're just the US Coast Guard come to visit to see if there's any interest in mutual assistance. If we run into the Army, we won't have a problem. And if we run into those SRF assholes, I don't think they'll shoot on sight and we can play it by ear."

"I wish I was sure about that 'won't be a problem' part as you seem to be," Luke said as they climbed out of the boat onto the floating dock.

"I'm not sure about it." Butler grunted. "I just think it's our only real option."

They climbed the ramp to the towering wharf then spread out as they walked toward shore on the concrete pathway. The wharf accommodated a two-lane road, and train tracks ran down the left side for the length of the structure. Luke turned and looked back down the wharf. Any structure built to bear the weight of a fully loaded freight train was one stout piece of work. There were three of them spread down the riverbank at regular intervals.

Butler took point, with Luke on his right some distance back, and the others spread out behind at intervals. They reached shore, and a paved road ran right and left through a thick stand of trees, paralleling the riverbank. The railroad tracks continued straight ahead, down one of the many rail sidings spread throughout the terminal.

"The road to the left will take us to the terminal offices," Butler said over his shoulder, turning in that direction through the trees.

They were a quarter mile down the road when it happened.

"HALT!" barked a voice from the trees. "GROUND YOUR WEAPONS, AND PLACE YOUR HANDS ON YOUR HEADS! COMPLY IMMEDIATELY, OR WE WILL FIRE."

Butler looked at Luke and shrugged before following the order. Luke turned to his men and nodded before following suit. When all their weapons were on the pavement, the voice rang out again.

"YOU MEN IN THE REAR, CLOSE RANKS. I WANT YOU ALL TOGETHER. THEN I WANT YOU ALL TO FACE THE RIVER AND DROP TO YOUR KNEES. KEEP YOUR HANDS ON YOUR HEADS."

They did as ordered, and soon heard movement behind them. A black-clad figure came into view, his M4 trained on the group. He wore a black uniform and was trailed by another man, an Army sergeant, who appeared to be unarmed. The frigging SRF.

"Don't even think about moving, or my friend behind you will light you up in a heartbeat," the SRF thug said.

"Hello, Hill," Butler said.

"Hi, Butler. It's been a while," the Army sergeant replied.

The SRF thug looked back and forth between Butler and the sergeant. "You girls know each other?"

"It's like I told you before," the sergeant said, "they're just Coast Guard. They come here all the time to help us with riverside security. It's just routine."

The black-clad SRF man seemed to relax slightly. "Yeah, well, we'll see about that. We'll take them back to the terminal building and call it in."

Sergeant Hill shrugged. "Suit yourself."

The man was about to respond when Hill looked down the road away from the terminal. "What the hell is that?"

The man turned, obviously puzzled, and Hill stepped close and smashed the man's face with a left elbow strike, pulling the man's sidearm from its holster with his right hand as he stepped back. He brought the gun around in one fluid sweep, transitioning into a two-handed grip and firing over the heads of the kneeling men. Luke heard a gasp behind them, and the clatter of a weapon on the pavement, but kept his eyes on the scene before him. Hill already had the first SRF man on his knees, his own gun pressed to the man's temple as blood gushed out his nose.

"Y'all can get up now, Butler," the sergeant called. "And I hope like hell there are more of you wherever you came from."

***

Two minutes later they had the SRF men hidden in the woods; the live one zip-tied hand and foot, and mouth duct-taped. Hill motioned them away so they could speak in private.

"How many more?" Butler asked.

"Only two here," Hill said. "They're over in the main terminal complex. But there seem to be a bunch of the bastards over at the nuke plant. I've been seeing chopper traffic in and out of there all day."

"The two in the terminal building will have heard your shot," Luke said. "They'll call in backup for sure."

Hill was shaking his head. "I doubt it. It's almost a mile, with thick trees all the way. That's a long way to hear a pistol shot. There's also a generator running, powering a window AC unit. A very noisy window unit. And these boys ain't what I'd call the most situationally aware troops, if you get my drift."

"What's going on, Hill? How long have these goons been here, and where is everyone else?" Butler asked.

"Everybody else in this case was me, the major, and Sergeant Brothers. The others either took off or never showed up in the first place. As far as these assholes," Hill said, "two chopper loads of them hit us day before yesterday. They showed up with some sort of bogus order we were to turn the terminal over to them. The major refused until he could clear it with our chain of command. That basically meant never, because we haven't had comms since the power went down. Anyway, they beat the major down, and when Brothers tried to intervene, he got a beat down for his trouble too. By that time they had a nine millimeter to my forehead, and I had no doubt whatsoever they'd use it."

"So they're holding the others in the terminal building?" Butler asked.

Hill shook his head. "They took 'em out by chopper. Maybe over to the nuke plant or maybe someplace else. I don't really know. They kept me here because they needed someone who knew the layout. They been dragging me all over the place, making me show them what's where. They're up to no good, for sure, and I had no illusions when they knew what I knew, I was toast. When I saw y'all and recognized Butler, I figured my best bet was to throw in with you folks."

Hill looked back toward the terminal. "And right about now, I'd say, would be a good time to get out of here."

"Negative," Luke said. "If the two left pick up on something wrong, a chopper could intercept us long before we got back upriver."

Butler nodded agreement. "We'd be sitting ducks on open water. What's their routine?"

Hill shrugged. "Well, they haven't been here that long, but so far they seem to change shifts by chopper every twelve hours at noon and midnight. A couple of 'em scour the hard copy bills of lading, tryin' to get a handle on how much there is here, while the other two drag me around to show them where things are. They swap off and argue about it a lot, since they all want the 'let's sit on our butts in the air-conditioning' duty. We were goin' down to check one of the rail sidings when we heard y'all's boat. They just pulled the vehicle off the road into the woods and waited."

"So they didn't come out specifically in response to our arrival or radio back to the others when they heard the boat?" Luke asked.

Hill shook his head. "Nope. Like I said, not the sharpest tools in the shed."

Luke looked at his watch. "So if they follow routine, we've got ten hours, more or less, before the next shift change."

"About that," Hill said, "presuming you think two days' experience qualifies as routine."

"How about weapons?" Butler asked.

"Just what you saw. M4s and sidearms," Hill said.

"No, I mean weapons here in the terminal? Is there anything easily accessible we can grab now?" Butler asked.

"Well, we got, or had I should say, our own security force, so there's an armory in the terminal police station. That's still under lock and key. And there are weapons in inventory, a lot of them, but they're a bit harder to get to."

Luke nodded and looked at Butler. "Okay, at a minimum I say we take out the two in the terminal building, alive if possible, then load out all available weapons and ammo. We sure as hell can use the firepower, and prisoners will give us some much-needed intel." They both looked at Hill.

He shrugged. "I'm in as long as it buys me a boat ride out of here."

***

Hill wasn't exaggerating the SRF men's lack of situational awareness. Long and Abrams donned the black uniforms of the two neutralized thugs and followed Hill as he walked nonchalantly into the small air-conditioned office in the main terminal complex. The waiting men looked confused, but not unduly alarmed, no doubt assuming the pair were new faces from the larger SRF contingent at the nuke power plant. They both had guns to their foreheads before they discovered their mistake.

With the new prisoners trussed up beside their first captive in the back of a commandeered terminal pickup, they walked across the parking lot to the terminal police station. Hill used a ring of keys retrieved from the pocket of one of the SRF men to unlock the police station and armory.

Butler and Luke entered the armory behind Hill, their eyes as wide as kids in a candy store. There were multiple rows of M4s standing at vertical attention, with cartons of ammo stacked on shelves behind them. Butler pointed at several boxes labeled night-vision gear, and racks of tactical gear, including body armor. Another shelf held cases of flash bang grenades. Luke shook his head in disbelief.

"Were you expecting a war?" he asked.

Hill grunted. "Your tax dollars at work. I never thought they needed all this crap, but nobody asked me. That's what happens in a government organization when you get a budget—spend it all or lose it next year."

Butler grinned. "Well, I can assure you, Sergeant Hill, that we'll put this material to the very best of use."

"You got that right," Luke said. "We need to get this stuff back to Fort Box ASAP, but I've been thinking, we need to know what the hell is happening over at that nuke plant too."

Butler shook his head. "Sounds like mission creep."

"You know I'm right," Luke said. "As soon as they know we've been here and gone, they're going to put more troops into this place. And for sure there will probably be more chopper overflights. If we're gonna find out what's going on next door, now is the time."

"All right. I can see that, but what do you have in mind? We have to get this stuff back to Fort Box."

"Maybe we can do both." Luke looked at Hill. "Are those patrol boats we saw tied up down at the wharf operational?"

"Absolutely," Hill said. "And both have full tanks of gas. That's standard operating procedure. Not that we had anybody to run them."

Luke nodded and turned back to Butler. "All right then. I think Long, Abrams, and Sergeant Hill here should load all of this gear and our three prisoners in those two boats and return to base. The rest of us will recon the nuke plant."

"I should go with y'all. I know the area," Hill said.

Luke shook his head. "Negative. I'd love to have you, but you're far too valuable. I think we'll be making some more trips to the terminal, and having someone who knows it inside and out will be a tremendous advantage. We can't risk you on a recon like this."

Hill scowled, then grinned. "Well, what do you know? For the first time in my military career, I'm too valuable to be expendable."

Everyone grinned, then Butler spoke. "Actually, there's a small tributary of the river that runs by the north side of the power plant. There are homes along that stretch with boat docks. That's how I know about it; I've towed a few disabled boaters back to their home docks. We can get pretty close. My only concern is the engine noise."

Hill shook his head. "I don't think you have to worry about that, at least during the day. A lot of folks on this end of the river have been using their boats for transportation. We been hearing boat motors for some time. Less, of course, since gasoline started running low, but we still hear one now and again. I doubt these boys will come looking for you even if they hear the motor."

"I hope you're right," Luke said.

Cape Fear River (Tributary)
Near Brunswick Nuclear Plant

Same Day, 5:35 p.m.

Butler eased the boat along, running dead slow on only one of the two engines and oversteering to compensate for the slight uneven thrust. They crept through the ever-narrowing tributary, looking across the marsh bordering the stream to the tree line and solid ground beyond. Ahead of them in the distance, high-voltage wires stretched through the air from left to right.

Butler pointed at the power lines. "We're almost to the power plant now. We should probably nose her in somewhere along here."

"Try to find a place where the channel gets as close as possible to the tree line," Luke said. "That marsh looks like cottonmouth central, and I'd like to minimize the amount of muck and marsh we have to wade through."

Beside him in the open door of the little cabin, Washington visibly shuddered. "Amen to that, brother. I do hate snakes."

"I'll do my best," Butler said, "but we don't have a lot of options here. I pretty much have to go where—"

"There!" They rounded a bend, and Luke pointed out a narrow inlet, barely wider than the boat, running through the thick marsh grass toward the tree line marking firmer ground.

Butler stopped the boat and studied the inlet. "Okay. I'll try it, but I'm gonna back her in. If we have to leave in a hurry, I sure as hell don't want to be backing out."

His companions nodded and watched as he turned the boat expertly and maneuvered stern first up the narrow inlet. The inlet dead-ended at the tree line, but Butler killed the engine thirty feet short.

"We'll paddle her back the rest of the way," he said. "I don't want to take a chance on damaging the propeller on a submerged stump."

Three minutes later, and to Washington's obvious relief, they only had to walk a few steps through mud and muck to solid ground.

"What now, LT… I mean Major?" Washington asked.

Luke shrugged. "We play it by ear, I guess. We'll work our way through the woods to the power plant, then take it from there depending on what we see."

The others nodded and followed Luke through the woods, maintaining their intervals. As the trees thinned, they moved more carefully from tree to tree until the power plant came into view.

"Son of a bitch," Luke said. He glanced over his shoulder as Butler and Washington moved up beside him. "What's that look like to you?"

They stared past him at a large area in the middle of an open field, surrounded by a tall chain-link fence with coils of razor wire running along its top. The area was rectangular, and each corner was topped with a tower, complete with the searchlight and machine gun. They could make out two figures standing in the nearest tower.

Inside the fence were row on row of large tents, obviously communal shelters. They heard shouts of children playing and saw an open area at the far end of the enclosure. People moved listlessly from tent to tent.

"It's a frigging concentration camp," Washington said as Butler nodded agreement.

"So much for a volunteer effort," Luke said.

He pulled a monocular from his pocket and looked beyond the fenced area toward the plant itself. There was a long row of tents outside the fenced area, and here and there civilians moved among them. He judged the SRF presence to be at least company strength, if not greater. Several choppers sat in the asphalt parking lot, and on the far side of the parking lot, tents were arranged in the orderly rows of an advance military base.

Luke passed the monocular to Butler, who looked, nodded, and gave the instrument to Washington.

"Looks like some civilians in the concentration camp and more in the tents outside. What do you make of that?" Butler asked.

Luke shrugged. "I don't know, but my guess is anyone outside the wire is cooperating with them, and those inside are less enthusiastic."

Butler nodded. "Makes sense."

"Yeah, and it looks like they plan to stay a while," Washington said.

Butler nodded again. "And between here and the military terminal next door, I expect there will soon be a whole lot more of them. Which makes the likelihood of them leaving us alone—"

"Somewhere between slim and none," Luke finished.

Washington looked thoughtful. "Maybe it ain't a bad thing, if they get the power back on, I mean."

"I got no problem with that," Luke said. "My problem is the way they're doing it, and what they intend to do with it after they restore it. They seem much more inclined to take things for themselves and toward consolidating control than helping others. Somehow I get the feeling if they get the power back, it's not going to help anyone but them."

"But what are they really up to?" Washington asked. "I mean, all we can tell is they're holding a bunch of prisoners."

"We got the three prisoners. Maybe we can get some intel out of them," Butler said. "I'm thinkin' we shouldn't push our luck."

Washington shook his head. "We're not going to learn too much from those SRF fools. Maybe how many troops and where they're from, things like that. But they're not likely to have a clue what's going on inside the power plant. They're not exactly geniuses."

Luke nodded. "Washington's right. If we want good intel, we're going to have to talk to one of those civilian 'volunteers.'"

"And how the hell we gonna do that?" Butler asked.

Luke checked his watch. "It'll be midnight or maybe a bit later before they change shifts at the terminal and figure out anything is wrong. We've got the night-vision gear we kept from the armory, so I say we wait until after dark and grab one of the civilians. It won't be full dark until nine or a little after, but if we grab him at ten, we can be almost back to Fort Box by midnight."

"Kidnap him? Are you nuts, Kinsey?" Butler asked.

"Think about it. It's probably our only shot at finding out what they're up to. I mean, do those people behind the wire look happy to you?"

Butler shook his head. "No. Of course not. But if we go around friggin' kidnapping people, how does that make us any better?"

Luke grinned. "Because we're the good guys." Washington grinned too and Luke continued. "Look, we keep him blindfolded until we get to Fort Box and make sure he doesn't see anything while he's there. We question him, learn what we can learn, and give him the choice of staying or coming back here. If he wants to come back, we just blindfold him and bring him partway down the river, then put him in a small boat and let him make his own way back here. No harm. No foul."

Butler shook his head. "All right. I guess it will work. But how did an honest Coastie end up running around with a couple of criminals like you."

"Just lucky, I guess," Luke said, and Washington grinned.

***

The sun set around eight, and thirty minutes later they heard the whine of an electric starter as a generator rumbled to life somewhere on the other side of the concentration camp. The reason became apparent as the search-lights on all four corner guard towers winked to life. Luke felt a momentary concern until it became clear the lights were focused on the camp, sweeping over the tents and playing over the fence lines. One by one, lights came on inside the tents, glowing through the fabric and setting shadows dancing on the tent walls. Individual lights bobbed through the gathering darkness here and there as people walked with flashlights, but there was no general outside lighting. Better and better, Luke thought.

They passed the time talking quietly, waiting for ten o'clock. Like the tents in the concentration camp, the tents outside the wire seemed to be shared facilities, which meant they had to catch a civilian alone, outside the tents.

Their 'collection point' was obvious, a row of portable toilets serving, but set some distance away from, the row of civilian tents.

At nine o'clock, lights began to wink off inside the tents, and Luke's concern grew. What if the bastards all went to sleep before ten? They couldn't hang around indefinitely, waiting for someone to wake up and come out to make a piss call. Fewer and fewer flashlights were bobbing between the tents or back and forth between the portable toilets. Then all the tents were dark except two. Then one.

Luke glanced up at the sky still dimly lit on the far western horizon. Close enough.

"Come on," he said, folding down his night-vision goggles as his two companions followed suit.

He led them in a crouching run over the open field to the row of toilets a hundred yards away. Since they couldn't know which toilet their quarry would choose, the plan was to wait until the man selected his toilet, then creep up behind the unit and grab him as he exited.

Washington was by far the strongest of the three, and by consensus, he was to grab the victim and clamp a hand over his mouth while Luke shoved a gun in the man's face to convince him not to struggle. Butler was to quickly duct-tape his mouth and zip-tie his hands before they hustled their captive back to the tree line and the boat beyond. It was going to go like clockwork.

Except it didn't.

They waited impatiently, staring at the last lighted tent, willing someone to come out and come their way. They heard voices through the still air, audible in the distance.

"Dempsey, will you put that book away and turn off the friggin' light! You know what time we have to get up in the morning."

"All right, all right. Keep your shirt on, Goodman. I'm gonna go take a piss and then I'll turn the light out."

Relieved, Luke saw the beam of the flashlight bobbing toward them. The first hint of trouble came when the bobbing flashlight got halfway to them, then stopped.

What the hell? Luke watched in his night-vision goggles as their mark shoved the flashlight under his arm and fumbled with his fly. He wasn't coming to the toilets. He was just going to take a leak on the ground.

Plan B. Luke got up and started running, circling wide off the gravel path so the grass muffled his footsteps as he approached the man from the rear. Twenty feet from the man, he had to step back on the path, and gravel crunched underfoot. Startled, the man whirled, and Luke's world went supernova as the piercing beam of the halogen flashlight hit him full in the night-vision goggles. Too late, he flipped up the goggles and closed his eyes.

He heard gravel crunch as the man backed away from him. "What the hell—"

The question was cut off with an emphatic *oomph*, and Luke felt a strong hand on his upper arm and heard Butler whispering in his ear.

"Washington cold-cocked him. Looks like he's down for the count, but be quiet. His buddy's moving around in the tent. I can see the shadows on the tent wall."

"Dempsey? What the hell you doing out there, talking to yourself? Come on, man. Get a frigging move on. I want to go to bed," came the voice from the tent.

They all kept their positions frozen in place, unsure what to do.

"Dempsey, God dammit! Answer me, you turd."

Butler whispered in Luke's ear again. "Get ready to run if this doesn't work out. I'll hold your arm to keep you from running into anything. Just follow my lead and run like hell."

Luke whispered back, confused, "If what doesn't—"

Butler called toward the tent, "Gotta take a dump. You can turn out the light. I got my flashlight."

"You catching a cold, Dempsey? You sound like hell. And you better not give it to me, you asshole."

"Screw you, Goodman," Butler called.

There was a muffled curse, and the light blinked off in the tent. Luke's sight was mostly recovered, and he flipped down his night-vision goggles to find Washington zip-tying their victim's hands. The man was out cold, and there was already duct tape across his mouth. *I hope like hell he's still alive,* Luke thought.

Luke helped Butler, and they split up Washington's gear so the big man could carry the prisoner. Washington reached down and picked up their prisoner effortlessly, throwing him over his shoulder as they all set off for the boat.

CHAPTER TWELVE

"That's a lotta gear, Lucius," Dave Hitchcock said, staring at the massive pile of boxes and assorted loose gear heaped on the deck of the *Miss Martha*.

Lucius Wellesley nodded. "And there's a pile that big or bigger on every one of the boats on this side. It's gonna be a bear to ferry it all to the lock wall in the skiffs then haul it all the way to the other end of the dock, then down the other end of the lock wall and back into more skiffs to spread it out among our boats." He sighed. "But I can't bring myself to leave it. We ain't likely to see any more spares or supplies from now on. We're gonna NEED this stuff, sooner or later."

Hitchcock nodded soberly, overwhelmed by the task in front of them. Then he smiled. "Why don't we do what those Coast Guard guys did?"

Wellesley cocked an eye. "What do you mean?"

"We could load the stuff into the skiffs on this side," Hitchcock said, "then move the loaded skiffs to shore at that narrow place the Coasties brought their boat over. They needed the boat ramp to pull out, but there's a much narrower place where it can't be more than twelve or fifteen feet across. After we nose the loaded skiffs into the bank, we set up like a bucket brigade to pass the stuff across that narrow neck of land to skiffs from the other boats. That would save us a lot of handling, to say nothing of hauling it up and down the lock wall."

Wellesley stroked his chin. "That's a good idea, Dave. And I think it may have given me a better one."

***

Wellesley eased the blunt nose of the *Miss Martha* into the massive concrete piling of the highway bridge. He touched it lightly, then slowly worked the boat's stern around until the towboat fit snugly in the narrow channel between the bridge piling and the slender neck of land separating the Intracoastal Waterway and the Calcasieu River. He looked up as Hitchcock stepped to the open door of the wheelhouse.

"How we lookin'?" Wellesley asked.

Hitchcock nodded. "The stern's about twenty feet off the bank, and we're dead on perpendicular, so we couldn't ask for a better setup." Hitchcock hesitated. "But you sure we should be doing this, Lucius?"

Wellesley shrugged. "I can't see as it's gonna make much difference. The only reason for the lock in the first place is to keep saltwater out of supposedly agricultural land, and depending on conditions, it's wide open more than half the time anyway. And the way things are going, I don't see anybody planting that land anytime soon, if they ever did in the first place. I been runnin' this stretch goin' on twenty years and never saw nothin' but swamp. Besides, it'll be a little hole, and if they want to fill it in later, it won't take more than a few truckloads of dirt."

"Well, if you say so. I guess you might as well let 'er rip," Hitchcock said.

Wellesley eased the twin throttles forward, and the *Miss Martha* pushed against the concrete piling holding her immobile. A powerful wash jetted aft from her flailing twin propellers, striking the canal bank and sending a boiling mass of muddy water over the narrow neck of dirt and marsh grass into the waters of the inlet beyond. The volume of water slowly increased as Wellesley went to full throttle, and the powerful prop wash from twenty feet away made short work of the dirt bank, opening a shallow channel in less than a minute. But he kept at it, and when he shut the engines down fifteen minutes later, there was a clear passage through the dirt bank almost as wide as the *Miss Martha*.

Wellesley maneuvered the big towboat out of the slot and brought her around expertly to lay against the bank some distance away to watch the proceedings. One of the flat-bottom aluminum skiffs all the towboats carried as tenders was making its way toward the newly opened hole, heavily loaded and deep in the water.

Sam Davis was operating the outboard, and Bud Spencer stood in the bow, with a long pole. Wellesley watched as Davis slowed and conned his skiff tentatively through the new channel as Spencer probed the bottom with his pole, checking the depth.

Then Davis was through, and Spencer dropped the measuring pole into the skiff and cupped his hands around his mouth.

"FOUR FEET OR MORE ALL THE WAY THROUGH, CAP!" he yelled, then lowered his hands to reveal a wide grin as he flashed Wellesley a thumbs-up.

Sam Davis grinned and waved as well before increasing speed and disappearing down the channel, around the lock to the *Judy Ann* waiting on the far side.

"I think this is gonna work just fine," Wellesley said.

"Damned if it ain't," Hitchcock said.

FORT BOX
WILMINGTON CONTAINER TERMINAL
WILMINGTON, NORTH CAROLINA

DAY 30, 7:35 A.M.

Levi Jenkins enjoyed the wind on his face as the boat glided across the glistening surface of the river toward Fort Box in the distance. Even this early in the morning the sun was formidable; it was going to be another hot one.

"You think this new plan is workable?" asked Anthony McCoy.

Levi looked over at his father-in-law and shrugged. "I don't know enough to say. Wright couldn't go into detail on the radio. It sounded like it might have possibilities as long as they don't try to ram it down our throats."

"Amen to that," said Vern Gibson, from behind them at the outboard. "We could all use some new neighbors as long as they're good, hardworking folks. But how do we know before they're our neighbors; that's my problem."

"Well, I guess we'll see, won't we? These guys are practical, so I'm sure they probably thought of that. Let's just keep an open mind and hear what they have to say."

They lapsed into silence, each with his own thoughts, as the boat covered the remaining distance to the Fort Box waterfront. They arrived under the watchful eyes of armed guards manning the rails of the container ships tied up to the wharfs. More guards than usual, it seemed to Levi. He mentally filed that away as Vern Gibson deftly maneuvered the little craft to the vertical ladder.

Levi fended the boat off the wharf pilings and tied up at the bottom of the ladder. The trio scrambled up to the dock.

"About time you river rats made it to town," said a voice just as Levi's head cleared the top of the ladder. He looked up to see Josh Wright's grinning face and outstretched hand, and grabbed the hand for an assist up the last few rungs.

Levi returned the grin. "Good to see you too, Sergeant... I mean Lieutenant Wright."

"All right, rub it in, why doncha?" said Wright, with a sheepish grin.

Levi laughed. "Every chance I get."

Wright greeted each of the other two men cordially as they cleared the ladder, then turned and led them toward the headquarters building. He started off at a brisk pace, but slowed to accommodate his guests, who looked around wide-eyed as they walked.

Vern Gibson shook his head. "Dang if it don't look different every time I come. I was just here ten days back, and there's a lot of changes. And a whole lot more people."

Wright nodded. "That's the point of this meeting. We're hoping to put some programs in place that will be beneficial to everyone."

His guests nodded noncommittally, and they walked in silence to the headquarters building. Wright led them into the former break room, now known as 'Conference Room A,' and nodded toward a pot of coffee on the sideboard.

"Fresh pot. I started it when we saw y'all on the river."

The three men grinned in unison. "Now that's what I call hospitality," Gibson said. "I don't suppose you might have any of that coffee we could take home, do you?"

Wright grinned back. "Just a full forty-foot container. Ask and you shall receive."

Vern Gibson laughed. "Well, this meeting is gettin' off to a good start. I can't be bought, but I can be rented. Especially if there's coffee involved."

They were still chuckling when the others arrived, with warm greetings and handshakes all around before they settled around the conference table, each with a steaming mug. Colonel Hunnicutt wasted no time fleshing out the proposed concept, with Wright, Butler, and Luke Kinsey adding details as appropriate. The three visitors listened silently but attentively. When Hunnicutt finished, the men from the river looked back and forth at each other, each waiting for the other to speak. Finally Levi broke the silence.

"How many of these fortified towns you figure again?"

"We were thinking twenty," Wright said. "One every mile or so up the river, alternating sides where we could. But that's the ideal, in practice we'll place them wherever the local folks will go along with it, as long as they're reasonably spread out."

"And you want to build them all at once?" asked Vern Gibson, his doubts obvious.

"Yes, or at least as many as we can. Besides the advantages the colonel outlined, our census here is increasing rapidly." He sighed. "So to be honest, we also have a lot of desperate people that need new homes."

No one responded, and the room lapsed into an uncomfortable silence. Finally Hunnicutt spoke. "I'd hoped for a bit more enthusiastic response."

"It's not that we don't like the concept, Colonel, but I think it's the 'desperate people' part that's giving us all a little trouble," said Anthony McCoy. "I'm sure we all like the part about towns and fortified positions and militias and all that. But you're basically talkin' about dumping strangers among us just because they're desperate and need a place to go. We're sympathetic, but I think we can all see the potential for this turning out to be a real bad idea."

Hunnicutt nodded. "Point taken. But if you like the basic concept, we're open to suggestions. How would you improve it? If you'll each give us your comments and criticisms, maybe we can still get to yes. Would you like to start, Anthony?"

Anthony nodded. "Okay, for starters, I sure wouldn't try building 'em all at once. I'd say start with one or two, maybe halfway out from here and the one furthest away. Say twenty miles out. It'll be a lot easier to get folks on the river enthusiastic about two towns than twenty. Just make those two towns bigger than you planned, then stick to the security stations everybody's already agreed to in between. If the towns turn out to be workable, and everybody likes them, we can always build more by expanding the security stations. But if not, we haven't wasted a whole lot of effort for nothing."

Hunnicutt nodded, encouraged by Anthony's use of 'we.'

"And another thing, we'll need assurances y'all don't use the river towns as dumping grounds for misfits. There are gonna be a lot of 'recruits' and you're not going to be dead right on every one of them. Some of them are going to fool you, and when you end up with fools like that Singletary, we don't want 'em on the river. We got enough homegrown fools without importing any," Anthony said.

Everyone laughed, and Hunnicutt nodded. "Agreed."

The laughter died, and Vern Gibson spoke. "We're all laughing now, but this is serious, Colonel. It's not just us three you gotta convince. I don't think the majority of folks up and down the river will buy it unless they have some say-so about their new neighbors. That's especially true if you're plannin' on asking them to donate the land for these towns." Gibson cocked his head and fixed Hunnicutt with a knowing look. "Which I suppose you are."

Hunnicutt nodded and was about to speak when Wright interrupted. "If I may, sir? I have an idea about that."

Hunnicutt made a go-ahead gesture.

"What if," Wright asked, "we set up a vetting committee? It could include mostly folks from the river farms, with maybe one or two advisers from Fort Box they trusted, who've had an opportunity to observe the potential recruits more closely and offer opinions. The committee could interview and approve anyone who applied to move to the river."

Vern Gibson nodded slowly, as did Levi and Anthony. "Might work," Gibson said.

Hunnicutt beamed. "Excellent! We're making progress. How about you, Levi? Do you have any suggestions or concerns?"

Levi laughed. "So many, I don't know where to start. But I think the plan is workable. However, I think we all know no matter what we decide here or what we plan, it's all going to fall to pieces at some point. We need to be prepared to be true to the CONCEPT while maintaining some flexibility."

The others nodded, and Levi continued. "But like Vern said, folks on the river have to buy into the concept."

Hunnicutt nodded and turned back to Gibson. "How do you like our chances, best guess?"

Gibson shrugged. "I'm thinkin' maybe sixty percent will go along after they think about it a bit, another twenty-five or thirty percent can be convinced, and ten percent will be dead set against it, just because they're dead set against everything."

"I'll take those odds. Can we ask you gentlemen to take the lead in discussing this with your neighbors?" Hunnicutt asked.

Vern Gibson sighed. "I'm not what you'd call real eager, but I guess I can do that. Assuming these other two jokers agree. I'm sure not doing it by myself."

Levi and Anthony nodded, and Hunnicutt's face was creased by a relieved smile. "Thank you, gentlemen. We really appreciate it."

His smile faded. "But now that we've settled that, I'm afraid I have less welcome news. It may not impact you immediately, but I thought you should know about it." He nodded at Luke. "Major Kinsey?"

"Yes, sir," Luke said, and turned toward their visitors. "Yesterday, we did a reconnaissance of the Military Ocean Terminal at Sunny Point and also the Brunswick Nuclear Station. The FEMA Special Reaction Force is occupying both facilities. We managed to take prisoners, and what we've learned from them is concerning."

"Ahh… isn't taking prisoners kind of like poking the bear?" Levi asked. "Maybe we ought to just leave those folks alone. Live and let live."

"Based on what we know, they don't intend to live and let live," Luke said. "They plan to build both of those facilities up as major SRF bases, and it's unlikely they will tolerate an armed presence nearby they don't control. In fact, under interrogation, the prisoners revealed they believe an attack against us is imminent."

"They're going to attack Fort Box?" Anthony asked.

Luke shook his head. "Not them, but someone. They had no hard intel, just rumors in their ranks. So the reliability is suspect, but we can't discount it. Rumors are a lot more accurate than people realize."

"If not them, then who?" Anthony asked. "The regular Army?"

Beside Luke, Hunnicutt shook his head. "They seem to think it would be a surprise attack, and I can't see the regular military attacking us without at least engaging us first and demanding our surrender. We're no match for the regular military, and they know it. Besides, they just don't operate like that, especially against fellow Americans. They would talk first and only attack as a last resort. Nonetheless, we're taking the threat seriously. We've been on increased alert since we heard about it."

Levi nodded. "I noticed extra guards."

"We've doubled up security everywhere," Hunnicutt said. "But it's stretching us thin. Which is another thing we wanted to talk to you about."

Levi looked confused. "But what can WE do…" He trailed off as he understood.

"Major Kinsey's force managed to capture almost a hundred M4s and a substantial amount of ammunition. We now have rifles without riflemen. We don't have time to vet and recruit people out of the refugee population. It's one thing to recruit a forklift driver or a cook, but we'd have to trust a recruit completely before we turned them loose inside Fort Box with a weapon. There just isn't time."

"You want volunteers from the river," Gibson said.

"Only until the threat passes," Luke said. "I'm sure Donny and Richard…"

Vern Gibson visibly bristled at the mention of his sons, then calmed and nodded. "Donny thinks highly of you, Major. I reckon if he knew you needed help, he'd be here in a heartbeat. Richard too, for that matter." He smiled ruefully. "Thing is, you ain't the one who's got to explain it to their mama."

"We know we're asking a lot, Mr. Gibson," Hunnicutt said. "And we wouldn't ask at all if we weren't desperate. But if Fort Box falls, I think it's only a matter of time before the FEMA thugs start moving upriver."

"Maybe, maybe not," Gibson said. "There's some who think we're too little to mess with. Out of sight, out of mind. Personally, I'm not of that school of thought, but I can't speak for my neighbors." He shook his head. "It's one thing to ask folks to buy off on settin' up these towns, but it's another to ask 'em to maybe stop a bullet."

"Agreed," Hunnicutt said. "We can only ask."

The room fell silent again as the river men mulled the request.

Luke broke it. "How many veterans do you estimate are on the river, Mr. Gibson?"

Gibson shrugged. "Countin' old Vietnam-era dinosaurs like me, more than a hundred I'd say, but I can't rightly be sure." He sighed. "I can't speak for anybody else, but I'll tell my boys and they can make their own decisions. And if they decide to come, I'm sure they'd be willing to go up and down the river and ask other folks."

"That's more than generous, Mr. Gibson. Thank you," Hunnicutt said.

"I'm in," said Levi quietly.

"Me too," said Anthony.

"Hell, Anthony," Gibson said. "What war are you a veteran of, the Spanish-American?" He turned to Hunnicutt. "If you're takin' old coots like Anthony here, I guess I'll sign up too."

"He's not taking Anthony," Levi said, glaring at his father-in-law. "One of us has to stay home and protect the family."

Hunnicutt held up his hand. "Gentlemen, I appreciate your willingness to help us, but Levi is right. We don't want to leave any family defenseless, so please make that clear to any of your neighbors who might be willing to help us."

***

After more discussion, the three civilians took their leave with promises to consult their neighbors on the 'town plan,' as it had come to be known, and the much more pressing issue of volunteers. Hunnicutt and Luke Kinsey saw them off at the waterfront, sending them on their way with five pounds of coffee apiece.

"Think we'll get any volunteers?" Hunnicutt asked.

"I think a few at least," Luke said. "Whether it will be enough is anyone's guess."

Hunnicutt nodded. "How's your exclusion zone plan coming?"

"We have all the signs posted and about half the barriers in place. And Wright started random patrols two days ago. They rousted a few refugee families that were squatting inside the zone and drove them back to the country club camp." Luke sighed. "But your prediction was accurate. It wasn't popular, and it's increasing resentment in the camp. Maybe it wasn't a good idea."

Hunnicutt sighed. "Resentment was inevitable anyway, if not about this, then about something else. It may as well be over something that actually enhances security."

UNITED BLOOD NATIONS HQ
(FORMERLY NEW HANOVER COUNTY
DEPARTMENT OF SOCIAL SERVICES)
1650 GREENFIELD STREET
WILMINGTON, NORTH CAROLINA

DAY 30, 11:35 A.M.

"So how many they roust all together?" asked Kwintell Banks.

"'Bout twenty, mostly from over around Newkirk Avenue," Darren Mosley replied. "But yesterday it was Wellington, and they puttin' those Exclusion Zone signs all along Seventeenth Street. Look like that the closest they want anybody to get to their fort."

"Who they rousting, black or white?"

Mosley shook his head. "Don't seem to matter. You squattin' in that exclusion zone, they gonna roust you."

Banks stroked his chin, considering this latest development and how he might use it to advantage. "How dat goin' down in the camp? What our spies there say?"

"All the 'fugees be seriously pissed, no matter the color. Thing is, about half the squatters they brought back to the camp was never there in the first place. And a lot of them had gathered a lot of stuff in the crib they was squatting in, and the soldiers only let them bring what they could carry. So those be double pissed," Mosley said.

Banks nodded, a plan forming in his mind. "When the next soldier patrol?"

Mosley shook his head. "They ain't regular now. They mix it up."

"All right then. We just gotta be ready for them whenever they come. I want you to have our guys in the camp get them 'fugees all riled up. Spread a rumor the soldiers run over a kid that was just asking for food or something like that. The worst the better. Get a crowd gathered around the camp entrance, so whenever the soldiers get there, they gotta run through it. Then block the road so they CAN'T get through, and start throwing rocks and bottles. The rest of the crowd will pitch in, guaranteed. You follow me so far?"

Mosley nodded, and Banks continued. "The soldiers likely won't shoot, at least right away, so the crowd will get bolder. When they good and excited, just have our guys slip away. If we lucky, at some point the soldiers will panic and shoot at the 'fugees or at least over their heads."

Mosley nodded again, then asked, "But what if they don't? Shoot, I mean."

"Then we do it for them. Have some of our boys hid nearby, and you give them the signal to shoot," Banks said.

"At the soldiers?"

Banks exploded. "NO, FOOL! THE 'FUGEES!"

Mosley nodded his head vigorously. "Oh yeah. I get it now. That smart, Kwintell. Real smart."

Banks sighed. "All right. Get your ass outta here and go take care of it."

Mosley bobbed his head again and scurried out of the conference room.

"Real crack team, Banks," scoffed a low voice from the end of the table.

Banks' heart raced. He swallowed the lump in his throat and did his best to hide his fear. "He all right. He just need supervision sometime. You know what I mean."

The man stared unblinking. He stood six feet six, and even sitting at the conference table he towered over Banks. His African DNA was clearly undiluted, and he was the blackest black man Banks had ever seen. It was almost impossible to tell where the black tee shirt stretched over his massive chest stopped and his bulging biceps started. His shaved head bore many scars, and there was a small gold ring in one earlobe. His only earlobe actually, the other was cut off in a straight line. If Rorke was pirate scary, this guy was insane-serial-killer-under-the-bed scary. Banks had difficulty keeping his composure in the man's presence. Rorke called him Reaper.

Reaper snorted. "Yeah, I know exactly what you mean. He's a frigging idiot."

Banks changed the subject. "This is all good. All the 'fugees bein' pissed at the soldiers, I mean. That can help us out a lot, we play it right. We got lucky on that one."

Reaper snorted again. "Only fools need luck. You do what I told you?"

"Yeah, but what you need—"

"I hope you're not about to ask me a question. You know I hate questions. As a matter of fact..." Reaper smiled and produced a Fairbairn-Sykes fighting knife seemingly out of thin air and buried the point in the wooden conference table. He released it, and as it stood quivering, upright in the table, Reaper pointed at the leather-wrapped grip. "Know what kind of leather that is, Banks?"

Banks looked at the knife handle and shook his head.

"It's the nut sack of the last fool to ask me a question without my permission," Reaper said. "I ask the questions. You give the answers. We clear on that, fool?"

Banks nodded, cowed, as he had been since Reaper and his small contingent had arrived the morning before. Like Banks and his gang, all the newcomers were African-American, but there the similarity stopped. The SRF troopers were hard men and openly disdainful of the gangbangers posturing as badasses. They arrived in Humvees laden with crates, which disgorged their cargoes then disappeared. The newcomers set to work immediately, confiscating pickup trucks from the UBN thugs or nearby parking lots. They brought an ample supply of gasoline in jerry cans, and by nightfall they had converted over a dozen pickups into 'tacticals' with the addition of machine guns and improvised armor. Banks had seen rocket-propelled grenades among the gear, and he was eager to know when his men would get access. Now he was afraid to ask.

"How many of these fools you got?" Reaper asked.

"Almost fifteen hundred, if you count the baby ganstas—"

"I'm not wasting an M4 on a third grader," Reaper said. "How many man-sized fools you have smart enough to tie their own shoes?"

Banks ignored the insult. "'Bout a thousand, give or take."

Reaper nodded. "I got four hundred M4s. Pick out your four hundred best men, and divide them into groups of twenty. One of my men will be in charge of each group, to teach them how to use—"

Banks bristled, terror momentarily forgotten at this affront to his authority. "These my men. I'm in charge. And the M4s just like the ARs, ain't they? We know—"

Reaper glared and looked pointedly at the knife still upright in the table.

"Course, we can always use some pointers," Banks finished lamely.

"You can use more than pointers. 'Cause every one of you fools is gonna be blasting away on full auto if I don't nip that in the bud. We gonna teach you to fire single shots or three-round bursts, no more. I see one fool firing on full auto, I'm gonna waste him myself. You got that, Banks?"

Banks nodded.

"We can't actually shoot; otherwise they'll hear it inside the fort. We're just going to have to do weapons familiarization by dry firing and hope these idiots of yours learn enough to keep from shooting each other when it's for real. As I said, each twenty-man group will be under one of my men, and the rest of us will man the tacticals and carry the RPGs. I want all fifteen hundred of your men on the front line with whatever they've got, and the four hundred men with the M4s will be evenly spread among them. The tacticals will be spread in the line along the front behind them, out of sight until they're needed and then coming out to provide suppressing fire against the crew-served weapons on the wall. Is that clear?"

Banks nodded again.

"Good," Reaper said. "You may now ask a question if you have one."

"Ahh… where you want me?"

"With me, of course. You're a fool, but you're not completely stupid. Riling up the 'fugees wasn't a bad idea, and it's going to make things a whole lot easier."

WILMINGTON REFUGEE CAMP
(FORMERLY PINE VALLEY COUNTRY CLUB)
PINE VALLEY DRIVE
WILMINGTON, NORTH CAROLINA

SAME DAY, 1:45 P.M.

Corporal Jerry Miles looked at the road ahead and cursed. Why did this crap always seem to happen on his patrols? First they stumbled across the gang rape, and Lieutenant Wright chewed his butt to hamburger even though he'd done the right thing, and now this. Three cars were across the road ahead, blocking the western entrance to the camp. They were surrounded by what looked like a far from friendly mob of refugees.

Miles sighed. "Slow down," he said to the driver. "We don't want to be in the middle of that."

"How we gonna get into the camp?" asked the driver.

"Well, not through there, that's for sure," Miles said. "This is shaping up to be a shit show, and we're not playing. Stop the vehicle."

The driver did as told, stopping well back from the crowd. But not far enough. The angry mob surged forward and encircled the Humvee. Curses filled the air and angry faces pressed against the windows. Miles reach for the radio.

"Box Base, this is Rover One. Do you copy? Over."

"Rover One, this is Box Base. We copy. Over."

"Box Base, be advised we have a situation. Our vehicle is surrounded by hostile civilians. Repeat. We are at the west entrance to the refugee camp, and our vehicle is surrounded by hostile civilians. Please advise. Over."

"Rover One, we copy. Stand by. Over."

Miles cursed under his breath again and looked out at the crowd, noise rising as they began to beat on the vehicle with their fists. The driver flinched as a large black man with gang tattoos hammered at his window with a fist-sized rock.

"We can't stand by too long," the driver said, wide-eyed.

The radio squawked. "Rover One, this is Box Base. Can you disengage without casualties? Repeat, can you disengage without casualties? Over."

"Box Base, unknown. Repeat, unknown."

There was a long pause before the radio squawked again. "Rover One, we copy. Do your best. You are clear for RTB. Repeat. You are clear for return to base. Advise when you have disengaged from civilians. Do you copy? Over."

"Box Base, we copy. Rover One out."

Miles snorted. "Yeah, assholes. I copy just fine. I just don't have a clue how to 'disengage without casualties,'" he muttered and turned to the driver.

"All right, back her out of here slow before they get the bright idea to start trying to rock the vehicle, and we have to hurt 'em to get loose. When we start backing up, hopefully the ones behind us will get out of the way and stack up around the other three sides of the Hummer. Keep gradually increasing speed backwards until you have a clear opening; then floor it, and get us the hell out of here."

The driver nodded, and the crowd behaved as Miles anticipated. At the first sight of an opening to the rear, the driver gunned it and they shot backwards, free from the mob. They barely cleared the crowd when the interior of the Humvee began to ring with clangs and bangs as the thwarted mob showered the vehicle with rocks and bottles.

"Don't stop!" Miles yelled as he glanced at the open street behind them. Then he jerked around at the sound of gunfire. In the space they'd just vacated, civilians at the front of the mob jerked in a macabre dance as bullets impacted them, and the crowd evaporated almost instantaneously, leaving a dozen bloody bodies on the street.

"I think we're about to have a very bad day," Miles said.

FORT BOX
WILMINGTON CONTAINER TERMINAL
WILMINGTON, NORTH CAROLINA

SAME DAY, SAME TIME

"Does he have a clue what's going on?" Hunnicutt asked.

Luke shook his head. "No, sir. Washington hit him pretty hard; then we duct-taped his mouth and eyes and flex-cuffed him. He didn't start moving around until we were well up the river on the way back, and we were careful not to say anything he could overhear. He's been blindfolded and restrained ever since. I had Dr. Jennings check his vital signs last night, but I didn't allow her to talk to him—"

"As well I know, Major," Hunnicutt said, "because immediately thereafter I got the good doctor's 'I won't be party to barbarism' speech, so thank you. I don't suppose you could have just grabbed one of the nurses instead?"

"I tried, sir. Dr. Jennings caught me and demanded to know what was going on. I figured it would be worse if I didn't tell her," Luke said.

Hunnicutt nodded, and Luke continued.

"Anyway, we've kept him disoriented, and I want to try to learn as much as I can from him without giving up anything. That way we can let him go without being too concerned he might leave with any usable intel."

"And you're sure he's voluntarily working for them?"

Luke shrugged. "He wasn't behind the wire in the concentration camp and he seemed to have the run of the place. So yeah, I'd say he was cooperating."

Luke gestured down to his SRF uniform. "He has no clue where he is or why he's here. He saw me for less than five seconds last night, but it was dark and I was in Coastie coveralls with night-vision gear hiding my face, so I doubt he recognizes me. I'm going to go in there in this uniform with food and water, and we'll just see what he says."

Hunnicutt sighed. "Do the best you can, Major. What we got from the SRF prisoners was vague at best; maybe understanding exactly what their plan is for the power plant will shed some light on things."

Luke nodded and glanced over at Hunnicutt's weary face. The man had aged visibly in just the short time Luke had known him. He stood now, a look of dejection on his face as he studied the floor.

"Problem, sir?" Luke asked.

Hunnicutt shook his head. "Nothing new, Major. I was just thinking how different our lives have become in a few short weeks. We were all just going our own merry ways, and now we're worried about 'enemy forces' and 'collaborators' and who the hell knows what else we never even thought about except maybe when watching an old war movie. Now it's all happening right in my hometown. It just all seems so unreal."

Luke said nothing for a long moment. "What did you do in civilian life, sir? If I might ask."

Hunnicutt smiled wanly. "Well, you might say I wasn't without combat experience. I was a high school principal."

Luke chuckled. "I didn't see that one coming."

"Well, we all have our stories, Major." Hunnicutt nodded at the door. "And right now, I'd say you need to see how much of Mr. Dempsey's you can pry out of him."

"Yes, sir," Luke said, and Hunnicutt nodded and set off down the hall.

Luke opened the door quietly and slipped into the room. It was formerly a large storeroom, a windowless cube in the middle of the building, recently turned into a makeshift isolation cell. There was a small table with two metal chairs, and a single bare light bulb. The prisoner lay on a cot on the opposite wall, zip-tied hand and foot, with duct tape over his mouth and eyes.

Luke set a paper bag and a bottle of water on the table, and the prisoner raised his head at the sound. Luke walked over to the cot.

"I'm going to slip a knife blade under the duct tape around your eyes and mouth to cut the tape, but I'm not going to hurt you. Nod if you understand."

The man nodded, and Luke cut the tape. As he tried to remove it, it was obvious the hair was going to be a problem.

"I'm sorry," Luke said, "but it's stuck in your hair pretty good, so I'm just going to jerk it off fast. This might hurt a bit."

The man nodded again, then flinched as Luke snatched the tape off first his eyes, then his mouth. He blinked at the light, then squeezed his eyes shut as Luke cut the plastic flex cuffs off his wrists and ankles and helped him sit up on the cot.

"I have some water, and there's a sandwich in the bag on the table, Mr. Dempsey," Luke said.

"Wh-where am I?"

Luke ignored the question and gently tugged the man to his feet and helped him walk unsteadily across the short distance to the table and sit. The man twisted the top off the bottle and chugged the water. Luke pulled another bottle from the leg pocket of his pants, and the man nodded gratefully before downing half of the second bottle, then pulled the sandwich from the bag and began to eat, barely chewing before swallowing.

The guy's half-starved, thought Luke as Dempsey attacked the sandwich. He was in his late thirties or early forties, with the red hair and fair skin of his Irish heritage. Half his face was covered by a purple and yellow bruise from Washington's fist. To Luke's relief, the man finished both the sandwich and the water without choking.

"Better?" Luke asked.

Dempsey nodded. "Wh-why am I here?"

"I think you know," Luke said.

The man shook his head vehemently. "I don't, really. I've been cooperating, ask anyone. I... wait, if it's about the start-up sequence, I can explain."

Luke merely nodded. "Please do."

"Look, I know you want the plant on line ASAP," Dempsey said. "I get that, we all do. But there are certain safety procedures we have to... I mean need to... follow. I'll take all the shortcuts we possibly can, but some things we just can't ignore."

The man was obviously terrified, almost at the point of babbling. What could induce such fear?

Luke shrugged. "You know the price of failure, Mr. Dempsey."

All color drained from the man's face, and the hideous bruise stood out in even greater contrast. "Please," he whispered, "please don't hurt my family. I... I'll do it any way you want me to."

Luke kept his face a mask. "And when did you last see your family, Mr. Dempsey?"

Dempsey looked confused. "Yesterday, the same as everyone else, when you let us all inside the wire for visiting hours." He paused. "But wait. If you're SRF, why didn't you know—"

There was a soft knock at the door.

"Excuse me, Mr. Dempsey," Luke said, rising and moving to the door.

He cracked the door to see Washington standing in the hallway, beckoning. He stepped into the hallway and closed the door behind him.

"What is it?" Luke asked.

"There's been some sort of problem at the camp," Washington said. "The colonel wants you up on the wall if you can break away."

Luke sighed and shook his head.

"What is it, Major? You don't look so good."

"We screwed up, Washington. Dempsey isn't a collaborator; they're holding his family hostage in the camp. That's how they're 'encouraging' all the people who are 'cooperating.'"

Washington looked puzzled, then a look of concern crossed his broad face. "You're worried those FEMA bastards are gonna think he took off and harm his family."

Luke nodded. "Maybe we got this guy's family killed."

Washington shook his head. "Probably not. Remember we grabbed the three SRF guys at the same time, and chances are, they found where our boat was pulled up in the mud. They'll likely just figure it for what it was."

"I hope you're right," Luke said. "But what's so important that can't wait?"

"I'm not sure. All I heard was trouble at the refugee camp; then the colonel asked me to come get you."

"All right, just let me tell Dempsey I'll be back later and then lock up here."

CHAPTER THIRTEEN

Luke hurried up the ladder to the top of the wall, to find Hunnicutt standing with Wright, staring in the direction of the refugee camp. He could hear gunfire in the distance.

"… and Miles' patrol was attacked by the mob, and someone opened fire on the crowd," Wright said. "There are fatalities and injuries, extent unknown."

"Dammit! I thought we told them—"

"Miles swears the fire came from a neighboring house, sir. He thinks it was bangers trying to stir things up."

Hunnicutt took off his helmet and ran a hand through his thinning hair as he muttered a curse. He glanced up as Luke arrived and turned back to Wright. "Major Kinsey is here, Lieutenant Wright, so go over the SITREP again, please."

Wright nodded toward Luke. "The refugees are rioting, but our folks are safe for the moment inside the swimming club perimeter, but it's going south in a hurry. I ordered the extraction protocol on my own initiative."

Hunnicutt nodded. "Good call. Status?"

"It'll be close, sir, but we should be okay," Wright said. "They have six up-armored Hummers and two school buses for the noncombatants. They'll exfiltrate from the country club east entrance on Pine Valley Drive in five minutes. Lieutenant Butler is organizing a relief column to roll out to support them if necessary. I turned Corporal Miles' patrol around with orders to hold the intersection of College Road and Pine Valley Drive, in case this is part of some larger attack we don't yet understand."

"Very good," Hunnicutt said. "Get our people out ASAP. Delay for nothing. Take only our people, our weapons, and vehicles. If anyone else objects, don't waste time arguing. Bring them out by force if necessary."

Wright nodded, then hesitated. "Confirm rules of engagement, sir?"

Luke saw Hunnicutt's jaw tighten. When he replied, it was slow and deliberate. "Scatter them with warning shots if possible. But you are weapons free at shooters' discretion. Don't take chances. All of our people are coming home alive."

FORT BOX
WILMINGTON CONTAINER TERMINAL
WILMINGTON, NORTH CAROLINA

SAME DAY, 3:10 P.M.

"Prior Planning Prevents Piss Poor Performance," Hunnicutt said with a satisfied nod as he stood on the wall an hour later and watched the little convoy roll through the gates of Fort Box. "SITREP, Wright?"

"No casualties, sir. Unless you count Dr. Jennings' pleasant disposition," Wright said. "She's madder than a wet hen and demanding to speak to you."

Hunnicutt sighed. "Which I'll do, sooner or later. But please hold her at bay until we get this mess sorted out."

Wright nodded. "Then I best go meet the convoy and give her a target. Though I'd rather trade fire with the bangers."

Hunnicutt chuckled and nodded his thanks, and Wright headed for the ladder down. Hunnicutt turned east and raised his binoculars. Smoke rose in towering columns from around the refugee camp. He shook his head.

He lowered the glasses. "What's it look like, Major?"

Luke shook his head. "Not good, sir. Washington and his team have eyes on the camp, or what's left of it. I sent them out with the relief column with orders to set up an overwatch. The rioting is general and aimless for now. They're burning everything in sight in and around the camp, but I think we can count on them heading this way. There's a lot of anger there, seeking a target."

Hunnicutt nodded and turned to Butler. "What was the camp census, Lieutenant Butler?"

"We stopped trying to estimate several days ago, sir," Butler said. "Given all the squatters in the surrounding neighborhoods, it was a near impossible task, but our best guess four days ago was at least thirty thousand."

Hunnicutt raised the binoculars again. "And they'll all be heading this way," he said softly as sporadic gunfire sounded in the distance.

WILMINGTON REFUGEE CAMP
(FORMERLY PINE VALLEY COUNTRY CLUB)
PINE VALLEY DRIVE
WILMINGTON, NORTH CAROLINA

SAME DAY, 5:40 P.M.

Kwintell Banks stood with Reaper by their technical, watching the mob on the golf course. All around the perimeter of the former country club, homes and businesses joined the club structures burning in the afternoon sun. Towering columns of smoke rolled skyward in the still air, and the acrid smell wafted across the now unkempt green expanse of the golf course.

Banks watched Darren Mosley at work. For all his shortcomings, Banks thought, nobody worked a crowd quite like Mosley. With Banks' permission, Mosley had dipped into the UBN provisions and handed out food and drink liberally, including cases of beer and whiskey. He was well on his way to convincing the mob he had all the answers.

It was a mixed crowd he addressed, black, white, and Hispanic refugees of all ages, some formerly middle class and others impoverished. They were all the same now: desperate people clinging to a miserable existence in squalor, surviving on inadequate rations of horrible food, all looking for someone to blame. Mosley was serving them up a target on a platter.

"… and that ain't all," Banks heard Mosley yell. "I was a soldier in there. North Carolina National Guard. Yes, I was. But I couldn't take it no more, couldn't live with myself. It's disgusting what they got inside, hidin' it away, not sharing with folks. Man, they got whole containers full of canned hams and shrimp and salmon. All kinds of shit. And what they feeding you? Crappy-ass boiled corn come off one of them skanky old foreign ships, probably full a rat turds, and not even American rat turds. Foreign rat turds. Chinese rat turds."

There were cries of agreement and outrage, scattered at first, then general as Mosley fired up the crowd.

"But you know what they ain't got? And what they want you to think they got a lot of? Ammunition. Oh, they got enough to make a show, but if we decide to go in there and take what we got coming, they can't stop us. They probably just gonna load up their boats and run away, just like they did here today."

Mosley paused and drank from the long-neck beer bottle in his hand. Refreshed, he redoubled his efforts, striding back and forth in the pickup bed, gesturing wildly to the crowd around him.

"You done this here today," he yelled, taking in the entire crowd with a sweeping gesture. "It was YOU who made them fool soldiers run. It's YOU they afraid of. I say we march right down to that dumb-ass little fort they built and DEMAND they give us the food they STOLE so we can share it out equal for everybody."

Mosley shot a look to Banks, who nodded, and Mosley turned back to the mob.

"WHAT DO YOU SAY? ARE YOU WITH ME?" Mosley screamed.

"YES!" the mob screamed in unison.

"ARE YOU READY TO GET SOME GOOD FOOD?"

"YES!" the mob screamed again.

"THEN GET YOUR ASSES IN GEAR, AND LET'S GO GET WHAT'S RIGHTFULLY OURS!"

With that, Mosley beat his fist on the top of the pickup, and the driver set out across the golf course, driving slowly as the crowd parted and fell in behind Mosley's truck like he was the Pied Piper, headed for Shipyard Boulevard and Fort Box beyond.

Banks looked over at Reaper. "What you think of my boys now?"

Reaper shrugged. "Any fool can talk big. We'll see how they do when bullets start flying, but this is a good diversion. We need to keep the guys with M4s and the technicals well back out of sight until we're ready to use 'em."

FORT BOX
WILMINGTON CONTAINER TERMINAL
WILMINGTON, NORTH CAROLINA

SAME DAY, 6:10 P.M.

Luke raced up the ladder. Hunnicutt stood on the wall with Wright and Butler.

"Lieutenant Washington says they're on the move, sir. Pretty much the entire mob as far as he can tell, with a few gangbangers mixed in," Luke said. "Things are about to get real, so I ordered Washington and his men to RTB."

Hunnicutt nodded. "Agreed. Please tell Lieutenant Washington I said well done."

He turned to Butler. "How many M2s do we still have along the river?"

"Two each on both the larger boats and one on the smaller boat. Plus a couple set up on the outboard side of the ships, placed to sweep the river in both directions." Butler hesitated. "Why, sir? You want to reposition them?"

"Some of them, yes," Hunnicutt said. "An attack from the river looks less likely, at least in the immediate future. What can you spare?"

Butler rubbed his chin. "We can take all four off the larger boats. The smaller boat is more mobile anyway, and between that gun and the two on the ship sides, we should be able to handle any threats from the river. At least long enough to reposition guns if necessary."

"Do it," Hunnicutt said. "Work with Lieutenant Wright here to reposition them. Space them evenly along the top of the wall to supplement the guns at each corner."

Wright spoke up. "We'll have to improvise, sir. We won't have time to armor them like the corner gun emplacements or the other firing positions."

Hunnicutt nodded. "I understand; use sand bags or whatever you can find. I doubt they'll be taking fire anyway. My hope is seeing them stretched along the wall will serve as an intimidation factor. The best battle is one you don't have to fight, gentlemen."

"Amen to that, sir," Butler said, moving toward the ladder to carry out his orders, with Wright close behind.

"You really think they'll attack, sir?" Luke asked.

"Hunger and desperation make people do extreme things," Hunnicutt said. "But I hope staring up at the wrong end of a row of M2s, with maybe a burst or two fired above their heads, will bring them to their senses. But if it doesn't... well, we'll just have to be prepared to deal with that."

Luke shook his head. "Even the dumbest of them should understand they're no match for armed soldiers in prepared positions with crew-served weapons."

Hunnicutt turned and looked to the east. "You would think so," he said. "But there are thousands of them, and as Stalin once said, quantity has a quality all its own."

***

The leading edge of the mob came into view twenty minutes later, surging up Shipyard Boulevard. Hunnicutt ordered the gate in the outer perimeter fence closed and locked, and reinforced it by having two of the container transporters block the gate completely with several containers pre-staged nearby for that purpose. The big machines completed the task and moved back inside the stout defensive walls of Fort Box itself, where they duplicated their efforts and barricaded the more substantial gate there as well. The defenders were as ready as they could be.

As the mob reached the fence, Hunnicutt got his first inkling of trouble. Rather than massing at the gate as anticipated, the mob spread down the fence line in both directions at the exhortations of a man in the back of a pickup and his minions. Fighting a rising unease, Hunnicutt adapted and ordered defenders spread more evenly along the threatened walls, in between the newly repositioned machine guns.

Beside Hunnicutt, Luke watched the mob flow down the fence line. "I'm not liking this. This looks way too coordinated for a rioting mob."

"Agreed, but we'll handle whatever they throw at us. Hopefully without a wholesale slaughter," Hunnicutt said.

Luke looked due west at the sun nearing the horizon. "I'm not sure the intimidation factor is going to work, sir. The sun's directly in their eyes now. They probably can't see the machine guns that well. Should we fire a burst over their heads to give them a clue?"

Hunnicutt looked west then glanced at his watch. "Let's not waste the show. We'll wait till they all have a ringside seat and light 'em up. How many are loaded with tracer?"

"Every other gun," Luke said, and Hunnicutt nodded.

They stood in silence and watched the mass of humanity flow against the chain-link fence, screaming and shaking fists and improvised weapons.

LOUISIANA STREET
2 BLOCKS FROM THE PERIMETER FENCE

SAME DAY, 6:50 P.M.

Banks stood in the street next to the technical, listening to the radio squawk and reduced to observer status as Reaper directed the operation. The technicals were spread evenly along the perimeter fence, one to two blocks back and out of sight from the fort walls. His own men, weapons concealed, were spread evenly at the back of the mob along the fence. They were anonymous faces in the crowd, with the bulk of the milling mass of screaming refugees between them and the guns of Fort Box.

All except for the baby gangstas. Fifty preteens were spread across the front of the mob near the fence, all volunteers eager to prove their worth to the UBN. The single qualification for their current task was sufficient strength to operate the bolt cutters they kept concealed in plastic garbage bags. They would strike at the first gunfire either from Fort Box, or if that was not forthcoming, from their brothers at the back of the mob. Their task was simple: cut the fence to ribbons along its entire length.

Banks glanced over at Reaper. "I don't like this. We shoulda made the signal something else. Them soldiers can shoot any time; what if we ain't ready?"

"What's important is that the fence gets cut. Exactly when makes no difference. If we made the signal something else, half those little morons would miss it. This way, all they have to remember is 'hear guns, cut the fence.' Even they can remember that," Reaper said. He narrowed his eyes. "And you let me worry about things like that. You're starting to get on my nerves again."

Banks fell silent, and Reaper looked down the street and grinned. A pickup approached, and Banks saw people in the bed. They were all women and children, refugees in ragged clothes with haggard faces. Their wrists were zip-tied, and terrified eyes showed over duct-taped mouths.

"Put them in the bed of the technical," Reaper yelled to the driver of the arriving pickup. "Zip-tie 'em to the rack, standing up, and make sure they can be seen."

Banks stared. "What the hell you doin', Reaper?"

Reaper grinned. "That's an unauthorized question, fool. But I'll give you a pass, seein' as how I'm in a good mood. That's 'enhanced armor.' When it hits the fan, the technicals are gonna be priority targets, so I'm givin' our heroes over there in Fort Box a little extra to think about before they pull the trigger."

Reaper's smile faded. "Now you ridin' with me. So get your ass up in the bed of that truck before I put you in a dress and mount you as a hood ornament."

FORT BOX
WILMINGTON CONTAINER TERMINAL

"GIVE US OUR FOOD! GIVE US OUR FOOD!" the mob chanted in unison, those nearest the fence shaking the chain link in time to the chant. Luke looked on with growing concern as Hunnicutt swept the fence with his binoculars, then dropped them to hang on his chest by the strap.

Hunnicutt sighed. "I guess it's time to offer a bit of discouragement, Major."

"Yes, sir," Luke said, raising the radio mic. "All tracer-loaded guns, repeat, all tracer-loaded guns, fire a short burst over the heads of the hostiles on my signal. Confirm. Over."

He listened as each gun confirmed promptly; then he gave the order. "All tracer-loaded guns, execute. Repeat, execute."

All along the wall, the guns barked, and fiery tracers shot out hot and straight, well over the heads of the screaming refugees. The chanting stopped at once, silenced by the fifty-caliber snarl. When the guns stopped scant seconds later, a deathly quiet fell over the fort and mob alike.

Like a hysterical person slapped back to sanity, the mob was shocked, and on the wall, soldiers held their breath, hoping this would end it. Hunnicutt raised the glasses again, scanning the faces pressed up against the fence, encouraged by what he saw. Maybe it would be this easy after all.

And then he saw an African-American boy perhaps twelve years old, perhaps younger, resolutely cutting through the chain-link fence with a pair of bolt cutters almost as big as he was. The cut was already two feet from the bottom of the fence and growing. Oh God, please not this, he thought, a lump in his throat. It took three tries to get the next order past his lips.

"Corporal Miles," he said to the rifleman kneeling to his right, "there is a perimeter breach directly in front of us. Take him out. Now."

Miles raised his M4, searching, then looked up at the colonel. "Sir, it's... it's a kid. I... I can't shoot a kid."

Hunnicutt's voice was shaking, "That's an order, Miles."

"But, sir—"

"PERIMETER BREACH!" came a scream from down the wall, followed by a second, then a third.

Things seem to go in slow motion for Hunnicutt, and he felt a steely calm run through him. He put a hand down on Miles' shoulder. "Take the shot, son," he said softly. "This is on me, not you."

The young soldier looked up with glistening eyes, bobbed his head once, and raised his rifle. The sound of the shot seemed to tear through Hunnicutt's own heart. He shook it off and turned to Luke.

"Pass the order, Major. Weapons free. Repeat, weapons free. Anyone inside the fence is a legitimate target."

The fence was fully breached in two dozen places before they got the situation neutralized. The mob reacted like a living thing, recoiling from the fence in panic, none even attempting to enter the newly opened breaks now blocked by dead children's bodies. Hunnicutt ordered a cease-fire and crossed his fingers.

But it was not to be. He heard sustained gunfire behind the mob, and like a blind and wounded beast, the massed humanity surged back toward the fence and Fort Box beyond, charging without thought, reacting to the immediate pain. It crashed into the fence with a horrific scream, those refugees nearest the fence unable to prevent themselves from being pinned against it. Some, the lucky ones, were forced through the multiple breaches. Free from the crush of the mob, they looked fearfully towards the fort walls, raised their hands in surrender, and huddled near the groaning fence, unable to retreat and terrified of going forward. Hunnicutt ordered his men to hold their fire.

But it was only a matter of time. Gunfire continued to come from the back of the mob, though the exact source was impossible to ascertain. The fence was leaning along its entire length with the press of thirty thousand refugees. Blood dripped from the chain link as faces and hands and arms and legs were mashed into the wire, far beyond the limits mere flesh could endure.

And then it happened. At places the mesh separated from the poles, and in others the poles themselves toppled over, concrete foundations breaking free of the ground like uprooted trees in a windstorm. Whatever their pattern, the failures occurred in quick succession, and in seconds the perimeter fence ceased to exist. The mob flowed toward the defenders like a fast-rising tide.

And on the tide came sharks. The shooters drove the mob forward at gunpoint, more visible now, but always careful to stay close enough to use the mob as cover. As they cleared the battered remnants of the fence, the shooters ran forward, mixing in the terrified and milling crowd to turn their fire toward Fort Box.

What they lacked in accuracy, they made up in volume. Hunnicutt heard a grunt, and he looked down to see Miles down, blood flowing from a shoulder wound.

"IT'S BANGERS. THERE MUST BE A THOUSAND OF THEM!" Luke shouted.

"TARGET THE SHOOTERS," Hunnicutt yelled.

Along the wall the defenders fired sporadically, coping with the near impossible task of differentiating between armed bangers and their human shields. The horrific roar of the battle increased, augmented by the sound of roaring engines and stuttering machine guns as the technicals burst from hiding and roared forward.

It was all about survival now, and every defender knew it without the need for orders or commands. The fire increased without regard to collateral damage as defenders began to fall. A machine gun fell silent, victim of sustained fire from two of the technicals. Another ceased to exist, hit by an RPG. The attackers' strategy was obvious, and by unspoken agreement, the defenders turned their fire on the technicals.

And paused. There was a perceptible lull in defensive fire as the defenders saw the technicals' ghastly human armor. But in the end, it could make no difference. Tracers streaked toward the technicals from the M2s and drew fire and RPGs in return. Riflemen pulled triggers again and again, tears rolling down their cheeks as their rounds tore through innocents to impact the monsters behind them. Each defender became an emotional island, the revulsion and shame at their own action fusing into a white-hot hatred of the bastards who forced them to it.

It lasted fifteen minutes—and forever. Here and there, a banger reached the wall with a grappling hook on a rope, but such penetrations were few and easily dealt with. In the end, the human shield strategy proved to be the attackers' undoing. The mass of refugees was packed so tightly against the walls, the bangers behind them couldn't reach the wall in any significant numbers. They found themselves a readily identifiable fringe at the back edge of the packed mob, and easy targets for the defenders. They fell in increasing numbers, and the more intelligent among them hid or dropped their weapons and burrowed into the safety and anonymity of the crowd.

When the attack stalled, the technicals changed tactics. Oblivious to the huddled refugees, they targeted their remaining RPGs at one small area at the base of the wall, hoping to force a breach. A half dozen explosions rocked the sidewall of a single container and opened a gaping hole. But the inside wall of the container held, and the surviving technicals fled the field. By dusk, it was over.

And the worst was just beginning.

CHAPTER FOURTEEN

Same Day, 10:30 p.m.

The guns fell silent in the gloaming, replaced by the heartrending cries of the dying and wounded. Hunnicutt forced himself to ignore it and concentrate on the tasks at hand. He ordered all available night-vision equipment spread along the wall and posted an overwatch. Anyone approaching the wall was labeled a threat and terminated. Anyone fleeing the huddled mass of refugees along the wall was allowed to leave unmolested unless they were armed, in which case they were to be terminated.

Those defenders without night-vision glasses worked by flashlight, assisting wounded comrades and carrying down the dead. They moved silently, on wooden limbs, and spoke in quiet monosyllables when they spoke at all, barely audible above the piteous cries outside the walls. More than one defender broke down and sobbed, and Hunnicutt had cotton balls brought up from the dispensary. They stuffed their ears and kept working.

***

Hunnicutt heard approaching footsteps and turned to see a flashlight bobbing toward him along the top of the wall. "That you, Luke?"

"Yes, sir," came Luke's voice.

"How bad?"

"Twenty-three, sir. Seventeen wounded and... and six KIA."

Hunnicutt didn't speak for a long moment. When he did, his voice had a detached, almost philosophical tone. "It sounds better somehow, doesn't it? KIA, I mean. Somehow less final than dead. Noble somehow."

Luke didn't respond, and Hunnicutt shook himself out of his funk. "Sorry, Major. How about the wounded? Are any of them..."

"Three are critical, sir. Dr. Jennings doesn't think one will survive the night, but she's optimistic about the other two."

Hunnicutt nodded, then realized Luke couldn't see him in the dark. "Very well. Continue to rotate personnel on the night-vision glasses every two hours. Everyone not on watch should get some sleep. I have a feeling we're going to need all the rest we can get."

"Yes sir," Luke said, but he didn't move away. "What about... out there?"

The moans and cries of the wounded outside the walls had subsided into background noise, punctuated by sporadic shrieks of pain and the crack of M4s as armed bangers attempted to leave the scene.

Hunnicutt shook his head. "We can't send anyone out there to help them until morning when we can reestablish a perimeter. We don't know how many hostiles are still in the mob, and there are at least a half dozen technicals still out there somewhere. Anyone outside the walls would be sitting ducks. You know that."

Luke sighed. "Agreed, sir. But with respect, I don't think you should be standing here dwelling on it either. You need rest too."

"I'll be down directly, Major, but thank you for your concern."

***

Despite his promise, Hunnicutt paced the wall all night, listening as the moans outside the fort faded. As if by agreement, his subordinates left him with his own demons. As the sky lightened in the east, Hunnicutt confronted the sight he'd been dreading. The carnage was even worse than he remembered. He sank down cross-legged on the hard steel of the container, buried his face in his hands, and wept.

After a while, he felt the warmth of the sun on top of his bowed head, then looked up, wiped his eyes with the back of his hand, and rose. There was work to be done.

***

Relief washed over Luke as Hunnicutt descended the ladder and started toward him with a determined step.

"SITREP, Major Kinsey," Hunnicutt said.

"We're maintaining overwatch, sir. There don't appear to be any more armed hostiles in the crowd. At some point during the night, they must have figured it out and begun to leave unarmed. Nor is there any sign of the technicals, but Lieutenant Wright is preparing a reconnaissance using the up-armored Hummers. Lieutenant Butler is seeing to the disposition of forces along the wall, and Dr. Jennings reports that two of the critically wounded are out of the woods. She expects them to make full recoveries. But I'm sorry to say the third casualty didn't make it, sir."

Hunnicutt's jaw tightened. "Who?"

"One of your folks, sir. Corporal Susan Phelps. She was—"

Hunnicutt nodded. "A driver in the transport group. She's from Hankins Corner. Engaged to be married next month; her boyfriend's name is… was Byron." He sighed. "Who else?"

"Corporal Miles—"

"I saw Miles get hit. It didn't look like a mortal injury, and I saw him being attended to—"

"He returned to the firing line and was hit a second time manning an M2."

"A good man," Hunnicutt said softly. "Who else?"

"Another guardsman, sir. I'm sorry, but I can't recall his name offhand. And two of the guys who came in with me, Corley and Abrams, former jarheads. And the Coasties lost Wilson and Fontaine. All the units lost someone."

"We're all one unit, Luke," Hunnicutt said.

"Well, if we weren't, we are now," Luke said.

Hunnicutt nodded, then looked toward the waterfront. Luke followed his gaze to see Levi Jenkins and both the Gibson brothers approaching, long guns slung and followed by a group of armed men.

"What's going on?" Hunnicutt asked.

"I took the liberty of radioing Levi to bring him up to speed and expedite the call for volunteers. We have no clue what we're up against."

Hunnicutt gave an approving nod just as the group reached them.

"Sorry we couldn't get here any sooner," Levi said. "We didn't have enough boats to move this many people at once without leaving the folks on the river short on transportation. Some of them just ferried us down and went back for the others. Can you top them up with fuel for the trip home?"

"Absolutely," Hunnicutt said, extending his hand. "Thank you for coming."

The three men nodded as Luke studied the group, trying to count heads.

"There's a lot more of you than I expected," he said. "How many?"

"This isn't all of us," Levi said. "We got about thirty here, but there are a hundred and fourteen all told."

"Outstanding. Thank you," Luke said.

Levi nodded toward the Gibson brothers. "Don't thank me, thank them. Turns out they're natural born recruiters. Where you want us?"

Luke glanced toward Hunnicutt. "I was thinking they could relieve our folks on the wall. As soon as we can get a new perimeter established, we have a lot to do."

Hunnicutt nodded grimly. "Let's get it done, Major."

***

Wright led his up-armored Humvees in a sweep through the nearby neighborhood. Finding it all clear, he ordered them back into a protective ring around Fort Box at the point formerly marked by the perimeter fence, and positioned them facing outward in mutually supporting positions. Only then did Hunnicutt allow Dr. Jennings and a team of volunteers to treat the still living among the fallen refugees.

If Hunnicutt had expected recriminations from Jennings, he got none, for even she recognized the impossible situation in which he found himself. Instead she combed through the shattered specimens of humanity, seeking signs of life. She found almost a hundred, including a dozen who were clearly bangers and four in the wreckage of the technicals who appeared to be something else entirely.

It was only at that point Hunnicutt and Jennings clashed, with the colonel insistent the former combatants be physically restrained and treated in a tent outside the walls of the fort. After a halfhearted and somewhat obligatory protest, Jennings let it go. Beyond her Hippocratic oath, she had no sympathy for the savages who caused this carnage.

After attending to the living, they turned to the dead, a task made more urgent by the weather and the southern sun. Their own honored dead were buried as they had fallen, together, a twenty-foot container their shared coffin.

Flags were no problem; the ever-resourceful Wright discovered a container containing two pallet loads of American flags among its mixed cargo, made in China, of course. He found folding cots from the same source, which they mounted permanently in the container turned sarcophagus, to hold the flag-draped remains of their fallen comrades. They welded the vents and doors shut while a backhoe made short work of the asphalt in a secluded corner of Fort Box and dug a perfectly rectangular hole to receive the container.

They left six inches of the container protruding from the ground as both a headstone and monument. The best welder in the group inscribed the names of each of the fallen in weld bead on top of the container. The improvised sarcophagus was lowered into the hole slowly and reverently, with full military honors.

Then Hunnicutt dismissed the company, and they set about the altogether more grisly task of dealing with the refugees. There were hundreds of bodies clustered near the walls or spread across the asphalt in a macabre tableau of violent death, and over a hundred more dead bangers facedown near the remains of the perimeter fence, weapons on the asphalt beside them.

Hunnicutt asked for volunteers and set the example by being the first volunteer himself, despite his rank. When almost everyone followed his lead, he divided them into five teams to finish the task as quickly as possible. They turned once again to their store of empty containers and positioned five twenty-footers on the asphalt as group coffins.

They handled the bodies as respectfully as possible, but the sheer volume of the task and the need to get the corpses sealed inside the containers before decomposition began mandated they work as quickly as possible. They reserved four of the containers for the refugees, and used the fifth for the bangers. It didn't seem fitting to bury the sheep with the wolves.

The work went mercifully quickly, and by noon it was complete. Hunnicutt left instructions for the disposition of the containers and went to his quarters to stand under the blasting hot shower for long minutes, his guilt at wasting precious water overcome by the need to feel clean. But he felt dirty to his soul and doubted he'd ever really feel clean again.

He'd just changed into a fresh uniform when he heard a tentative tap at his door. "Come," he said. The door opened and Luke stood in the threshold.

"We're ready, sir," Luke said.

Hunnicutt nodded. "Thank you, Major. It will take me a moment to collect my thoughts. Please have the garrison assembled in thirty minutes."

Luke nodded and started to leave, then turned back to Hunnicutt. "What can you say after something like this, sir? Words just seem so... so inadequate, somehow."

Hunnicutt smiled sadly. "My thoughts as well, but I have to give them something, some... I don't know, some closure somehow. They've just been through a horrific ordeal. If they can't put it behind them, it'll eat at us like a cancer."

Luke shook his head. "But how?"

Hunnicutt hesitated, thinking. "Ever heard of the 'conscience round,' Luke?"

"You mean like the blank they loaded at random in a firing squads' rifles, so no one was sure whether or not they fired the killing shot?"

Hunnicutt nodded. "We'll have to do some difficult things to survive, but some things—things like we did yesterday, if we have to do those things too often, our humanity won't survive."

"But it's done, Colonel. And it can't be undone. So how can you—"

Hunnicutt held up his hand. "I don't know, Luke. But hopefully it will come to me in the next half hour."

***

Thirty minutes later, Hunnicutt stepped out of the HQ building into the afternoon heat and strode across the asphalt to their newly designated cemetery. As ordered, the garrison was formed up in ranks in front of four neatly excavated holes in the asphalt. The coffin containers were lined up neatly to one side, one of the half doors slightly ajar on each container, as Hunnicutt had ordered. He glanced toward the walls of the fort and saw the river volunteers standing at attention, facing inward toward the cemetery, except every third man, who faced outward to maintain a watch. *Good folks, those river people*, Hunnicutt thought.

He spotted Luke at the head of the garrison and motioned him over to hand him four sealed Ziploc bags and a roll of duct tape.

"Major, please see that one of these bags is taped securely to the inside door of each container, then have them sealed and prepared for burial."

"Yes, sir," Luke said, and went about the task as ordered.

Hunnicutt watched Luke in whispered conversation with the senior non-com before returning to his place at the head of the garrison. Five minutes later the task was complete, and Hunnicutt heard the screech of the locking bars as the containers were sealed for the last time. He waited until everyone returned to ranks, then extracted a folded paper from his pocket. He took a deep breath and began to speak.

"We gathered earlier today to perform the sad and solemn task of honoring our fallen comrades. We come together now to pay our respects to those who, through no fault of their own, fell before our guns. These were not evil people, but victims. Not our victims, but victims of those who would use and manipulate them. They were driven not by hatred, but by fear and desperation, and taken advantage of by evil men. Though they died by our hands, it was not by our intention, and I know there is no one among us who does not wish with all their heart and soul this tragic outcome could've been avoided."

Hunnicutt unfolded the piece of paper.

"I've prepared a statement and placed a copy in each of the coffin containers. I did so in anticipation of some future time when normalcy is restored. I would like to read it to you now."

There was a murmur in the ranks, which Hunnicutt ignored.

"In these containers lie the remains of eight hundred and fifty-two souls, known only to God, who died by my hand and on my orders on the thirtieth day of April, 2020. I accept full and sole responsibility for these deaths and am prepared to provide a full accounting of my actions at such time as a legitimate government is established to hear my account.

"At no time or in no way did any of the officers or troops serving under my command act except at my direct orders. Collectively and individually, they behaved properly and honorably and maintained the highest standards of the American soldier.

"We lay these souls to rest, on this, the first day of May, 2020. May God have mercy upon their souls, and upon mine.

"Colonel Douglas David Hunnicutt, Commanding

"Wilmington Defense Force

"Fort Box

"Wilmington, North Carolina"

Hunnicutt folded the paper and slipped it back into his pocket.

"And on a personal note," Hunnicutt said, "let me say that I have never had the honor of commanding or serving with a finer group of people."

There was no loud cheer or shouted response, nor did he expect one. Rather there were scattered nods and a glistening eye here and there. They knew what he was doing, and whether it mitigated their collective guilt or not, they loved him for it. The feeling grew into an almost palpable thing, and the healing began.

"Major Kinsey," Hunnicutt said, "please proceed with the interment."

Luke nodded and motioned to the heavy equipment operators, who mounted their machines and began to lower the containers to their final resting places. Throughout the garrison, people bowed their heads or murmured prayers or placed their hands over their hearts. Halfway through the interment, the clear sweet notes of 'Amazing Grace' rang out across the Fort, and the group turned to see Donny Gibson on the wall, singing a cappella. One by one, the river men on the wall joined him, as did the garrison. The last note sounded as the final container was laid to rest in the mass grave.

The lump in Hunnicutt's throat made it difficult to dismiss the formation.

MUNICIPAL WASTEWATER TREATMENT PLANT
RIVER ROAD
WILMINGTON, NORTH CAROLINA

DAY 31, 3:20 P.M.

Luke rode in the lead vehicle as the little convoy wound its way down River Road. There were five vehicles in all: two Humvees front and back, with the container transporter riding in the middle. The technicals were still unaccounted for, which necessitated any trip outside the immediate area of the fort to be of sufficient strength to repel an attack.

If the burial of their comrades and the refugees was an emotional task, no such positive or respectful feelings were attached to the disposal of the remains of their attackers. This was simply taking out the trash, and Wright's suggestion of a suitable disposal site won quick and universal acceptance. Luke nodded to the driver and they made a right turn into the sewage treatment plant.

It didn't take long to find the holding pond. They stopped alongside and Luke got out of the Hummer. He motioned for the transporter to drop the container as far as possible up the sloping berm surrounding the pond. The driver did as ordered, managing to leave it teetering on top of the berm at a crazy angle. The transporter moved away, and one of the Humvees nosed up to the end of the container, and tires spinning and engine roaring, tipped the container the rest of the way over the berm, into the fetid waters of the pond.

Luke and his men watched as the container drifted to the middle of the pond, slowly sinking as water rushed in the holes they'd drilled in the bottom.

"Ashes to ashes, shit to shit. May you all burn in Hell," Luke said.

"Hallelujah, amen," one of his men added, with a derisive snort.

"You reckon they might pollute the pond?" another asked, to general laughter.

"Let's saddle up and get out of here," Luke said, and they all moved back to their vehicles.

Day 32, 7:10 a.m.

Rorke heard the muted thump of the chopper blades muffled through his headphones as they circled high above the fort. Far below, heavy equipment was moving new containers in to replace those damaged during the attack.

"They're rebounding pretty fast," Rorke said into his mic. "And it looks like they have a lot more people on the wall, and some of them aren't in uniform."

Beside him, Reaper shrugged. "I don't think it makes much difference, General. Bodies alone won't make much difference, and they have to be low on ammo now. A Guard unit in peacetime wouldn't have had a very big ammo load out to start with, and they can't have much left. We ain't gonna sword fight them; another attack like the last one and they're finished."

"You got anybody left to attack them WITH, especially after what happened?"

Reaper laughed. "Funny how it happens, isn't it? The bangers are mostly shot to hell and useless. We might get a little more mileage out of them somewhere, but I seriously doubt we'll get them to throw themselves at that wall again. They're dumb, but they're not completely stupid. But the refugees, that's a different story. Most of them are cowed, right enough, but some are white-hot mad at the fort for killing their friends and relatives. They're so pissed they don't seem to connect with the fact it was us that threw them under the bus, and those that have a clue blame the bangers, not us. We play our cards right and spread some of those MREs around, I think I can recruit us 'Indigenous Force Act Two.' It will just take a little patience, that's all."

"How much patience?" Rorke asked.

Reaper shrugged again. "Two, three weeks tops."

"You have two, and another fifty advisers. But at two weeks and one day, I want possession of that fort and all of their supplies. Is that clear?"

"Crystal, General," Reaper replied.

Rorke nodded and looked down at the fort. "Well, it wasn't the success I'd hoped for, but we've hurt them badly at little cost. As you say, they must be low on ammunition and are undoubtedly demoralized at having slaughtered the very people they were trying to save." He smiled. "They may even disintegrate on their own. Anyway, they're much less of a threat than they were two days ago, and they're no longer squandering my supplies on the refugee rabble. We'll just let them sit there until we're ready to take them out for good."

FORT BOX
WILMINGTON CONTAINER TERMINAL
WILMINGTON, NORTH CAROLINA

DAY 32, 8:15 A.M.

"You're sure?" Hunnicutt asked, looking around the table at what he'd come to think of as his war council. Luke Kinsey and Joel Washington were there, as was Josh Wright and Mike Butler. As a courtesy, Levi Jenkins and the Gibson brothers were now sitting in, representing the river volunteers.

Washington nodded. "Absolutely, sir. They're SRF, and the mercenary scum, not the recruits from regular forces like us." He looked toward Luke for support.

"Washington's right, sir," Luke said. "I recognize them too. Two of them were in Jacksonville when we were."

Hunnicutt grunted. "Well, too bad none of the wounded ones made it. I'd have loved to get some intel out of those bastards."

Across the table, Mike Butler shrugged. "Well, a half dozen of the bangers did survive, and they seem pretty pissed at their 'advisers.' Every one of them identifies these SRF thugs as being from 'the pirate in the chopper.' I think that's pretty definitive."

"It's Rorke, all right," Luke said. "They all describe him to a T."

"Pretty smart, actually," Wright said. "I mean, they risk a few of their own guys and throw the bangers out as cannon fodder. It's quite a force multiplier. If they win, they bought a cheap victory, and if they lose, they haven't lost much."

Hunnicutt sighed. "And when we won, we didn't really win anything, except staying alive to fight another day. How do we stand?"

Butler glanced at his legal pad. "We picked up almost two hundred M4s from the fallen bangers and scavenged six M240s from the disabled technicals, along with some ammo for each. But that's our Achilles' heel. We burned through ammo like a house afire." He shook his head. "No way we could survive another attack like that, even if the mob is carrying clubs."

Hunnicutt nodded. "You think your friend Sergeant Hill would guide a little trip to the Military Ocean Terminal?"

"Absolutely, sir," Butler said. "But I'm pretty sure SRF will have more forces guarding the place now, especially after our previous trip. It will be tough to sneak in and out with enough ammo for our entire force."

Hunnicutt shook his head. "That's not exactly what I had in mind." He turned to Luke Kinsey. "How's Dempsey doing?"

Luke shook his head. "I almost wish I hadn't told him. When he finally accepted we'd snatched him and his family was still back behind the wire, he's been going crazy."

"Understandable, but we need to get him calmed down, because I think we're going to need him," Hunnicutt said.

"I'm a bit confused, sir," Butler said. "What's the Duke Power guy got to do with any of this, and if we're not going to slip in and steal ammo, what's the plan?"

Hunnicutt smiled enigmatically. "Gentlemen, in another life, I was a history teacher, and despite my love of my home state, I've always harbored a deep and abiding admiration for Joshua Lawrence Chamberlain and the Twentieth Maine. Are you all familiar with Colonel Chamberlain's defense of Little Round Top during the Battle of Gettysburg?"

A few heads nodded, some more confidently than others.

"Chamberlain was in a somewhat similar situation," Hunnicutt said. "Out of ammunition and besieged by a larger, seemingly more capable force, it appeared his only option was surrender. But he—"

"Ordered his men to fix bayonets and charged, breaking the back of the attack and saving the day for the Union," Josh Wright finished.

"Exactly, Lieutenant Wright. Exactly." Hunnicutt's face hardened. "I'll be damned if I'll sit here waiting for this man Rorke to crush us like a bug. He's about to find out some bugs have a deadly sting."

CHAPTER FIFTEEN

Six Days Earlier
Day 26, 7:20 p.m.

Matt Kinsey shifted uncomfortably against the hard bottom of the boat and leaned forward to relieve the pressure on his aching arms. His hands were behind him, bound at the wrists with duct tape, and the edge of the seat he'd been forced to lean against for the past two hours had restricted circulation. He was losing feeling in his fingers.

The Cajuns had separated them, placing Bollinger in the Coast Guard boat with the two underlings while Kinsey rode in the Cajuns' boat with the older man who'd done all of the talking. They backtracked up the channel north to Calumet and from there into the Atchafalaya River, only to leave the main channel of the river an hour later to wind their way through a maze of twisting, narrow bayous beneath towering cypress trees. Kinsey was facing backwards, and he watched the Cajun at the outboard deftly maneuver the boat through the narrow channel, the electric trolling motor up and out of use at his side.

"I can't feel my hands," Kinsey said. "You think you could adjust these bindings?"

The Cajun glared at him and spat over the side.

Kinsey tried a different approach. "What's with the trolling motor?"

"You writing a book, *couyon*."

Kinsey shrugged. "Just curious."

The Cajun said nothing for a long moment then shrugged himself. "When we leave the bayou, we like to be quiet."

"How'd you find us?" Kinsey asked. "I know you couldn't see us."

The Cajun smiled. "Just lucky, *couyon*. We drain diesel from the barges. All those tank barges have pump engines, and the engines have fuel tanks, *non*? Even if the barge is empty, there's fifty or sixty gallons of fuel there, and the tanks are nice and high—easy to drain into the cans in our boat."

Kinsey tried to keep the conversation going. "You know we had nothing to do with what happened to your family. We're not even here on an official mission. I'm just trying to find my family in Baton Rouge."

The Cajun's face hardened. "So when you try to scare me, you're Coast Guard, but when you're caught and tied up, you're just a simple man trying to find his family. Very convenient, *couyon*. But a fancy boat, M4 rifles, and night-vision equipment, they tell a different story, eh? Besides, you ain't from Baton Rouge or anywhere around here. You're a Yankee, for sure. There's no family in Baton Rouge."

"I'm from Wisconsin originally," Kinsey said, "but my wife's maiden name was Melancon, and my daughter goes to LSU. She's on the soccer team."

"And your wife, she is in Baton Rouge?"

Kinsey shook his head. "She passed some years back, and I haven't heard from my daughter since this all started. I hope she's with my sister-in-law's family in Baton Rouge."

The Cajun said nothing, suddenly intent on something ahead. Kinsey twisted at the waist, straining to see. In his peripheral vision, he could just make out the stern of the Coast Guard boat rounding a huge cypress tree, the trailer close behind, into an even narrower channel. The Cajun reduced speed, and seconds later followed the Coast Guard boat into the smaller bayou.

"Where are we going?" Kinsey asked.

The man ignored him, and fifteen minutes later the boat bumped against a low wooden dock where several men waited. There was a hurried exchange in a combination of French and heavily accented English, and Kinsey and Bollinger were dragged from the boats and hustled down a path through the cypress swamp to a clearing with a dozen houses on an island of high ground in the wetland, the term 'high' being relative. All the houses were constructed of rough-cut cypress planks, gray with age, but there the similarity ended. Some were small, little more than sheds, but others were large and sprawling and looked as if they'd been added on to willy-nilly. They'd all been there awhile, that was obvious.

Kinsey's appraisal was cut short as he and Bollinger were marched up the rickety wooden stairs of one of the smaller buildings and forced to the floor. Their captors bound their ankles together with duct tape and left without saying a word, closing the door behind them. A padlock rattled in a hasp and then silence.

"What are we gonna do now, boss?" Bollinger asked.

Kinsey shook his head. "Damned if I know. Looks like the only way in and out of this place is by boat. Do you think you can find your way out if we stole one?"

Bollinger looked skeptical. "Lots of twists and turns, and all this swamp looks alike. We must have passed a couple of dozen little interconnecting channels. Even if we can steal a boat, I doubt anyone could get in and out of here without knowing the landmarks. I'm thinking that's why they didn't bother to blindfold us."

"Either that, or they don't figure on leaving us alive long enough to try to escape," Kinsey said.

***

Andrew Cormier peeked into the darkened room. His daughter-in-law sat at the bedside in a straight-backed chair, silently reading a Bible in the light of a kerosene lamp. A floorboard creaked as he shifted his weight, and Lisa looked up and put a finger to her lips. She rose quietly to join him, softly closing the bedroom door behind her.

"How is he?" Cormier asked.

"He's been in and out of consciousness since we got the bullet out. But he's in a lot of pain, so I think it's better when he's unconscious. He has a fever, so I'm afraid the wound is infected. I only wish we had a real doctor and antibiotics and better pain medication and..." The woman shook her head, unable to continue.

Cormier nodded sadly then shrugged. "We have what we have, *cher*. And my son is a strong man." He pulled the woman into his embrace and whispered in her ear, "And besides, it takes more than one bullet to kill a Cormier, *eh*."

She nodded and her body moved in what could have been a laugh or sob or both, and he put his hands on her shoulders and held her at arm's length. She looked gaunt and hollow eyed, with the pain of a lifetime written prematurely across her young face.

"But, *cher*? Maybe you should be resting—"

The woman shook her head and gave him a wan smile before gently disengaging his hands. "I'm a Cormier now too, Pop." Her face hardened. "And I won't shrink into a shell because of... because of what they did to me."

Cormier could only nod, not trusting himself to speak. After a long moment, he found his voice.

"We caught two of the bastards this afternoon."

She stared at him, blood in her eye. "FEMA?"

He shrugged. "They dressed like Coast Guard and claim they're looking for family, but who knows? And even if they are, it doesn't mean they're any better than the FEMA bastards. The world has gone crazy, *cher*, and we're safer here with the old ways. We trust no one who isn't from the bayou. We'll survive here like our ancestors did, and any *fils putain* stupid enough to come in after us will be gator food."

Andrew Cormier had been a gentle man, a good father and husband, quick with a joke and equally quick to laugh at one. All that changed two horrible weeks ago in a once well-kept suburb of Lafayette. He'd been away from the house at the time, out with his neighbors on bicycles, scavenging for food. He'd returned to find his home ransacked, his wife murdered and his son near death, and his daughter-in-law naked and tied spread-eagled to a bed in the back of the house. He'd cared for his son and daughter-in-law as well as he could, buried his wife in the backyard, and then loaded his family in his truck and, bass boat trailing behind, used their small hidden store of gasoline to get to the only refuge he could think of, the bayou. He was tortured daily by thoughts he should have made the move the day the lights went out.

For many modern-day Cajuns, 'the bayou' was a place shrouded in myth, but not for Andrew Cormier. His father left the twisting waterways and Cypress swamps as a young man and settled in nearby New Iberia, but Andrew spent each summer on the bayou with *grandpere* and *grandmere*, speaking the blunt, archaic and unadorned peasant French of the Cajuns and learning the old ways. His grandparents died within a month of each other, just two months before he graduated from vocational school. He'd never returned to the bayou, but neither had he forgotten what he learned.

He began life in 'the real world,' as he called it, as an air-conditioning technician, guaranteed steady employment in Louisiana, and eventually started his own business. He hadn't wanted to move to Lafayette, but his wife was from there, and the larger population offered good business opportunities. Opportunities that fueled a lifestyle he'd been far too reluctant to abandon, even with the writing on the wall.

Others joined him daily in reclaiming the scattered and weathered little communities hidden among the Cypress swamps of the Atchafalaya. Men and women like himself, not far removed from life on the bayou, who instinctively shed the now useless trappings of modern life. They were a people whose peasant ancestors had marched as foot soldiers under William the Conqueror and later swore curses instead of allegiance to George the Third. A people who prospered in the bitter winters of the Canadian Maritimes and the steamy swamps of Louisiana. A people with survival in their genes and, when crossed, blood in their eyes.

"What are you going to do with them?" she asked.

"Don't worry, Lisa. The boys and I will take care of it."

"But what if they're... you know. Not like the FEMA thugs. What if they're what they say they are?"

"They got a radio, so I figure they have to know what the government is doing. The way I look at it, anyone still running around pretending to be part of the government likely IS part of the government or at least close to it. The only difference is this time we got them before they got us. And we ain't the only ones who lost people. All the people here want some payback, *cher.*"

"I want payback too," she said, "but aren't you at least going to talk to them or have a trial or something?"

"I have talked to one of them. Says he's going to Baton Rouge lookin' for family and his wife's maiden name was Melancon. Which proves exactly nothing. How many Melancons you figure are in Baton Rouge?"

"I don't know. A lot, I guess. But is that all he said? What's HIS name?"

Cormier shrugged. "Didn't ask, don't care. But he did say he has a daughter who plays soccer at LSU."

The woman looked thoughtful. "Tim and I went to a game last year. Maybe if we know the name, I might be able to remember if there was a player by that name. At least we'd know if he was telling the truth about that."

"Even if he is, so what? He's still—"

Lisa put a hand on his arm and looked into his eyes. "Pop, I know you're hurting about Mom and you haven't had a chance to process it because you've been too busy taking care of us. But this isn't you. You can't just cut up two men who may be innocent just because of what they're wearing."

He returned her gaze. "Yes, I can," he said, then paused. "But maybe you're right. We talk a bit more first."

***

Kinsey and Bollinger sat up as the rickety steps squeaked and they heard the padlock rattling in the hasp. The door swung open with a plaintive squeal and they squeezed their eyes shut as a bright flashlight painted their faces.

"Okay, *couyon*, question time," said a familiar voice. "What are your names?"

"I... I'm Matt Kinsey, and this is Dave Bollinger."

"Tell me about your daughter. The soccer player."

"What do you want to know?"

"Her name, for starters."

"Kelly. Kelly Kinsey. Her friends call her KK for short."

Kinsey heard murmurs and realized there were at least two people behind the light. He heard a woman whisper.

"What position does she play?"

"Goalie. But why the hell do you want to know—"

The light retreated abruptly and the door closed, but he didn't hear the padlock.

"What the hell was that about?" Bollinger asked.

"I don't know," Kinsey said, "but maybe I shouldn't have said anything. If something happens to Kelly—"

He was interrupted by heavy footfalls on the stairs outside, several men this time. The door flew open again and four men burst in with flashlights. He and Bollinger were hoisted to their feet by hands under their armpits and dragged outside and across to a larger building, the toes of their bound feet digging furrows in the dirt. Soft lantern light spilled from the windows of the building, casting another set of wooden steps in a soft glow. Not that they needed the light. Their captors half dragged, half carried them up the steps and through the front door to dump them unceremoniously into straight-back chairs in the center of a large sparsely furnished room, across from the head man.

"Now, Coast Guard," the man said, looking at his watch, "you have exactly five minutes to convince me I shouldn't cut you up for gator bait."

***

It took closer to thirty, but Kinsey started liking their chances a lot better when the allotted five minutes passed with none of the Cajuns unsheathing a knife. Their captor insisted on a blow-by-blow account of everything that had happened to them from the time of the blackout, jumping on anything that seemed the slightest far-fetched and demanding more in-depth answers.

Finally, Kinsey finished, and there was a long silence punctuated only by the breathing of the people collected in the room. Their captor rose to unsheathe a large hunting knife, and Kinsey's heart fell. *I guess I wasn't that convincing after all*, Kinsey thought as he watched the man approach slowly, his step deliberate.

He stopped in front of Kinsey's chair, just out of range of a two-footed kick, and squatted to look Kinsey straight in the eye.

"I got a good ear for BS, and I don't think anyone could make up a story like that," the Cajun said.

Kinsey heaved a relieved sigh as the man reached down and sliced the duct tape binding his ankles, then motioned for Kinsey to rise and turn so he could cut the tape from his hands. Kinsey rubbed his wrists and rolled aching shoulders as the man freed Bollinger.

"Andrew Cormier," the man said, turning from Bollinger to sheath the knife and extend his hand to Kinsey.

Kinsey took the man's hand. "Matt Kinsey," he said.

The Cajun grinned. "Yeah, I think we been over that."

"So we have," Kinsey said. "So what now?"

"I suggest y'all get settled down in the bayou. You gonna be here a while."

Kinsey shook his head. "Negative. I have to get to Baton Rouge."

"That may be a problem," Cormier said.

SOMEWHERE IN THE ATCHAFALAYA RIVER BASIN
NORTH OF MORGAN CITY, LOUISIANA

DAY 27, 9:20 A.M.

Cormier shook his head. "It won't work. I mean, your floating trailer's a good idea, but I still don't think you'll be able to get around the locks at Bayou Sorrell and Port Allen. Plus there's a lot of people up and down that stretch. The good people gonna take a shot at you for being feds, and the bad people gonna shoot you to take your stuff. It won't work, Kinsey. I doubt you make it halfway."

"We have to make it work," Kinsey said, tapping a point on the chart spread out on the table between them. "Port Allen Lock is directly across the Mississippi from LSU, and my sister-in-law's house is just southeast of there. It can't be much more than a mile from the river. I figure that's the most direct and quickest way in and out."

Cormier shrugged. "Figure all you want, *couyon*. Y'all go that way and you're dead meat."

Kinsey blew out an exasperated sigh. "Look, Andrew. I have to get there—"

"I didn't say you couldn't get there. I said you can't get there that way." Cormier put his own finger down to the chart and traced a line. "You need to go up the Atchafalaya. It's mostly farmland and woods on either side, and when you get to the Mississippi, there's a couple of different places you can cross over the levee without an audience, eh."

Kinsey followed Cormier's pointing finger, his doubt obvious. "But that's twice as far, and when we reach the Mississippi, we'll be over fifty miles up-river from Baton Rouge, maybe twice that with all the river bends."

"And you'll be alive," Cormier said. "You can't do your family much good if you're dead."

Kinsey fell silent, then gave a reluctant nod and studied the proposed route. "There's a few towns along the way, do you think we'll have any problems there?"

Cormier shook his head. "They're small places, and the river is plenty wide. You can stay to the far side of the river and blow right by before anyone can think about it."

Kinsey shook his head. "You're forgetting something, aren't you? We still have to tow the trailer to get over the levee into the Mississippi. I don't think we'll be 'blowing by' anybody with that thing in tow."

"We ain't takin' the trailer," Cormier said.

"What do you mean we're not taking the trailer..." Kinsey trailed off and stared at Cormier.

"And what do you mean WE?" Kinsey asked.

Cormier nodded. "I figured me and a couple of the boys will take a little boat ride with you. We'll take aluminum boats. If we tie off to yours, you got enough power to take us all up the river pretty fast. And the aluminum boats are light enough that we can manhandle them over the levee. We leave your Coast Guard boat on the Atchafalaya side."

Kinsey was speechless. "But why? I mean we appreciate it, but why are you helping us?"

Cormier shrugged. "A lot of reasons. Maybe because every time there's a hurricane, it was always the Coast Guard we see with helicopters, pulling folks off rooftops. Getting the job done while everybody else seems to be running around with their finger up their ass. Maybe because I've been thinking about this ship of yours over in Texas, and think maybe having some friends outside the Bayou might be a good thing. We're self-sufficient in everything but gasoline, and you tell me they got plenty of that." Then Cormier smiled, but there was no humor in it. "And maybe because my only son is lying in the next room near death. He is in God's hands, and there is nothing I can do here. But maybe while we're out, we catch a few of these

FEMA bastards to bring home and pass a good time, eh? Everybody was a little disappointed we didn't get to chop you two up for gator bait."

Kinsey chuckled politely, not altogether sure Cormier was joking. "Whatever your reasons, I appreciate it," he said. "When can we leave?"

"We'll get everything ready and leave at first light tomorrow," Cormier said.

"It's still morning; we could get out of here today."

"'Cause there's planning to do," Cormier said, putting his finger on the map again to indicate a bend in the river. "There are a lot of things we have to think about, and this is a big one right here. There aren't so many places to run into trouble going this way, but there could be a lot of trouble in one place, *eh*?"

Cormier removed his finger, and Kinsey looked at the point indicated, the Louisiana State Penitentiary at Angola, bounded on three sides by the wide Mississippi.

"There are a lot of bad, bad people there," Cormier said. "And I'm bettin' by now they're out and maybe on the river, and—"

"And we gotta get by them," Kinsey said.

CHAPTER SIXTEEN

DAY 28, 11:15 A.M.

The Atchafalaya River flows south, though much more directly than the Mississippi, its sinuous cousin to the east. Bollinger was at the wheel, guiding their strange little convoy over the sluggish brown surface of the river at twenty-five knots. They ran three abreast, a sixteen-foot aluminum boat lashed tight and unmanned to either side of the Coast Guard boat. Cormier and two of his men rode in the Coast Guard boat with them.

As Cormier promised, they left the Cajun village at first light and wound their way through a maze of bayous for a good hour before reaching the main river. Kinsey attempted to memorize the path, but was hopelessly lost by the sixth turn in the first fifteen minutes. The only thing he was sure about was that they were leaving by a different path from the one they used coming in. Cormier watched him scrutinizing the banks closely and laughed.

"Good luck remembering the way, *couyon*. The bayou, she is changing all the time. Tomorrow she will look very different, *non*? You have to know the things that do not change, and for that you will need a lifetime or a teacher. And I think no Cajun is going to be schooling outsiders anytime soon. We will be friends, I think. But we will come visit you when we want to talk, not the other way around."

Kinsey shrugged and grinned back. "Fair enough, I suppose. If I had a secure place, I wouldn't be too eager to share it with anyone either."

They'd ridden upriver mostly in silence as they made their way through cypress swamp and pine forest, passing the occasional ramshackle tin-roof shack five to six feet off the ground on pilings, with an almost obligatory tumbledown dock jutting a few feet into the river. But no people. At one point Kinsey commented on the deserted feel of the place, and Cormier just smiled.

"Oh, there are people there, *mon ami*, and we are in their gun sights. Trust me on that," Cormier said, then pointed ahead at a bridge looming in the distance.

"We're makin' good time," Cormier said. "That's the I-10 causeway, so we're halfway to the Mississippi. We'll reach the levee in time to get the boats over in daylight, and we want to go downstream in the dark anyway."

Kinsey nodded and watched the top of the bridge, looking for threats but finding none. Bollinger kept the boats to the center of the river as they motored beneath the double concrete span, and Kinsey noticed an opening in the trees ahead on the right bank. As they drew abreast of the small clearing, he glimpsed flashes of white between the trunks of the pine trees and after a moment made out the familiar shapes of recreational vehicles. A dozen people lined the bank, mostly men, but here and there a woman or a child. They stared at the passing boats in sullen apathy.

"An RV park?" he asked Cormier.

Cormier shook his head. "Not a park, I think a squat. Likely they were running from Baton Rouge in their RVs and made it here before they ran out of gas. Luckier than some, I suppose. They have shelter and they can fish from the river, and they're hidden from I-10 by the trees. But by now, I suspect they are as desperate as everyone else."

Kinsey nodded and turned his gaze back upriver. There were more than enough desperate people in this cruel new world; right now the only ones who mattered to him were his family.

"We'll be coming up on Krotz Springs in an hour or so, and after that there are four small river towns scattered between there and the Mississippi levee. How much faster can we go?" Cormier asked.

Kinsey moved to the door of the little cabin and looked into where Bollinger stood at the wheel, then glanced down at the throttle lever. He moved back to where Cormier stood astern of the cabin. "We have a bit of throttle left. Your boats are dragging us down, but I think Bollinger can get another ten knots out of her if need be. Why? Do you expect trouble?"

Cormier shrugged. "These days, I always expect trouble. Then I can be happy if it doesn't happen. I just want to know what our options are if we run into it."

Despite Cormier's worries, they made it by Krotz Springs and the other villages upriver without incident. They stayed to the opposite bank, as far from the towns as possible, and accelerated past at full speed. The sun was well on its way toward the western horizon when Cormier pointed to a channel to the right.

"That's the channel to the Lower Old River lock. I think that'll be the easiest place to cross."

Kinsey nodded and moved into the little cabin with Cormier close behind. Space was tight, so Cormier stood just outside, where he could talk to both Coasties. Kinsey ordered Bollinger into the side channel, and they all stood silent as he negotiated a bend and came to a split in the smaller channel.

"The right fork goes to the lock. Take the larger fork to the left," Cormier said. "That's the old riverbed, and it dead-ends at the Mississippi levee."

Bollinger did as ordered, and they approached the dead end, a narrow sandy beach. Beyond it, a grassy slope rose like a great wall, filling their vision from left to right.

"That thing must be a hundred feet high," Bollinger said.

Cormier shook his head. "More like fifty or so," he said. "But it will seem like a hundred when we're trying to carry a three-hundred-fifty-pound boat. That's why I picked this spot. There's grass on both sides, so we can drag the boats up and slide them down the other side."

Kinsey looked up at the towering levee. "You sure this is gonna work?"

"No," Cormier said. "But I'm sure five of us have a better chance of getting aluminum boats over the levee than you two had of getting your Coast Guard boat weighing many times as much around those locks, trailer or no trailer."

"Point taken," Kinsey said.

It went surprisingly well. They stripped everything from the first boat to lighten the load, and Cormier produced wide web strapping they slipped under the floating boat in two places as lifting straps. Grunting and straining, they walked the boat out of the water and across the little beach, two men on either side, with the fifth man lifting the stern.

They set the boat down at the foot of the levee, and Cormier ordered one of his men up the slope with one end of a long rope. While the man climbed, Cormier tied the other end of the rope to the bow ring of the boat and then waited for his man to reach the top and take up the slack. By prearrangement, the others positioned themselves around the boat, and on the count of three, pushed and pulled for all they were worth, sliding the boat up the slope through the long grass as far as possible. The man with the rope gathered in the slack as the boat advanced to a stop, then braced himself, the friction of the boat on the slope sufficient to help him keep it from sliding back. In a dozen heaves they had it resting on the crest of the levee and started back down for the second boat.

More confident now, they loaded both outboards, trolling motors, and other gear in the second boat after first positioning it at the base of the levee. It made the boat heavier, but it would be faster and easier than carrying the heavy gear up the steep slope piecemeal. Twenty minutes later, the second boat rested beside its twin on the levee.

Gravity was their friend now, but the big concern was the boats might slide down too fast and damage their thin aluminum hulls on a hidden rock. They sent them down the slope bow first, with the rope tied off to the transoms now, and two men holding back on the rope. Two others guided the boat down the slope, while the fifth walked in front, checking for any obstacles that might damage the boat. They had the boats in the water and fully outfitted just as the sun reached the horizon.

Kinsey turned to Cormier. "Who you gonna leave with our boat?"

Cormier nodded to one of his men. "I'm leaving Breaux. I told him to move it into the little inlet up in the trees to the right of the beach. You see it?"

"I was going to suggest it," Kinsey said. "When should we take off?"

Cormier looked west, then turned back to Kinsey. "This channel puts us in the Mississippi directly across from the prison farm, but a wooded island in the middle of the river will screen us from sight. And I doubt anybody is in the fields of the prison farm at night, or maybe at all now. I say we wait until full dark, maybe two hours, then take off. We lash the boats together, so we don't lose each other in the dark, and go on the trolling motors, using y'all's night-vision goggles. We'll hug the west bank until we get well past the prison; then we can stay close to whichever side is least inhabited."

"The trolling motors are gonna be slow," Kinsey said.

"They also going to be pretty quiet," Cormier said, "and we're gonna have a strong current behind us. But we do need to save the batteries, because we definitely need quiet when we go through Baton Rouge. We switch to the outboards when we're safely past the prison, then go back to the trolling motors to go through the city."

Kinsey nodded, and they took advantage of the waning light to eat a meal. Then they said their goodbyes to a forlorn Breaux, the man obviously irritated he'd drawn the short straw and boat-sitting detail, and watched him scramble up over the levee and out of sight.

The minutes dragged for Kinsey. Being this close to his family and unable to fly downriver grated on his nerves. But ever so slowly the sky darkened until finally they were wrapped in the inky blackness of a post-event night. After whispered conversation with Cormier, they cast off and moved down the short channel and into the stream of the mighty Mississippi.

They moved on a single trolling motor, propelling both of the lashed boats, and Kinsey was amazed how quickly the bank slipped by in his night-vision goggles. Cormier had been right about the current.

By mutual agreement, Cormier's man, Bertrand, was at the helm, wearing one of the Coasties' pairs of NV goggles. Kinsey and Bollinger were alternating overwatch duties, trading off the other pair of NV goggles every half hour to keep their eyes fresh.

It was near the end of Kinsey's first watch when the channel turned almost due south. He glanced over to where Cormier sat, staring into the dark.

"We're turning due south," Kinsey said softly. "We're past the prison, right?"

Cormier nodded in the green-tinted world.

"That wasn't too bad," Kinsey said.

"It ain't going downstream I was worried about," Cormier said. "It's clawing back against this current with the outboards blastin'. We won't be exactly hard to spot."

"They might hear us," Kinsey said. "But it will be night, and we have the NV equipment."

"They might have it too. You ever think of that?"

"Yeah, but I've been trying not to," Kinsey said.

MISSISSIPPI RIVER
SOUTHBOUND
JUST NORTH OF BATON ROUGE

DAY 29, 1:25 A.M.

Their approach to Baton Rouge was signaled by increasingly large fleets of idle river barges tied up along both banks and glowing green in Kinsey's night-vision goggles. They made a sharp bend to the right, and a bridge loomed across the river in the near distance.

"That's the 190 bridge," Bertrand said softly. "Should I kill the outboard?"

"*Oui,*" Cormier replied, and the rumble died abruptly as Bertrand switched back to the trolling motor.

The quiet was eerie, but short-lived. As they moved closer to the city, Kinsey heard sporadic gunfire, and here and there distant fires flared green in his glasses.

"You sure you can recognize this place, Kinsey?" Cormier asked.

"I'm not sure of anything," Kinsey said, "But the place I saw on the chart was just south of the I-10 bridge and almost directly across from the Port Allen Lock. If we start hugging the east bank at the bridge, we should be able to spot it. Besides, any dock in the area should work. We'll be close to LSU and I know the way from there. We just cut across the campus to Connie's neighborhood."

When Cormier spoke again, there was doubt in his voice. "Just how much do you know about Baton Rouge?"

"Not a lot," Kinsey said. "We visited Connie fairly often, but my brother-in-law always did the driving around town. Why?"

"Because not every neighborhood around LSU is a good one, and it sounds like we're headed right into the projects," Cormier said. "The locals say to stay off streets named after presidents if you don't want to end up dead. And that's when things were normal; I can't imagine how it is now."

"Okay, what's the alternative? Beyond this short stretch, there are no other good landing spots for at least four miles. That would make it a long hike to Connie's house, to say nothing of getting back to the boats. Besides, I know my way from the LSU campus, but we get too far away and we're gonna be groping around in the dark with no clue where we are."

Kinsey heard Cormier sigh. "No, you're probably right. We'll just have to slip past the projects. It's the middle of the night, and if we don't show a light, we should be okay. The LSU veterinary school is right near the river. We can use that as a landmark."

"I-10 bridge coming up," Bertrand called softly from the stern. "What y'all want me to do?"

"Hug the east bank," Cormier said. "Let's see if we can find Kinsey his dock."

Bertrand did as ordered, and the bank grew more distinct in the green glow of Kinsey's NV goggles. They passed a dock almost immediately under the I-10 bridge. Kinsey shook his head and waved Bertrand forward. The riverbank was lined with large blocks of empty and idle barges now, and Kinsey was beginning to worry the dock he was looking for would be blocked. Then he saw it through an opening in the blocks of barges, a floating dock with a crane in place, tethered to shore by a movable ramp designed to accommodate the changing level of the river.

"That's it," Kinsey said. "Take us in."

Bertrand reversed the trolling motor to slow the boats, but momentum and the current behind them were strong. The boats slowed ever so slowly as the little electric motor strained. It was obvious the motor could not counter the powerful current, and for a long, terrifying moment, Kinsey was afraid they'd be swept past the dock. But the Cajun handled the joined boats expertly, maneuvering them so they bumped along beside the dock at much reduced speed, allowing Kinsey to grab one of the ropes hanging down from the dock, no doubt placed there for that very purpose. Kinsey held them alongside in the current as Bertrand killed the trolling motor and rushed to tie them up securely to the dock. Only then did Kinsey release his grip on the catch rope.

"I think we should be safe using the headlamps here as long as we keep them in low-intensity red-light mode," Cormier said. "Anyone who spots us from across the river can't get to us, and we're well below the levee, so we don't have to worry about anyone spotting us from this side."

"Agreed," Kinsey said. "But first Bollinger and I should take the NV glasses and sweep the area to make sure we're alone. We can't stumble ashore lit up like Christmas trees."

"Okay," Cormier said. "But hurry, eh? We need to do this fast. This place ain't gonna be too healthy in daylight."

Kinsey murmured agreement, and Bertrand passed his NV goggles to Bollinger. Moments later, the Coasties were moving up the sloping ramp toward solid land, night vision in place and M4s at the ready. The ramp terminated in the well-worn gravel parking lot of what had previously been McElroy Fleet Services, empty except for a battered flatbed truck of indeterminate but ancient vintage.

The offices were in a utilitarian metal building, the windows smashed and front door standing open. They entered to find the large one-room structure ransacked. Metal desks and filing cabinets were overturned, no doubt savaged by looters frustrated at the lack of anything of value. They exited the building and made their way around the periphery of the parking lot, examining the open shops and work areas. All were vacant and vandalized. Satisfied the area was secure, Kinsey signaled Bollinger, and they started toward the dock.

"I wonder if that heap runs," Bollinger said as they neared the old truck. "A ride sure would be sweet."

Kinsey stopped and opened the truck door, grimacing as it squeaked. "Not locked, but good luck finding any keys."

"Not a problem, boss," Bollinger said. "I wasn't always the model citizen you know and love. I have a few skills from my misspent youth."

Kinsey grunted and raised the hood. "Surprise, surprise. No battery. It's probably the only thing of value the looters found. I doubt anyone wanted this old beater, but you're right, it's worth a shot. Let's go get the others."

Cormier looked in their general direction as they moved across the dock in the darkness, obviously locating them by sound. "That you, Kinsey?"

"It is," Kinsey replied. "And we found—"

"We got a problem," Bertrand blurted. "I clicked on my light to check the lines, and the stern line is already chafing. We can't leave the boats tied up like this and bouncing around on this current; if one line breaks, the other will go quick. And what if we don't make it back before daylight? We can't just leave the boats here in plain sight. We gotta find a hiding place out of this current."

Kinsey cursed and turned his NV goggles toward the riverbank. He was scrutinizing a block of empty barges lashed together and moored to the tree-lined shore downstream when Bollinger spoke.

"Maybe we can take them around the downstream end of these barges into the backwater between the barges and the bank," Bollinger said. "Nobody will be able to see them from either the dock or the river, and the trees will screen them from the bank. There can't be much surface current there."

Kinsey nodded. "Looks like our best shot, but first let's get our gear ashore." Kinsey turned to Cormier. "Andrew, we're done with the trolling motors, right?"

"*Mais* yeah," Cormier replied. "They ain't gonna do no good against the current. We go back upstream on the outboards. Why?"

"Because I want one of the batteries." Kinsey told them about the old truck.

They got their gear ashore, including a battery and a five-gallon can of gas, working in the soft warm glow of their red headlights. Given his claimed expertise, Kinsey left Bollinger working on the truck with Bertrand's assistance while he and Cormier hid the boats. As hoped, they found a protected backwater between the barges and the riverbank and tied the boats up securely to a tree. By the time they'd slogged up the muddy riverbank and through the trees to the parking lot, their two companions were ready to try the truck.

"Ready when you are, boss," Bollinger said from the driver's seat.

Kinsey nodded, then grimaced as Bollinger touched two wires together under the steering column and the starter ground loudly, followed immediately by the roar of an unmuffled exhaust as the engine caught.

"Shut it down!" Kinsey hissed, and Bollinger complied.

"We can't drive around in that," Kinsey said. "We may as well take out an ad."

But Bollinger was already out of the truck and on his back in the gravel, inching under the truck with his headlight. He emerged with a diagnosis. "The exhaust system is Swiss cheese, but I saw some sheet metal scraps in one of the shops. I can patch it, at least temporarily."

Cormier looked at his watch. "It's two thirty. We don't have much time."

Bollinger ignored the Cajun and fixed his gaze on Kinsey. "Five minutes now can save us an hour later. It's worth a shot, boss."

Kinsey looked from Bollinger to Cormier. "Okay. Five minutes. No more."

Bollinger was moving before Kinsey finished speaking, and emerged from the nearest shop moments later with a handful of sheet metal scraps of various sizes. He tossed them on the ground, then rummaged in his pack for a roll of duct tape. He motioned for Bertrand to assist, and dove under the truck again. Kinsey and Cormier watched as Bollinger periodically asked for a piece of sheet metal and Bertrand passed it under the truck. Kinsey kept glancing at his watch.

"Time's up, Bollinger," Kinsey said. "Get out of there and let's—"

"Almost done, boss. One more minute, two max."

And so it went for ten. Kinsey was about to drag Bollinger out feet first when the man scrambled out, grinning. "Done!"

"And how long is friggin' duct tape gonna last?" Kinsey asked.

Bollinger shrugged. "Ten or twenty minutes or until we catch fire, whichever comes first. I figure it'll keep us quiet enough to get past the projects and to your family's house, and that's all we need, right?"

"Let's hope so," Kinsey said. "Give it a try, but shut it down if it's too loud."

Bollinger slid into the driver's seat, and Kinsey cringed again as the starter ground. But this time the engine was much quieter; still not exactly a whisper, but not a roar.

"All right, I'll drive. Bollinger, get in back with night vision and an M4. Andrew, you guys ride front or back, whichever you want," Kinsey said.

"Back," Cormier said. "Even if we can't see nothin', if Bollinger starts shooting we can shoot in the same direction. Maybe we get lucky, eh?"

"Fair enough," Kinsey said, sliding behind the wheel as Bollinger got out.

"Just a minute, boss," Bollinger said, and disappeared around the back of the truck. Kinsey heard several loud whacks and the sound of something breaking.

"Dammit, Bollinger!" he hissed. "Can you make any more noise—"

"Sorry, boss," Bollinger said softly. "Just takin' out the brake lights."

"Okay, okay. Let's go," Kinsey said.

He settled behind the wheel of the idling truck, and moments later, Bollinger knocked on the cab, signaling everyone was ready. Kinsey put the truck in first gear and crept out of the parking lot and up the steep incline to the top of the levee. He turned right, down the road on the levee crest rather than descending to the mean streets below. The higher vantage point would make it easier to avoid an ambush and give Bollinger a clear field of fire.

Any pretensions to stealth quickly evaporated when he shifted into second gear and the raucous sound of mechanical mayhem rose from the ancient transmission. He cursed and shifted back to first, and the transmission quieted. He built up sufficient speed to shift directly into third, hoping it wasn't gone as well, and heaved a relieved sigh as the truck slid smoothly into higher gear. The old beater moved quietly along the crest of the levee, 'quiet' being a relative term. In less than a mile he spotted a large office complex to his left at the foot of the levee: the vet school. He slowed, looking for a way down, and spotted a wide sidewalk angling down the side of the levee to the street below.

He stuck his left hand through his open window and pointed at the sidewalk. Bollinger knocked quietly on the top of the truck cab in acknowledgment and Kinsey started down. All went well until he bumped across a high curb and into the street, and cursed at the loud, grating sound of the truck dragging bottom. The impact was followed immediately by a rumbling roar, announcing he'd just undone Bollinger's makeshift repairs to the exhaust system.

***

Kinsey gritted his teeth and cursed himself for not vetoing the use of the truck immediately. But it was too late now. If anyone was around, they'd already heard, and since that was the case, the truck would minimize the time to Connie's house. He muttered another curse and rumbled east on the first street he came to.

He was unfamiliar with the campus this near the river and drove six or seven blocks before he saw Tiger Stadium looming in the glow of his NV goggles. Reassured, he accelerated and the old truck rumbled through the dark.

Stadium Drive took him to Highland Road, where he made a sharp right. Connie's house was less than a mile away, and for the first time since they left Texas, Kinsey felt optimistic. He fantasized about getting his loved ones back to the safety of *Pecos Trader*, but his daydream was interrupted by frantic knocking on the truck cab.

"WHAT?" Kinsey yelled out the open window, the roaring exhaust system negating any need for silence now.

"I THINK THE DUCT TAPE IS ON FIRE! THERE ARE FLAMES SHOOTING OUT FROM UNDER THE TRUCK!" Bollinger yelled.

"WE'RE ALMOST THERE," Kinsey yelled. "HOW BAD IS IT?"

"WHO THE HELL KNOWS? JUST KEEP GOING," Bollinger replied.

Kinsey mashed the gas, trying to coax a bit more speed out of the old beater. He almost missed the turn to Connie's subdivision, but he braked hard, managing to negotiate the left turn on to Sunrise Drive with his passengers still aboard. Then he slowed, remembering the numerous speed bumps along the quiet tree-lined street, a point of some irritation and frequent complaints from his brother-in-law. Flickering light illuminated the trees beside the truck as they passed, evidence of the growing fire under the truck.

He drove as fast as the speed bumps would allow, and bits and pieces of the exhaust system clattered to the pavement as they lurched over each bump. But whatever was falling off didn't seem to have duct tape attached, because the flames continued to grow beneath the vehicle. *How much of that crap did he use?* Kinsey wondered as the truck moved forward. The engine noise was deafening now, precluding even shouted conversations.

Kinsey spotted the entrance to the gated community ahead. The ornamental wrought-iron gate was closed, and he wondered if the old truck would hold together long enough to force it open. There was a sharp crack as a bullet shattered the windshield a foot to the right of him, and he slammed on the brakes just as the front wheels were starting over yet another speed bump. The combined assault transmitted through the steering system and jerked the wheel from Kinsey's hands and the truck veered into the trunk of a massive oak tree. Only the relatively slow speed prevented the collision from being worse.

He pushed himself back from the steering wheel, thankful his tactical vest had spread the force of the impact. He'd be bruised, but there were no broken ribs. But his self-congratulations were brief as the smell of gasoline from a broken fuel line drove him from the cab. Bollinger and the two Cajuns were still on the truck bed, disentangling themselves from a heap against the back of the cab. Another round ricocheted off the street near Kinsey and whined into the distance.

"Get the hell off there and away from the truck!" he yelled at the others. "There's a gas leak somewhere and this heap is liable to blow, and the fire is silhouetting us for the shooters."

Kinsey was dragging a groggy Bertrand off the flatbed as he spoke, and Cormier and Bollinger were gathering their weapons and gear. They were on the ground in seconds, moving away from the burning truck into the shadows and safety of the massive oaks on the opposite side of the street. They barely reached cover when the air was split by a thunderous explosion and the night flashed bright for a brief instant as the gas tank exploded.

The truck continued to burn; no need for night vision now. Kinsey flipped up his goggles and peeked around the tree trunk to see something he'd missed earlier. The guardhouse by the gate, occupied in better times by a lethargic and geriatric rent-a-cop, was now sandbagged. He could just make out heads popping up over the sandbags for a quick look: two or possibly three men. A shout rang out across the distance.

"YOU ARE SURROUNDED! DROP YOUR WEAPONS AND STEP INTO THE LIGHT WITH YOUR HANDS ON YOUR HEADS."

Kinsey was contemplating his response, when Cormier made it for him.

"MAYBE YOU SHOULD DROP YOUR WEAPONS, *COUYON*, BEFORE I THROW A GRENADE IN YOUR LITTLE HOUSE, *EH*?"

"I REPEAT," the man at the gate yelled, "DROP YOUR WEAPONS AND STEP INTO THE LIGHT WITH YOUR HANDS ON YOUR HEADS."

Something about that voice? Relief washed over Kinsey as he shouted a reply. "ZACH! ZACH DUHON! IS THAT YOU?"

There was a long silence. "WHO WANTS TO KNOW?" the voice replied.

"MATT. MATT KINSEY."

More silence. "IF YOU'RE MATT, STEP INTO THE LIGHT AND WALK TOWARD US AND KEEP YOUR HANDS WHERE I CAN SEE THEM."

Kinsey stepped out from behind the tree, hands on the top of his head, and walked toward the gatehouse. When he was halfway there, a tall man moved from behind the sandbag barricade and rushed to meet him. They embraced in the area in front of the gatehouse, then stepped back, both embarrassed by the gesture.

"Man, it's good to see you," Zach said. "We thought you were—"

"Is Kelly okay?"

"She's fine," Zach said. "And she'll be more than fine when she sees you."

Zach looked toward the trees in the shadows. "Is Luke with you?"

Kinsey shook his head. "No, but he's safe. He's in North Carolina."

"I'm relieved to hear it," Zach said, and grinned. "You want to bring the rest of your folks in. I promise we won't shoot them."

Kinsey turned and motioned the others forward. When they arrived, he made quick introductions all around, and they all turned toward the gate. Zach's fellow guards were a bit less welcoming, holding their weapons pointing downward, but leaving no doubt they were prepared to raise them at the slightest provocation.

"They're okay," Zach said. "This is my brother-in-law and he vouches for the others."

One of the guards shook his head. "You know the rules, Duhon. We're not supposed to let anyone in without approval from the council."

"I don't think that applies to family," Zach said. "But if you want to go wake up Fat-Ass Fontenot at three in the morning, be my guest. Meanwhile, I'm taking these boys to my house. You know where to find us if anybody has a problem with that."

The two men held their ground for a few seconds, as if contemplating pressing the point, but seemed to think better of it. They both stepped back to let Zach pass. Zach clicked on a headlamp to light their way and started down the middle of the street. Kinsey and his comrades turned on their own headlamps and fell in beside Zach. Kinsey held his tongue until they were well away from the gate.

"I get the impression there's no love lost there?"

Zach shrugged. "They're all right, but the longer this drags on, the more strained things get. We were doing okay for the first two or three weeks. There was rioting and looting after the first few days, but the governor called out the guard and they were able to contain a lot of it. Then as it got worse, most of the guardsmen just left and went home to protect their own families, and those that were left were tasked with defending the governor's mansion."

"Have you had any trouble?" Kinsey asked.

Zach nodded. "Yeah, at first the looters were running all over the place. But we've only got the one way in and out, so me and a few of my neighbors set up a guard on the gate. The wall around the community isn't much of an obstacle, but between that and guys with guns at the gate and a roving neighborhood patrol, it was enough to encourage the bad guys to look elsewhere. There were a lot more vulnerable places around."

"So what happened?"

"Fat Ass Fontenot happened, that's what. He's retired, but he was some sort of corporate bigwig. He ran for city council a couple of times but always lost, but for all that he has a pretty good line." Zach shrugged. "With things like they are, some people aren't thinking straight, if they ever thought straight to start with. They want someone to tell them what to do, so Fontenot took it upon himself to start beating the drum for a 'community council.' A lot of us just figured he was a blowhard and ignored him, but that turned out to be a mistake. More than half the residents went along with it, and the next thing we know we got the council, and surprise, surprise, the council elected Fat Ass as president. He didn't do much for the first week, but then he started trying to control things, and it's gone from bad to worse."

"Worse how?"

"Like now everybody is supposed to pool their food and supplies for the COUNCIL to distribute. Except the people on the council, and most of the people who voted for it, don't have anything to contribute. Hell, we can't even get most of them to take a turn at guard duty, but they want to run things." He shook his head. "Most of us have resisted, but they're getting more aggressive, and like I said, things are getting tense."

"Actually I'm relieved to see you in such good shape," Kinsey said.

"You can thank Connie for most of that," Zach said. "You know how she loves her garden. She wouldn't even let me put in a pool because she didn't want to give up the garden space, and she took up over half the storage room in the garage for the stuff she canned out of the garden."

Kinsey grinned. "You can take the girl out of the country, but you can't take the country out of the girl."

Zach snorted. "You got that right. Anyway she had another idea. We had two freezers in the garage full of fish and game, and our neighbors on either side had pretty much the same. And between the three households we had a couple of little Honda generators, so we moved the generators around and ran the freezers three or four hours a day to preserve the food. Then we pooled our propane bottles, and Connie and the other ladies used the gas grills and camp stoves to can as much of the meat as possible. And when they ran out of propane, we started pruning our trees real hard and finished the job on wood fires in the backyard. When they ran out of canning jars, we started eating the frozen stuff and consolidating the rest in one freezer. We didn't lose any of it at all; we either ate it or canned it."

"Pretty smart," Kinsey said. "What about water?"

"We had a rain barrel, and I helped the neighbors rig tarps for rainwater. We treat it with a few drops of Clorox for drinking. One of our neighbors has a pool, and we've been using buckets for washing and flushing toilets.

The pool's half-empty now and it's gettin' kind of green, but it's better than nothing." Zach shrugged. "It sucks, but it's doable."

Kinsey nodded, and Zach shot a worried sidelong look at his companions and lowered his voice. "Ah… about that, Matt. We don't have much left, maybe a week for the folks we're supporting. I don't think—"

"Relax, Zach," Kinsey said. "I've got a safe place in Texas, and I came to get you all. It's not without its challenges, but there are plenty of supplies for at least the immediate future."

Zach's relief was visible, even in the peripheral light of the headlamps; then he looked concerned again.

"What's the problem?" Kinsey asked.

"It's not just us," Zach said. "Reba and George are here with their two kids, and so are my folks. And we've always been tight with our neighbors; they're like family, especially now. We can't just leave them here to fend for themselves. I wouldn't feel right about it, and I know Connie won't leave them."

Kinsey was quiet a long moment. "How many?"

Zach was quiet, mentally counting. "Seventeen."

Crap, thought Kinsey.

CHAPTER SEVENTEEN

Kelly Kinsey sat on the couch beside her father, a hand slightly resting on his forearm. She'd hardly let him out of her sight since they woke her. For all her nineteen years, she was very much a little girl again, unwilling to be separated from her dad for even a moment. Kinsey gave her hand a reassuring pat and turned his attention back to the group. He sighed. Nothing was easy.

After a joyous and emotional reunion, his plan derailed almost immediately. The quick race upriver under the cover of darkness never happened, and he sat now in a group meeting in Zach and Connie Duhon's living room, discussing 'options.'

"We appreciate you coming, Matt," Connie Duhon said, "but I don't see how this ship is an improvement on our situation. We all have gardens planted and enough supplies to last until they start producing, if we're careful. We get plenty of rain, so drinking water isn't a problem, and we're already rigging more tarps to replenish the wash water in the swimming pool." She shook her head. "It's not perfect here, but I doubt any of us want to go to some strange ship. And what about these convicts you mentioned? It sounds like we're safer here."

Around the room there were nods and murmurs of agreement. Kinsey nodded as well, suppressing a surge of secret, guilty relief as his life just got a hell of a lot less complicated. Still, they were family, and his own conscience wouldn't allow him to leave it at that.

"It's not without its dangers," he said. "I've been up front about that. But in the long run, it's the better option. You've done great here, but you've got no reserves. When you get right down to it, you're one failed garden crop away from starvation in increasingly hostile territory. But if you don't want to come, that's your call. I came here mainly for Kelly, so the rest of you can make up your own minds."

Connie hesitated. "Aren't you forgetting something? Kelly is an adult now. She has a say in the matter."

Kinsey was dumbstruck. He'd been so focused on getting here and so relieved at finding Kelly well, it never even occurred to him she might not agree to his plan. He turned and saw the indecision on her face.

"Kelly, honey, what DO you want to do?"

"I want you to stay here. Why can't you do that?"

"Because I have obligations there too," Kinsey said. "A lot of people are depending on me, and I really think it's the best option in the long run. You're scared; we all are, but I need you to trust me on this."

Kelly shot a look at her aunt Connie, who almost imperceptibly and perhaps unconsciously shook her head. Kelly looked conflicted, then turned back to her father.

"If… if you think it's best, Dad, I'll come."

Kinsey reached over and folded his daughter in a hug as he fought down a lump in his throat.

"Okay," he said, releasing her, "that's that. We'll leave as soon as it's good and dark. I'm sorry the rest of you—"

"Just a minute, Matt," Zach Duhon said, then turned toward his wife. "Connie, let's not be hasty." He glanced across the room to two men standing on either side of the door into the dining room. "Things are getting a lot worse with the council." He hesitated. "I'm not so sure how long it's going to be safe here."

"What do you mean, Zach Duhon? You've been telling me Fat Ass Fontenot was just a big blowhard and nothing to worry about."

"He is, but he's managed to control the council, and three days ago they started taking food and supplies by force, for the 'community store.' The only reason they haven't messed with us is they know we have six men and we're all armed. But we're one of the few places neighbors have banded together, and Fat Ass's group is getting stronger all the time. Even folks who should know better are going along for self-preservation. When they finish all the easy marks, I think we're next."

"And you're just telling me this NOW?"

Zach shook his head. "And why would I tell you before? So y'all could all go crazy worrying about it too? I haven't had a decent night's sleep since it all started." He nodded to the men standing near the door. "Me, George, and

Jerry have been trying to come up with a plan, but I think maybe Matt's offer is the best answer."

Kinsey listened, conflicted and thinking of his earlier conversation with Hughes. Seventeen people was considerably more than Hughes was expecting.

His thoughts were interrupted by a loud knock.

"DUHON! GET YOUR ASS OUT HERE!" yelled a voice from the front porch.

Zach rose and walked to the door as Kinsey gently disengaged himself from Kelly's hand and rose to follow. The others in the room followed suit.

Zach opened the front door to face a man standing at the glass storm door. He was in his sixties, red-faced, and agitated. Overweight despite the times, the man was dressed casually but expensively, as if about to play eighteen holes. However, his clothing was rumpled and dirty, and he had graying stubble on his cheeks. He looked like a fat, homeless golf pro.

Zach pushed the storm door open and stepped onto the porch, forcing the older man back. The man's eyes widened as Kinsey and the others crowded out behind Zach, filling the small porch. It was almost comical to watch him scamper down the two steps to stand on the sidewalk, just out of reach. As Redface stood there trying to recover his dignity, Kinsey looked beyond him into the front yard. There were six armed men there, and two more stood on either side of a pickup backed into the driveway.

"What do you want, Fontenot?" Zach asked.

The man ignored the question. "You've crossed the line this time, Duhon. You know it's against the rules to let outsiders inside the perimeter. Who are these people?"

Duhon started to reply, but Kinsey touched his arm. "I'm Chief Petty Officer Matthew Kinsey, US Coast Guard," he said. "And who might you be?"

The man puffed up. "I'm Ronald Fontenot, president of the Community Council."

Kinsey nodded. "Congratulations."

He suppressed a smile as the older man turned redder still, but the others on the porch were less diplomatic and laughed out loud. Fontenot turned back to Zach Duhon.

"Folks around here are sick and tired of you acting like the rules don't apply to you, Duhon. First you hoard food and supplies, and now you're harboring outsiders. By order of the council, these men are to leave the community immediately, and you are further ordered to turn over all your food and supplies. They'll go to the community store, and you will receive your fair daily distribution, just like everyone else." He inclined his head toward the pickup truck. "Now start loading it into the truck. If you refuse, I am authorized by the council to arrest every person in the household eighteen years old or older. Is that clear?"

Kinsey saw Zach tense, and he put his hand on his own sidearm. He was about to respond when a voice rang out from the side of the house beside the garage.

"What is clear, *couyon*," Cormier yelled, "is that you don't know what the hell you're doing. 'Cause, you see, I got me five shells fulla double-ought buck in this old Model 12, and I can take out all your men standing there all grouped together. And I mean right now."

Fontenot stared at the corner of the garage, where only the barrel of Cormier's shotgun was visible. "You're bluffing."

"No, he's not, and neither am I," came Bollinger's voice, and Kinsey looked to the right to see the barrel of an M4 protruding from the opposite corner of the house.

"Me neither, *Gros Tcheu*," called a voice from above, and there were titters of laughter from the porch at the use of the Cajun for 'fat ass.'

Kinsey smiled. Bertrand! He must be in an upstairs window.

Fontenot made a strangling sound of impotent rage, and his men, never too enthusiastic to begin with, were decidedly less so when faced with armed resistance. They all took obvious care to keep their hands away from their weapons, and one actually had his hands raised.

"This isn't over, Duhon," Fontenot finally managed.

"Oh, I think it is," Zach said. "Now get the hell off my property, Fat Ass."

Fontenot stalked to the truck and motioned his men to follow. He got in the passenger side as his men piled into the bed, and the truck sped away.

"He's right about one thing," Kinsey said. "I don't think it's over."

Zach nodded. "I know. Let's go talk some more about your ship."

***

"But we can't leave tonight," Connie Duhon said. "We have to pack all the stuff, and most of the food is in jars, so we have to pack well to keep them from breaking."

Kinsey shook his head. "No way, Connie. I'm not even sure we can get all the PEOPLE up the river, much less supplies. Everyone gets one small bag, a change of clothes, toothbrush, stuff like that, along with enough food for three days. Each person will carry their own bag, except for the kids, who carry as much as they can. We'll divide the rest of the kids' food among the adults."

Andrew Cormier stood in the dining room doorway, his arms crossed as he leaned against the door jamb and watched the confused back and forth of the meeting. He broke his silence.

"Y'all need to take every gun and bit of ammunition you have. It don't spoil, and if you don't need it, you can trade it."

Kinsey nodded. "Good idea." He turned to Zach. "How you fixed for gas? We brought enough for our own small outboards plus a bit extra, but some of that went up with our truck. I'm not sure we have enough fuel left for that gas-hog boat of yours."

Zach shrugged. "There's most of a tank in the boat plus what we have left around here. We stopped making scavenging runs when the gangbangers ran wild, so all the cars have at least a little left. We can siphon it and leave just enough in a couple of cars to get to the river. The problem is, other than a few gas cans for our lawn mowers, we got nothing to put it in. And speaking of the boat, how the hell we gonna get it in the river? There aren't any boat ramps near where y'all are tied up."

"Just make sure it's loose on the trailer and back it down the bank," Cormier said. "We'll keep a rope on it to make sure it don't get away from us in the current."

"But the bank is mud. How will I get the car… oh yeah, I don't guess it matters, does it?" Zach said.

Cormier grinned. "It'll be a one-way trip. And I'd have all the windows down and my seat belt off if I was you, just in case the car slips in the mud and keeps going. We don't have time to chase nobody downriver on the current. Not that we could find 'em in the dark anyway."

"I really love that car," Zach mumbled.

"If we can't take all the food," Connie said, "I'm not leaving it for Fat Ass. I'm going to give it to the Wilsons and the Trahans on the next street over. They—"

"No, you're not," said Kinsey and Cormier in unison.

"Why not?" she demanded.

"Because word will spread we're leaving, and Fat Ass would likely try to shake us down for the gas or make some problem," Zach said.

"Why would he care? He'll be happy to see us go."

"Only if he can make a big show of kicking us out," Zach said. "We don't have time for his drama."

"Agreed," Kinsey said. "We'll leave at ten. I'd like to leave later, but we have to make it past the prison while it's still dark. We can't afford any delays." He looked pointedly at Connie.

She bristled. "You don't worry about me. And if we have to leave food anyway, as soon as we get packed and ready, I'm feedin' us all until we pop," she said.

SAME DAY, 9:15 P.M.

Kinsey stifled a yawn as he walked into the kitchen and accepted a cup of strong black coffee from Zach. Gathering the supplies for the trip had been finished before noon, and true to her word, Connie had set about preparing a feast. No longer constrained by the need to conserve, the Duhons and their neighbors pitched in with a vengeance, and cook fires topped by cast-iron cookware had sprouted across the privacy-fenced backyard. By midafternoon the dining room table groaned with the weight of a sumptuous buffet of the rich Cajun food Kinsey had grown to love since marrying into the Melancon clan.

Full from the meal, almost two days without sleep had caught up with him, and his eyelids grew increasingly heavy. When it became obvious the rest of his team was in the same shape, Connie and Zach had insisted they sleep while the rest of the group finished departure preparations. Kinsey had agreed, not without reservations.

"The others up?" Kinsey asked.

His brother-in-law nodded in the light of the lantern. "About a half hour. They're out checking the cars now." Zach smiled. "Makin' sure we didn't screw anything up."

Kinsey ignored the dig. "Everything go okay?"

"Yeah, we decided to put all the gear and supplies in the boat, that way we can get on our way in a hurry. Since the boats will be lashed together for stability, we can redistribute the load among the three boats en route," Zach said.

Kinsey nodded and took another sip of coffee. He looked down at the cup. "This stuff could resuscitate the dead."

Zach laughed. "Yeah, well, the way you were snoring, I figured you needed to be resuscitated."

Kinsey chuckled and turned toward the door to the garage, cup in hand. Zach followed him out.

The garage was also lantern lit, and the far bay held a large center console fishing boat with an equally large outboard motor. The Duhon's SUV was backed up to the open garage door and hitched to the trailer. Kinsey reached up and turned on his headlamp so he could see better, then walked over and looked in the boat. He sighed.

"I see Connie's fine hand here," Kinsey said. "What part of one small bag per person didn't she understand?"

Zach shrugged. "You know Connie, she's kind of like a force of nature. Besides, there is one bag per person, there's just a little extra, that's all."

Kinsey played his light over a collection of boxes and bags, then shook his head. "Zach, we have to hump all this stuff over a fifty-foot-high levee, and even if we get it to Cormier's place, there's no way we'll get it all to Texas. I haven't even figured out how I'm going to get all the PEOPLE there."

He played his light over boxes as he spoke, stopping on one with distinctive markings. "What the hell is this?"

Zach looked embarrassed, but he quickly recovered. "What does it look like? It's a case of Jack Daniel's."

"Dammit, Zach—"

"Trade goods," Zach said. "I'm figuring it will be valuable, and I'd rather give up booze than ammo."

Kinsey let out a resigned sigh. "Okay, I'll grant you that, but here's the deal. One, if you folks want this stuff over the levee, YOU hump it, not me or any of my guys. Two, you do that AFTER you help us get the aluminum boats over. And three and most important, if at any point it slows us down or we can't find a reasonable way to carry it, we're dumping it, and I won't tolerate any bitching about it. Are we clear?"

Zach nodded his head. "Absolutely."

"Okay," Kinsey said. "What about life jackets?"

"We got regular life vests for the four kids, but after that it's a bit of a hodgepodge. Between the three houses we've got a mismatched collection of life jackets, ski vests, and ski belts. I think we'll have enough for everyone to have some sort of flotation, with maybe a few old ski belts extra," Zach said.

"Bring 'em," Kinsey said. "They're light, and you never know when they'll come in handy. How about glow sticks, got any?"

Zach glanced at the pile of supplies in the boat and grinned. "I suspect we do, why?"

"Break some out and tie one to each flotation device. If anyone goes overboard, they can activate it. Otherwise we don't have a chance of recovering anyone in the dark in that current."

Zach nodded just as Bollinger walked in, flanked by Cormier and Bertrand. Bollinger nodded toward the boat and shot Kinsey a questioning look. Kinsey shook his head, then shrugged, and Bollinger grinned. "Looks like you lost that one, boss," he said.

Kinsey ignored the remark. "How's everything else look?"

"Pretty good," Bollinger said. "They found a bunch of empty gallon milk jugs to collect the gasoline. They're out by the driveway, but we'll load them in the boat before we take off."

Kinsey nodded, suppressing a mental picture of the overloaded boat and trailer rolling backwards down the riverbank and straight to the bottom of the river. "What about a route?"

Cormier spoke up and nodded at Zach. "I showed Duhon here where the boats are on a street map. We should let the locals get us there. If we run into trouble, they'll have a better idea how to bypass it."

"You okay driving with the NV gear, Zach?" Kinsey asked.

"Do we HAVE to go dark?" Zach asked. "I mean, if everything goes well, we'll just reverse the route you came in on until we hit River Road and head north beside the levee. Running fast with lights, we can get to that intersection in five minutes tops. We keep a shooter with the NV stuff in each car, and if we run into trouble we can't avoid, we stop and kill the lights until the shooters take care of it. But I honestly think we'll be okay; I mean, if anybody sees or hears us, we'll likely blow past them before they can react. Even if someone decides to chase us, it'll take 'em a minute or two to get organized, and by then we'll be at River Road and dark again. We have to go dark the last half-mile stretch anyway to sneak past the projects and over the levee, and you guys wearing the NV gear can take over driving for that. We just stop, switch drivers, and haul ass, quick and quiet."

Kinsey nodded. "Well, even with the lights on, I guess we can't possibly be more obvious than we were coming in."

Cormier laughed, and Bollinger looked indignant until Kinsey grinned to take the sting out of his jibe. Only Zach seemed unamused.

"Problem, Zach?" Kinsey asked.

Zach shook his head. "That last half mile worries me big time. Y'all tied up next to some of the worst projects in Baton Rouge. If we attract the wrong kind of attention, we gotta get over that levee and upriver fast."

CHAPTER EIGHTEEN

Their plans aside, they did go dark for the first very short leg of the journey. They stuffed both SUVs full to capacity and beyond, every seat occupied, with wives on their husband's laps and, in places, children perched on top of parents. Kinsey and Bollinger wore the NV gear and eased the vehicles through the subdivision to a side street a block from the entrance gate.

Taking out the guards was child's play; they weren't expecting an approach from the rear. Both surrendered without heroics when they felt the M4 muzzles touching the backs of their necks. The Coasties bound the guards' hands behind them with duct tape and eased them to the floor to wrap their ankles as well. Then they whistled for Zach.

"Gene, Pete," Zach said as he entered the little guardhouse. The pair squinted in the harsh light of his headlamp, glaring at him over duct-taped mouths. "We're leaving now," Zach said, "and we won't be back. I checked the schedule and see Bill and Dan are set to relieve y'all in two hours. You're all good people, despite how Fat Ass has your heads twisted up, so I'm gonna give you a little present."

The glares turned to looks of interest.

"We left all the food and supplies we couldn't carry in our garages. When Bill and Dan let y'all go, you can go get it and split it four ways. Fat Ass has no idea what we had, so he'll think we took it all. Nobody but y'all will know when we left, so if you leave Bill and Dan tied up until morning, you got all night to move and hide it and nobody will be the wiser. I don't care one way or another, but I'd rather y'all have the stuff than Fat Ass. 'Cause make no mistake, anything that goes into his 'community store' is gonna end up where HE decides, not the community."

The men exchanged a glance, then shrugged and nodded to Zach. He nodded back and exited the guardhouse.

"Feelin' better?" Kinsey asked.

"I am," Zach said. "The thought of leaving anything for that bastard was irritating the hell out of me. It was like he won somehow."

***

As Zach predicted, the run to River Road was uneventful. They raced through deserted streets, headlights blazing, with the unencumbered vehicle in the lead and the SUV towing the boat following. They pulled up in front of the veterinary school scarcely three minutes after leaving their subdivision. They killed the lights on the cars, and Kinsey and Bollinger flipped down their NV goggles and changed places with the drivers to head north up River Road. The vehicles swapped places, with Bollinger in the lead, towing the boat. He was to cross the levee first and head immediately to the riverbank while Kinsey followed behind. As soon as they crested the levee and dropped down toward the river and out of sight from town, Kinsey would use the chase car's headlights to light up the riverbank to aid launching and departure preparations.

All went well until Bollinger approached the road up the levee and slowed to make what was almost a U-turn. Kinsey was almost blinded as red lights flared.

"I thought we took the bulbs out of the brake lights?"

"It's the trailer," Zach said. "Someone must have plugged in the lights out of habit. It was in back before, so nobody noticed, and with the lights off, nothing showed until Bollinger braked."

Kinsey shot a look to his right, into the heart of the projects.

"Maybe nobody saw it," Zach said.

"Maybe not yet," Kinsey said, "but Bollinger doesn't even know he's doing it, and you can be sure he'll hit the brakes again at the top of the levee before he heads down. That's gonna be a great big flashing red sign fifty feet in the air. As dark as things are, it'll be visible for miles, and it might as well read VICTIMS HERE."

"What are we going to do?"

Kinsey shook his head. "Improvise."

In the short time it took Kinsey to make the tight turn to follow Bollinger up the levy, he had a plan.

"All right," he said to Zach, "I'll bail out on the crest and take up a defensive position. Take the wheel and turn on the lights; the cat's out of the bag now anyway, so it won't make any difference. Use whatever light you need to get the boat launched and everything ready to take off, but send Cormier or

Bertrand back up here with the other set of NV gear. We'll hold off any visitors, and when you're ready to go, sound the car horn and we'll come running."

"Got it," Zach said as Kinsey bumped over the crest of the levee and skidded to a stop. Both doors flew open, and Zach jumped behind the wheel as Kinsey settled into the grass on top of the levee, eyes focused on the mean streets below.

Kinsey was studying the mob forming at the foot of the levee when Bertrand plopped down beside him five minutes later, puffing from his run up the steep slope.

"What you got, Coast Guard?" Bertrand asked.

"Twenty or thirty bangers, best I can tell. So far they're just milling around, but they keep looking up this way. We'll have company sooner or later," Kinsey said.

Bertrand was studying them now, and he grunted agreement. "Maybe we ought to discourage them."

"We will, but let's wait until they actually start up the levee. I'd like to drag this out as long as possible to give the others time to get the boats ready. I doubt these bangers are military geniuses, but they have a lot of cover down there if they decide to use it, and they'll shoot back at our muzzle flashes. Don't let them fix your position. Shoot, pull back behind the crest, then pop up someplace else; shoot and move, shoot and move. Got it?"

"This ain't my first rodeo, Coast Guard," Bertrand said.

"Army?"

"Travel to exotic places, meet interesting people, and kill them," Bertrand said. "I'm a sucker for a catchy motto."

Kinsey chuckled. "Okay, I'll shut up now."

"So much for waiting," Bertrand said. "Here they come. I'll take the fat guy on the left."

Kinsey sighed. "I'll take the tall one in the middle."

No sooner had Kinsey spoken than Bertrand's rifle barked, and the fat banger stumbled and fell. Kinsey fired a three-round burst, and the tall banger joined his fallen comrade. Both defenders dropped back below the levee's crest, and when they rose again in different positions several yards apart, the situation at the foot of the levee had changed dramatically. The bodies of the men they'd shot lay unmoving at the foot of the grassy slope, but the others had scattered, no doubt to positions in and around the houses lining the opposite side of River Road.

"THEY CAPPED FAT DOG AND T-BOY!" someone shouted.

"YO, WHOEVER Y'ALL ARE UP THERE, WE GONNA MESS YOU UP! AIN'T NOBODY DISRESPECTIN' US IN OUR OWN HOOD."

"Is it just me, or are they pissed?" Bertrand asked.

"Just as long as they stay pissed off down there, it doesn't matter."

Kinsey had hardly finished speaking when his position atop the levee allowed him to glimpse the flash of headlights several blocks away. Then there was another, and within seconds, he could see a steady stream of vehicles pouring out of the surrounding neighborhoods and heading in their direction.

"I'd say they have radios," Kinsey said. "It looks like we've stirred 'em up."

"Not good." Bertrand shook his head. "With enough shooters, they can keep raking the top of the levee to keep our heads down while the rest climb right up in our laps."

"Ya think?" Kinsey asked, then flipped up his NV glasses and looked back down the levee toward the river. There was a pool of light at the riverbank, and he could see moving figures. "What's taking them so long?"

"Uh-oh," Bertrand said. "Look toward the vet school."

Kinsey heard the distant throaty snarl of motorcycles and, a half mile south, saw headlights bouncing up the slope of the levee at an angle.

"They get up top, and we're flanked," Bertrand said. "And the boats are lit up like Christmas trees down there. They'll be sitting ducks."

"Let's go!" Kinsey said, and he started down toward the river at a run, Bertrand hot on his heels.

The scene below reminded Kinsey of some surreal tableau from the tragic past. The boats were lashed three abreast, floating in the shallow water near the riverbank, with the larger fishing boat in the center and a smaller aluminum hull on either side. They rode low in the water, and the huddled mass of passengers and heaps of supplies were cast in sharp relief by the harsh glare of the car headlights. Kinsey saw Zach removing the cowling of the big outboard on the fishing boat. He ran to douse the headlights of the nearest car while Bertrand scrambled and slid through the mud of the riverbank to the second vehicle. In seconds everything was plunged into darkness, and a howl of protest rose from the boats.

"Dammit!" yelled Zach through the darkness. "Who turned off those lights? I can't see what I'm doing."

Multiple flashlights flashed toward Kinsey.

"Shield those lights and get ready to get out of here," Kinsey said. "Every banger in Baton Rouge is about to come over that levee."

"The outboard keeps dying. I can't—"

He was interrupted by the roar of approaching motorcycle engines, and headlights popped over the crest of the levee and raced down toward them.

"Better do something quick," Kinsey said. "These guys are just the scouts and there are a whole lot more where they came from."

He turned and braced his M4 on the hood of the car and opened fire on the approaching cycles. He heard Bertrand do the same from the other car. Their first rounds hit the lead cycle almost simultaneously, and it dropped sideways in front of two bikes following closely behind. All three bikes went down in a tangled mass of steel and flesh, the riders' screams echoing above the sound of the crash. Two bikes trailing the leaders managed to swerve around the wreck, but Kinsey and Bertrand took them out. But there was no time to celebrate victory; the headlights of more bikes and cars began pouring over the levee.

"READY OR NOT, HERE WE COME!" Kinsey yelled as he and Bertrand stumbled and slid down the muddy riverbank and splashed into the water.

They were waist deep when they reached the boats, and willing hands reached out to drag them aboard. Kinsey heard the muttering pop of the smaller outboards, but nothing from the fishing boat motor.

"It's no use," he heard Zach say. "I can't get it going."

"Bollinger?" Kinsey said into the dark.

"Here." Kinsey turned and was relieved to see Bollinger sitting at the small outboard, glowing green in the NV goggles. He wormed his way down the boat, stepping over people sitting terrified in the darkness, until he was within arm's reach of Bollinger.

"Put your hand out. I'm going to hand you the NV gear. Put it on and get us the hell out of here. Where's Cormier?"

"Here," called Cormier. "I'm at the other outboard."

"The same for you, but just keep your motor straight ahead and let Bollinger do the steering," Kinsey said.

"Do you want me to pass Cormier my glasses?" Bertrand asked.

"Negative," Kinsey said. "We might need you to shoot somebody."

He looked back toward the levee, a hundred yards away, and watched headlights stream down the slope into the parking lot. With no light to attract the bangers' attention, and the roar of the bangers' own cars and motorcycles drowning out the outboards, they had a bit of time. However, it wouldn't take the bangers long to find the cars on the riverbank and figure out where they should be looking. When that happened, the sound of their outboards would give them away; they needed to get out of range upriver as soon as possible.

He felt the boat buffeted by ever stronger currents as they moved into the river, and watched impotently as headlights and powerful flashlights cut the night ashore. Then he heard raised voices ashore over the low conversation of his fellow passengers, and the lights began to converge on the riverbank near the cars. The bangers' vehicles began to die one by one, and he knew it wouldn't be long before they heard the outboards, if they didn't already.

"Can't you and Cormier get any more juice out of those sewing machines?" Kinsey asked quietly.

"They're having all they can do to make any headway at all," Bollinger responded. "They're not exactly designed for this."

Kinsey said nothing as powerful beams of light began to stab out from shore, motorcycle headlights and handheld spotlights no doubt, dancing across the water in search of what the bangers could hear but not yet pinpoint. One seemed more aggressive than the rest, the beam sweeping toward them.

"See it, Bertrand?"

"I got him," Bertrand replied, and his M4 barked. The beam of light veered off at a crazy angle.

"Kill those outboards," Kinsey said abruptly.

"But what—"

"DO IT!" Kinsey said, and the two men complied.

"Let's hope they didn't see the muzzle flash," Bertrand said softly.

"On the contrary, let's hope they did. Now everyone be absolutely quiet," Kinsey said.

No longer fighting the powerful current, the odd little convoy floated free on the powerful flood, streaking downstream in the dark past the bangers on the riverbank. Kinsey held his breath as they floated by barely fifty yards from the bank and said a silent prayer they wouldn't be captured by a probing beam. But with no sound to guide them, the bangers were momentarily confused and concentrated their search in the direction they had last heard the sound and seen the flash. Kinsey had no doubt the bangers would eventually put it together, but all he really needed was five minutes on the swift current to put them beyond the range of the bangers' lights and guns.

He gave it ten.

"Okay, boys," Kinsey said. "Crank up the outboards and let's find a place on the far bank to get this mess straightened out."

Mississippi River
West Bank
One Mile South of Port Allen Lock

Same Day, 11:20 p.m.

Their temporary refuge was another backwater between a wooded stretch of the west bank and a string of abandoned barges. They pulled into the gap, the empty barges hiding them from Baton Rouge across the river.

"Okay," Kinsey said. "Bertrand, get up on that barge and keep watch. The rest of you, get some lights on and get this squared away. We've already lost too much time. Bollinger, you're our mechanical genius, give Zach a hand with his engine."

"No genius required," Bollinger said. "I already told him he's got bad fuel."

Kinsey looked at his brother-in-law. "How old is the gas in your boat, Zach?"

"We haven't use the boat since last summer, but I added fuel stabilizer... anyway I THINK I added stabilizer." He shook his head. "To be honest, I don't really remember."

Kinsey sighed and bit back a rebuke. "All right. Bollinger, help me out here. What are we lookin' at?"

"I got no clue until I get into it, boss. At a minimum we have to dump the tank and put in new gas. After that, it depends on what we're dealin' with." Bollinger turned to Zach. "You got a spare fuel filter?"

Zach shook his head.

"Tools?" Bollinger asked.

Zach reached in his pocket and produced a small adjustable wrench and a couple of screwdrivers.

"Friggin' lovely," Bollinger muttered.

"I got a toolbox," Cormier volunteered. "It ain't much, but it's better than that."

Bollinger thanked Cormier and moved over to accept the toolbox the Cajun produced from underneath a seat. He took it and moved back to the big outboard.

Kinsey worked his way back to where Bollinger and Zach were about to tear into the engine. He spoke softly. "Will we have enough gas to make it now?" he asked Bollinger.

Bollinger shrugged. "No way of knowing, but it'll be close, that's for sure."

"Okay," Kinsey said. "You and Zach do the best you can. I need to talk to Cormier."

Bollinger nodded and Kinsey worked his way across the crowded vessels closer to Cormier. "What are your thoughts on our little flotilla?"

Cormier shook his head. "We're unbalanced and too heavy. We didn't have time to rearrange anything before the bangers showed up, but we need to spread stuff out." Cormier glanced at Connie Duhon. "And get rid of some of it. And we need to think about the outboards. We're gonna have to run them all now to make any speed against the current with this load, and we can't have three people steering. We should just tie the tillers of the small boats so the outboards are pushing straight ahead, then steer with the motor on the big boat in the center."

"Makes sense," Kinsey agreed, then looked back at the pair working on the motor and lowered his voice even more. "What if they can't get the motor going? You think we can make it in the smaller boats?"

Cormier looked at Kinsey as if he were insane. "Even with just the people we'd be dangerously overloaded. We planned on bringin' back four or five people, not seventeen. No way we'd make it in less than a full day, if we made it at all. You saw how they was strainin' against the current. I doubt they could go over five or six miles an hour by themselves, not to mention being unstable like hell in this river. But you know that, I think."

Kinsey nodded. "Yeah, I do, but I was hoping you might see something I missed." He sighed. "Oh well, can you take care of setting up the smaller outboards and getting the gear redistributed?"

Cormier nodded. "Mais oui."

Kinsey turned to his sister-in-law, "Okay, Connie, you can see for yourself we're overloaded. I'll let you choose, but I want you to lose at least half of it; then you and the others help Cormier redistribute it between the boats evenly. Are we clear?"

"Yes, Matt. And I'm sorry."

"Not a problem, let's just get this done."

"Don't throw away them glow sticks," Cormier said. "I'm gonna need some of them."

"What for?" Kinsey asked.

"Just an idea," Cormier said. "It's easier if I show you than tell you."

***

The others finished their respective tasks long before the engine was ready, and as they waited, Kinsey watched Cormier implement his idea and smiled as the Cajun explained it to him.

That was the bright spot; things were going much worse with the engine repair. Kinsey checked the time repeatedly as Bollinger tore into the outboard with Zach's help. It was over two hours later before they got the motor off to a sputtering start. Bollinger wiped his hands on a greasy rag and looked over at Kinsey and shook his head.

"I cleaned everything that's cleanable with the tools at hand. I'm hoping it smooths out when we run it under load. But I doubt she can develop full power." Bollinger shrugged. "She'll get better or she won't, and it's even money either way. I'm sorry, boss. I did the best I could."

"I know you did, Bollinger. We'll just give it a shot and hope for the best." Kinsey shot another worried glance at his watch and called Bertrand down from the barge.

They put the kids and nonswimmers in the fishing boat, along with most of Connie's much-diminished load of supplies. Adult swimmers were in the aluminum boats on either side. The Coasties took full control of the NV gear again, though Bertrand returned his set with obvious reluctance. Bollinger took the wheel of the larger fishing boat, and Kinsey provided overwatch with his M4 as they moved upriver.

The big engine sputtered and popped, but overall performed better than expected. But it was almost two in the morning, and they had to cover seventy miles against the current before daylight, a bit over three hours away.

Presuming they made it at all; the noise from the outboards was significant and if they couldn't be seen, they could certainly be heard. They still had to get past the bangers and God knew who else.

"What you think, Kinsey? Time for my toy?" Cormier asked.

"Do it," Kinsey said, and Cormier squatted at the back of the fishing boat, working on the two surplus ski belts now festooned with chemical glow sticks. He bent the sticks one by one, his face illuminated by the eerie green glow as they activated; then he stood and tossed the ski belts out the back of the moving boat. The boat raced onward, leaving the glowing ski belts in its wake and with Cormier paying out the line attached to them and coiled at his feet with the end secured to a cleat near the boat's stern. The line finished paying out and went taut, towing the glowing ski belts in line twenty feet apart, racing along a hundred feet behind the boat.

"What the hell?" asked Zach Duhon.

"We killed some of those bangers and they're pissed off," Cormier said, "and Kinsey thinks they got radios. So who knows what we're going to run into. For sure, we ain't gonna sneak by with these outboards, and if they shoot at the sound, they might even hit somebody, especially if there's a bunch of 'em. I figure we give 'em something to shoot at that ain't us, far enough away that even if they're lousy shots, they won't hit us."

"Think it'll work?" Zach asked.

"Don't know," Cormier said. "But sound is hard to pinpoint in the dark, and if you heard an outboard in a general direction and saw something speedin' through the water, what would you shoot at?"

They hugged the west bank, keeping well out of range of the bangers from the LSU area until they passed under the I-10 bridge and moved back to the center of the river. Suddenly, the bridge erupted in gunfire, with muzzle flashes visible along half its length. Kinsey grinned as the surface of the water near their glowing decoys was peppered with splashes that looked like green pinpricks in his NV glasses.

"Looks like it's working, Andrew," Kinsey said.

"Let's just hope we can get through Baton Rouge before they figure it out," Cormier replied.

But their luck held. They were fired on three more times, each time with the same result. When they finally passed under the US 190 bridge, Kinsey heaved a sigh of relief and focused on their real enemy, the clock.

An hour later, the clock gained an ally.

"We're sucking fuel like there's no tomorrow," Bollinger whispered, worry in his voice.

"Will we have enough?" Kinsey asked, equally quiet.

Bollinger shrugged. "No way to tell. The motor's running flat out. It's settled down a little, but still not running anywhere near normal efficiency. Throw in the extra resistance of the current on this lash-up we're pushing, and fuel efficiency is in the toilet anyway."

"Suggestions?"

"Not really," Bollinger said. "If I slow down to conserve fuel, it'll take longer to get there and pretty much guarantee we're limping past the prison in daylight."

"Should we lighten the load more?"

Bollinger shook his head. "I don't think it matters unless you're planning on throwing people overboard. Nothing else is heavy enough to make much difference, and we're pretty well-balanced now; changing things might even make it worse. Avoiding the strongest currents will help. We got nothing but farmland on either side now, so I'll hug the banks and take every bend on the inside radius. Whether it helps enough is anyone's guess."

"Do what you can," Kinsey said.

So they clawed their way upriver through the darkness. Around them the others rode in quiet uncertainty, wives leaning against husbands' shoulders, and kids sleeping in mothers' laps. Two hours later, they swept around a long bend and began to head due west as the sky lightened in the east.

Kinsey glanced back east. "How far you think?" he asked Bollinger softly.

He almost jumped out of his skin when a voice answered out of the darkness from the seat in front of him. "Let me have the glasses, and I'll tell you."

"Geez! You scared the crap out of me," Kinsey said.

Cormier chuckled. "Nervous, Coast Guard?"

"Hell yes," Kinsey said, taking off the NV glasses and reaching over to press them against Cormier's chest so he could accept them by feel.

The big Cajun put the glasses on and studied the riverbanks. "We're about five miles from Angola Landing, I think. We ain't gonna make it past the prison in the dark. Keep to the left bank from now on. The channel to the levee is about two miles beyond the prison landing."

They rode in silence under a lightening sky, and Kinsey imagined the outboard was getting louder with the rising sun. People were starting to stir on their seats, and Cormier and Bollinger took off the NV glasses.

Kinsey strained to see the far bank of the river. "You think there'll be anybody at the landing, Andrew?"

Cormier shrugged. "Who knows? I'm hoping all the cons like their beauty sleep. Even if they see us, we're out of range, so they'll have to chase us. If they don't have a boat ready, we might get a big enough lead to slip behind the island and up the channel to the levee without them seeing which way we go."

"Your lips to God's ears," Kinsey said.

The landing was clearly visible across the river now, and Kinsey saw boats tied to the dock. He saw no movement and said a silent prayer the cons were all asleep and there was no one to hear the roar of the outboard.

They were in the swiftest part of the current now, forced to the outside of a sweeping river bend to maintain their distance from the prison landing. Their progress slowed perceptibly, and Kinsey realized the big outboard WAS louder as it strained against the increased load. Just two more miles and they'd be home free. Kinsey turned his attention from the prison dock and stared upriver, willing them forward.

They'd covered a half mile when Bertrand spoke.

"Trouble," he said, and Kinsey turned and followed the man's pointing finger. Behind them, a boat was leaving the prison dock. Kinsey watched as it cut across the river diagonally to fall into their wake, growing larger with each passing minute.

"They're gaining on us," he said.

Bertrand raised his rifle, but Kinsey reached up and pushed it down, nodding toward the passengers. "Let's not start a gunfight just yet. We're a much bigger target and have a lot to lose."

Bertrand nodded, and Kinsey turned to Cormier. "Think we can lose them behind the island, Andrew?"

Cormier shook his head. "Doubtful. They're already too close and gaining. They'll be right on our butt when we turn up the channel."

Kinsey muttered a curse. "All right," he said. "It probably won't help, but let's start lightening the load." He tossed one of Connie's remaining boxes over the side.

There was some hesitation; then the others began to toss things over as well.

"How we looking on fuel?" Kinsey asked Bollinger.

"Running on fumes," Bollinger replied. "But I think we'll make it."

The words had hardly left his mouth when the big outboard sputtered, coughed three times, and fell silent.

"Or not," Bollinger said as their speed dropped dramatically, and the pitch of the two smaller motors changed as they coped with the suddenly increased load.

"We're screwed," Bollinger said.

CHAPTER NINETEEN

DAY 30, 5:50 A.M.

Kinsey looked back. He could make out five convicts in the boat, and he saw one of them point to a jettisoned box as they flashed by it. The con shouted something to the others, and Kinsey saw them all laugh. They knew they had won the race and were enjoying the victory.

Then it hit him.

"ZACH! Put that down."

Zach looked confused, but set the case of Jack Daniel's he'd been about to jettison on the deck. Kinsey pushed past the others to get to him at the stern.

"Take your ski belt off, and buckle it around the booze. Make sure not to cover the markings on the box."

"What are you—"

"DO IT!" Kinsey screamed, and Zach hastened to do as ordered. Kinsey reached over and began to untie the tow rope for Cormier's decoy, which still trailed the boat. Zach finished buckling the whiskey in the ski belt, and Kinsey pulled ten feet of the tow rope in and handed it to Zach, letting the loose end trail on the deck at their feet.

"Don't let this go," Kinsey said as he dropped to his knees and began tying the end of the rope to the ski belt encircling the case of whiskey. When he was done, he gave it a tug to make sure it was secure, then ordered Zach to toss the slack back over the side.

"Cormier and Bertrand," Kinsey said, "get to the small outboards. Slow down to just hold us in place against the current, but DON'T stop. Then be ready to haul balls when I give the order."

"We ain't haulin' anything with this rig, but we'll do what we can," Cormier replied as he and Bertrand maneuvered through the crowded boats to take control of the two functioning outboards.

Kinsey looked astern, judging the distance to the oncoming boat, as he waited for the Cajuns to get into place. When they were there, he said, "Cut speed now."

He heard muttered curses from the passengers as the speed dropped further, and he slipped the whiskey over the stern and let it go, watching briefly as it fell behind in the boat's wake. He stood and faced the others.

"You're going to have to trust me on this, folks," Kinsey said. "I want everybody to turn and face the oncoming boat, with your hands over your heads."

"Are you nuts?" Zach asked.

"Do it," Connie said as she raised her hands as ordered.

One by one, the others followed Connie's lead. Kinsey turned back to face the oncoming boat himself and raised his own hands.

He heard the motor on the convicts' boat change pitch as, unsure what was happening, they cut their own speed. They closed the gap steadily, but not as rapidly as before. The whiskey floated between the two boats, moving ever closer to the cons. When he thought they were close enough to hear him, Kinsey shouted across the gap.

"WE SURRENDER."

Kinsey heard angry muttering behind him; then after a moment's hesitation, a cheer went up from the convicts' boat. About that time, one of the cons shouted and pointed at the whiskey, and the boat veered toward it and circled it, preparing to pull it aboard.

Kinsey held his breath as the cons' boat passed over the semi-submerged towline, then smiled as the plaintive sound of mechanical mayhem announced the rope had wrapped in the propeller and jammed it tight. As soon as he heard the cons' motor stop, Kinsey reached for his M4 and began to shout.

"GO! GO! GO! EVERYBODY DOWN. EVERYBODY DOWN."

He steadied himself against the slight rocking of the boat on the current and began firing at the cons, dropping one immediately and sending the rest diving for cover. He heard firing beside him and glanced over to see Bollinger, M4 at his shoulder.

"Hold your fire," Kinsey said, "so we're not both changing mags at the same time. We don't have to take them out, but one of us has to keep their heads down until we're out of range."

Bollinger grunted his understanding and his gun fell silent as Kinsey continued to fire well-placed single shots anytime one of the cons showed himself. The distance between the boats widened as the disabled craft bobbed downstream on the swift current, and Kinsey's overloaded and lashed-together boats clawed their way slowly upstream on the small straining outboards.

When they were out of range, Kinsey lowered his rifle and swiveled to look upriver.

"How much farther?" he called to Cormier.

"A bit over a mile, I'd say," Cormier replied. "But we're barely moving and the big boat's nothing but drag now. We gotta lose it or it will take us more than a half hour to get there, and for sure we ain't got that much gas."

Kinsey nodded. "Bollinger, you and Zach go through our empty gas cans and those milk jugs and drain every last drop that's left. Split it between the gas tanks on the smaller boats while I divide everyone between the two smaller boats. Then we'll figure out how to separate."

Bollinger's task didn't take long, as 'every last drop' from the various gas containers amounted to less than a cup, which he and Zach dutifully split between the two boats. Dividing the people was more difficult, as Kinsey had to move them one at a time so as not to destabilize the delicate equilibrium of the overloaded boats. It took five long minutes with Kinsey making on-the-fly assessments of each passenger's weight before he had both boats loaded more or less equally, with him in the bow of Cormier's boat and Bollinger in the bow of Bertrand's.

"Okay, folks," Kinsey said, "we're really overloaded, so please keep as close to the centerline of the boats as you can, and don't move around. We're going to separate from the center boat, then bring the two boats back together and tether them side by side as we move upstream. That way, if one of our motors runs out of gas, we should still have enough power to at least maneuver both boats to the west bank. Everyone ready?"

There were murmurs and fearful nods, and after he confirmed Cormier and Bertrand were ready, Kinsey loosened the bow lashing on his own boat and held it wrapped around the cleat, ready to be thrown off at a moment's notice. Bollinger duplicated his actions in the other boat as Kinsey called back and had men untie the stern lashings completely.

"Okay, Bollinger," Kinsey yelled, "we separate on the count of three. Are you ready?"

"Affirmative," Bollinger replied.

"ONE, TWO, THREE!" Kinsey yelled and threw the line off the cleat as Bollinger did the same, and Zach's fishing boat slipped from between the two boats and fell astern. No longer encumbered by the dead weight of the larger boat or tied together, the smaller boats surged forward at different speeds and separated.

"CORMIER," Kinsey yelled, "HOLD YOUR COURSE AND SPEED. BERTRAND, BRING YOUR BOAT ALONGSIDE, BUT CAREFULLY! THE BOW WAVES WILL FORCE US APART, SO DON'T PUSH IT. JUST GET CLOSE ENOUGH FOR US TO PASS LINES."

The Cajuns handled the boats deftly, and soon the boats were running side by side, just feet apart and tethered together bow and stern. The rest of the short trip was uneventful, and they'd just turned out of the current and into the still backwater of the Lower Old River when Bertrand's outboard sputtered to a stop and his boat bumped back alongside of Cormier's.

"Pull in the slack and lash them side by side," Kinsey ordered, then looked back at Cormier. "Think we have enough gas to make the levee, Andrew?" he asked.

Cormier shrugged. "Maybe, maybe not, but we can paddle from here if we have to."

Kinsey nodded, relief written on his face.

Cormier grinned. "Relax, Coast Guard. The hard part's over. Now we just gotta get back to the bayou."

SOMEWHERE IN THE ATCHAFALAYA RIVER BASIN
NORTH OF MORGAN CITY, LOUISIANA

DAY 30, 4:20 P.M.

As Cormier predicted, the trip back to his bayou stronghold was uneventful. The extra manpower made getting the aluminum boats and gear over the levee easier, and the addition of more armed men discouraged any who might have considered challenging them on their return trip down the Atchafalaya. They arrived in the late afternoon, and Kinsey saw Cormier's daughter-in-law, Lisa, standing on the little dock.

"How'd she know we were coming?" Kinsey asked.

Cormier scoffed. "Seriously, Coast Guard? You don't understand by now nothing moves on the bayou we don't know about?"

"Okay, dumb question." Kinsey nodded to where Lisa stood, smiling. "But she does look happy to see you."

Cormier nodded, and as they neared the dock, Lisa called across the gap, "Tim's much better, Pop. The fever broke last night, and he demanded breakfast this morning. I think he's gonna be all right."

Kinsey saw Cormier swallow hard, then blink away sudden tears before he looked skyward and crossed himself. He laid a hand on the big Cajun's shoulder and the man turned to him, grinning from ear to ear, but he could only bob his head, as if he were incapable of speech.

Cormier stepped across the gap between the boat and the dock without waiting for the boat to be secured, and raced away with Lisa, eager to see his son.

***

Cormier seemed like a new man when he came back down to the dock twenty minutes later to find Bollinger and Kinsey still on the Coast Guard boat.

"Where's everybody else?" he asked.

"Some of your folks are showing them where to bed down for the night," Kinsey said. "Bollinger and I figured we'd stay here to plan our trip to Texas. We appreciate the help, but we don't want to abuse your hospitality."

Cormier shrugged. "We'll take anyone who wants to stay, as long as they pull their weight. They're Cajuns too." He paused and looked from Kinsey to Bollinger. "You too, Coast Guard, if you want."

The offer took Kinsey by surprise. "Thank you, Andrew. That's very generous, but I have to say I'm surprised."

"It's no mystery. They were doing okay in Baton Rouge, so I think they'll be willing to work. The bayou and our gardens will provide our food, and it rains enough here that freshwater is no problem. Finally, we can use the extra manpower, both for survival and defense," Cormier said.

Kinsey thought about it a moment, then nodded. "I'll put it to them. I suspect some of them will accept."

"What about you two?" Cormier asked.

"I'll be going back to the ship," Bollinger said quickly. "I appreciate the offer, but I'd feel like I was deserting my friends when they need me."

Kinsey was nodding. "Same here."

Cormier nodded. "*Je comprends.*"

They lapsed into silence a moment before Kinsey spoke. "It may be crowded, but if we reduce the number going back, maybe we can fit them all into our boat."

"Too bad we can't get word to Wellesley to wait for us," Bollinger said. "He should be taking off any time, but our rescue took a lot less time than we figured, thanks to Andrew. If we can get to the lock before he leaves, we can put some of the folks in one of the push boats and all go back to Texas together. I don't really look forward to having a boatload of noncombatants if we get into another gunfight."

Cormier shrugged. "Why not call him on your radio?"

Kinsey shook his head. "Even if he's still at the lock, that's over a hundred miles from here. The VHF won't reach that far."

Cormier rubbed his bearded chin. "I know a lot of people between here and there. Some worked on crew boats, and others own shrimp boats. We could probably set up a relay to pass word to him, if you want to try."

Kinsey nodded enthusiastically and reached for the VHF handset, but Cormier stopped him with a raised hand and shook his head.

"No transmitting here. We have to go on the river, and I want to be moving while we transmit. I don't want to take the chance on anyone locating us from your transmission." Cormier looked at the sky. "It'll be dark in a couple of hours. We take your boat on the river with your NV glasses, almost down to Morgan City."

SAME DAY, 10:20 P.M.

They went south almost to Morgan City before Cormier felt comfortable transmitting. Bollinger killed the engine and Kinsey nodded at Cormier. The big Cajun picked up the handset and began speaking French.

"What's with the French?" Bollinger asked.

Cormier shrugged as they waited for a response. "I figure if any FEMA assholes are listening, they're probably less likely to speak Cajun than English."

Kinsey nodded. "Good point."

Cormier called several times before he raised anyone, but when he got a response, he explained he was attempting to relay a message to the push boat *Judy Ann*. The message was simple, consisting of only 'Kinsey coming. Please wait.'

After almost an hour and three relays, the message was apparently delivered, with the last relay link switching to English for Lucius Wellesley's benefit. The radio squawked in Cajun, and Cormier bobbed his head at the two Coasties. He acknowledged the transmission then lowered the mic and looked at Kinsey quizzically.

"What is it?" Kinsey asked.

"There was a reply," Cormier said. "Wellesley said, 'Trouble in Texas. We are holding here.'"

Kinsey felt a chill run down his spine. He thought about the reply a moment.

"Pass the word for Wellesley to try to find a French speaker among his guys. We need to discuss this a bit more."

CHAPTER TWENTY

US MARITIME ADMINISTRATION RESERVE FLEET
MCFADDEN BEND CUTOFF
NECHES RIVER
NEAR BEAUMONT, TEXAS

THE PREVIOUS DAY
DAY 29, 5:10 A.M.

Chief Mate Georgia Howell eased open the aft door of the enclosed life-boat, struggling to do it quietly with one hand. She stepped out onto the almost nonexistent rear deck, set the bucket down on the two-foot-wide shelf, and used both hands to close the door for privacy. That is, if pissing outside in a bucket, floating in the middle of a river between the massive hulls of two gigantic, but empty and unmanned, ships could be considered private. Lifeboats didn't have toilets, and they certainly weren't designed for coeducational occupancy. *Here's hoping I don't fall overboard*, she thought as she dropped her pants and squatted over the bucket. Just another thing women had to worry about that guys didn't, pissing in an enclosed lifeboat during the apocalypse.

She finished and pulled up her pants, then emptied the bucket overboard and dropped to her knees, leaning down to rinse the bucket in the river. The sky was lightening in the east now, and she'd be able to see well enough to navigate in fifteen or twenty minutes; she was considerably less quiet when she opened the door.

"Up and at 'em, guys. It's almost daylight and we'll be taking off in a few minutes. I'm leaving the bucket just inside the door. Do whatever you need to do and get something to eat and drink. This is likely to be a long day." She heard sleepy acknowledgments, then closed the door and leaned back against the cabin to watch the eastern sky.

She wanted an early start, her theory being miscreants were unlikely to be early risers. It was nine miles to the boat club, and she figured they could make it in three hours max, even against the current in the lumbering life-boat, but they had to pass some pretty crappy sections of town. Her 'boat of many colors,' as she came to think of it, might blend in well with the natural riverbank in the dusk, but it would still stick out like a sore thumb in broad daylight in an industrial area. She wanted to be safely docked at the boat club before the lowlifes woke up.

The lifeboat door cracked open tentatively, and she shifted to make room as it opened wider and Juan Alvarez stepped out and emptied the bucket over the stern. Then he dropped to one knee and repeated the ritual she just performed, though his longer arms made it much easier to reach the water's surface. Alvarez finished the task, rose and leaned through the open door to pass the empty bucket to one of the others inside before turning back to Georgia.

"So what's the drill, ma'am?" he asked.

"We'll head upriver as soon as we can see," Howell said. "It's mostly vacant land or industrial areas on both sides of the river, but if we have any problems, I expect they'll be from the west bank, probably closer to downtown. I want you and Jones watching that side, with Jimmy and Pete on the other. If we have any problems, I suspect it'll be near Riverfront Park. Other than that, we play it by ear."

Alvarez nodded. "Yes, ma'am. Rules of engagement?"

"I'm not second-guessing anyone," Howell said. "If it looks like we're in danger, fire at your own discretion. But remember, there are just five of us, so if we draw the wrong kind of attention, we're toast. The plan is to get in and out as quietly as possible."

"Copy that, ma'am. We'll be ready when you are."

***

They were moving ten minutes later. The east bank of the river was mostly undeveloped almost all the way to downtown Beaumont, and their camouflage paint job in the dim light of early morning still afforded some protection. *Use it while you got it*, Howell thought as she steered to starboard and hugged the east bank.

Despite the plodding pace of the underpowered lifeboat, they passed the Exxon-Mobil refinery on the west bank and were approaching Harbor Island Terminal in just under two hours. It was full light now, and the boat was readily visible. A railroad bridge spanned the river ahead and she steered as close as she dared to the right bank and called softly to the others. "Look sharp. Riverfront Park coming up on the left bank, just after the railroad bridge."

There were murmured acknowledgments, and Howell put her hand on the throttle, unconsciously trying to press it forward, even though the lumbering boat was topped out. But the park was deserted, the area devoid of activity in the early morning hours. Minutes later she heaved a relieved sigh when she negotiated a sharp right turn and left the downtown area behind her to pass the old shipyard on her left.

"Almost there," Howell said. "Fifteen or twenty minutes max."

They rounded another turn to the left, and through the viewing port at the conning station, she saw the I-10 bridge looming across the river just ahead. The tops of abandoned cars were visible above the guardrail the length of the bridge.

"Alvarez," Howell said, "can you see the bridge from the gun ports? We'll be sitting ducks for anyone on the bridge, and we don't have any armor on the top of the canopy."

"Negative. It's too high. We best move outside."

"Do it," Howell confirmed, but the two Coasties were already moving toward the back door and front entry port of the lifeboat. In seconds, they were standing on the bow and stern, M4s pointed up toward the bridge ahead.

"Have you given any thought to live-aboards, ma'am?" Alvarez asked Howell through the open rear door of the lifeboat, never taking his eyes off the bridge. "Some of the boats in this yacht club likely have generators and what have you. If I owned one, that's where I'd be."

"Agreed," Howell said, hands on the wheel and her own eyes fixed up at the bridge as they approached. "But I also figure the last place I'd stay is in an urban marina when I could duck out of sight into a wooded inlet upriver where nobody could get to me by road." She hesitated. "But you're right, it's better safe than sorry."

Howell cut speed abruptly as they moved under the bridge, steering hard left toward the strip of wooded land lining the western riverbank under the bridge.

"What are you doing?" Alvarez asked.

"We're only a hundred yards from the yacht club channel," Howell said. "It's to the left, just past these trees. We'll go ashore here under the bridge and do a little recon from the safety of the trees. The boat will be directly under the bridge, so no one can spot it from above."

"Good idea," Alvarez said. "Jones and I will—"

"Negative," Howell said. "I need to see it myself. It'll be me and you while the other guys watch the boat."

WEST END OF I-10 BRIDGE
BEAUMONT, TEXAS

The police cruiser was parked at right angles across the highway in the westbound lanes, barring nonexistent traffic. The windows were open and its occupants sat in a lethargic daze. They were unkempt and unshaven, and a successive series of circular sweat stains emanating from the armpits of their rumpled shirts tracked the number of days since their last uniform change as surely as rings marked the age of a tree.

One of them stirred. "This sucks! The sun ain't hardly up, and you can already fry an egg on the road. Turn on the AC."

The driver shook his head. "You know the orders; fifteen minutes of AC every hour after eight. We got a while yet, and if Spike catches us wasting gas, we're dead meat. So quit bein' a whiny pussy; you're gettin' on my nerves."

"Come on, who's gonna know? There ain't nobody around but us, and I don't even know why we're here. Nobody's traveling the interstate anymore. We ain't pulled any pussy or plunder off the bridge in a week."

"Everybody's gonna know when you get drunk again and start running your mouth. These orders came straight from Spike. Have you forgotten what he did to Miller last week when he screwed up?" The driver shuddered. "He is one mean dude, and I ain't gonna cross him. And if Spike wants us here, we're here. That's all there is to it, so quit your bitchin—"

The driver cocked his head. "Hear that?"

"I don't hear nothing—"

"It's a boat. Not an outboard, something else," the driver said.

His partner shrugged. "Still don't hear nothing."

"That's 'cause it's stopped now, numb nuts," the driver said, reaching for the radio mike. "I'll call it in; you go see if you can spot it."

"Up yours," his partner said, motioning to the bridge jammed solid with abandoned cars. "We can't drive, and I ain't walking all the way up there in this heat to see some boat that ain't even there. If you're so damned anxious to see what it is, YOU go, and I'LL call it in. Maybe I'll turn on a little AC while I'm at it."

The driver glared. "Am I going to have to kick your ass, Cecil? You do remember the last time, right?"

Cecil cursed under his breath. "All right, dammit, but you come with me. If I have to tromp around in this heat, I want company. And besides, we shouldn't call it in unless we really see something; otherwise they'll have us chasing our tails all over the place."

The driver considered, then nodded. They got out, the driver grimacing when Cecil slammed his door. "Think you can make any more noise, asshole?"

Cecil snorted. "Like it matters. Let's get this done. And when we get back, we WILL be turning on the AC."

It was nearly a half mile walk from the foot of the bridge to the center of the river, and the two cons arrived sweat-soaked and irritable.

"We're here, genius," Cecil said. "So where's your boat."

"Keep it up, Cecil, and your ass is going in the river." The driver looked over the guardrail. "Don't worry, it's not much of a fall; but, oh yeah, you can't swim, can you?"

Cecil stepped back from the guardrail and changed the subject. "What about that marina down there? Reckon the teams hit it yet?"

The driver shrugged. "Probably not. There's a lot of low-hanging fruit out there, and plenty of stuff in mid-county. I doubt they've had time to get this far north."

"Wonder what's in all them covered docks? I can't see nothin' but roof from up here."

The driver glanced at his watch. "Not our problem. Let's head back. By the time we get to the car, we can run the AC."

**

"That was close," Howell whispered to Alvarez as the men above them moved away, their voices fading. "It was a good thing we heard the car door."

Alvarez nodded and whispered back, "Sound carries a long way when it doesn't have to compete with a thousand other sounds. It's like being in a library twenty-four seven."

"I don't hear them anymore. You think they're gone?"

Alvarez glanced at his watch. "Let's give them five more minutes, just to be sure."

Howell nodded, and they waited in silence until Alvarez nodded and moved silently from beneath the bridge. She followed through the scrub brush and trees. They reached the bank in minutes, and Alvarez parted the brush to reveal covered docks across the man-made access channel. What had been invisible to the cons on the bridge above was all too visible at water level. The berths were largely unoccupied, validating Howell's theory of the likely behavior of any boat owners lucky enough to have reached their boats.

"What do you think, ma'am?" Alvarez asked.

"Looks like only about a third of the berths are occupied, and I don't see any activity, so I'm guessing the boat owners aren't around. There's plenty of room for us under cover, but I'm concerned about the noise, especially since our arrival drew a look."

Alvarez nodded. "I was thinking the same. That enclosed boat won't paddle worth a damn, but we can walk it around to this point on a rope. We'll be less than a hundred feet across to the docks, with no current up in this side channel. We should be able to paddle it that far without any problem, right up into one of those covered berths." He shook his head. "But it's not getting in I worry about, it's leaving."

"We'll worry about that when the time comes."

***

They pulled into an empty berth between two large cabin cruisers, and the Coasties worked in tandem to check and clear the abandoned boats in the covered berths. When they confirmed all the boats were unoccupied, they turned their attention to the yacht club grounds while the *Pecos Trader* crewmen checked the boats more closely. Alvarez and Jones returned a short time later, both grinning.

"What's the deal?" Howell asked.

"All clear, ma'am," Alvarez said. "And we're grinning because all the boat owners who bugged out left their vehicles here—"

"And left hidden keys," Howell finished his sentence.

Alvarez's grin widened as he held up three magnetic key holders.

"There's almost forty cars out there," he said. "It stood to reason some folks would suffer from lack of imagination as far as hiding places go. We got wheels, and the marina has aboveground tanks for both gas and diesel. The departing boat owners hit 'em hard, but there's some left. We can drain out enough to supplement the fuel we brought."

"Terrific," Howell said. "We're looking good all around. Six boats are big enough to accommodate folks, all with generators and toilets and at least some fuel. We won't risk running the generators and we'll flush with buckets, but at least we'll be able to house people while we gather them up. And maybe we can take some of these boats with us. It's cramped on the ship now and likely to get a whole lot worse."

The next decision was how to deploy. After mulling it over, Howell decided not to leave a guard on the lifeboat. Jimmy and Pete knew the way to most of the other crewmen's homes, and she needed both of the Coasties for security. If cons or gangbangers found the boat, the only thing an out-gunned defender could do was die. They came together, and they would stay together.

The storage buildings housing trailered boats yielded enough gas cans to drain the club's tank. They loaded their newfound bounty and several of the cans they brought into the three 'borrowed' vehicles, and Howell held her breath as they tried the engines. Each started smoothly and ran quietly, much quieter than their boat engine. *Maybe this will work after all,* she thought from the passenger seat as Jimmy Gillespie drove through the yacht club gate and turned north on Marina Street.

716 WILLIAMS ROAD
BEAUMONT, TEXAS

SAME DAY, 10:40 A.M.

Jimmy's parents' house was closest, and he figured his family would congregate there in an emergency. Howell was also hoping for a read on the situation ashore and figured it was better to stay together until they had one. They worked their way to the far north edge of town through older, less traveled neighborhoods, some blighted and run-down, others neatly maintained and resistant to the march of urban decay. All the while, they were ever vigilant for 'cons turned cop' or any other threats.

The deserted streets were eerily quiet, as if the populace had fled at the sound of their engines. Here and there the flash of a face at a window or movement of a curtain told them they were being watched, but not welcomed. The houses got more and more run-down and farther apart, and many seemed deserted as they moved north on potholed streets.

"Mom and Pop have both lived up here since they were kids," Jimmy said. "My brothers and I tried to get them to move, but they wouldn't hear of it. We finally just left them alone."

Here and there, the run-down homes were separated by vacant lots, and Howell glanced woodland through the openings.

"Are we still in the city?" she asked.

Jimmy snorted. "Barely, but it depends on who you ask. If you asked the property tax people, the answer is yes. But if you're looking to get a pothole fixed, the answer is no."

They rode on in silence for another few minutes before pulling to the curb across from a modest but neat frame dwelling. Alvarez pulled up in the center of the deserted street, abreast of them, to form a sheltered area between the two vehicles. Jimmy got out between the cars and Howell joined him.

Jimmy stared at the house.

"What is it, Jimmy?" Howell asked.

Jimmy swallowed. "I've been thinking of nothin' else for a month, and now I'm scared. What if… what if they're…"

She put her hand on his arm. "I'm sure they're fine, Jimmy," she said, then paused. "But—"

"But if they're not, I gotta know that too," Jimmy said, and moved from between the cars to start across the overgrown lawn.

He was halfway to the door when it burst open and a slim red-haired woman darted across the porch and over the lawn into his arms. She was sobbing and laughing at the same time, clinging to Jimmy like she'd never let go. Seconds later, two small boys, twins by the looks of them, ran out of the house and wrapped their arms around their parents' legs. Jimmy separated himself from his wife with difficulty and scooped up a boy in each arm, whereupon his wife wrapped all three of them in a hug. The boys' facial resemblance to Jimmy and flaming red hair left no doubt as to their parentage.

Howell smiled. At least something was working out.

More people emerged—men, women, and a few kids. All the men and some of the women were armed, and they were all smiling, some less confidently than others as they studied Howell and her group and shot nervous glances up and down the street.

An older woman, obviously Jimmy's mother, separated herself from the group and rushed toward him, a man close behind her. Jimmy's wife gave ground grudgingly and let the older woman hug her son.

"Dang, boy," said the older man, "Y'all scared us to death rolling up like that and sittin' there. We almost shot you."

Jimmy grinned. "That would've been a fine homecoming, Pop."

The two other men in the group bore a strong family resemblance; brothers, Howell concluded. One of them shot a worried glance up and down the street and spoke.

"We best get those vehicles out of sight," he said.

The second brother nodded and ran to open a wooden gate beside the house, revealing a narrow passage into the fenced backyard. Jimmy turned to Howell, but she was already moving to their vehicle and ordering the others to do the same. Seconds later, she rolled through the narrow opening into a surprisingly spacious backyard.

The lot was narrow and deep, well over an acre, she guessed, and hidden from street view by the bulk of the modest house. It was screened on both sides by a tall wooden privacy fence, which ran well back into the yard before it was replaced by an even taller, impenetrable-looking hedge around the remaining border of the large lot. Behind the hedge at the back of the lot, she could see the towering trees of thick woodland; no neighbors there.

On closer inspection, the 'modest' house was a bit less so, with a substantial extension on its back side. Fruit trees ran down either side of the long yard, and she could see a large garden to the rear, with the green splash of growing plants. There was a three-bay garage, with what looked like an attached shop, and a small aboveground swimming pool. Half a dozen vehicles of various types were parked around the garage, including a boxy delivery truck with Lone Star Marine printed on the side in large letters, underneath an even larger stylized logo of a ship painted like the Texas state flag.

She parked her SUV next to the other cars and got out as Alvarez and Pete Brown followed suit. The others followed the cars through the gate, and one of his brothers closed and barred it as Jimmy's father separated from the group and walked over, his hand extended.

"Earl Gillespie," he said as Howell shook his hand. "We sure appreciate y'all gettin' Jimmy home."

Howell smiled. "He more or less got himself home. We just came along for the ride. I'm just glad we found you folks all okay. It's been pretty rough all over."

Earl Gillespie nodded. "It has that. We been blessed with not having to get out much since all the meanness started. We catch rainwater for drinking and cooking, and we cut a hole in the back hedge and dug us a latrine in the woods. There's enough deadfall back there so we got plenty of firewood for cooking and such, and plenty of wash water from the swimming pool. It ain't exactly what we're used to, but we been gettin' by—better than most folks, I reckon."

"It sounds like it," Howell said. "What about food?"

"We still had stuff in the pantry and things we put up from the garden last year—" he nodded toward the Lone Star Marine truck "—but mostly we been eatin' outa Mike's truck."

Howell looked confused.

"That would be me, Mike Gillespie," one of Jimmy's brothers said. "I drive... or drove, I guess, for a local ship chandler. When we have a real early morning delivery, we load up the night before and the driver takes the truck home. That way we can go straight to the ship in the morning. Except when the power went out and all the traffic lights were down, everything was all screwed up, so I tried to wait it out. When we finally figured out what was going on, I brought the truck over here. It wasn't a real big order, mostly canned goods and noodles and stuff, but we've been able to stretch it."

Earl Gillespie shook his head. "We're blessed to have it, but we been eatin' some weird stuff."

Mike Gillespie grinned. "It was for a Korean ship, so you might say some of the canned stuff is a little 'exotic.'

Earl shuddered. "Eyeballs and assholes is what it is."

"EARL GILLESPIE, mind your language," Mrs. Gillespie said.

"The truth is the truth, Dorothy," he said.

Howell suppressed a grin and changed the subject. "What's up with the fake cops, Mr. Gillespie?"

He shook his head. "Call me Earl. And it ain't good. After the first week or so, the gangs and no-goods were running wild, and the cops couldn't seem to keep a handle on 'em. Then the cops changed and started putting 'em down hard, just shoot first and no questions, no Miranda rights, none of that stuff. Just bang, you're dead. At first folks thought that was okay until they realized the cops were cons and they were only killing the bangers to keep all the loot for themselves."

"Did anyone do anything?" Howell asked.

Earl shrugged. "Like what? All the cops are dead, and from what we hear on the radio, the National Guard seems to be tied up in Houston and Dallas and San Antonio, places like that. And from the rumors about FEMA, we sure as hell don't want them here, so who's left?"

"I just figured people would fight back," Howell said.

"We are. They come around here, and they'll get ventilated and they pretty much know that," Earl said. "They don't seem real eager to take up anything resembling a fair fight. After they put down the bangers, they seem more than happy to stick to folks who can't fight back. If you have a few armed men and you're minding your own business, they'll like as not leave you be unless you're sittin' on a big load of goodies they know about. That's why we been real cagey about the truck. The only other time they seem to strike hard is if they think someone's trying to get resistance organized. I guess they figure that's a threat."

Howell nodded, silently processing the information. Earl cleared his throat and looked pointedly at Pete Brown and Alvarez.

"One other thing you should know," Earl said. "If you ain't white, they'll pretty much shoot you on sight, no questions asked."

Howell saw both men stiffen. She turned her attention back to Earl. "Do you know how many of them there are or where they are?"

"There's a bunch of them, for sure," Earl said. "But we been seeing less of them in the last few days. I'm figuring they're low on gas, so they're not moving around as much. The boys say they're sticking to the major intersections and roads in and out of town."

"That's right," Mike Gillespie confirmed. "We know other people through the town who are scraping by. One of us goes out a couple of times a week on a bicycle to connect with them and share news. The rumors are the cons control mainly Jefferson County, but like Pop says, lately they're keeping to major streets and intersections in the more populated areas. That makes sense if gas is an issue."

"Well, that's something, anyway," Howell said. "We may be able to bring in our folks without drawing undue attention."

"Bring 'em in where?" Earl Gillespie asked.

"To the ship, Pop," Jimmy said. "*Pecos Trader* is anchored in the river down near the reserve fleet. We came ashore to get everybody and take them to the ship. We got plenty of food and water—"

"You mean you're not staying here? You can't leave, Jimmy! You just got home," his wife said.

Jimmy turned to his wife. "I'm not going back by myself. I want y'all to come with us—"

"This is my home. Our home," Earl Gillespie said. "It might not look like much to some folks, but I'll be damned if I let a bunch of convict trash run me off. Besides, we're way off the radar here, and I'm thinkin' a ship in the river's gonna stick out like a sore thumb."

Howell nodded. "You're right, Mr. Gillespie. Earl. In fact, we've already had some run-ins with the convicts, so we're very much on their radar, and coming with us might be more dangerous in the short run. But even if you stay here, you can't be invisible forever. And when the cons get strong enough, I think you can expect a visit."

Earl Gillespie shook his head. "I can't say I like livin' like a scared rabbit in a hole, but this is pretty sudden. We need to think on it."

The rest of the family all started talking at once, and Howell raised her hands. "I know it's a big decision, folks, and I'm sorry I can't give you more time, but we're burning daylight and I need a decision one way or another. However, we will give y'all some privacy. We'll wait in one of the cars while you folks talk it out."

Earl shook his head. "It'll be hot in the car. Y'all wait out here in the shade and we'll go in the house to talk."

There were murmurs and nods of agreement, and the family followed their parents up across the deck and to the back door of the house, Jimmy in the rear. He gave Howell an apologetic shrug.

"Ten minutes, Jimmy. No more," she whispered.

***

At twenty minutes, Howell glanced at her watch and was about to start across the deck just as the back door opened and Earl emerged, followed by the rest of his clan. He approached slowly, a solemn look on his face. She prepared herself for bad news.

Then he grinned. "So tell me, y'all got anything to eat on this ship besides noodles and assholes?"

CHAPTER TWENTY-ONE

BEAUMONT YACHT CLUB
560 MARINA STREET
BEAUMONT, TEXAS

DAY 29, 4:35 P.M.

Howell bit back a curse as a small boy ran past her down the enclosed dock, squealing as he was chased by a second. She grabbed the second kid's arm and pulled him up short.

"Get back to your boat, NOW!" she hissed, and the boy's eyes went wide in his dark face, and his lip started trembling.

Howell immediately regretted her action and softened her tone. "I know it's tough," she said, "but there are very bad people close by, and if they hear you, they might find us. Do you understand?"

The boy nodded solemnly and glanced over at his brother, subdued since Howell had captured his sibling.

"I didn't mean to be loud, ma'am. Me and Clarence was just playing chase, that's all," the boy said.

"I know you didn't," Howell said, "but you have to be real quiet, and you have to tell your friends, okay?"

"Yes'm," the boy said and motioned his brother to follow and turned down the dock. They were running again inside of ten steps, but no longer screaming. *That's something, at least*, thought Howell.

"Not exactly a low-profile operation," said Alvarez. "I didn't figure on so many."

Howell shook her head. "Neither did I. I guess success has its downside. How many so far?"

"Over fifty, with more sure to come," Alvarez said. "Way too many to keep under wraps for long, especially if the cons have men stationed up at the foot of the bridge."

"Did you get 'em all fed?"

"Jones and I passed out food," Alvarez said. "Since it looks like we're headed back tomorrow anyway, I gave 'em all they wanted. Some of 'em were near starving."

Howell nodded absently. "Good."

"What's the problem, ma'am?" Alvarez asked.

"Just wondering how pissed the captain's going to be at the number of new mouths to feed," she said.

Alvarez grinned. "Well look at the bright side. If we need help getting out of here, we have a lot more shooters. Everyone that's come in so far has been well armed."

Howell laughed. "God bless Texas."

Alvarez chuckled as well and Howell turned her attention back to the line of rapidly filling boats.

After convincing the Gillespies to join them, she'd been faced with a decision. All three of the Gillespie men volunteered to help, and Jimmy argued persuasively that with the extra vehicles and manpower, it made more sense for Howell and the Coasties to go back to the yacht club to protect the families and get them settled in as they arrived. Unable to fault the logic, Howell had reluctantly conceded the point.

They were three for five so far, with Jimmy and Pete having safely collected their own families and one other. More than 'families' actually, as groups of survivors generally included extended family, friends, and neighbors grouped together for protection. Thus a significant portion of the people she'd collected had no connection to the ship, and she was worried about Hughes' reaction.

Of the missing families, one was gone without a trace, their home abandoned. The second were apparent victims of the cons 'ethnic cleansing,' and the weeks-old crime scene was beyond grisly. Jimmy could only describe it in general terms as 'horrible,' and Pete wouldn't speak of it at all, shaking his head with jaw clenched and rage in his eyes. Given the condition of the remains and their lack of tools, burying multiple bodies was impossible. After an impromptu prayer in the front yard, the late arriving 'rescue party' burned the house to the ground; a crematorium of sorts and the best they could do for a shipmate's family.

Howell shook her head to clear the tragic image from her imagination and turned at the sound of tires on gravel outside.

"I hope they got the other families all right," she said.

Alvarez nodded as the door to the enclosure swung open and Jimmy and one of his brothers ushered in a group of new arrivals.

"Where you want them, ma'am?" Jimmy asked.

"Wherever they can find room on one of the boats, Jimmy. They're all pretty full." She looked toward the door. "Any more?"

Jimmy shook his head. "No, ma'am. The other house was... we had to burn it."

Howell felt a lump in her throat. Unable to speak, she nodded, and Jimmy hurried his charges down the dock just as Pete came in.

"I... I'm really sorry, Pete," she said.

Pete nodded but didn't speak.

"How's the gas in Mr. Gillespie's truck?" she asked.

"About half a tank. Why?" Pete asked.

"Because I have one last job to do."

Pete nodded. "The chief's wife?"

"Ex-wife," Howell corrected.

"We'll come with you," Pete said.

Howell nodded, and Pete walked down the dock to where the new arrivals were wrangling with the occupants of the largest cabin cruiser while Jimmy tried to keep things under control. Howell ignored the altercation, happy to let Jimmy and Pete handle it.

"How you want to do this?" Alvarez asked.

"I'll take you, Pete, and Jimmy," she said. "We'll leave Jones in charge, with the Gillespies to help. They all seem pretty capable, Earl in particular. Let's put them to trying to organize our getaway while we're gone. If they can keep these folks undercover and busy, the less chance they'll do something stupid to call attention to themselves."

"Works for me," Alvarez said. "You think there's enough daylight to get to this woman's house and back?"

Howell nodded. "She lives in town, and if she's not there, we just come straight back. Trust me, I'm not gonna waste time on this bitch."

***

They made good time, using a technique Jimmy and Pete perfected during earlier forays, avoiding main streets to parallel them in residential areas. When they couldn't avoid a major intersection, Jimmy scouted ahead, silent on the bicycle they carried in the truck bed. A double-click on his radio signaled all clear.

They stayed north of I-10 and crossed under US 96 on Delaware Street, a route scouted earlier. They ducked south off Delaware as soon as possible and made their way westward on secondary streets before Howell stopped a block from their destination. It was an upscale area of large homes set on larger lots, with privacy fences hiding backyard swimming pools.

"According to Dan, it's the next left," Howell said. "1616 Windsor Court at the end of the cul-de-sac."

"This Trixie's done all right for herself," Jimmy said, looking around. "These are some nice little shacks."

Howell grimaced. "Dan paid for it. He signed it over as part of the divorce settlement. According to Captain Hughes, he didn't even fight it. He said it meant nothing to him if he had to live in it alone." She shook her head. "Even after he caught her…" Howell trailed off. There were few secrets on a ship, and the whole crew knew of the well-liked but socially awkward chief engineer's short-lived marriage, at least in a general way. But as angry as she was at her friend's situation, discussing a fellow officer's private life with crewmen was straying out of bounds.

Jimmy nodded. "It's strange how a man can be so smart about everything else and so dumb about women. I reckon the chief was just thinking with the wrong head."

She ignored the remark. "Take the bike and check it out. I don't want any unpleasant surprises."

Jimmy nodded, unloaded the bike, and pedaled away.

Howell waited tensely for the double-click, impatient to complete an unpleasant task and secretly hoping they'd find another vacant house. She was fairly sure 'rescuing' Trixie was a mistake, but she'd promised to make the effort, and a promise was a promise.

Ahead, Jimmy rounded the corner at full speed and skidded to a stop beside her open window.

"There… there's a police cruiser," he said, breathless.

"Where?" she asked.

"In the friggin' driveway."

They all got out of the truck.

"We obviously can't just roll in beside them," Alvarez said. "Let's check it out on foot."

Howell nodded, looking around. She spotted a long driveway across the street, which turned to disappear behind a large home.

"We need someplace to stash the truck. Alvarez, you and Pete check out that house. Give me two clicks on the radio if it's vacant."

Alvarez took the radio from Jimmy and the men took off as Jimmy threw his bike into the truck bed. Minutes later, she heard the all clear and pulled into the driveway to hide the truck behind the house.

They moved down the cul-de-sac cautiously, to positions overlooking Trixie's driveway; Alvarez and Jimmy on one side behind a parked car, with Howell and Pete opposite, hidden behind a hedge.

Howell shook her head. "We need to figure out what's going on here. I don't want to go in blind."

She'd hardly finished speaking when the front door opened and two uniformed men came out, trailed by a blonde with an obviously enhanced anatomy, wearing sandals and a see-through negligée. The woman had her arm around the shoulders of a similarly clad girl of perhaps fifteen. The girl's body language telegraphed fear and shame.

Howell swallowed her rage. Trixie. She had no use for the bitch, but she'd thought her better than this.

"She's just learning," Trixie said. "She'll be better next time."

"She better be," one of the cons said, "and a helluva lot more enthusiastic. You got a good setup, Trixie, and if you expect to keep eatin', you best make sure these little bitches get trained up right."

Trixie laughed and fondled the con's crotch. "Don't worry about that, big boy. Besides, I made up for it by taking care of you both, didn't I? Was I enthusiastic enough?" She draped herself over the con and stuck her tongue in his ear, then jumped back playfully as he grabbed at her.

Pete whispered, "Murderin' bastards."

"Yeah, and obviously Trixie doesn't need rescuing," Howell whispered back, still watching the driveway. "We'll wait until they go and then get the hell out of—"

BLAM!

Blood and brains splashed Trixie as the con beside her dropped like a rock, and Trixie started screaming. The second con stumbled back toward the patrol car, looking in all directions and clawing at his holster.

Howell whirled to see Pete standing, his dark face a mask of hatred, the M4 at his shoulder.

"DAMN IT, PETE!"

BLAM! BLAM!

The second deputy dropped, dead before he hit the ground.

Howell cursed and rounded the end of the hedge, running toward the screaming woman. "Trixie! Shut the hell up!"

Trixie stopped, confused. "Who the hell are—"

The other three were in the driveway now, and Howell pointed to the dead cons.

"Drag them into the garage and pull the car in after them," Howell said, glaring at Pete. "We're gonna be real lucky if those shots don't draw a crowd."

"You ain't seen what we seen, Mate," Pete said. "All these sons of bitches need killing."

Beside Pete, Jimmy nodded agreement.

"Sure they do," Howell said. "But we still have to get the families back to —"

"Hey! You're that bitch from Danny's ship," Trixie said. "You're going to be sorry you ever—"

Howell turned. "Get inside. You got some explaining to do."

"I don't have to explain a thing to—"

Howell backhanded her, and Trixie stumbled back, catching her sandal on the edge of the sidewalk to sprawl on the overgrown lawn.

"That was my backhand," Howell said. "If you'd like to feel my rifle butt, keep it up. Now get inside."

Trixie scrambled up and fled into the house. Howell looked at the frightened girl and motioned her after Trixie with a nod.

Trixie tried a different tack in the living room. "I'm gonna tell Danny how you treated me. Then we'll see who has the last laugh, bitch."

Howell pushed her down on a sofa. "Sit. And shut up. If you open your mouth again except to answer a question, you're gonna lose some teeth."

The woman glared and Howell turned to the girl. Her look softened. "What's your name, honey?"

"L-Lana," the girl said.

"That's a pretty name," Howell said softly. "We're not going to hurt you, Lana. But I need your help. Is there anyone else here?"

The girl nodded. "J-just the others. L-like me—"

"MATE?" yelled a voice from the kitchen.

"IN HERE," Howell yelled back, and Jimmy Gillespie rushed in.

"You need to see this," he said. "The garage."

Howell nodded. "Watch Trixie. If she tries to get up, shoot her."

"My pleasure," Jimmy said.

Howell was unprepared for what she found in the three-bay garage. The two corpses sprawled in one bay, and the middle bay held the police car, but in the third was a wire cage perhaps ten feet square. The door stood open, and cowering in the far corner were three naked girls, all in their early teens. Alvarez stood at the cage door with his back to her, but he turned at her approach, a look of helplessness on his face.

"They won't come out, and I didn't want to scare them anymore. I thought maybe a woman…"

Howell nodded. "Go find something for cover, blankets, bedspreads, anything. Bring it out, then y'all stay in the house."

Alvarez nodded and turned to go.

"Oh. And get the kid in the living room something too, and ask her to come out here."

TRIXIE'S HOUSE
1616 WINDSOR COURT
BEAUMONT, TEXAS

"What the hell did you expect me to do?" Trixie asked. "They caught me right after the blackout and put me in a horrible cell in that prison." Her lower lip began to tremble. "And they… they raped me."

Howell looked down. "Cry me a river, bitch. That 'wounded victim act' might work on Dan, but I see through you like glass."

Trixie sneered. "Screw you. A girl's gotta get by."

"And let's welcome back the real Trixie," Howell said. "You know, I could almost buy it; the whole 'surviving by your feminine charms' thing, I mean. It's the training these children to be sex slaves I have a little trouble with."

Trixie shrugged. "Get real. This is a win-win. They were already sex slaves and they had it a hell of a lot worse in the cells with the cons having twenty-four access. This way I got to have my own place, we all got better food, and the cons have to travel to us, which really cuts down on the visits. I'm teaching them to be survivors."

"No, you're raping them just like the cons."

Trixie glared, and Howell walked over to where Alvarez sat at a built-in bar, watching the interrogation.

"Real friggin' humanitarian, ain't she?" Alvarez said. "The question is what the hell we gonna do with her?"

Howell shook her head. "I'd like to shoot her right between the eyes, but I guess we have to take her back to the ship."

The color drained from Trixie's face at the mention of going to the ship, and Howell laughed.

"What's the matter, Trixie? You worried Dan is finally gonna find out just what a bitch you are?"

"I… I just don't want to disappoint him, that's all," Trixie said.

Howell snorted and turned back to Alvarez. "How are the girls?"

Alvarez shrugged. "Better since we let them into her closet to find clothes. Jimmy and Pete found some food for them in the pantry. They're packing it down like there's no tomorrow, so I don't think Trixie was sharing much of that 'better food' she mentioned."

Howell looked concerned and moved toward the kitchen. "We shouldn't let them gorge themselves. They could get really sick."

"I have to pee," Trixie said from the couch.

Alvarez looked at Howell, who nodded agreement and continued to the kitchen. Once there, she found Jimmy and Pete way ahead of her, trying to withdraw some of the food they'd initially set out. But the girls' pleading was heartbreaking, and she could see indecision on the men's faces. Howell interceded and firmly but kindly moved the food out of sight into a cabinet, then turned to the now agitated girls. She had just calmed them when Alvarez came in.

"Uhh… we've got a problem, ma'am. The bitch went out the bathroom window. You want us to go find her?"

"Good riddance, I say," Jimmy said, and Pete nodded.

Howell shrugged. "Solves a problem, actually. I guess she didn't want to go to the ship."

At the mention of the ship, the girl Lana flinched and started shaking her head.

"Lana, honey, what's the matter?" Howell asked.

The girl was on the verge of tears. "Don't… don't take us to the ship. The convicts will get us again."

Howell wrapped her in a hug. "There are no convicts on our ship, and I won't let anybody take you. Okay?"

Lana shook her head vehemently and pulled free of Howell's embrace. "You… you don't understand. He was bragging he had almost two thousand men… and… and he's gonna kill all the men on the ship and make whores of all the women and take—"

"Who, Lana? Who's going to do this and when?" Howell asked.

"The one they call Snag; today or tomorrow, I think… I… I'm not sure. He was drunk last night so I couldn't understand everything he said, but I know it's soon. He was bragging about it to Trixie."

Howell suppressed her rage. That bitch! "Who's Snag?"

"He's one of the boss convicts. He's skinny and real mean, with bad teeth and stinky breath. When he's drunk, he brags a lot and… and he likes to hurt us."

Howell pulled the girl back into a hug and held her until she calmed. "No one's going to hurt you now, honey. Not when I'm around."

She straightened and released Lana to dig in her pocket for the truck keys and toss them to Alvarez.

"Alvarez, bring the truck around. Jimmy, you and Pete find some trash bags and collect anything of use. We're rolling in five."

CHAPTER TWENTY-TWO

Howell rolled out of the driveway in the cop car, with Lana sitting beside her and the other girls in the backseat. The cop car was Alvarez's suggestion, and a good one. If they were attacked, she could get the girls to safety while the men in the truck fought a rearguard action. As an added bonus, the cop car radio might give them an early warning if the cons were onto them.

There was no picking their way cautiously down side streets now. They had to warn the ship, and the sooner the better, but she had the families to think about too, and they had no hope if they were cut off on land. Her best bet was to get on the river southbound as soon as possible, then break radio silence to warn the *Pecos Trader*.

She raced east on Delaware, with the truck close behind. Their plan was simple. If they encountered cons, she was counting on the cop car to confuse them, at least momentarily, and she would swerve around them as Alvarez and Pete popped up from the truck bed and unloaded on the cons in full auto. Even if they survived, the cons would be reluctant to give chase. All she really needed was a little breathing room.

She flew under US 96 and across North 11th Street at ninety miles an hour and scant minutes later made a sharp right south on Magnolia, tires squealing. She glanced at her rearview mirror to confirm the truck was still with her, and let out a relieved sigh when she saw it negotiate the turn. They were going to make it with no problems, as far as the yacht club, anyway. The radio crackled.

"Unit 18 to base. Repeat, unit 18 to base. Over."

"This is base. Go ahead 18."

"Base, Trixie flagged us down in Rogers Park. She claims a bunch of people off that ship killed Red and Leon at her house and tried to kidnap her. She wants to talk to Snag. Over."

"Wait one, 18. I'll try to confirm. Over."

There was a brief lull, then the radio squawked again. "Unit 7, this is base. What is your situation? Over."

The call was repeated three more times as Howell raced south on Magnolia. It changed when she made the left onto Elm Avenue.

"Unit 7, please respond. Damn it, Red, talk to me. Over."

She'd just made the final turn onto Marina Street when the dispatcher gave up and switched back to Unit 18.

"Unit 18, this is base. Proceed to Trixie's house and confirm. Over."

"Base, we're rolling into the driveway now, and there's a big puddle of blood. I think you better call Snag. Over."

"He's already on the way. Did Trixie say anything else? Over."

"Yeah. She overheard one of 'em say something about the yacht club by the I-10 bridge. She thinks that's where they're headed. Over."

"Roger that, Unit 18. Confirm the situation at Trixie's, then check back in for orders. Base out."

Howell's blood ran cold as she heard the dispatcher begin routing units to the yacht club and sending others to various places south along the river. They're probing, she thought, and when they get a fix on us, we're screwed.

She slowed as she approached the entrance to the club and stuck her arm out the window to wave the truck past. Running up unannounced on the Gillespie clan in a police cruiser wasn't likely to produce a happy ending.

She followed the truck in and skidded to a stop in front of the enclosed dock, confused by the scene before her. People, mostly women, were digging in the narrow grassy strip immediately next to the dock, shielded from view from the bridge above by the dock house itself. They were shoveling the dirt into black plastic bags held open by children. Here and there men were disappearing into the dock house with the half-filled bags while elsewhere along the back of the long dock building, men were removing sections of corrugated sheet metal.

What the hell?

Howell ordered the girls out of the car just as Alvarez and the others joined her. She asked Pete to find one of the families to look after the girls, and as he hustled away, Howell turned to Alvarez.

"They're onto us and headed this way and also setting up a gauntlet all along the west bank of the river between here and the *Pecos Trader*. I don't know what the hell is going on here, but we need to load up and leave, and now. I'm thinking we jam everyone in three or four of the fastest boats and run for it. Any suggestions?" Howell asked.

Alvarez grimaced and shook his head. "It doesn't matter how fast the boats are, ma'am. If they're already setting up south of us, they'll be in place when we pass, and those boats are only wood and fiberglass. They might not sink us, but they'll chew the hell out of the boats and anyone in them. We've got a better shot in the lifeboat, at least we can shield some of them."

Howell cursed. "But it can't hold everyone, and even with the current we won't make over five or six knots downstream and it's twelve miles back to the ship. That's a long time to be under their guns, and I'm not sure our makeshift armor will stand up to that either."

"We're almost ready," said someone behind her.

Howell turned to see Earl Gillespie, dirt on his hands and his shirt soaked with sweat.

"Earl, stop whatever you're doing. We need to get out of here," Howell said.

Earl nodded. "We just gotta finish the sandbags."

Howell looked confused. "Sandbags?"

"Well, dirt bags, actually. We found a couple of boxes of heavy contractor bags in the club office and some shovels in the maintenance shed. I figured if we piled dirt bags behind that sheet metal... hell, just come look."

Howell followed Earl into the enclosed dock and shook her head in admiration. The bridge level of the closest cabin cruiser was obscured by a length of the corrugated sheet metal, as was the open deck near the stern.

"I figured anybody shooting at us will be on our right side, so we only rigged up that side of the boats to save time," Earl said. "We tied a triple thickness of that sheet metal to the rail, then piled up dirt bags about two foot thick behind 'em. I don't know if it'll stop everything, but I figured it's a hell of a lot better than nothing. We protected the boat drivers and made a covered shooting position on each boat. We can put the young'uns and anyone who ain't drivin' or shootin' in that lifeboat of yours, where there's already protection. Then we run these other boats as a screen on the right side, between the lifeboat and the bank."

Howell was speechless.

"Something wrong?" Earl asked.

"Hell no," Howell said. "How did you get this done so quickly without attracting attention?"

Earl shrugged. "I've found when you put folks to work, hard work anyway, they usually quiet right down. It's hard to run your mouth when you need all your air to breathe. And givin' young'uns something to do and makin' 'em feel important tends to keep 'em from runnin' around like wild injuns. The hard part was gettin' the sheet metal loose without making too much noise."

"Great job, Earl. We just need to get everyone situated—"

"In progress," Earl said. "Five or ten minutes max."

Howell saw Alvarez glance south, even though he couldn't see the bridge on the other side of the dock house. "We still don't have any protection on top," he said. "If they get shooters on the bridge before we get under it, we're toast."

Howell nodded. "Those guys from the foot of the bridge are probably already there. Think you can take them out?"

Alvarez shrugged. "Piece of cake if they're dumb enough to stand at the guardrail and give me a shot. But I'll need Jones. If there are multiple targets, we need to take them down fast. If any get to cover, it will become a standoff, and that means we lose."

"Do it," Howell said. "And take a radio, but use it sparingly."

"Copy that. I'll go find Jones." Alvarez jogged away.

Beside her, Earl looked at the boats and sighed. "They're all leanin' more than I like. I wish we had time to load some weight on the other side to compensate."

Howell shook her head. "You did just fine, Earl. If we make it through this, it will be thanks to you and your boys. And I'm sorry I got you into this. I guess y'all would have been safer where you were."

Earl shrugged. "Maybe in the short run, but like you said, they'd have come for us sooner or later. Anyway, it ain't me I'm worried about, it's the young'uns."

Day 29, 6:05 p.m.

Alvarez peeked around the thick trunk of the tree next to the clubhouse and cursed. The con standing at the guardrail was an easy shot, but he could see the guy talking to someone behind him, out of sight farther back on the high bridge. His radio double-clicked; Howell requesting an all clear.

"What the hell are we supposed to do?" he hissed. "If I give her an all clear and we can't take them all out, she's screwed."

"Maybe not," whispered Jones from the next tree. "When those boats crank up, I'm betting it'll draw all those turkeys to the rail. Then we can have a turkey shoot. We either take 'em down fast, or we don't, and if we still have an active shooter, you can warn her in plain language before they back out of the docks." Jones paused. "It is what it is, bro. I don't think you have much choice."

Alvarez sighed and keyed the transmit button on the radio twice, and from up the channel to their right, multiple powerful engines rumbled. Alvarez smiled. Just as Jones predicted, the turkeys came to the turkey shoot. There were four of them lining the guardrail.

"I got the two on the left," Jones said.

"I got the two on the right," Alvarez confirmed. "On three. ONE. TWO. THREE."

The M4s barked four times in quick succession, and three of the cons tumbled over the guardrail to splash into the river below. The fourth man, Jones' second shot, grabbed his left shoulder and hesitated a split second too long before attempting to drop down behind the cover of the guardrail. The Coasties' guns barked as one, and the con joined his brothers.

Alvarez double-clicked the radio and got an answering signal from Howell before breaking cover to run across the yacht club lawn to the bulkhead at the edge of the channel. Earl Gillespie pulled alongside in the leading screen boat just as they arrived, his boat listing to starboard from the weight of the improvised armor. He barely slowed as the Coasties leaped across the narrow gap and scrambled behind the improvised shooting position.

"Welcome aboard, boys," Earl yelled. "I hope y'all brought plenty of ammo, because I don't think there's gonna be a shortage of targets."

***

Howell hugged the left bank as she ran downstream at a blistering seven knots behind the screening vessels. As they cleared the bridge, she raised her radio.

"*Pecos Trader, Pecos Trader,* this is Howell. Do you copy? Over."

Jordan Hughes' voice answered immediately. "We copy loud and clear, Georgia. Over."

"*Pecos Trader,* we're at the I-10 bridge southbound, with sixty-seven survivors. We are coming in hot. Repeat, coming in hot. Over."

"We copy, Georgia. The cavalry is on the way. Repeat. The cavalry is on the way. Over." She heard the stress in his voice.

"NEGATIVE! Repeat, NEGATIVE! We have intel an attack on your position is imminent. Repeat, attack on your position imminent. You may need all your resources. Over."

There was a long pause; then the radio squawked again.

"We copy. Do you have details of attack? Over."

"Negative. Repeat. Negative. Nothing but a possible, repeat, possible time of today or tomorrow. Over."

The river narrowed ahead and took a sweeping bend to the right, forcing the little convoy closer together and uncomfortably close to the old shipyard in the inner radius. The radio continued to squawk, but Howell ignored it as she conned the lifeboat through the turn.

Earl Gillespie's lead screening boat had just drawn abreast of the shipyard when all hell broke loose. There was a shooter behind every piece of abandoned equipment and junk pile, all pounding the screening vessels at point-blank range. The radio squawked again, and Howell raised it to her mouth without taking her eyes off the river.

"We're kind of busy now, Cap. I'll check in if... when we get clear. Howell out."

The screening vessels were being pounded, but Earl's makeshift armor was doing the job, due in part to their attackers' weaponry. Most cons were diverted from patrol, armed with handguns and tactical shotguns. Accuracy was spotty at best, and though they could easily hit the screening vessels at close range, stopping them was a different story. The engines were low in the boats, and it would take a fantastic stroke of luck to hit the control cables. The boats were hit repeatedly above the waterline, but the operators crouched behind protection and drove on.

After the initial terrifying onslaught, the tables turned. The defenders loosed a deadly accurate fire from M4s and ARs and a variety of long guns far more accurate than the weapons of their attackers. Convicts fell and began to lose their appetite for the fight.

The boats swept around the tight shipyard bend, guns blazing, and the river widened to allow them to move out of the effective range of their attackers' weapons while maintaining their own accurate fire. Then the river bent left and narrowed again, once more exposing them to fire from convicts scattered along the shore in Riverfront Park. But here too, superior accuracy carried the fight and soon scattered their attackers.

The children were frightened into silence by the violence of the onslaught, but rather than calming their fears, the slackening fire fueled them, and the children all began to cry.

Howell flinched at a loud crack and saw a hole in the fiberglass canopy in front of her just as another round penetrated six inches to the left of the first, missing her completely. All of the kids were screaming now, and several women were praying. She keyed the radio, shouting over the noise.

"Alvarez, do you copy? Over."

The speaker clicked twice.

"Sniper on the railroad bridge ahead. Over."

The speaker clicked twice, followed a few heartbeats later by the distinctive sound of multiple three-round bursts from the screening vessel ahead of her.

Alvarez's voice came over the radio. "Clear."

They crept under the railroad bridge and past the city docks at their glacial pace, giving better than they got. The river widened a bit more as they neared the Exxon-Mobil refinery, and she hugged the undeveloped east bank as closely as she dared to put as much distance as possible between her little fleet and any shooters.

Then the firing slackened before stopping completely. She could see nothing from behind her screen and she keyed the radio.

"Alvarez, what's happening? Over."

"I'm not sure. They seem to be leaving. Over."

"Roger that. Keep your eyes open. Howell out."

They were a good ten miles from the *Pecos Trader*, almost two hours at this speed. It seemed unlikely the cons would abandon the attack, especially given what she'd heard on the cop car radio. What the hell were they doing?

JEFFERSON COUNTY COURTHOUSE
1149 PEARL STREET
BEAUMONT, TEXAS

DAY 29, 6:35 P.M.

Spike McComb stood on the small observation deck near the top of the courthouse, fuming as the little convoy crept from under the railroad bridge and made its way downstream. He lowered the binoculars and turned to glare at Snag, who was fidgeting nervously.

"I told you this was gonna happen. These assholes are doing whatever they want right here in our territory. And now they go makin' a recruiting trip right under your frigging nose, Snag."

Snag began to protest, but Spike cut him off. "And then, they fall in your lap, and this is the best you can do?"

"Spike, we only had a half hour, and we still got—"

"You got shit for brains, is what you got, Snag," Spike said. "Now get on the radio and move everybody south, and get some of those boats you been roundin' up on the water. But call the armory first and make sure they get their butts over to the launching ramps with long guns and ammo."

"But, Spike, we're gonna need those boats for the attack—"

Spike's eyes narrowed as he glared, and Snag shut up. "As I was saying, pick your best marksmen and put a couple in each boat. I want two or three more guys with shotguns in each boat. The riflemen will keep the shooters' heads down so the boats can get within point-blank shotgun range; then I want the shotguns to unload on the boats right at the waterline. They ain't nothing but fiberglass, and we can sink 'em right from under 'em."

"I dunno, Spike, we're gonna have to get pretty close. Are you sure it's worth maybe gettin' a bunch of the boys shot up before—"

"I swear sometimes, Snag, I don't think there's one of you sumbitches who can think beyond the end of your dicks. Now just why do you figure the people on the ship would come ashore to gather up MORE people? And they came for Trixie, and she says her ex is on the ship. So just think about that. I mean, they can only carry so much food, and they only got so much room, so why get more crowded and share your food with somebody unless those somebodies are..."

Spike waited expectantly for Snag to make the obvious connection and fill in the blank. Snag screwed his face up a moment, followed by a smile of understanding.

"Pussy?"

Spike's face purpled. "FAMILIES, YOU MORON! The crew's families must be on those boats. And if we got the families, we won't NEED to attack; we'll have 'em eatin' out of our hands. Now get going, and have some boats standin' by to pull survivors out of the river. They won't do us much good if they're dead."

Snag turned and raced for the stairway, but Spike called after him.

"On second thought, maybe we can use the dead ones. Make sure to collect any bodies too, especially kids. We'll pile 'em in a boat and send 'em to the ship with one of the survivors, just so they get the point about what's gonna happen to the rest of them if they keep messin' with us." Spike grinned. "Ain't nothin' says surrender like a buncha dead kids."

CHAPTER TWENTY-THREE

NECHES RIVER
APPROACHING HAWKINS SLIP
BEAUMONT, TEXAS

SAME DAY, 7:05 P.M.

"I knew it was too good to last. We got company," Alvarez said to Jones.

He turned and was about to yell up to Earl, but saw him already waving to the other boats and moving to tighten the cordon around the lifeboat. Alvarez's radio squawked.

"Talk to me, Alvarez. What's up?" Howell asked.

"Six boats of shooters coming out of the slip ahead," Alvarez said. "Hug the left bank as close as you can, and we'll pull in tight around you in a semicircle and try to keep them away. Over."

"Roger that," Howell said, and Alvarez watched her inch the lifeboat even closer to the east bank.

Jones raised his M4. "Here they come—CRAP!"

Jones ducked behind their sandbags and Alvarez instinctively followed suit as a dozen rounds splattered into their improvised armor. Jones was clutching his right ear; blood flowed between his fingers.

"Son of a bitch got me in the ear," Jones said. "I think this bunch is a little bit better equipped, and they can sure shoot straighter."

Alvarez nodded and took off his booney hat to raise it above the sandbags on the muzzle of his rifle. It immediately drew heavy fire, and he pulled it down and stuck his finger through a neat hole.

"They're serious about keeping us down," he said, "but we can still screen the lifeboat, so I don't get it."

The roar of the outboards on the approaching boats grew louder, almost deafening, but not loud enough to mask the blasts of automatic shotguns seemingly only a few feet away. Their attackers sped by in line, now intent on savaging the second boat in the screen. As they came into view astern,

Alvarez and Jones opened fire at the last attack boat in line as it sped away. Two men fell in the boat, including the driver, and the boat veered off to the left at a crazy angle, uncontrolled and out of the fight.

"They ripped us a new one just below the waterline," Earl yelled down. Alvarez turned back forward to see Earl out from behind his sandbags and leaning over the starboard side, peering down at the hull.

"How bad is it?" Alvarez yelled.

"It ain't good," Earl yelled back. "We was already leanin' right from all these sandbags, so any water coming in is gonna stay on that side, and we're just going to lean more and more. Like as not we'll sink, if we don't flip over first."

"How long?" Alvarez asked.

"How the hell should I know? I ain't no sailor. I was in the Army."

Alvarez watched the remaining attack boats speed upriver and execute a long arcing U-turn to roar back downriver, hugging the far bank. He had no doubt they'd repeat the maneuver downstream and come roaring back on another strafing run. He turned back to Jones.

"How are the other boats?"

Jones shook his head. "We got it worst, but they all took hits. None of them will take much more of this."

Alvarez nodded. Their own boat was listing noticeably more to starboard now, and moving sluggishly. He looked downriver as their attackers completed the turn.

"Earl, cut speed and fall back against the next boat," Alvarez yelled. "If we can tie off to her, at least we can protect her hull. They can't shoot her through us."

Earl nodded and cut speed, and in seconds they were bumping along the starboard side of the second boat in the screen. They barely had time to get tied off and back behind their sandbags before their attackers returned.

They could do nothing but absorb the blow, then fire on their retreating attackers. Three more screening vessels were badly damaged, one so badly it sank almost immediately, and its three occupants scrambled aboard the next screening vessel in line. The remaining damaged vessels had enough reserve buoyancy to stay afloat, with the more severely damaged quickly roped together and towed as a screen for their two less damaged sisters.

With surprise no longer a factor, the outcome of the third attack was a bit different. The defenders were a compact mass now, much more difficult to suppress, and no longer engaging their attackers piecemeal. When the line of attack boats roared toward them the third time, they met the concentrated fire of a dozen rifles and broke off the attack long before they were in shotgun range. They sped out of range downriver to circle and wait, like hyenas waiting for a wounded gazelle to bleed out.

That was the good news. The bad news was that the gazelle WAS bleeding out. The more severely damaged boats rode ever lower in the water, and they lost a second when they were five miles from *Pecos Trader*, cut loose to sink as they rearranged their makeshift screen.

"You thinking what I'm thinking?" Alvarez asked.

"If you're thinking we're going to be screwed when the river opens up to that big anchorage where all those old reserve fleet ships are, I guess I am," Jones said.

Alvarez nodded. "That's two miles of open water where we can't hug the bank. We can try screening the lifeboat on both sides, presuming we have at least two screening boats still floating, but all the sandbags are on the starboard sides..."

Alvarez and Jones both looked up at the distant roar of outboards UP-RIVER. A lot of outboards. "Or maybe not," Alvarez said. "Sounds like our friends have called in reinforcements."

"What the hell are we gonna do?" Jones asked.

Alvarez didn't hesitate. "Put Pete, Jimmy and the rest of the Gillespie brothers in the lifeboat. Keep all the noncombatants low in the boat and a shooter at every gun port. Maybe they can keep those hyenas downstream off the lifeboat long enough for Howell to get it to the ship. You and I and everybody left will cut loose from the sinkers and take the two good boats back upstream to engage the bunch coming downriver. We'll try to slow these bastards down long enough for Howell to get the families to the ship."

"You know that's at least a half hour, maybe more, right?" Jones asked.

Alvarez merely nodded.

"And you know your plan sucks, right?"

Alvarez nodded again.

"Just checking," Jones said. "For the record, if we don't survive this, I'll be seriously pissed off at you."

NECHES RIVER
NEAR OLD MANSFIELD FERRY ROAD
SOUTH OF BEAUMONT, TEXAS

Earl Gillespie drove back upstream toward the island they'd passed just a few minutes before in their downstream flight. The island split the river evenly, with the deeper, dredged shipping channel on its west side and an equally wide but shallower channel to the east.

As they neared the island, Earl slowed the boat, and fifty feet away, his counterpart in the other boat did the same. The sound of multiple powerful outboards could still be heard in the distance upstream, just around a bend.

"Which side of the island you reckon they'll come down?" Earl Gillespie asked. "I mean, I DO figure you mean to set an ambush, seeing as how we have two slow, sluggish boats with bellies full of water, against God knows how many faster, maneuverable ones. Thing is, sounds like we gotta set it fast, and if we pick the wrong side of the island, they'll just cruise on past."

Alvarez was already nodding and pointing to the west channel. "There, those empty barges moored against the island. We'll leave some bait to draw them into this channel then ambush them from the barges. Get us to the upstream end of the island, quick."

Earl turned into the west channel, and the second boat fell in behind. When they reached the north end of the little island where the channel split, Alvarez ordered Earl to stop a hundred yards inside the entrance to the west channel and put them alongside the second boat. He shouted over to the man at the wheel.

"Drop your anchor, then cut power and come aboard our boat. We'll leave your boat as bait, and when they stop to check it out, we'll open up on 'em from those barges," Alvarez said.

"The anchor will drag in this current," the man replied.

"It doesn't matter. It only has to slow the boat enough so it's still visible when they come around that bend," Alvarez said. "Which may be any minute, so move it."

The man was moving before Alvarez finished speaking, putting out the anchor as the others switched boats. Less than a minute later, Alvarez glanced nervously upriver and pointed Earl toward the first in a line of empty barges moored against the shore of the little island. He shouted instructions as they moved toward the barge.

"Okay. We'll split up. Jones, pick four men and we'll land you on this first barge." Jones nodded, and Alvarez continued. "Does anyone else have combat experience; before today, I mean?"

One man raised his hand.

"All right, you pick four men and we'll drop you at the second barge. That will leave Earl, me, and two men here on the boat. We'll pull out of sight downstream behind the third barge and engage targets of opportunity or any boats that make it downstream past you. Clear?"

There were hesitant nods, and Alvarez continued, looking at Jones and the other newly created squad leader.

"Spread out on the barges, and find something solid for cover. I don't know how many boats to expect, but it sounds like a bunch. If you get over-whelmed, do the best you can. If you have to retreat, jump into the mud and water on the shore side of the barges and crawl into the brush cover on the island. We'll reform on the opposite side of the island if it comes to that."

"When do we engage?" Jones asked.

"You'll be in the best position to see what's going on, so you decide when to fire, and when YOU open up, everyone else will fire at will. Got it?" Alvarez looked around the group. They were all nodding now, a bit more confidently.

"One last thing," Alvarez said. "A still target's a lot easier to hit than a moving one, so target the boat drivers. That should slow down their response as well."

He finished just as Earl pulled alongside the first barge. One by one, the men stood on the bridge rail and crawled up aboard the tall barge. He left Jones deploying his group and moved on to the second barge to repeat the operation. Two minutes later, Earl nosed the boat in behind the third barge, and Alvarez boosted himself up and moved across the barge to crouch at its edge, where he had a better view upstream.

He smiled as the first few boats rounded the bend at high speed, then slowed and made for the west channel and the bait boat. His smile faded quickly.

"Sweet Mother of God," he whispered to himself as he watched boat after boat turn into the west channel. They were powerboats of all types, no doubt looted from dealerships and private garages. He stopped counting at fifty, and the only thing they all had in common was they were all faster and more maneuverable than his own waterlogged vessel. He turned and moved rapidly back across the barge to yell down at the boat.

"Plan B, Earl. Pull the boat completely out of sight between the barge and the bank, and everyone climb up here and spread out. There's no way we could survive engaging this force on the water. We'll add our guns to the fight from this barge," Alvarez said.

Alvarez barely had his men positioned when Jones opened fire, prompting a fusillade from the second barge as well. It went as planned, and a dozen boat drivers dropped.

Except the plan hadn't included so many boats. Though the first strike was deadly, it wasn't disabling, and the other boats started moving again immediately. They'd stirred up a hornet's nest, and the hornets were pretty pissed.

Even though the distance was greater, Alvarez ordered his group to open fire, in hopes it would spread the cons out and draw some of the hellacious fire away from the first two barges.

Alvarez crouched behind the block of a pump engine, firing in disciplined three-round bursts, while the others fired from their own spots of cover.

"Hey, Alvarez," called Earl, from behind a hatch coaming.

"What?" Alvarez replied.

Earl flashed Alvarez a nervous grin. "Jones was right. Your plan sucks."

NECHES RIVER
JUST NORTH OF MCFADDEN BEND

Howell started to pull the lifeboat door closed after the last of the men had come aboard, but Jimmy Gillespie stopped her.

"I'm thinking we should keep a shooter here," Jimmy said. "And the same for the forward access hatch. Between that and a shooter at the gun ports on either side, we won't have any blind spots."

Howell nodded. "Makes sense. They'll probably start circling us like a pack of wolves anyway. We can at least try to hold them at bay until we get to the ship."

Jimmy nodded to Pete, who picked his way to the forward access hatch through the women and children seated on the deck. Jimmy's two brothers did the same, taking positions at the improvised gun ports on opposite sides of the lifeboat. Movement was difficult, with the boat full to over twice its rated capacity. Howell had ordered all the passengers to get as low as possible, and they were taking up almost every square inch of real estate the bottom of the lifeboat had to offer, in many cases on top of each other.

Howell headed downriver as fast as the lumbering lifeboat would go, wondering how long it would be before their attackers engaged. She didn't have to wonder long.

"Here they come," Pete said from the front hatch.

"They may not realize we have teeth," Howell yelled. "Make the first shots count. You only get to surprise them once."

"They're forming two lines to run down both sides," Pete yelled. "I'll take the lead boat on the left."

"I got the right," Jimmy yelled from behind her. She glanced back through the open door and only then realized he had used the closing dogs on the open door as footholds to boost himself up so he could steady his rifle on the top of the fiberglass canopy and shoot over it.

She watched through her viewing port as the attacking boats separated, two in line to her left, and three to her right. They grew larger as they raced toward her, and she had all she could do to keep from screaming SHOOT! SHOOT!

But she needn't have worried. She heard Pete's M4 in the front of the boat, and the driver of the lead boat slumped at the outboard, and the boat veered off at a crazy angle. Then Jimmy's gun barked, and like Pete, he had targeted the driver, striking the man in the arm.

The driver jerked, sending his boat smashing into the now driverless boat from the left column, capsizing both. The following boats only narrowly avoided the wreck and spread out wide to either side of the lifeboat, guns blazing.

Howell heard the strange double THWACK of bullets passing high, through and through the fiberglass canopy, punctuated with the altogether more terrifying sound of rounds striking the steel plates protecting her position. But most of the fire was directed at the front hatch, below which Pete now crouched, out of sight.

So intent were they on the front hatch, the cons roared past on either side oblivious to the side gun ports. The Gillespie brothers rewarded their inattention by shooting two cons out of their boats, one on each side.

The attackers roared past out of sight. Howell willed the lifeboat downriver as she heard Jimmy in the open doorway behind her, blazing away at the boats as they raced away upstream.

"GOT ONE OF THE BASTARDS!" she heard him yell, followed by, "THEY'RE COMING BACK!"

Jimmy's gun was their only defense now, as he was the only one who could see the attacking boats. She heard repeated three-round bursts as he fired, punctuated by lulls and muttered curses as he changed magazines.

"GET DOWN, MATE!" Jimmy yelled as he backed down the short steps into the lifeboat and fired aft through the open door.

Howell rolled out of the coxswain's chair to drop on top of him just as bullets shredded the unprotected fiberglass at the back of the canopy and tore through the coxswain's chair where she'd been sitting seconds before.

"Sorry, Jimmy," she said. "And thanks."

Jimmy only nodded. "This ain't good, ma'am. They stay back here on our ass, and we can't steer. Plus we only got one shooting position, and they'll have five or six guns on it. All they have to do is creep up close and start laying into us with those shotguns."

No sooner had Jimmy spoken than the back fiberglass bulkhead behind the coxswain's seat exploded as it was shredded by multiple loads of buckshot. Round after round tore through the bulkhead until all that was left was a ragged spiderweb of glass fibers. The coxswain's chair was destroyed, and the steering wheel hung at a crazy angle. All the children were screaming and crying out, and she had to yell to be heard above the bedlam.

"It doesn't matter now," Howell said. "Nobody's gonna be steering. But the engine is still running, so I hope—"

Another fusillade destroyed what was left of the fiberglass bulkhead, and debris rained down on their heads. When Howell looked up again, the throttle control was hanging by a single wire as the engine sputtered to a halt. Behind them, she heard the outboards cut back to a guttural rumble. They were there waiting, no doubt with all their guns trained on the lifeboat.

"Y'ALL THROW YOUR GUNS OVERBOARD AND WE'LL GO EASY ON YOU. BUT IF ANY MORE OF US GET HURT, Y'ALL ARE GONNA REGRET IT. THAT'S A PROMISE."

"What we gonna do, ma'am?" Jimmy asked.

Howell thought a moment. "As long as we stay low below the steel plates, I think we're safe enough. And they can shoot as many holes in us as they want, but they're not likely to sink us with all the extra buoyancy there is in a lifeboat. I don't think they're too eager to come charging in and get shot either, so it's a standoff as long as we're still armed."

"So what we gonna do?" Jimmy asked again.

Howell shrugged. "Stall and wait."

"Wait for what?"

"The cavalry," Howell said, reaching for the radio. "The ship's less than three miles away now. They can send the patrol boat out for a quick punch in the face, then rush back to cover the ship—"

But Hughes had apparently anticipated the situation. She lowered the radio as a new sound penetrated the bedlam of the screaming children and praying women—twin outboards, and big ones. She'd hardly processed the sound when it was blotted out by the sweet tune of a large-caliber automatic weapon. They raised their heads in unison just in time to see the cons' boats, and the cons in them, shredded by machine-gun fire. It was hard to watch, even though she had no doubts the men dying would have done the same to her, or worse.

She was still staring when the radio squawked.

"Mate? Georgia? Are y'all okay?" She recognized Torres' voice.

"That you, Magician?"

"That's me," came the reply. "First you see 'em, then they're dead. Any casualties? On our side, I mean?"

"We're okay here," Howell said, "but there are more cons coming down-river. A lot of them. Alvarez and Jones took some guys up to try to cover our escape. You have to help them."

"Roger that," Torres said. "Captain Hughes gave me fifteen minutes to bring y'all in, and I have ten left. Can you get back to the ship?"

"Don't worry about us, Magician. The current is with us and we'll paddle if we have to. Go help Alvarez, and hurry!"

***

Torres raced upriver at forty knots toward the sound of distant gunfire. It was measured at first, the intermittent three-round bursts of disciplined fire, but that soon dissolved into a continuous roar—fully automatic weapons or a whole lot of undisciplined shooters with semiautomatics. He had no doubt it was the latter.

The man beside him shook his head. "Sounds like a war."

Torres nodded. "And as long as it keeps up, we know our guys are in the fight."

He held that thought, an ear cocked to the sound of battle, straining to hear who might be carrying the day. But the disciplined fire was slacking, and the battle began to sound one-sided. Finally the firing stopped completely, a lull followed by separate individual shots. Torres' blood ran cold. Executions?

The building roar of powerful engines replaced gunfire, growing louder as his boat flew upriver. Ahead, the river divided into two channels around an island, and racing toward him out of the left channel was an armada of small craft, perhaps twenty or thirty boats. He saw the muzzle flashes and heard a bullet whiz by his ear before he heard the shot itself.

"Let 'em have it," he called to the bow gunner and was answered by the roar of the machine gun.

Heavy rounds tore into the approaching boats as if they'd hit a brick wall. The first wave stopped dead in the water, blasted to bits, and the following boats ran over the debris, either capsizing at speed or fouling their propellers.

It was over in seconds, with a few boats in the extreme rear turning to escape upstream while Torres circled what was left of the convict armada, his machine gunner blasting anything that moved. He saw a head surface to gulp air then submerge. He stopped, and as the boat drifted, the gunner turned back to him, his eyebrows raised in a question.

"We need intel," Torres said. "I want a prisoner."

The gunner nodded, and they floated silently, drifting down the river with the mass of debris. When the head didn't reappear, Torres surveyed the debris field and pointed toward the hull of a flat-bottom aluminum boat floating upside down.

"Put a burst through the far end of that hull over there," Torres said.

The gunner complied.

"WE'RE GONNA UNLOAD ON THAT HULL IF YOU DON'T COME OUT IN FIVE SECONDS. FIVE. FOUR. THREE..."

A head bobbed up beside the overturned boat. "Don't shoot. I'm unarmed," the man said.

"Swim over here, and don't try anything funny or we'll shred you. Got it?" Torres said.

The con swam over, and Torres ordered him to place his hands on the edge of the boat so the gunner could flex-cuff his wrists. Only then did they drag him into the boat and flex-cuff his ankles as well. They dumped him facedown in the bottom of the boat.

Torres started up the left channel around the island.

"Damn!" the gunner said. "Would you look at that?"

Drifting toward them on the current were scores of boats, many with bullet holes above the waterline, with dead cons sprawled in more than a few. Here and there along the west bank were more boats, obviously run aground by dying cons unable to control them.

The gunner shook his head. "Ain't this something. But where the hell are Alvarez and Jones?"

Torres shrugged and crept up the channel, finding no sign of the Coasties or their companions. At the north end of the island, he turned back downstream via the eastern channel. As he neared the southern end of the little island, a man in Coast Guard overalls stepped out of the brush and waved. Relief washed over Torres as he nosed the patrol boat into the little beach.

The relief faded when he saw the look on Alvarez's face.

"How bad?" Torres asked.

Alvarez took a deep breath. "Bad enough. Jones lost part of his ear and took another one in the shoulder, but I think he'll be all right. Two other walking wounded, both arm wounds. But we... I... lost one. His body's up on the barge."

"Who?" Torres asked.

Alvarez looked away, gazing downriver. When he turned back, his eyes were glistening. "A really good guy," he said. "Jimmy's dad, Earl Gillespie."

CHAPTER TWENTY-FOUR

M/V *Pecos Trader*
Sun Lower Anchorage
Neches River
Near Nederland, Texas

Day 30, 6:45 a.m.

They buried Earl Gillespie on a ridge of slightly higher ground running along the edge of the marshy island next to the ship. They used their single body bag, and Kenny Nunez, the bosun, worked through the night building a coffin. Jimmy Gillespie was well-liked on board, and there was no shortage of volunteers to dig his father's grave or help in any way possible to ease the burden on the Gillespie family.

Hughes scheduled the service for sunrise, with the shore party limited to family and those shipmates chosen to finish the burial. But everyone on board crowded the bow of *Pecos Trader*, standing in respectful silence while the brief ceremony played out below them. Everyone, that is, except Torres and a group of Coasties, who stood watch facing the river, alert to any threat.

Having never conducted a funeral, Hughes stuck to the Lord's Prayer and the Twenty-Third Psalm. He sat with Mrs. Gillespie as the patrol boat ferried them the short distance back to the ship's accommodation ladder.

"I'm sorry this was so quick and... basic, Mrs. Gillespie. I promise if... when things settle down, we'll try to do better," Hughes said.

Dorothy Gillespie shook her head. "Y'all did just fine, Captain. We appreciate what everyone's doing. And I doubt things will settle down for a while yet, if ever. Earl liked the river, so he'll be just fine here. If you want to make promises, just promise me I'll be beside him when my time comes."

Hughes swallowed hard and nodded. Dorothy Gillespie gave him a sad smile and reached over to pat his hand.

***

Hughes sipped coffee and glanced around the table at his council, noting strain and tension in each face. The events of the last day made it clear just how desperate their situation was.

"I'm thinking they saw the chance to grab hostages and tipped their hand," Torres said. "No way they deployed that many boats so quickly unless they were already staged for something. Besides, that tracks with what our prisoner says."

"Did you get any more out of him?" Hughes asked.

Torres shook his head. "He's definitely a peon and dumber than a rock besides. But he told us they've been collecting boats, and the rumor is they're going to attack very soon. It might actually be a good thing a few of the boats got away. None of these assholes strike me as heroes, and I doubt many of them will be eager to come charging up to the ship in an open boat now."

"Any confirmation on numbers?" Hughes asked.

"Pretty much the same thing the girl from Trixie's…"

The Coastie glanced nervously toward Gowan, but the chief engineer lowered his gaze to the table and said nothing.

"The girl from the woman's house said," Torres continued, "two thousand. But I suspect he's just parroting whatever he's heard. I doubt the dumb bastard could count to twenty-one without taking off his shoes and unzipping."

Chuckles eased the tension, and Hughes nodded. "Be that as it may, we have to assume an attack is imminent, and that it will be a big one. What's our head count now?"

Georgia Howell glanced down at her notes. "Assuming the entire original crew as shooters, plus the Coasties and the guys from the refugee group minus the wounded, we have forty—"

"Make that forty-three," Laura Hughes said. "The girls and I can all handle firearms, and I'm sure a number of the other women can as well."

"I stand corrected. We have plus forty-three shooters, which may exceed our gun inventory anyway." Howell looked at Torres.

Torres checked his own notes and shook his head. "I think we're okay there. We have eight M4s, the three AKs we took from the Cubans, three machine guns, also counting the one we took from the Cubans, two Barrett sniper rifles, and a few guns from Captain Hughes' place, as well as a mixed bag the new folks brought in yesterday. But we scavenged the boats Alvarez and his guys shot up, and got about two dozen more, mostly shotguns, handguns, and ARs, along with a fair amount of ammo. We'll be able to put a gun in the hand of anyone willing and able to use it."

"What about the other stuff we took from the Cubans?" Hughes asked.

Torres shook his head. "I don't see the grenades as being very useful unless the convicts actually get into the deckhouse and we're trying to hold them at bay as we fall back—not a scenario I want to contemplate—and we only have four grenades anyway. As far as the RPG goes, we only have the one. I think they're only accurate to around a hundred and fifty yards, and none of us have ever fired one, not to mention the fact the thing is like thirty-year-old Soviet surplus." He paused. "But weapons aren't really the problem."

Hughes nodded. "Numbers."

"Exactly," Torres said. "It's still forty or fifty shooters, many of them novices, against, depending on who you believe, up to two thousand convicts."

"Suggestions?" Hughes asked.

"A few," Torres said.

M/V *Pecos Trader*
Captain's Office

Day 30, 10:15 a.m.

Hughes took another sip of coffee, his fifth cup of the day. He'd miss it when it was gone and thought about stretching it out, but it was one of the few bits of normalcy left, and he vowed to indulge himself as long as it lasted.

"How about the towboat guys?" Laura said. "Thirty-seven men would almost double our defensive garrison."

Hughes shook his head. "Maybe, but they have no weapons, and we can't arm more than a few of them. And with an attack imminent, there's no way I can send out an escort to bring them in. The same with Kinsey. I can't let anybody stumble into this mess without warning them. They just have to stay away until it's settled, one way or another."

"How are you going to warn Kinsey? He's out of VHF range," Laura said.

"I can't, but I CAN reach Wellesley and warn him to stay put. He might be within VHF range of Kinsey, but even if he's not, Kinsey has to pass right by him at Calcasieu Lock. He'll be warned, one way or another."

Laura nodded, and Hughes drained his cup and rose from his chair. "I'd best go up to try Wellesley."

DAY 30, 1:40 P.M.

"How many again?" Spike McComb demanded.

"Uh... sixty-seven," Snag said, louder the second time.

"Sixty-seven boats? Your morons lost sixty-seven of my boats and didn't bring back one frigging hostage?"

"It ain't like they did it on purpose, Spike. I mean, they are mostly dead, after all," Snag said. "And boats ain't really the problem; there's plenty of boats lying around to gather up. Hell, there's one in every other garage."

Spike smashed his desk with his fist, and Snag jumped.

"WELL, WHAT THE HELL IS THE PROBLEM, SNAG? WHY DON'T YOU TELL ME?"

Snag flinched, but for once he held his ground. "That machine gun, that's what," he said, and held up his hands to stop what he knew would be Spike's immediate response.

"And don't go calling me a whiny pussy," Snag said. "That gun swept the boys off the water like a new broom, and there ain't none of 'em too enthusiastic about bein' the next targets. It don't matter if we have FIVE thousand men if they cut us up before we even get close."

Spike glared at Snag. "And what's your excuse for up by the shipyard and the railroad bridge where they shot the hell out of us? They didn't have no machine gun there."

"Yeah, but they had those sandbags to hide behind, and we didn't have enough time to—"

A strange look crossed Spike's face and he cut Snag off with a wave of his hand.

"Wh-what is it, Spike?" Snag asked. "The boys did the best—"

"Shut the hell up," Spike said. "I'm thinking."

Snag started to open his mouth again, but Spike silenced him with a glare. Then slowly, the corners of Spike's mouth turned up into a smile.

"Thanks, shit brain," Spike said. "It's a good thing one of us around here can think. We still got those tugboats we captured and the turds who were driving 'em?"

Snag nodded. "The boats are down in Port Arthur, but they won't do us no good. They're slow as hell."

"You let me worry about that. How about the boat drivers?"

Snag shrugged. "We threw 'em in the forced labor pool. I reckon they're still there, if they're alive. Why?"

"Go find one. I have an idea," Spike said.

M/V PECOS TRADER
SUN LOWER ANCHORAGE
NECHES RIVER
NEAR NEDERLAND, TEXAS

DAY 30, 5:20 P.M.

Hughes engaged the joystick of the bow thruster, eyes focused on Howell far away on the bow and leaning over the bulwark to peer at the water below. Howell's fist shot up and Hughes immediately released the joystick and watched the bow of the *Pecos Trader* inch starboard a few feet more before stopping. He spoke into his radio.

"How's it look, Mate?"

"I think we're there, Captain," she replied. "The bow is fifty feet off the island, and we're stirring up mud."

Hughes keyed his radio again. "How's the stern looking?"

"I think we're where you want, Captain," the second mate said. "We're maybe seventy-five or a hundred feet from the bank of the channel."

"Copy that," Hughes said. "You can secure from the bow and stern. Georgia, let's get a little ballast in her. Just enough where she's touching good in the mud, but don't wrinkle the bottom or get her stuck tight. We might get to leave here someday."

"Copy that," came Howell's reply, and Hughes cradled the mic and walked out to where Torres stood on the starboard bridge wing, looking out over the flat marsh and nodding his head.

"Happy, Mr. Torres?"

"As a clam, Captain. We couldn't really ask for a better defensive position," Torres said.

"I sure as hell hope so. I'm not really in the habit of putting my ship aground, even lightly."

Torres smiled and nodded, and Hughes looked out over their new position. The anchorage was deep enough to allow him to bring his fully loaded ship over five hundred feet up the southern leg of the oxbow, to where the channel not only got shallower but narrowed. There Hughes had swung *Pecos Trader* at right angles across the channel, effectively turning it into two bodies of water connected only by two extremely narrow and easily defended passages around either end of the ship.

Torres pointed up the oxbow channel. "This is perfect. They can only get to us by boat, and the only way they can get a boat to the starboard side is running it directly under our bow or stern or coming the long way around from the upriver entrance to the oxbow. And we'll see anything coming up that channel at least a half a mile before they get to us. It'll be a shooting gallery. Alvarez and me up on the flying bridge with the Barretts, can pretty much defend this whole side of the ship. We'll supplement that with the Cuban machine gun, since we don't have as much ammo for it. That leaves everybody else to defend the port side."

Hughes nodded. "We'll definitely have a height advantage. Where you gonna place the other machine guns? The port bridge wing?"

Torres shook his head. "That's actually TOO high to defend the gaps at either end of the ship. If they run in under the guns, it will be hard to depress the muzzles enough to target the attackers if they manage to get close to the ship. We'll put our machine guns on the main deck at the bow and stern so they can defend the gaps and have interlocking fields of fire to cover the whole port side. Then we'll spread the rest of our shooters out along the port side rail. We just need to improvise some cover."

"Chief Gowan is already working on that," Hughes said, and shook his head.

"What's the matter, Captain?"

"I was just thinking of all the rules we had in normal times. No matches or cigarette lighters on deck, all electrical equipment to be certified explosion proof, all tools to be non-sparking, and on and on." Hughes shook his head again. "And now we're standing here, calmly planning a frigging war on the main deck of a tanker loaded with diesel and gasoline. Thank God the inert gas system is working."

Torres shrugged. "Changing priorities, I guess. The chance of getting blown up by a spark doesn't even move the threat needle compared to being captured by a bunch of murderous convicts." He paused. "And about that, I think we got a pretty good shot here, but we need a fallback plan."

"I'm listening," Hughes said.

"Our whole strategy is based on superior firepower to keep them at bay, but guns jam or run out of ammo or get taken out by a lucky shot or fail for a dozen reasons you never thought possible. If that happens and they get aboard in any numbers, we're screwed," Torres said.

"That seems kind of obvious, Torres. Are you telling me this just to scare the crap out of me, or do you have a plan to get us unscrewed?"

Torres smiled. "Well, maybe less screwed would be more accurate. We need a fortified fallback position, and we need to prepare it now before things go to hell."

Hughes stroked his chin. "A citadel?"

"Exactly," Torres said.

DAY 32, 10:40 P.M.

Hughes stood on the bridge wing in the darkness, exhausted from two days of tension and constant work, looking downstream to where lights hidden from direct sight by the intervening tank farm cast a pale glow in the sky. He could hear the faint strains of country music muted by the distance. What the hell were those assholes doing?

He turned at a sound at the wheelhouse door.

"Cap?" called Dan Gowan.

"I'm here, Dan," Hughes said, and the beam of a small flashlight illuminated the deck as Gowan made his way over.

"We all set?" Hughes asked.

Gowan snorted. "I've been all set for a day or more. We'll have some nasty surprises for them if they get on deck, but I'm hopin' it won't come to that."

The silence grew until Hughes broke it. "You ready to tell me what's been eating you? You haven't been your usual charming and argumentative self."

Gowan sighed. "I reckon you know, Jordan. It's Trixie. I'm so sorry."

"She's just a conniving bitch, Dan. There's nothing you could do about that."

"Yeah, but if I hadn't been such a dumb ass, Georgia wouldn't have gone after her. Then maybe Jimmy's dad would still be alive and Jones and those other boys wouldn't be shot up. Any way you slice it, that's on me," Gowan said.

"Dan Gowan, you stop that nonsense this minute!"

Both men turned to the door at the sound of Laura Hughes' voice and watched the flashlight beam bob toward them in the dark.

"I mean it," she said. "You WERE being a dumb ass, but you're certainly not the first man to act stupid because some bimbo waggled her silicone implants at him. But now it's time for you to STOP being a dumb ass and put this behind you. Nobody blames you, and I know that for a fact, so knock off the pity party. We all need you at one hundred percent, and we can't afford to have you moping around. Is that clear?"

Hughes heard Gowan take a step back in the dark. "I... I guess so. But I still think—"

"That's just it, you're NOT thinking, because otherwise you'd be thinking about those four girls Georgia and the others saved," Laura said. "Do you think for one minute that Earl Gillespie or Jones or the other guys who were wounded would've left those girls in that house if they knew about it, whether Trixie was involved or not?"

"No, but I—"

"It was Earl's decision to stay with Alvarez and delay the cons to protect his family and the others. His decision, Dan. Not yours. I didn't know the man, but I'm pretty sure from the sons he raised he'd have made that decision ten times out of ten, even if he knew it was going to put him in the ground." Laura stopped for a breath, then continued before Gowan could protest. "And if you still think you owe a debt to Earl Gillespie, then apply yourself to keeping the rest of his family alive. I'm pretty sure he'd be happy with that program, so if you want to do penance, there it is."

She stopped, and the silence grew.

"Feel better now?" Hughes asked into the darkness.

"Well, yeah. Actually I do," Gowan said.

Hughes laughed. "I was talking to Laura." He grunted as she threw an elbow into his ribs. "Hey! That hurt!"

"Serves you right," she said, and Hughes heard footsteps as his wife moved to hug Dan Gowan.

"You're a good man, Dan Gowan, but sometimes you are a dumb ass. That Trixie's not fit to shine your shoes, so good riddance."

Hughes heard soft thumps as Laura patted Gowan's back, and burst out laughing when he heard Gowan say wistfully, "But she does have spectacular tits."

"Ouch! Damn, Laura! I was just kidding."

But Hughes' laughter was infectious, and soon the others joined him. One problem was solved, at least; he only wished they could all be solved as easily.

The laughter died and Gowan said, his voice cracking slightly. "Thank you, Laura. I really do feel much better," then more matter-of-factly, "I gotta go see how my napalm is coming along."

"Napalm? What the hell are you up to, Dan?" Hughes asked.

Gowan's light flicked on as he moved away. "I'll explain tomorrow after I test it."

"What's that all about?" Laura asked as they watched Gowan's light bob away.

"With Dan you never know, but I guarantee it will be original," Hughes said.

"He's such a nice guy," Laura said. "He really needs someone, especially given how screwed up everything is. We all need someone to hold on to."

"Laura," Hughes said, warning in his voice.

"What?" Laura replied, all innocence. "Just thinking out loud, that's all."

"Yeah, and we all know what that can lead to—"

"Relax, Captain, sir. I have nothing but the good of the crew at heart," she said, then changed the subject quickly before he had time to object further. "What do you think is going on with the lights and music downriver?"

"Not a clue," he said. "But I doubt it's anything good."

CHAPTER TWENTY-FIVE

Spike stood in the glare of the harsh work lights and watched as the workers put the finishing touches on the barges. He glanced upstream as the sound of the revelry in the park next door momentarily crested, allowing it to be heard above the muted roar of the portable generators in the little shipyard. He turned to Snag.

"You sure the barges are gonna be ready by daylight? I don't want these assholes next door to peak and crash too soon. I want the good part of the high to be finished and for them to be in the agitated and mean phase; otherwise we'll have to reschedule. We've already given that ship too long to get ready as it is," Spike said.

"We're good," Snag said. "They're finishing the last barge now. All four will be ready at daylight, just like you wanted." He smiled. "And it don't matter how much time we give the ship, 'cause they ain't gonna be ready for this. Using their own idea against 'em is genius."

"Presuming they ain't figured it out," Spike said. "I worry about that radar. Did you do what I told you?"

Snag nodded. "To the letter. We picked barges that were already close by and moved 'em here a little bit at a time. That's what took us so long. They'd have to be staring at the radar all the time to catch us moving 'em, and now we're so close it don't matter. Besides, even if they see us coming, there ain't a thing they can do about it now. It's perfect."

Spike grunted, hiding his pleasure at the praise. "If it works. Those machine guns might have armor-piercing stuff."

"That's the beauty of it, Spike. We found plenty of plate in the shipyard, and weight ain't a problem because the barges are empty anyway. We used a double thickness of three-quarter-inch plate for the shields and stuck two inches of plywood from Home Depot in between." Snag grinned and shook his head. "Ain't nothing gonna get through those shields. We can drive right up to the side of that ship and say howdy do."

Spike nodded, then jerked his head toward the sounds of revelry upriver. "Those assholes gonna be ready? Shields or not, the first ones out from behind them and up those stairways are gonna be stopping some bullets, and I don't want it to be our regular guys."

"They'll be ready," Snag said, and smiled as he shook his head. "I gotta hand it to you there too. When you had us set up meth production right after we busted out, I didn't know what the hell you were doing, but it was a stroke of genius is what it was."

Spike returned the smile. "What's the final count?"

"Almost eight hundred, give or take. They're all over there now havin' a high ol' time. I got some of the boys pushing 'em all the meth they can handle, and we threw 'em some of the used-up whores from the cells." Snag laughed. "It ain't like they can tell the difference."

"How about the second wave?" Spike asked.

"Relax, Spike," Snag said. "I done just like you said. I left enough guys scattered through the stations to keep the niggers and the beaners from gettin' any ideas, and the rest are ready to close in for the kill—almost five hundred of 'em. It's gonna be epic, man!"

Spike nodded, satisfied. He looked upriver and stroked his beard. "Okay, you done a good job on this, Snag. But you still got a long night ahead of you. Stay here and make sure they finish up on the barges; then just before sunrise, get on over to the park and whip those idiots up a bit. Give 'em the standard speech about the ship being fulla mud people and race traitors who have food and supplies that rightly belong to us. You know the drill."

"Gotcha," Snag said. "You can count on—"

"I ain't done yet," Spike said. "We need to make sure these morons take out any machine guns. So tell 'em anybody who captures a machine gun can have their pick of the women captives. Hell, tell 'em they get their pick of TWO women captives."

Snag nodded. "Will do, Spike. Are you really gonna—"

"Of course not. We'll just give 'em some more meth and they'll forget about it anyway."

M/V *PECOS TRADER*
SUN LOWER ANCHORAGE
NECHES RIVER
NEAR NEDERLAND, TEXAS

DAY 33, 5:05 A.M.

Georgia Howell stood on the port bridge wing, gazing downriver toward the glow of the mysterious lighted area now fading against the predawn sky. The music stopped an hour earlier, replaced by the muted sound of faraway shouts and cheering. That too stopped a few minutes earlier, giving her a strong uneasy feeling. Something was about to happen.

She moved into the wheelhouse and went straight to the radar, doing a double take as she saw a target separate from the riverbank and proceed upstream toward them at a leisurely pace. She reached for the phone, then thought better of it and sounded the general alarm. Only then did she pick up the phone and call Jordan Hughes.

***

Hughes was sleeping fully clothed and woke instantly at the clanging of the general alarm. He swung his feet over the edge of the bed and was pulling on his boots when he answered the bedside phone to hear Howell's voice.

"Captain—"

"On my way, Georgia," he said as he hung up and finished lacing his boots.

Laura was beside him by the time he stood. She wrapped him in a tight hug.

"Is this it?" she asked into his chest.

"Probably," Jordan said, and Laura turned her face up and kissed him.

"I love you," Jordan said. "Be careful, and tell the girls I love them."

Laura nodded and hugged him tighter.

"I have to go, love," he said.

She released him and busied herself with her own boots as he dashed out the door and up the steps to the bridge. He joined Howell at the radar and heard hurried footsteps clang on the metal stairs to the flying bridge—Torres and Alvarez moving into position with sniper rifles.

"What ya got, Georgia?" he asked.

"Looks like a push boat and multiple barge tow," Howell said. "We won't have a visual until she makes the next bend; then we should be able to see her across the marsh with the binoculars. But something else bothers me." She pointed at the screen. "What do you make of that?"

Following close behind the towboat was a large, amorphous, flickering ghost of a target. Hughes looked at it and shook his head. "I'd say it was a whole lot of fiberglass and wood pleasure boats running close together."

Howell nodded. "That was my take."

"How long before we have a visual?" Hughes asked.

"Five minutes, maybe ten. Then another ten before it gets here."

Hughes nodded and walked over to kill the clanging general alarm. "We have a lot of nervous folks out there; I better give them an update." He picked up the PA system mic, and his voice boomed through the deckhouse and across the open deck.

"We have a target on radar approaching from downriver, with an approximate ETA of twenty minutes. We are assuming it's hostile until we know otherwise. We will have visual contact in five to ten minutes and I will update you at that time. Please stay vigilant and watch upstream as well as down. If you see anything suspicious, please pass the word to the bridge. Thank you."

Hughes hung up the mic and gazed down at the main deck. He watched Laura move to her position on the port side near the center of the defensive line, with their twin daughters Jana and Julie in tow, and silently cursed them all for their stubbornness. Laura had seen through his plan to station her in the infirmary to await casualties and quietly but firmly informed him she would do more good on the firing line. Then she had to reap what she'd sown when their twins insisted on joining her.

In the end, it had been fifteen-year-old Julie's logic that carried the argument. "So let me get this straight," she'd asked innocently. "We'll be LESS likely to get hurt if the convicts actually DO get aboard?" Even in the stress of the moment, the memory brought a smile. She was destined to be a lawyer, that one, except there weren't any more lawyers.

There were fine folks falling in all along that defensive line as he looked down on the main deck. Two Coasties manned the machine gun aft while Jones, despite his injuries, had insisted on handling the gun on the bow. He was assisted by Pete Brown, who hadn't recovered from finding the massacred families. Gone was Pete's quick smile and easy laugh, replaced by the weight of perpetual sorrow and suppressed fury even the presence of his family failed to lift. He only seemed comfortable with Jimmy Gillespie, Jones, and the other members of the earlier rescue mission, as if the shared experience had bonded them more closely than family.

The rest of their new Coastie shipmates not otherwise assigned and those survivors and crewmen with military experience were spread along the firing line to support the inexperienced. Hughes sighed. They were as ready as they'd ever be. He turned back toward the radar, but Howell was gone. He found her on the port bridge wing, peering through binoculars across the flat marsh toward the distant river bend.

"A little early, aren't you?"

She lowered the binoculars and turned to him with a sheepish grin. "Patience isn't one of my virtues."

Hughes laughed. "Believe me, after four years I've figured that out."

Her smile faded. "Are you as scared as I am, Captain?" she asked quietly.

"Frigging terrified," Hughes said. "And if I could move us all out of harm's way, I'd do it in a heartbeat, but this isn't exactly a speedboat we're on."

Howell nodded and raised her binoculars again to stare downstream.

"What do you make of that?" she asked.

Hughes raised his own glasses.

He muttered a curse, then called to the Coasties on top of the wheelhouse. "HEY TORRES! DOES THAT DEFENSIVE PLAN OF YOURS HAVE AN OPTION B?"

***

Torres stood on the bridge wing and lowered the binoculars. "They're shields all right," he said. "But I doubt they're armor plate, and I don't know how thick they are. We might be able to punch through them, but the problem is we don't know what the target is on the other side. That's an awful big area just to shoot and hope. We might do better with the wheelhouse on the tugboat. It's armored too, but I'd say that's our best shot to keep 'em away."

Hughes nodded and looked downstream at the approaching tow. The boat was made fast to the opposite side of the barges, using the bulk of the barges themselves plus the shields atop them to screen the boat. Only the top of the towboat's wheelhouse peeked over the bulk of the barges, and it was shielded as well. He rubbed his chin, wondering how they intended to push the barges up to the ship without seeing it, then realized they didn't have to. *Pecos Trader* was a stationary target; all they had to do was move into position using landmarks on the opposite riverbank, then push the barges straight across the river and up against the ship.

"Well, we have to try something," Hughes said. "Can you hit the wheelhouse from here?"

Torres looked at Hughes as if he found the question insulting and yelled up to the flying bridge. "ALVAREZ! PUT THREE ROUNDS INTO THE WHEELHOUSE ON THAT BOAT."

Alvarez responded by firing three shots at short intervals. All produced loud clangs which echoed across the water, but nothing more. The barges continued toward them as if nothing had happened.

"Well, that sucked," Georgia Howell said.

There were nods from the small group on the bridge wing, which now included Dan Gowan.

"How about the RPG?" Hughes asked.

Torres shook his head. "Maybe if we could hit the boat, but she's way out of effective range for an RPG, and nothing else we have will work. We might have a shot with concentrated rifle fire if we could see the rest of the boat, but it's hidden behind the barges. We need a friggin' mortar."

Gowan nodded and started toward the wheelhouse door. "Be right back," he said.

M/V *Tilly*
Neches River
Approaching *Pecos Trader*

Same Day, 5:19 a.m.

Snag almost lost control of his bladder when the first round slammed into the wheelhouse shield. He was cowering on the deck with the ashen-faced towboat captain when the next two rounds impacted scant seconds later. He pulled his Glock and shoved the muzzle against the captain's head.

"Get back up there and drive this boat," Snag said. "Or it ain't bullets from outside you'll need to worry about."

Trembling, the man did as ordered, and Snag scrambled to his feet as well, thankful none of his underlings had witnessed his momentary weakness. He looked at the shielding and smiled. He'd had a feeling Spike was gonna send him on the boat, and he'd tripled protection here just to be on the safe side. He hadn't survived as long as he had by being dumb.

***

Hughes watched Dan Gowan rush across the bridge wing to the steps up to the flying bridge, carrying a cardboard box. First Engineer Rich Martin

285

was close behind with another. Hughes and the others fell in behind the engineers as they raced up the steps to their improvised air cannon.

"Dan," Hughes said, "I don't think throwing chunks of concrete at them is gonna do much good."

Gowan was shaking his head as he swung the muzzle around toward Rich, out of breath from his recent run down the stairs and back. "Not... concrete," he said. "Homemade... napalm."

Hughes was confused. "What the hell are you talking about—"

Rich Martin, a little less winded, filled in the blanks as he and Gowan worked. "It was the chief's idea, Captain. He had Polak go through all the stores and equipment and gather up all the Styrofoam packing material he could find. Then we dissolved it in gasoline, 'cause that's really all napalm is, jellied gasoline. Anyway, it worked. You set this crap on fire and it's hard to put out, and what's more, it sticks pretty good to whatever it touches. We filled up a bunch of aluminum soda cans. If it works like we hope, they'll split open on impact and spread this stuff all over the place."

Gowan was nodding emphatically as they worked and Rich talked.

Hughes looked downriver. "Can you reach them?"

"I don't know," Gowan said. "But this stuff is a lot lighter than concrete, so we should be able to shoot farther with the same air pressure." He looked back toward Rich Martin. "You ready, Rich?"

Rich nodded. "Ready as I'll ever be," he said, with a napalm round started into the muzzle of their makeshift cannon and his broomstick ramrod close at hand.

"All right," Gowan said. "Light her up and shove her home, but make sure not to let any of it get on you, because it's not coming off."

Rich finished and Gowan swung the muzzle downstream toward the approaching target. "I got no idea if I can even hit them," he said. "I'm just going to try to get one somewhere on target; then we'll fine-tune it from there. Man the firing valve, Rich. I wish we'd had time to work on these sights some more," Gowan muttered as he looked down the barrel. "Okay, Rich. Ready. Set. Fire!"

Rich cycled the quick closing valve open and closed, and there was a loud pop as four hundred and fifty pounds of air pressure flung the improvised round into the air, and the group watched it arc toward the target.

"I think it went out, Chief," Rich said.

"And I overshot them," Gowan said, disappointment in his voice as the round sailed over his target by a wide margin. "I figured it would drop more, and I was trying to compensate."

He barely finished speaking when the round impacted a paved road running along the river's edge. Flame bloomed across the width of the road, a broad circle of fire burning brightly.

Rich grinned. "I guess it didn't go out after all."

Gowan was already swinging the muzzle down. "Load another. I think I've got it now. These are light enough not to drop much at all."

The next round impacted one of the shields on the barge, leaving a large circle of flame burning on its surface. Gowan turned his attention to the towboat shield and managed to hit it with the third round, the other two rounds leaving more burning spots on the barge shields.

"See if you can drop one on the towboat itself," Torres said.

Gowan shook his head. "The aimed trajectory is too flat. To hit the boat, I'd have to aim up in the air and try to drop it straight down. And since we can't see most of the boat, I wouldn't really know if we were hitting it or not. But if I keep hitting the wheelhouse shields, maybe the burning stuff will drip down on the boat and set it on fire."

"Do it," Hughes said. "It's not like we have anything else to hit them with."

***

Snag saw something sail overhead to hit the riverbank and burst into flame.

"What the hell was that?" he asked aloud, but the terrified towboat captain only shook his head.

The fire ashore was followed a minute later by dull thuds from the barge, followed by excited shouts. As Snag was trying to work out what was happening, something struck the wheelhouse shield with a resounding THUD, followed seconds later by shouts of 'FIRE ON DECK!'

Snag felt panic rising. He pulled his gun again and shoved it in the captain's face. "What the hell is going on?"

"How would I know? I've been right here with you," the terrified man replied.

Snag jammed the muzzle of the gun hard into the captain's cheek. "DO SOMETHING!"

"Okay, okay. I'll... I'll try. But you only left me one man—"

THUD! Another round hit the shield, and the terrified deckhand burst into the wheelhouse.

"Whatever that stuff is, it's burning all over the bow. I used up a fire extinguisher, and that knocked it down, but it came right back," he said.

"Start the fire pump and get a hose on it," the captain yelled, and the man nodded and rushed out of the wheelhouse just as another round impacted the shield.

***

Hughes glanced at his watch and studied the flaming vessels continuing toward *Pecos Trader* undeterred. "They might be burning, but they're not stopping," he said aloud to no one in particular. He turned, his eyebrows raised in a question, as Georgia Howell came out of the wheelhouse.

"From the radar plot, it looks like they'll be directly across from us in five minutes, and it won't take them more than five more to cross the river and jam those barges against our side," she said.

Hughes turned at another shout of exultation.

"I think we're getting the hang of this," Gowan yelled as he swiveled the muzzle back toward Rich to load another round. Hughes nodded; by his timing, they were getting off four or five rounds a minute.

The wheelhouse shield was engulfed in flames now, and Torres pointed to one of the scattered places where the napalm burned on the barge shields. "Look at that white smoke pouring out around the edges of those shields. Something is burning behind them. I bet they got wood reinforcement."

Gowan shrugged. "The wheelhouse shields are burning pretty good. We may as well give the others a little attention."

He depressed the muzzle a bit to target the barge shields. By the time the barges were almost abreast of *Pecos Trader* across the river, the shields were burning for their entire length.

***

"I can't stop it, Captain," The deckhand said between gasps. "I hit it with water, and the fire just floats on top. Fact is, I spread it; some of the flames floated aft and set that pile of mooring lines on the stern on fire. And the lines to the barges are burning too. If they part, we'll lose the tow."

Snag listened in disbelief and stifled a cough. The thick synthetic mooring lines were impregnated with dirt and grease, and their noxious smoke mingled with the wood smoke from the burning plywood in the barge shields to engulf the wheelhouse in a thick funk. On the barges, he could hear angry shouts, no doubt directed at the ship raining fire on them. At least he didn't have to worry about the meth heads calming down. He jammed his pistol into the captain's head again.

"We lose these barges before they're jammed up against the side of that ship, and you're dead."

"But I... I can't control the lines burning—"

"Then you better make sure we get across the river sooner rather than later," Snag said.

The man nodded and rammed the throttles further forward in hopes of coaxing a tiny bit more speed out of his ungainly tow.

Snag looked aft from the wheelhouse at the flock of boats sheltering around them in the shadow of the barges. Close-packed and hard-pressed to maneuver in the tight space, they nonetheless managed; none of them wanted to become easy targets for a machine gun.

The boats held the second wave: five hundred hard-core members of the Aryan Brotherhood of Texas. But on the edges of the swarm were boats full of sacrificial meth heads, armed to the teeth and outfitted with boarding ladders and grappling hooks. To this group Snag had also promised the pick of the women captives to the first man who boarded *Pecos Trader*. He smiled. Dumb asses, all of them. It never seemed to occur to the meth heads the man or men capturing the machine gun AND the first man aboard from the small boats couldn't ALL have first pick of the captives. Not that it mattered. Presuming they lived, all they were getting was more meth.

Snag watched the west bank recede as the boat maneuvered the barges across the river toward the ship, the boats clustered in the shadow of the barges following like so many mechanical ducklings.

***

Hughes stood on the bridge wing as the burning barges crept toward them in a line parallel to the ship. He saw gaps near the tops of the burning shields, each perhaps four to five feet wide. Through the gaps he glimpsed platforms and what he took to be handrails, and then he understood; they'd built shielded stairways up from the decks of the barges to allow the cons to rush aboard the main deck of the *Pecos Trader* from a dozen sally ports. Hughes looked over to where Torres stood at the rail, well aft of him on the bridge deck, with their single Cuban RPG on his shoulder.

"Ahh... he's getting pretty close, Mr. Torres," Hughes called, just as flame shot out the rear of the tube on Torres' shoulder, and the grenade flew across the gap toward the shielded wheelhouse of the approaching push boat.

Things seemed to move in slow motion as the projectile moved straight toward its target, then veered sharply at the last moment to miss the boat by a foot and explode harmlessly in the river two hundred feet beyond the approaching threat. Hughes muttered a curse and looked back to where Torres was lowering the tube from his shoulder, a scowl on his face.

***

Snag flinched as the grenade flew past the wheelhouse of the push boat and exploded in the river beyond. A rocket! They had frigging rockets!

He jammed his gun into the captain's cheek again.

"How much longer, damn you?" he demanded.

"T-ten minutes! Ma-maybe less," the terrified man stammered.

Snag glanced nervously at his watch. "If it's eleven, you're a friggin' dead man."

***

"Can we pull our people back and set up one of the machine guns to sweep the port side as they try to board?" Hughes asked.

Torres shook his head. "I'm betting they're going to try to shoot the gaps on either end of the ship with the small boats and hit us on the starboard side too. We need the machine guns to plug those holes. Besides"—Torres nodded down the deck—"if we hit those shields at an angle, any ricochets might take out the opposite machine gun. There's just too much of a likelihood of friendly fire."

Hughes looked at the barges again and gave a nervous nod. "I guess this is the 'no plan survives first contact with the enemy' part, right?"

Torres nodded. "But we should pull back from the rail to the centerline like you suggested and divide our shooters into groups, each to concentrate fire into one of the barge sally ports. And half of each group should be ready to switch fire to the starboard side as needed. We'll use the Cuban machine gun as planned to target any boats that make it to the starboard side of the ship, and Alvarez and I will stay up top as overwatch to help deal with anyone who makes it aboard."

Hughes nodded, moving toward the stairs. "I'll get them organized—"

Georgia Howell moved to cut him off. "That's my job, Captain."

"Negative, Mate. Stay here and warn us if something is developing, and be ready to sound the signal if it looks like we're about to be overrun—"

"No, sir! You're commanding. You need to see—"

"And I'm commanding from the front and telling YOU to follow orders. Are we clear?"

"But, Captain... Jordan..."

"My family's down there, Georgia. I won't stand up here and watch them being shot at. It's just... it's just too hard. Are we clear?" The question was softer this time.

"Clear," Howell said softly.

Hughes turned toward the door, then hesitated. "What about the kids and noncombatants? That all squared away?"

Howell nodded. "Forted up in the steering gear room. Polak and one of his guys are down there with twelve gauges. They'll shoot anybody coming in who's not us."

Hughes nodded and moved to the central staircase. He glanced to port as soon as he reached the open deck. The barges were less than fifty yards away now, and he could see movement through the gaps of the sally ports. He moved along the defensive line, pulling his people back to the centerline of the vessel to find cover as best they could, and formed them into groups charged with defending the section of railing across from each barge sally point.

Task done, he found cover behind a pipe support in view not only of his designated sally port, but Laura and the girls in the next group further aft. If they retreated back to the deckhouse, he'd make sure his family didn't get left behind in the confusion. The barges were ten feet away now, inching closer.

"I never expected to be here doing this."

He turned to see Dan Gowan standing beside him, facing the approaching barges with a Winchester .30-30 in his hand. His cheek bulged from a huge wad of chewing tobacco.

Hughes nodded and turned back toward the barges. "Me neither. But don't let me catch you spitting that nasty—"

His voice was drowned in a maelstrom of noise as the machine guns opened up on the bow and stern, and a savage war cry sounded from hundreds of crazed meth heads on the barges.

CHAPTER TWENTY-SIX

Snag stood in the wheelhouse window of the towboat and gave the hand signal. Engines roared, and boats peeled off the outside of the swarm into two roughly equal groups to jet at full speed around opposite ends of the barges, bound for the narrow gaps at either end of the ship. He heard the machine guns and seconds later felt a shuddering thud through his feet as the barges impacted the ship's side.

"Now you better well hold them there, if you know what's good for you," he said to the towboat captain.

The man looked relieved. "Nothing to it now. As long as I keep the engines going ahead and don't touch the steering, we'll stick here like glue."

"You don't have to do anything else?" Snag asked.

"No. That's it…"

The man realized his mistake a split second before Snag shot him in the forehead.

"Good," Snag muttered. "I got things to do, and I was worried about leaving you alone."

Snag moved down the inside stairway and found the young deckhand cowering in the main deck passageway. The boy put up his hands. "Don't kill me, mister, please! I'll do anything you want."

Snag smiled. "Relax, son. I won't shoot you as long as you're straight with me. Now what's the best way for us to get off the boat?"

"Starboard side's burning like hell, but the port side is all right. I can show you," the boy said.

"No need," Snag said, then shot the boy in the head and moved toward the port side. He exited the deckhouse and waved one of the boats over. He was about to jump aboard when he glanced toward the barges and saw the still figures of meth heads at the back of the mob. That wasn't right; they should all be pressing forward.

He motioned for the boat driver to wait, then ran forward to climb the ladder on the port push knee at the front of the towboat. When his head was above the barge deck, he yelled at the milling mob.

"THE TOWBOAT IS ON FIRE AND SINKING!" He pointed to the burning shields on the barges. "AND THESE BARGES ARE FULL OF GASOLINE! Y'ALL NEED TO TAKE THAT SHIP AND TAKE IT NOW SO YOU CAN GET OFF THESE BARGES AND WE CAN MOVE THEM AWAY! AND DON'T TRY TO JUMP IN THE WATER, IT'LL SOON BE COVERED WITH BURNING GASOLINE. PASS THE WORD!"

Word spread through the back of the mob like fire through the nonexistent gasoline. The pressure from the back of the mob would likely counter any developing lack of enthusiasm at the front. Snag smiled. Sometimes you just had to know how to motivate people.

***

Hughes braced his rifle against the vertical stanchion, firing economically. Their impromptu plan was working better than he'd dared hope. Though sheltered behind their shields, the screaming cons were fully exposed when they topped the improvised stairways to drop over the rail on to the ship's deck, and the defenders' massed fire into each sally port was keeping the corks in all the bottles. Moreover, the growing piles of dead and wounded at the top of each stairway seemed to be noticeably diminishing the enthusiasm of those attackers still behind the shields.

The success of the main deck defenders left Torres and Alvarez little to do on the port side, but as the machine guns fell silent, Hughes heard the sporadic boom of the sniper rifles engaging targets to starboard. He keyed his radio.

"Captain to bridge. Request SITREP. Over."

"The boats swarmed the gaps. The machine guns took some of them out, but there were just too many and too close. Estimate thirty to forty boats made it to starboard. Repeat. Estimate thirty to forty boats made it to the starboard side. Snipers and bridge machine gun are trying to engage, but most of the boats are sheltering close to the hull where they can't be seen well without our guys exposing themselves to massed return fire. Do you copy? Over."

"I copy. Can we re-task the lower machine guns to starboard? Over."

"Negative. There are still a lot of boats behind the barges. If we change the guns, it will only get worse. We need to—"

Loud clangs from behind him on the starboard side diverted Hughes from the situation in his immediate front.

The PA system boomed. "GRAPPLING HOOKS AND BOARDING LADDERS SIGHTED STARBOARD SIDE. STAND BY TO REPEL BOARDERS STARBOARD. REPEAT. STAND BY TO REPEL BOARDERS STARBOARD SIDE."

Hughes glanced up and down the line as the designated defenders responded, then turned himself and walked a few steps to starboard to crouch behind another pipe support. Gowan was there, focused on the rail where the top end of a boarding ladder appeared.

"Isn't this some John Paul Jones shit?" Gowan asked.

Hughes was about to answer when a would-be boarder scampered up a boarding ladder and reached for the handrail. Hughes raised his rifle, but inexplicably, the attacker lost his grip and screamed as he fell from sight. Elsewhere down the starboard side, other boarders were falling, without a shot being fired.

"What the…"

"Damned if it didn't work," Gowan said.

"Damned if WHAT didn't work?" Hughes asked.

"Rich and I greased up all the handrails last night." Gowan glanced over with a lump-jawed grin. "I didn't want to bother you with it, seeing as how particular you are about keeping the main deck clean and all." He turned back toward the starboard rail and shot a stream of tobacco juice on the deck, then turned back to Hughes and grinned even wider, the picture of satisfied innocence.

"How is it you can piss me off even when you're doing something good?" Hughes asked.

Gowan shrugged. "Just a knack, I guess."

But Gowan's smile faded at the clang of grapples and boarding ladders in two dozen more places along the side. Then an attacker was up and over, ignoring the rail and diving over it to roll on the deck. The man scrambled for the cover of a set of mooring bitts, but was shot several times before he got there. Incursions increased, each ending with a dead boarder. They were containing the assault, but using half their defensive firepower to do it. The gunfire increased in intensity behind them, and Hughes glanced nervously back over his shoulder.

Something had changed. The attackers were no longer probing tentatively from the sally ports, but vomiting out of them as if pushed from behind. Most were shot down at the rail, but the sheer volume and speed of their advance ensured a few made it to the ship's deck. Some, but not all of those, fell to the guns of the overwatch; Torres and Alvarez were split now, port and starboard, and the surviving attackers found cover on board and began to return fire.

Hughes flinched as a bullet ricocheted off a pipe beside his head—from the wrong direction.

"DAN," he shouted, "PASS THE WORD! EVERY OTHER SHOOTER TO STARBOARD SHOULD SWITCH BACK TO THE PORT SIDE!"

"I'M ON IT," Gowan yelled back.

Hughes nodded and moved back a few steps to port in a crouching run. He glanced aft, relieved to see Laura and his twin daughters unharmed, firing steadily. But here and there along the line, he saw defenders down. He swallowed his panic and sighted down his rifle to take out an attacker.

"It's like they're friggin' crazy or something," said Jimmy Gillespie beside him. "I swear the last two bastards I shot were grinnin' like idiots."

Hughes' radio squawked.

"Bridge to captain. Over."

Hughes keyed his mic. "Go, Georgia."

"They've broken out forward, just aft of the forecastle. We've lost control of the forward sally port and they're pouring aboard." Hughes heard the stress in her voice and glanced forward to see the backs of defenders falling back toward him, running backwards from one place of concealment to the next, firing as they fell back.

"It's time, sir," said Howell over the radio.

"What about the guys on the bow?" Hughes asked.

"Cut off," Howell said. "The boarders are all the way across the deck and have hooked up with the attackers to starboard. The guys on the bow can't turn the machine gun on them without risking that any misses will hit your position. There…. there's nothing we can do for them."

Hughes felt a hundred years old. Lose two good men… or risk everyone? He swallowed. "Sound the signal."

The air was split with the mournful sound of the ship's whistle and the raucous clanging of the general alarm, competing with but not blocking out the gunfire. Up and down the line, designated shooters held their positions as the rest fell back toward the deckhouse, establishing new positions to cover the retreat of the others. They leapfrogged aft, carrying their casualties with them, with Hughes always in the rear. He'd leave no one else behind.

The deck behind them filled with attackers spilling through the now un-defended sally ports. With strength in numbers and the tide of the battle going in their favor, they grew increasingly bold and aggressive, and Hughes was only twenty feet ahead of the surge when two seamen slammed the wa-tertight door of the deckhouse behind him and dogged it down tight. He gave an approving nod as they lashed the dog handles so it couldn't be opened; then he started up the stairs for the bridge.

They were secure for the moment. As a precautionary measure before the attack, Georgia Howell had supervised the unbolting and removal of all the external stairways and ladders for the first two levels of the deckhouse and machinery casing. They'd hoisted them to the top of the machinery casing with chain falls, where they now rested in a jumbled heap, out of reach and of no use to the attackers. They'd also closed and secured all the steel doors anywhere on the deckhouse below the bridge and fitted heavy sheet-metal covers on the insides of the thick glass of the non-opening windows. No one was getting at them easily, but neither was anyone inside getting out.

When he got to the bridge, he found Howell on the radio, confirming all possible entrances were locked down tight. He walked out to the port bridge wing, where Torres had his Barrett sniper rifle resting on the wind dodger, peering forward through the scope. Hughes heard a noise above him and looked up to see the Coasties from the stern setting up a second machine gun on the flying bridge. He glanced toward the bow and his blood ran cold.

"Good Lord," Hughes muttered.

Beside him Torres nodded. "As soon as y'all got inside, most of the cons started for the bow. Looks like they're real interested in that machine gun."

Hughes glanced at the bow again and then back up at the flying bridge. Torres followed his gaze.

"Can we—"

"Not a chance," Torres said. "Jones and Brown have shifted to deal with the threat, and we can't tell exactly where they are in that mob. If we open up with the machine gun, we're as likely to hit them as the bad guys. Alvarez and I have the same problem. It takes a lot to stop these fifty-caliber rounds. I could shoot through a tango and take out Jones or Brown without know-ing it."

***

"To your right!" shouted Pete Brown, and Jones whirled to drop a charg-ing attacker with his Glock before ducking back behind the cover of the an-chor windlass.

"We're screwed," Jones said. "We can't open up with the machine gun, and we can't hold out long with just my Glock and your AR."

"Why not use the machine gun? We're shooting aft anyway." Pete snapped off a shot to the left.

"Too risky," Jones said. "Even if we hit the cons, it will keep on going right through 'em and maybe hit our folks as well. Even if they all made it back to the deckhouse, it's only thin steel. That gun will open it up like Swiss cheese. Besides—"

"Y'ALL SURRENDER AND WE'LL GO EASY ON YOU. BUT IF YOU MAKE IT HARD ON US, IT'LL GO TEN TIMES HARDER ON YOU. GIVE UP AND GIVE US THE MACHINE GUN AND WE'LL PUT YOU ASHORE AND LET YOU WALK AWAY," yelled a voice from aft.

"Sounds like they really want this gun," Pete said.

Jones nodded. "And they'll get it, one way or another, if we don't do something. Then our guys in the deckhouse don't stand a chance."

"Got any ideas?" Pete asked.

Jones snorted. "You know as well as I do there's only one. We gotta ditch it, but we can't reach the rail from here. We gotta get closer."

Jones surveyed the situation. "It's thirty or thirty-five feet to the rail on either side, and maybe fifty straight forward to the bow," Jones said. "The bow is farther, but I'll still have the anchor windlass between me and most of the shooters, at least partway."

"We should draw straws or something," Pete said.

Jones just looked at him. "Like it matters. Shoot me now or shoot me later. Besides, I got the gimpy arm and just the Glock. You can provide much better cover fire with the AR."

Pete nodded. "When?"

"No time like the present," Jones said. "Get ready to empty a mag at 'em, and as soon as you start shooting, I'm off. With any luck I'll have it over the side before they figure out what's going on. On three?"

Pete nodded, and Jones picked up the M240 with his good arm, took a deep breath, and began to count. When Pete leaped up to fire, Jones was off like a shot. He'd covered two-thirds of the distance when two rounds slammed into his back simultaneously. He heaved the machine gun as he fell, hoping against hope it would clear the rail.

***

Pete was changing mags when he heard the M240 clatter to the deck. He looked back to see Jones face down and unmoving, with the machine gun on the deck beyond him, ten feet from the bow. Pete slapped the fresh magazine home and rose without hesitation, running backwards as he fired.

A round slammed into his left shoulder, and he sprawled across Jones' body as a dozen more rounds pierced the space he'd occupied a scant second before. His left arm useless, he clawed at the deck with his good hand and pushed with his feet to move forward on his belly as bullets ricocheted off the deck all around him. He reached the twenty-five-pound gun and rolled over on his back to grab it with his good right hand and sling it toward the bow in an awkward toss, then rolled over again and crawled after it, oblivious to the whine of bullets off the deck around him. One struck him in the shin, but still he crawled as he heard boots pounding towards him.

He reached the gun and looked up at the solid steel of the bulwark, towering four feet above him. It might as well be forty.

Then he spotted the bull nose chock penetrating the bulwark and crawled toward it, summoning the strength to lift the butt of the gun and rest it in the opening. He used his good leg to push himself forward a bit more and grabbed the barrel of the gun with his good hand and heaved, gratified when it slipped through the chock.

And hung up at the tripod.

He reached to free it as a shadow loomed over him.

"DON'T TOUCH THAT GUN, NIGGER!"

He looked up to see a big man approaching, not ten feet away, gun at his shoulder. With a speed Pete didn't know he possessed, his right hand shot out and freed the tripod, and the machine gun disappeared to splash into the river below.

Pete Brown smiled. "Bite me, cracker."

He felt the first round penetrate his gut; then his attacker's head exploded.

***

"You got the bastard!" Hughes said, lowering the binoculars. "Keep the rest of them off him!"

Beside him, Torres squeezed off another shot, and Hughes heard Alvarez's gun bark from the other bridge wing as well.

"We'll try," Torres said, his eye still glued to the scope, "but it looks like he's already wounded and it's only a matter of... wait. It looks like they're losing interest."

Hughes raised his binoculars. With the treasured prize no longer on offer, the mob was turning back toward the deckhouse. They moved down the deck in a wave, screaming like injured and enraged animals. Hughes lowered the glasses.

With an icy calm he didn't quite understand, he turned to Torres. "Mr. Torres."

"Yes, sir," Torres replied, equally formally.

"Let's kill as many of these bastards as we possibly can, shall we?"

Torres responded, his jaw clenched, "It'll be our pleasure, sir."

Torres yelled up to his men on the machine gun, and they opened fire, driving the attackers to cover as Torres and Alvarez pitched in with the Barretts. Elsewhere from the flying bridge and along the bridge wings, other shooters joined the line, eager to avenge their shipmates. Hughes walked to the telephone.

"Engine room, Chief," Dan Gowan answered.

"You ready, Dan?"

"Just waitin' on the word."

"Do it," Hughes said.

"One nasty surprise, comin' right up," Gowan said, and hung up.

Hughes went back to the bridge window and waited. Their attackers were spread out over the main deck now, taking advantage of the ample opportunities for cover there to move on the deckhouse, despite the defenders' fire. He spotted the old fire hose, visible in places as it snaked under the deck piping toward the bow, multiple lengths joined together and lashed at intervals to the stanchions supporting the centerline pipe rack. The after end of the hose was connected via a jury-rigged fitting and some Gowanesque chicanery Hughes didn't want to know about to the engine room waste oil pump.

The hose was mostly obscured by deck piping, but Hughes picked out a visible section and waited. Soon it pulsated and a long black puddle formed along the centerline of the ship as used lube oil flowed from the perforations cut every three or four feet along the full length of the hose. It spread like a giant inkblot, covering the deck to run down the slight slope of the deck to each edge. In a nod toward pollution prevention, they'd plugged all the scuppers and deck drains, so the oil pooled at the edges of the deck and ran aft to run down each side of the deckhouse toward the stern.

Frantic cries rose from the main deck as startled attackers scrambled to escape the spreading oil, to no avail. In less than a minute, the previously pristine deck of *Pecos Trader* became one gigantic oil slick, and Hughes' grimace morphed to a smile as attackers attempted to move on the deck below and slid from behind their cover. Rifles barked along the wind dodger as the defenders dispatched the newly exposed attackers.

Hughes walked to the console and dialed the phone.

"Cargo control room, Chief Mate."

"All right, Georgia," Hughes said. "The deck's fully coated. Use all the ballast pumps and let's get her off the bottom and put as much starboard list on her as you can. When you get all the ballast shifted, transfer cargo to help out if you have any slack tanks."

"I'm on it," Howell said, and hung up.

Hughes nodded at the familiar sound of the hydraulic deep well pumps coming up to speed.

SUN OIL DOCK
NECHES RIVER
NEAR NEDERLAND, TEXAS

Spike McComb cursed before lowering the binoculars to grab his radio. "What the hell is going on, Snag? Over," he snarled into the radio.

There was a long pause before Snag's tentative reply. "Uhh… we got a problem, Spike."

"I CAN SEE THAT, SHIT BRAIN! WHAT IS IT?" Spike demanded.

"I can't see from where I am, but I sent some of the boys around in a boat. It looks like the bastards pumped oil all over the deck to make it slippery, then started tilting the ship. The meth heads are all sliding to the low side against the rail, and there ain't no cover. They're gettin' the hell shot out of themselves and they're all starting to jump in the water. We fished a few of them out, and they say there's no way in hell anybody can cross that deck." Snag hesitated. "Uhh… what do you want me to do, Spike? Uhh… over," he added as an afterthought.

Spike controlled his urge to scream while he thought through the situation. "All right. The meth heads ain't much of a loss anyway. I wanted to capture those damn sailors, but it ain't worth getting our hard-core guys shot up. We'll have to settle for just killing 'em all. How many of your boats got flare pistols?"

"I don't know," Snag said. "A lot of them, I guess."

"Okay, listen up."

Hughes nodded as the last few living attackers clawed their way over the piles of bodies to fling themselves into the river. Below him the surface of the water was black with oil leaking over the side, and here and there an oil-coated head bobbed as their would-be attackers swam for shore. The boats previously attacking the starboard side had long since fled back to the safe cover of the barges.

He heard a cargo pump wind up to speed and remembered in the excitement, he'd forgotten to let Georgia Howell know they had enough list. Along the centerline of the ship, liquid sprayed from a pipeline in countless places and the pungent smell of gasoline assailed Hughes' nostrils. He cursed and raced into the wheelhouse and up the canted deck, hamstrings straining, to reach the console phone and dial the chief mate.

"Cargo control room, Chief Mate speak—"

"SHUT DOWN! THE CARGO PIPING IS SHOT FULL OF HOLES!" Hughes yelled.

"On it," Howell said, and Hughes heard the pump winding down almost before she finished speaking.

"Secure the pump. Close all the remote valves," Hughes said.

"Roger that," Howell said.

Hughes hung up as a red-faced Dan Gowan appeared in the door from the central stairway. "Damn! Getting up those stairs with this list is a bear. It's enough to give you a heart—"

Gowan was interrupted by the strident buzz of an alarm from the inert gas panel. Both men made their way to the panel across the tilted deck, but Gowan arrived first and silenced the alarm.

"What the hell? We're losing inert gas pressure on the cargo tanks. I'll go below and check out the system." He turned to go, but Hughes shook his head.

"It's not the system. I bet the IG main is shot up, just like the cargo piping," Hughes said. "The cons were using all the deck piping for cover, and we were unloading on them with everything we have. That piping is all mild steel, not armor plate. For that matter, we likely have holes in the main deck into cargo tanks as well. We're probably losing the inert gas blanket to a hundred leaks."

Gowan looked back at the panel. "We still have at least some positive pressure, but it's falling fast, and we can't patch the leaks until these assholes leave." Gowan shrugged. "All we can do is keep the system running and hope for the best."

Hughes nodded. "And everything on deck's been sprayed with gasoline. Let's get the fire pump going and wash down the deck with a fire hose from up here, at least as far as the stream will reach."

Gowan nodded and started back down to the engine room while Hughes eased back down the sloping deck to the console to inform Georgia Howell of the plan. Before he called, he hesitated and looked out over the chaos of what had just a few hours before been the pristine deck of his ship. *God help us if they get men up on deck now,* he thought. A single muzzle flash could ignite a firestorm that didn't bear thinking about.

CHAPTER TWENTY-SEVEN

Snag looked the abandoned towboat over carefully before motioning his own boat back alongside. The starboard side of the towboat was still burning, but the fire hadn't yet engulfed the little deckhouse or spread to the port side of the boat. A pile of moisture-laden mooring lines smoldered on the stern, the water trapped in the fibers producing a loud hiss as the moisture flashed to steam and mixed with smoke from drier sections of the line now burning. The steam-smoke combination boiled from the pile to wreath the entire boat in a thick cloud of noxious and foul-smelling mist. The lines securing the boat to the barges were burned through, but as the late towboat captain predicted, they were no longer needed. The towboat's propellers still churned the water, pinning the barges against the side of *Pecos Trader* as surely as if the captain was still at the helm.

Snag's boat bumped against the port side of the towboat, and he and his henchmen scrambled aboard. A half dozen more boats awaited to disembark their convicts in turn as Snag barked orders.

"You two"—Snag pointed to two men—"y'all go to the engine room and the galley and round up anything glass or breakable with a screw top. It don't matter what it is, just empty it out and bring the containers up on the barge."

The men eyed the burning towboat unenthusiastically before giving reluctant nods and disappearing inside. Snag turned to the other men filing aboard, most lugging gas cans taken from other boats in their little flotilla. One carried a case of beer bottles.

"The rest of y'all haul those gas cans up the push knee and get on the barges. Spread out even behind the shields and start fillin' those bottles," Snag said.

The man with the bottles muttered something under his breath, and Snag moved across the deck in two strides and got in the man's face. "You got something to say, Murphy?"

"I said I don't see why we had to dump the beer. Fightin' is thirsty work. That's why I brung it. Besides, how do you know this is even going to work? That's a big steel boat, and last I heard, steel don't burn too good."

"It's a big steel boat fulla gasoline," Snag said. "And if we can make a big enough fire, it'll catch, one way or another. Now you gonna stand there and give me lip, or do what I told you? Or maybe you want me to get Spike on the radio and you can tell HIM it's a dumb idea. I'm sure he'd love to hear it, seeing as how it's his idea after all."

Cowed, Murphy stared at the deck and shook his head. Snag shoved him forward and motioned for the other convicts to follow, then fell in behind them.

M/V *Pecos Trader*
Port Bridge Wing

Hughes stood on the port bridge wing with Gowan, holding on to the wind dodger to steady themselves against the slope of the deck as they cast nervous glances toward the barges beside them. The napalm had burned itself out, but smoke still rose from the edges of the shields as the plywood behind them continued to smolder. More smoke rising from behind the barges indicated something on the towboat was still burning as well.

"At least we don't have any more open flames close to us," Gowan said.

"Thank God for that," Hughes said. "A fire is about the last thing—"

"Ready, Captain," said Georgia Howell, from near the wheelhouse door.

Hughes looked over to where Howell stood beside two seamen, holding a fire hose pointed over the top of the wind dodger and aimed at the main deck below. He nodded, and one of the seamen opened the combination nozzle, sending a powerful stream of water downward to smash violently against the steel deck. At Howell's direction the men played the stream across the deck immediately in front of the deckhouse, starting on the high port side and sweeping the stream to starboard, flushing the accumulation of gasoline and used lube oil across the deck and over the side.

Howell turned back to Hughes. "I'm not sure how far we'll be able to reach—"

They all looked forward as something clanged loudly on the deck, and a fireball bloomed near the port cargo manifold.

"What the hell..." Hughes turned back to Howell. "Georgia, get some water on that—"

A dozen more projectiles flew over the smoldering shields on the barge and smashed on the main deck. In seconds, the deck was a raging inferno as the Molotov cocktails ignited not only their own fuel but the gasoline not yet flushed away. Hughes hadn't fully absorbed what was happening when fireworks erupted from the gaps between the barge shields into the labyrinth of piping along the centerline of the ship. Fiery projectiles ricocheted crazily in the complex maze before falling to the deck to continue to burn brightly, setting off even more gasoline fires, which raced across the ship to the starboard side.

"Flares!" Gowan said. "What's next?"

His question was answered immediately as even more Molotov cocktails flew aboard, and another volley of flares danced their crazy dance in the piping. In less than fifteen seconds, the entire main deck of the *Pecos Trader* was a raging inferno. Hughes glanced up to the flying bridge and saw Torres and Alvarez with their sniper rifles, scanning for targets on the barge.

"CAN YOU TAKE THEM OUT?" Hughes called.

Torres shook his head. "THE SMOKE FROM THE SHIELDS IS TOO THICK. WE CAN'T EVEN SEE THE SALLY PORTS."

Hughes turned back to see Georgia Howell pointing, directing the fire hose at various targets, but it was too little, too late. Hughes held on to the rail behind the wind dodger and made his way down the sloping deck.

"It's no use, Georgia. Just concentrate on keeping the fire off of us. Get as many hoses as you can on the front of the deckhouse. Set them on spray, and tie them off to the rail up on the flying bridge to make a water curtain on the front of the house—"

Howell was shaking her head. "It's better not to tie them off. If we keep people handling the hoses, they can make sure no hot spots develop."

Hughes shook his head in turn. "Unless I miss my guess, our convict friends don't have any intention of letting us stand in the open and fight the fire. There are still a lot of them out there in boats, and I suspect any minute they're going to swarm and mass fire on the deckhouse to keep us all inside while it burns down around us. Rig the hoses to keep water on the front of the house unattended so nobody has to stand out here exposed."

Howell nodded and started shouting orders as Hughes turned back to Dan Gowan.

"If you have anything left in your bag of tricks, now would be a good time to trot it out."

Gowan shook his head. "I'm afraid the bag's empty, Cap."

***

Snag kept his boat under the overhang of the ship's bow, where he could see down the starboard side without exposing himself. He motioned the boats with his lieutenants closer and went over the plan again. You couldn't say things enough with this collection of morons.

"All right, Drake," Snag said. "You got fifty guns. Y'all's job is to shut down them machine gun and sniper rifles. Nothing else. Take 'em out if you can, but if you can't, it don't really matter. Mainly y'all just have to keep them off the rest of us. Keep your boats spread out so they can't target you easy. You got that?"

Drake nodded, and Snag turned to the next boat.

"Hopkins, you and your boys shoot up their boats. Spike's pissed, and he don't want nobody coming off now, even if they decide to surrender. They're all going to burn up right on that ship. Any questions?"

Hopkins shook his head, and Snag turned to the last boat.

"Nolan, you and your boys just shoot at anything that moves. Take out any other shooters and especially anybody who looks like they're fighting the fire. Hopkins and his guys will join y'all after they take care of the boats." Snag smiled. "Then we can all back off and wait for the bastards to fry. There ain't need for anybody to be a hero here."

M/V *PECOS TRADER*
BRIDGE

Hughes squatted with the others on the deck of the wheelhouse, well back from the doors and windows, trying to find a solution when he knew there wasn't one. They lost three people before being driven back into the wheelhouse, and anyone so much as showing themselves in a window became a target for a dozen guns. He looked at Georgia Howell.

"The boats?" he asked, raising his voice to be heard over the roar of the high-velocity tank vent valves on the flaming deck outside.

She shook her head. "Both the lifeboats and the fast rescue boat were chewed up resting in their davits. It doesn't take much concentrated fire to put a fiberglass boat out of business. We loaded the patrol boat on the stern, so it's not as easy a target. It might be okay, but we're sure not going to evacuate all these people with one boat and a couple of hundred convicts shooting at us."

Hughes looked at Gowan. "How much time you think we have?"

Gowan shook his head. "The deck's hotter than a firecracker, and the gas blanket on top of the cargo is expanding; that's what's poppin' the vent valves. At this point, the pressure in the cargo tanks is so high the fans can't push inert gas in, even if the IG main wasn't shot full of holes. That's the bad news. The good news is the inert gas is being replaced with expanding gasoline vapor but no oxygen, so the mixture in the tanks is probably too rich to support combustion. I think what's burning is the vapor shooting out of all the bullet holes in the deck and piping."

"How long, Dan?"

Gowan heaved a sigh. "Until the deck starts to fail and the pressure equalizes. Then oxygen will rush in and we'll likely have the first in a series of explosions or at best an unstoppable fire. I'm thinking an hour, maybe less."

Hughes nodded and was about to speak when the VHF squawked.

"*Pecos Trader, Pecos Trader*, this is Kinsey. How do you copy? Over."

SUN OIL DOCK
NECHES RIVER
NEAR NEDERLAND, TEXAS

Spike McComb watched the flames and smoke boiling up from the deck of the *Pecos Trader* and smiled; it was about friggin' time those morons did something right. He'd wanted to capture the ship, with all their stores and supplies, but that was an unknown payoff. He didn't mind risking the meth heads, but his power was based on force, and he couldn't afford to risk good soldiers. At least the troublemakers would be out of his hair now.

As he lowered the binoculars, something caught his eye downriver: a towboat pushing a couple of empty barges. What the hell? He raised the glasses again and saw not one towboat but two, both pushing empty barges and running side by side, as if racing. The name of the nearest was *Judy Ann*.

Spike watched, puzzled. The mystery was solved a heartbeat later when the Coast Guard patrol boat roared out from between the barges, followed by an armada of small craft bristling with armed men, all headed for the gap between the stern of the burning ship and the bank.

Spike cursed and reached for his radio.

Andrew Cormier sat in the driver's seat of the big airboat and looked over at Bertrand, who occupied the driver's seat of a slightly smaller model running next to him. They'd 'liberated' the airboats from a swamp tour operation Bertrand knew about near Lake Charles, and there was plenty of gasoline available in the barges abandoned at the Calcasieu Lock.

Bertrand nodded. Cormier returned the nod and turned to look back over what Kinsey had jokingly called the 'Cajun Navy.' Over two dozen boats of various types moved along, hidden from sight between the barges. They were all very fast and carried heavily armed men, and a few women, from both the cypress swamps of the Atchafalya and the ranks of Lucius Wellesley's towboat crews. People who made loyal friends and very bad enemies, and who in just one short day had come to view the term Cajun Navy with more than a little pride.

Cormier faced forward in time to see Kinsey's hand signal from the Coast Guard boat. He nodded his understanding, then stood up in full view of the other boats and wound his right hand above his head in a circular motion, then pointed forward at the Coast Guard patrol boat.

"*ALLONS!*" Cormier shouted, his voice booming above the muted rumble of the outboards creeping along in their moving hideaway.

The Coast Guard boat rocketed from between the barges toward the gap between the stern of the *Pecos Trader* and the shore. Bollinger was at the helm, and Kinsey and a half dozen armed Cajuns literally rode shotgun. The airboats followed, running side by side and close together fifty yards back, with the rest of the little armada following at the agreed interval.

The Coasties were first through the gap, hugging the bank and shooting past the stationary convicts, firing as they passed, not so much a threat as a distraction as they roared past the convicts and raced away up the oxbow channel. The cons were all still tracking the Coast Guard boat when the airboats roared through moments later, side by side. Bertrand glanced over at Cormier, who nodded. As the boats began to separate, a man in Cormier's boat fed a half-inch-diameter cable into the water between them. The boats diverged quickly, and when they were fifty feet apart, the wire shackled securely to the heavy fan frames of each boat leaped out of the water, stretched taut between the boats, a scythe running two feet above the surface at sixty miles an hour.

The other Cajuns in the airboats blazed away at the confused convicts while Cormier lined up on a half dozen boats in a rough line and roared toward them with Bertrand at his side. They bracketed the convict boats, and their improvised scythe put twenty men in the water in seconds, not all of them in one piece. It was as effective as it was bloody and barbaric, and terrified convicts began to flee toward the gap near the bow of the *Pecos Trader*.

The Coast Guard boat executed a tight turn and raced back toward the convicts, guns blazing, just as the remainder of the Cajun Navy burst through the gap and fell on the fleeing convicts from the rear. Though outnumbered five to one, the Cajuns attacked with a ferocity and confidence that totally unnerved the convicts. The rout was complete.

The first few boatloads of convicts fled through the gap under the bow, but a collision soon blocked the only escape route. Boats jammed together in a confused knot, unable to flee the tightening ring of approaching Cajuns, who poured fire into the convicts as they came. Some convicts fought back while others raised their hands. All of them died.

M/V *Pecos Trader*
BRIDGE

Hughes reached for the radio as the gunfire died. "Kinsey, this is *Pecos Trader*. Request SITREP. Over."

"We're good here. Can you contain the fire? Over," Matt Kinsey replied.

"Unknown. We'll try, but please get all the boats you can spare to our stern so we can start evacuating our nonessential folks in case we can't. Over," Hughes said.

"Roger that. Do you need manpower? Over."

Hughes looked over at Howell and Gowan, who shook their heads in unison.

"Negative your last. Please just concentrate on getting our families off. Over."

Kinsey acknowledged, and Hughes hung up the mic and turned to the others. "All right. Let's break out the fireman suits and see if we can get some foam—"

Gowan reached over and put his hand on Hughes' shoulder. "She's gone, Jordan. If the cargo piping was shot up, the firefighting systems were as well. And even if they weren't, everything on deck has been engulfed in flames, and if it's not melted, it's red hot or close to it. We go pumping cold water into it, it will crack wide open." Gowan paused. "I don't want to write her off either, Cap, but the only thing we're likely to do if we try to fight this fire is get more people killed. That's the bottom line."

Hughes looked away and stared out the bridge window, his view of the raging fire distorted by the water gushing over the glass from the hoses rigged on the flying bridge. He could feel the heat, despite the water curtain, and he knew Dan Gowan was right. He blew out a sigh.

"You're right, but we might be saving these people just to starve to death. Most of our extra supplies were in the containers on deck, and they're toast. And even if we get everyone ashore, there's no way we're going to have time to even save what we have here in the deckhouse."

Gowan rubbed his chin. "We might be able to do something. Let me and Georgia work on that while you figure out where the hell 'ashore' is. I expect there's still plenty of pissed-off convicts on the other side of the river, and there's nothing over here but marsh and mosquitoes."

***

Thirty minutes later Hughes stood at the stern rail, alternating between casting worried glances forward at the raging fire and watching his crew help the families over the stern rail and down the rigid aluminum ladder to the deck of the barge below. He'd been relieved when Lucius Wellesley pushed the empty tank barge up against the stern and held it there with the *Judy Ann*. It was a much shorter drop and allowed them to use one of the aluminum extension ladders they had on board rather than subject everyone to the terror of the swaying rope ladder dangling over a small boat.

It also freed up Kinsey and the Cajuns. They transferred a machine gun back down to the Coast Guard patrol boat, and Hughes nodded as he watched the well-armed patrol boat providing security for the evacuation. On the other side of the ship, Cormier and his Cajun Navy were moving among the convicts' boats, scavenging weapons, ammunition, and the boats themselves if they weren't too badly shot up. Hughes looked over as Georgia Howell joined him at the rail.

"All done," she said as the rest of the crew filed out of the deckhouse and took their place in line to descend to the barge. "We formed a human chain and passed things hand to hand down to the engine room. All the storerooms are cleaned out, but we just had to stack it wherever we found room down there. God only knows if we'll ever be able to find anything, but if the deckhouse goes, the stuff should be all right until we can come for it." She looked back toward the fire. "Whenever that is. How long you think it'll take her to burn herself out?"

Hughes shrugged. "Until the cargo's gone, I guess. God knows she won't sink; we're only a foot or two off the bottom."

Hughes heard the muffled wail of the CO2 sirens and looked up as Dan Gowan and Rich Martin rounded the corner of the machinery casing, both red-faced and sweating.

"We got the engine room closed up tight, and we're flooding the space with CO2," Gowan said. "Kind of strange, actually, using something designed to fight an engine room fire to prevent it from happening to begin with. But whatever works, right?"

"Whatever works," Hughes agreed. "That it, then?"

Gowan nodded. "I'm leaving the emergency fire pump running to keep the water curtain on the deckhouse as long as possible. It might not help, but it can't hurt."

"Then let's get out of here while we still can," Hughes said, and the group took their place at the back of the now short line waiting at the ladder. Hughes was the last one down and took a last long look at *Pecos Trader* as she died a fiery death. It was almost like losing a family member, and he swallowed a lump in his throat and climbed over the rail and onto the ladder.

But his real family waited on the barge, and he gave Laura and the girls a hug as crewmen lowered and stowed the ladder and the *Judy Ann* pulled the barge away from the ship. He left his family and made his way down the length of the barge to climb down one of the push knees to the short foredeck of the *Judy Ann*. From there he made his way up to the wheelhouse.

"Captain Wellesley?" Hughes asked as he stepped into the compact wheelhouse.

Lucius Wellesley extended his hand. "Call me Lucius."

Hughes took Wellesley's hand. "Only if you agree to call me Jordan."

Wellesley smiled. "Deal," he said. "And it's nice to meet you face-to-face, Jordan."

"I expect it was nicer for me," Hughes said. "Y'all saved our asses."

Wesley shrugged. "That was those other fellas. I'm just the bus driver."

"It was a bit more than that, and you know it. But I'll say I'm grateful and leave it at that," Hughes said. "You know where we're going?"

Wellesley nodded. "I've been up the Neches a time or two."

The men fell silent as the *Judy Ann* pushed the barge upriver under Wellesley's expert hand. In less than five minutes, the river widened dramatically into the expanse of the McFadden Bend Cutoff, home to the US Maritime

Administration's Reserve Fleet. Clusters of empty, unmanned ships, most far beyond their useful economic life, floated moored together in groups, held in reserve against a far different, and now unlikely, type of national emergency.

Wellesley nodded to starboard. "Which one?"

Hughes pointed. "We may as well check out the biggest group."

Wellesley nodded and steered toward a group of ten ships of various types and sizes moored side by side near the center of the wide expanse of water. He moved in slowly, looking for the best place to put the barge alongside.

Hughes studied the aging ships as they approached, his seaman's eye focusing laser-like on spots of bleeding rust and other signs of indifferent maintenance. He shook his head and sighed.

"Welcome to home, sweet home," he said under his breath.

CHAPTER TWENTY-EIGHT

Bear Mountain Bridge
Hudson River—West Bank
Appalachian Trail
Mile 1400 Northbound

One Day Earlier
Day 32, 6:35 p.m.

Wiggins moved the last few feet through the thick woods and stopped at the six-foot-high wooden fence, Tex at his side. They'd left the Honda hidden in the woods almost a mile away while they checked out the bridge approach.

Wiggins grasped the top of the fence and pulled himself up a few inches to peek over the top, holding himself there a few moments to study the approach before lowering himself back down to stand beside Tex.

"Well?" Tex said.

"It's manned all right," Wiggins said. "But I'd have been amazed if it wasn't."

"FEMA?"

Wiggins shook his head. "I don't think so. It's more like an ambush setup. There are cars parked haphazardly, like they stalled, with a zigzag gap through them about a car-width wide. It looks passable, but you'd have to take it dead slow. Whoever is manning the roadblock is staying out of sight between the pillars of the tollbooth. I spotted an elbow sticking out from behind one and what looked like cigarette smoke drifting up from behind another, so there's at least two of them. I'm thinking freelance. FEMA will likely get around to it sooner or later, but they're probably concentrating on the interstate crossings up- and downstream. This is about the most remote crossing we're likely to find."

"Maybe we can buy our way across," Tex said.

Wiggins shook his head. "More likely they'll kill us and take everything we have. And I doubt there's only two of them. On a positive note, if this end is blocked, the other side is probably open. We need to watch a while before we figure out what to do. Let's pile some deadfall and rocks against the fence to stand on."

Tex nodded, and they set to work. Ten minutes later, they had a serviceable if somewhat rickety platform, which allowed them both to peer over the fence at the tollbooth fifty yards away. They didn't have to wait long.

Three bicyclists approached from the west: a middle-aged couple and a teenage girl of perhaps sixteen. All had bulging packs on the handlebars of their bikes, and all looked dirty and road weary. The man and woman wore sidearms.

The man held out his hand and stopped in the road, eying the blocked tollbooth warily. There was conversation, and the woman pointed to the gap between the cars. The man nodded, then drew his pistol and started forward alone, steering with his left hand.

As he neared the tollbooth, there was a sharp crack, and his head exploded in a geyser of blood. He dropped the pistol and rolled forward a few feet before death overcame inertia and the bike toppled over.

Two rough-looking men in camo leaped from behind the tollbooth pillars, both bearing ARs pointed towards the woman and the girl.

"RUN, CARLY," the woman screamed, clawing at her holster, obviously intent upon covering her daughter's escape.

"She does, she's gonna have a big hole in her," said a voice behind the woman.

She spun, leveling her gun at a third man ten yards behind them, with a shotgun leveled at her daughter.

"Drop that shotgun and get out of the way, or I'll kill you," the woman said.

The bearded man laughed. "Maybe you will, but the question is, can you put me down before I pull the trigger and blow a great big hole in Carly here? And even if you do, don't you figure my friends are gonna kill you? And they'll be pissed you killed me. Too bad there won't be anybody but Carly here to take it out on. So go ahead and shoot, bitch."

Wiggins watched the woman's shoulders slump; then she slowly lowered the gun. The man was on her in a heartbeat, backhanding her so violently the gun flew from her grasp and she went down in a tangle with the bike between her legs. The girl screamed and scrambled off her bike to help her mother, but the men from the toll booth dragged her away to duct-tape her hands behind her as the third man knelt and did the same to the fallen woman.

Wiggins heard footsteps on the pavement to his right and saw four men running toward the action from a stately stone building across a narrow parking lot.

"Well, what have we got here?" said the first to arrive. "A little feminine company for the night."

"YOU ain't got shit, Atwood," said one of the men from the tollbooth. "You know the deal. Whichever watch takes spoils gets first dibs. And that ain't you."

"Don't be an asshole, Hollingsworth. You guys all have the watch until midnight. We'll just warm these ladies up for you. How about that?"

"How about you go catch your own pussy," Hollingsworth said. "'Cause these bitches are stayin' tied up in one of the cars until we get off watch. You guys can have sloppy seconds tomorrow afternoon."

"All right, if you're going to be like that about it. They have any other good stuff?"

"We ain't exactly had time to look, now have we?" Hollingsworth said. "They got a couple of pistols for sure. We'll sort through the packs together at change of watch, just like always."

Wiggins saw Atwood nod, and as the excitement of the encounter faded, so did the volume of the conversation. He heard no more. He touched Tex's arm, and they lowered their heads slowly to avoid attracting attention, cautious despite the distance and their cover. When they were fully concealed behind the fence, Tex spoke first.

"We won't be negotiating with these assholes," she said.

Wiggins nodded. "We have to take them out. One good thing is at least we know how many of them there are. I'm thinking they must be holed up in that stone building over there, and that they all turned out at the sound of gunfire. Four guys came from the building, so I figure two watches of four guys each. The fourth guy on each watch is probably—"

"Hiding in a car on the bridge," Tex finished his sentence, "so he can cut off the escape of anyone coming across the bridge who has second thoughts when they suspect an ambush at the tollbooths. Just like the guy that sneaked up behind the two women on this side."

Wiggins smiled briefly. "Great minds."

PUSH BACK

Wiggins knelt behind a rock in the dark, trying to ignore his stiff muscles. He'd moved into position hours before, and kneeling motionless was taking its toll. The fence had covered his move away from the tollbooth to the west end of the bridge approach, but then things got dicey. Without the fence for cover, he'd waited for the partial darkness of dusk to work his way back through the scattered foliage into a position behind where the backup man hid in the strip of wooded verge bordering the highway. He'd moved cautiously, torn between rushing to take advantage of the fading light, yet terrified a snapped twig or stumble might betray him.

An unnecessary worry, as it turned out. He'd heard the faint sounds of a heavy rock beat as he got close to his target's position and realized the man was listening to music turned up loud enough to leak around his headphones. Wiggins had breathed a relieved sigh and settled in to wait.

They'd decided to strike after the midnight shift change, on the theory they were all at an equal disadvantage in the dark, and if they were able to get past the toll booth, the man on the bridge would be unsure what was happening until they roared past him. That was the theory, anyhow.

Wiggins tensed as he heard someone approaching from the road, then ducked further behind his rock as he saw a flashlight bobbing closer.

"Who's there?" asked a voice.

"It's Baker, numb nut. Were you expecting the friggin' Easter Bunny? Besides, don't tell me you broke the night-vision glasses."

"I didn't break 'em. The battery is low, that's all."

"Didn't you bring a spare?" Baker asked.

"I forgot it. Don't you have one?"

"Yeah, I got one," Baker said. "Just like YOU'RE supposed to—"

"Give it a rest, Baker. Squattin' out here in the bushes sucks, and I'm not in the mood to take any crap. Just once I'd like to get the bridge side and sit in a nice soft car seat. Who's got the bridge end for your shift, as if I didn't know."

Baker snorted. "Atwood, who else? Rank has its privileges."

"Yeah, well, I'm getting a little sick of that too. But whatever, I'm hauling ass. I don't want the party to start without me. You have a great night."

"Yeah, screw you too, Hardy," Baker said.

Hardy laughed, and Wiggins heard him moving back toward the road. He flinched, startled, as Baker turned on the red night light of a headlamp and sat on a nearby rock. The man sat facing away from Wiggins with his head bent, apparently changing the battery in the night-vision goggles.

Wiggins fingered the thick, two-foot section of rebar he'd found on the roadside and hesitated only a split second before rising and closing the gap separating him from Baker. He raised the club as he came, and it struck the man's skull with a crunch of sickening finality. Baker toppled over soundlessly, and Wiggins stood staring down, his heart pounding.

Slowly his heart rate dropped, and Wiggins glanced at the luminous dial of his watch. It was just after midnight, and Tex was due in less than thirty minutes, but their opponents' night-vision capability changed everything. They'd assumed the sentry on the bridge was out of the equation until they'd taken out the men on the toll booth and started across the bridge. However, if the bridge sentry clearly saw what was happening at the toll booth and engaged too soon, not only could he pin them down, the firing would alert the others off watch. Game over.

Wiggins looked down at the dead man and cursed. He'd seen the opportunity and reacted without thinking it through, but he should have waited. Maybe he could have faded back and cut through the woods to intercept Tex on the road, and they could make a new plan that accounted for their enemy's NV capabilities. But what if he missed her? She'd be heading into a trap without a clue things weren't going according to plan.

He muttered another curse. It was too late for second-guessing anyway. If they pulled back now, the dead man would put the marauders on high alert, and he and Tex would have zero chance of surprising them. No, he had to make it work. He'd just have to take out the bridge sentry first, quickly and quietly, then run back to support Tex.

Wiggins stooped and pulled the still-glowing headlamp from Baker's head and put it on, ignoring the wet stickiness, then scooped up the fallen NV goggles and examined them in the red glow of the headlamp, relieved to find the battery compartment closed. The man had made the battery swap, so Wiggins didn't have to hunt through the weeds for an errant battery. He doused the headlight and powered up the night-vision goggles. The night became like an eerie green day, almost like an old video game.

He stuck the rebar in his belt and turned to go, then stopped. The dead man was about his size. Wiggins swallowed his distaste and wrestled the camo shirt off the corpse and pulled it on over his own. After a stop at his hiding place to scoop up one of the M4s they'd taken from the FEMA SUV, Wiggins trotted back the way he'd come; he didn't have time to waste.

The privacy fence shielded him until just past the tollbooths. From the end of the fence, it was a dash across a half-empty parking lot to the pedestrian walkway along the side of the bridge, separated from the roadway by a waist-high concrete wall. If he could make it to the wall without being spotted, he could stay below it and crawl onto the bridge without being spotted.

He peeked around the fence toward the tollbooth and said a silent prayer of thanks for the NV gear. Unlike the daytime operation, the night guards seemed unconcerned about being seen at a distance and leaned side by side against the stone wall of the tollbooth, chatting and smoking. He nodded to himself and planned his route to the shelter of the pedestrian walkway.

He took a zigzag course, from car to scattered car, and five minutes later huddled against the low wall of the walkway, the guards less than thirty feet away on the opposite side. He could hear them plainly and was terrified they might hear his labored breathing.

He checked his watch: fifteen minutes until Tex arrived, and the long crawl coupled with the need to do it silently was going to take time. He set out, the rough antislip coating of the walkway biting into his hands and knees. As he passed the stone building, he heard muffled music through the thick walls, punctuated by what sounded like a scream. He ignored it and crawled. Terrible things were happening in the world, and he couldn't fix them all.

The next challenge was location; Wiggins had no idea how far out the bridge sentry was or whether he was facing back over the bridge or toward the tollbooth. In the end, Wiggins decided the man wouldn't be too far out, so he'd crawl until he was sure he was past, then count on Tex's approach to draw the man's attention toward the tollbooth.

The plan was for Tex to come in slowly with only her parking lights on, as if she were using the minimal lights necessary to see. She'd quickly kill the lights when she saw the situation at the tollbooth, then stop like she was surprised and evaluating the situation. At that point, she was to play it by ear, doing whatever was necessary to hold the tollbooth guards' attention while Wiggins took them from the rear. They figured the bridge sentry would know something was going on, but counted on him not being able to see enough to matter until it was too late. They'd been wrong there, but Wiggins now planned to use Tex's arrival as a distraction.

He crawled cautiously, gauging progress by the vertical stanchions of the handrail to his right. He'd just passed a hundred and fifty feet when he caught a whiff of cigarette smoke from over the low wall. Thank God for bad habits.

He moved another thirty feet to make sure he was past the sentry, then risked a peek over the wall, moving very slowly to keep from attracting attention. He saw the glowing end of a cigarette in the drivers' side window of an SUV forty feet back toward the tollbooth. He could see the tollbooth guards clearly as well, and a chill shot through him as he realized if either of them took a few steps to the side and looked in his direction, they now had an angle to see him clearly as well. He slowly sank back behind the wall and hoped Tex arrived before one of the guards decided to stretch his legs.

The clock now slowed to a crawl, and Wiggins hugged the low wall and sweated until he saw the dim parking lights of the Honda turn into the entrance ramp. Across the wall and back toward the roadblock, he heard the squeak of an opening car door and pulled himself up cautiously to peep over the wall.

The bridge sentry was standing behind the open door of a late model SUV, watching the toll booth. Wiggins crawled over the waist-high wall silently and moved forward, pulling the rebar from his belt as he approached. He'd closed half the distance when he kicked a pebble. It skittered along the roadway as the bridge sentry turned.

Wiggins dropped the rebar down beside his leg and sped up. He needed to disorient the man before he yelled or got a shot off.

"Atwood! It's me, Baker," Wiggins said as the man completed his turn, facing Wiggins ten feet away, looking insect-like in the green glow of Wiggins' NV goggles. Wiggins knew his NV gear made him look the same to the man and hoped Baker's voice wasn't distinctive.

"Baker! What the hell? What are you doing out here? You're supposed to..."

Atwood connected the dots far too quickly and reached for his sidearm when Wiggins was still five feet away. Wiggins leaped the last few feet, bringing the rebar up as he charged, driving the end into Atwood's throat with all his weight behind it. The rough rod tore through the carotid artery and punched out the back of the man's neck. Atwood's cry died on his lips, and blood sprayed on Wiggins' stolen camo shirt. The man clutched the open car door and sank to the pavement.

Wiggins disarmed him and threw his pistol over the side of the bridge, then dragged the still-gasping man well away from the vehicle. He looked back toward the tollbooth. Tex had stopped as agreed with her lights off, but the two guards had moved only a short distance toward her and stood staring at the Honda.

He looked back down. Atwood wasn't dead, but he soon would be and was no longer a threat. Wiggins started for the tollbooth, then thought better of it and came back to collect the rebar. He grasped the end firmly and put a foot on Atwood's chest, trying to ignore the pitiful sounds as he reclaimed his most effective silent weapon.

"What do you make of that?" Stanfield asked.

"I think Baker's screwing off," Hargraves replied. "He should have that shotgun stuck in the driver's face by now. I bet the son of a bitch is sacked out again."

"What should we do?"

"How the hell should I know what we should—"

He was interrupted by the sound of an opening car door as the driver exited the vehicle, followed by a seductive feminine voice.

"Evening, boys. I just want to cross without any trouble. I'm sure I can make it worth your while."

"You alone?" Stanfield yelled.

"Yep. Just a poor girl trying to get home the best way she can."

"Step away from the car with your hands in the air, then turn in a full circle, real slow," Stanfield said.

The men watched as the woman complied.

"She's a looker, even in these NV glasses. I like the little ones. What do you think, Stanfield?" Hargraves asked quietly.

"I think she seems willing, and we can have a nice little party through the night takin' turns in one of the cars. Atwood won't care if we let him go first. We won't even have to tie her up until she figures out we're not gonna let her leave."

"What if it's a trap or something?"

Stanfield snorted. "Look at her. She's maybe five feet tall and weighs a hundred and nothing. She's got no visible weapons, and we won't let her go back to the car to get any. I say we put her in one of those cars and have ourselves a party. I'm going to go search her. You stay back and keep your eyes open and cover me. Then you keep an eye on the girl and I'll holler at that dumb ass Baker to get his butt out here and help me make sure there aren't any unpleasant surprises in the car."

"Roger that," Hargrave said, and Stanfield started toward the woman, pistol in hand.

***

Wiggins' heart pounded as he crouched behind the tollbooth pillar and watched the scene unfold. He'd heard Tex's shouted inducement and watched as the two men discussed it, too low for him to hear what they were saying. They were only partially turned away from him, and he didn't think he could close on them before one of them saw him.

He could challenge them with his Sig or the M4, but what if they called his bluff? They were much more likely to do so at a distance than they were at point-blank range. He needed them both to focus fully on Tex so he could get closer. His heart sank as they separated.

One of the men started toward Tex, pistol drawn, and the other stayed behind, both with their backs to him now. He covered the distance to the closest in long silent strides and raised the rebar to deliver a crushing blow to the back of the man's head. Wiggins was inured to the violence now. It would haunt him later, but not now, not with Tex's life on the line.

Wiggins grabbed the man as he fell, almost toppling from the weight before stabilizing himself and easing the man to the ground. The second man continued towards Tex, oblivious to the action behind him. Wiggins had almost overtaken him when the man heard him and spun, pistol leveled.

"Don't shoot! It's Baker," Wiggins tried for a repeat.

But the dead man lying on the pavement behind Wiggins gave lie to the claim, and the guard fired without hesitation, but missed. Wiggins flung the rebar underhand with all his might, knocking the man's NV goggles askew as Wiggins jogged left.

Sightless now, the man fired repeatedly at where Wiggins had been, until Wiggins drew his own Sig and shot the man three times, center mass. The man fell, and Wiggins stood trembling, his heart pounding.

"Bill?"

"Here, Tex," Wiggins said. A flashlight came on.

"TURN THAT OFF!" Wiggins said.

Tex complied. "But how—"

"Wait there," Wiggins said, stooping to strip the NV gear off the dead guard. He pulled his own glasses off and looked through the guard's. Dead. Optics didn't like being smacked by rebar. He dropped the damaged gear and hurried to the first guard he'd dropped, to find his NV gear working. He hurried back to Tex with it.

"NV gear. Put it on and grab one of these guys' M4s. We'll divide their extra mags. The guys in the house will likely be out here any minute."

"Let's just crash the bridge," Tex said. "The guy further out is probably confused. We can get past them if you drive and I lay down suppressing fire."

"The guy on the bridge isn't a problem," Wiggins said. "Creeping through that obstacle course they've set up is. We'll never make it through in time, and if they catch us in transit, they'll just hunker down behind the concrete wall of the pedestrian walkway and shoot us to pieces at point-blank range. It'll be a friggin' shooting gallery."

"Speak of the devil," Tex said, pointing toward the stone house, where flashlights bobbed. "They're coming."

Wiggins studied the bobbing flashlights. "They traded off the NV gear during the watch change, and they wouldn't be using flashlights if they had any more. Now we have it and they don't."

Shouts now accompanied the bobbing flashlights.

"Uhh... I think maybe we should curb their enthusiasm while we figure this out," Tex said.

"All right. Grab a gun and let's separate a bit and both fire a short burst toward the lights to send them to cover, then move in case they return fire at the muzzle flashes. On three?" Wiggins asked.

Tex stooped to pick up the fallen guard's rifle and nodded, and she walked away a few paces. Wiggins counted down, and they both fired a three-round burst, then scrambled thirty feet to the right. Sure enough, the pavement where they'd been standing erupted in sparks.

"What now?" Wiggins asked.

Tex shrugged. "You've been right so far about what they'd do, so why not turn this into OUR shooting gallery."

BEAR MOUNTAIN BRIDGE
PEDESTRIAN WALKWAY NEAR TOLL BOOTH

"Who the hell's out there, and where are our guys?" Saunders asked.

"How should I know?" Hollingsworth said. "The chickenshits likely ran off. I never did trust that Atwood."

"What are we gonna do?"

"I can tell you what we AIN'T gonna do. We ain't gonna move from behind this wall until we know what we're facing," Hollingsworth said.

An engine started to their left, somewhere along the entrance ramp to the toll plaza. It seemed to move toward them as they listened.

"Now that's more like it. The dumb ass is gonna try to shoot through our little obstacle course." Hollingsworth grinned. "We'll chew him up. Lay those three big flashlights on the wall, pointing toward the obstacle course, but everybody pick out a firing position at least ten feet away from the lights in case they draw fire. When I hear him stuck in the obstacle course, I'll give the word to light him up; then you guys turn on your lights and jump back to your firing positions. After that, it's just a turkey shoot."

***

Tex stared at the backs of the four men lined up along the wall, oblivious to her presence. Gaining her present advantageous position had been no more difficult than walking through the pitch-black night down the middle of the paved driveway to the parking lot.

She thought about what she was about to do. It was murder, really. Or was it? No, murder was what was done to her parents and many good people like them by scumbags like the four in front of her. This was an execution, and a just one. Wiggins had volunteered, but someone needed to create a diversion to keep all of their opponents focused on the same place, and Bill had done more than his share of killing.

Tex felt a flash of remorse at what they'd become. Mild-mannered Bill Wiggins, well liked on the ship for his quick smile and even temper, a man who seldom raised his voice much less his hand to anyone. A man who just killed four human beings without hesitation. They weren't the same people they were just a few short weeks ago; their 'old selves' couldn't survive in this new world. And she would survive. Tex pushed her misgivings to the back of her mind and studied the men in front of her.

She heard the Honda and watched the men prepare their trap. She could hear them clearly, and their laughter and apparent enthusiasm for the task erased any lingering doubts. It was over in four three-round bursts, and she walked over and pointed one of the large flashlights skyward so as not to blind Wiggins. She flashed a signal in the air and watched through the NV glasses as the SUV approached the roadblock and zigzagged through the obstacle course.

She turned and looked east, over the bridge. They were lucky this time, again. She wondered where their luck would run out.

CHAPTER TWENTY-NINE

DAY 33, 00:55 A.M.

They found the women locked in a storeroom, beaten and thoroughly traumatized. Tex comforted them as Wiggins checked out the stone building, originally some sort of local museum.

One room was crammed with guns and ammunition of all types, and another held canned goods, MREs, and other nonperishables—all undoubtedly looted from refugees. A carport held the greatest treasure, two rows of red plastic gas cans of various sizes, all full. Here was the fuel to get home—all the way home.

He returned to find Tex sitting with the women in the glow of a Coleman lantern, drinking instant coffee she'd found and prepared on a nearby camp stove. Wiggins shot her a questioning look. She gave a hesitant nod and he moved to a couch across from the women.

"Bill, this is Fran and her daughter, Carly," Tex said.

Wiggins nodded. "Nice to meet you ladies."

Fran nodded, but Carly just stared at the floor. The silence grew.

"I… uh… I'm sorry about your husband," Bill said.

The woman shook her head. "We only met John three weeks ago, at our hotel in Scranton. We all live near here and he was helping us get home. He's a… I mean he was a good man. Did you find… I mean is his…" She trailed off, unable to finish.

Wiggins shook his head. "I'm sorry. His body's not there. They probably dragged it into the woods, and I'm afraid we don't have time to search. We need to be far away when the sun comes up. More bad guys might turn up at any time."

The girl whimpered and moved into her mother's arms. Tex glared at Wiggins and he gave a helpless shrug.

"We can't ride the bikes in the dark," Fran said. "But we live near Lake Carmel—only about twenty-five miles. Tex said... I mean I thought maybe... can you take us there?" Her plea was heartbreaking.

Except Wiggins couldn't afford a broken heart. He shook his head. "No, but there's plenty of gas, and I'm sure I can get one of the cars in the parking lot running for you. We'll gas it up, give you food and guns for protection, and you can go on your own."

"But Tex said you were following the Appalachian Trail," Fran said, "and it crosses Route 52 not three miles from our house. So it's not really out of your way. And you could rest at our house a bit and sleep in real beds. And—"

Wiggins raised his hand to cut the woman off and glared at Tex. "See you outside a minute, Tex?"

He started for the door without waiting. Tex found him pacing in the dark, ready to explode.

She didn't give him a chance. "Look, Bill. Those women have been through a lot. I thought we could—"

"YOU thought. No, actually, you DIDN'T think. She doesn't just want a ride, she wants us for protection against the unknown, can't you see that? What happens if their house is burned down or full of gangbangers or subject to any one of a hundred horrible, screwed-up conditions now common in our new *Mad Max* world. What then? Do we just say 'see ya' and drop them in the bad guys' laps? Do we take them with us? Or do we get guilt-tripped into taking them to a friend or relative's house, which will further delay us?"

Wiggins blew out an exasperated sigh. "Look, Tex. I'm glad we saved them, but we can't keep saving them. I'm worried about my OWN family. If they can't make it twenty-five miles on their own with guns, a car, and a full tank of gas, they sure won't be able to cope with whatever disaster they find when they get there. I can't be responsible for that. I WON'T be responsible for that. My family comes first. Sorry, but that's just the way it is."

Silence grew. Finally Tex nodded.

"I didn't think it through," she said. "It's just they're so traumatized, I wanted to offer comfort. I let my heart overrule my brain, and in this world, that's a recipe for disaster." She paused. "That said, it's done and we are going in the same direction. I think we can help them without getting further entangled."

Wiggins sighed. "Okay, then how do you see that playing out? I damn sure don't want to be a houseguest or guilted into taking them to Aunt Suzy's."

"We figure our closest point of approach to their house. If they're right, it's a few miles at most. How much food and gas is there?"

"More than we can possibly carry in two cars," Wiggins said.

"Okay. We load up the Honda and another car with as much as we can carry. We'll go heavy on gasoline in our car, but they just need enough gas to get home. We'll give them all the food and water they can carry and whatever weapons they think they can handle. How many sets of NV gear do we have?"

"Three, if the set of the guy on the bridge wasn't damaged. Why?" he asked.

"Are you going to give them a set?"

"No way. We'll be able to drive at night now, with one of us driving and the other as security. I'm not giving that up. Presuming the third set's working, we'll keep it for a spare. It's like Levi says, 'two is one and one is none.'"

"All right. I'll drive them in the second car, using the NV glasses and following you. Even going a roundabout way to stay close to the AT, it shouldn't take more than an hour to reach the point we part company. We find them a side road to hide on and leave them there. They drive the few miles home at first light. By then, we'll be far away. I hope everything goes well with them, but whether it does or not, it's no longer our concern. What do you think?"

"Works for me," Wiggins said. "Let's get on it. You bring them up to speed and start trying to find a working car. I'm going to look around for a charger for the NV batteries. If we're lucky, there'll be a solar-powered one."

"I'm on it," Tex said.

I-84 AND MOUNTAIN TOP ROAD
NEAR STORMVILLE, NEW YORK

DAY 33, 3:40 A.M.

They dropped the women off at the intersection of State Route 52 and Mountain Top Road and proceeded on their way after making sure the women's car was well concealed in the wooded verge. It was clear Fran wanted them to accompany her home, but Wiggins was resolute. They parted company stiffly with a curt nod from Fran and no word of thanks.

Thirty minutes later they sat in the Honda, stopped on the narrow ribbon of blacktop called Mountain Top Road. Wiggins studied the bridge ahead over the broad lanes of I-84, alert for any signs of a trap.

"What do you think?" he asked.

Tex shrugged. "It's pitch black, with no lights on the interstate or background light at all, and the bridge looks clear. If anyone was using so much as a flashlight down on the interstate or in the woods, the NV would probably show it. I think it's clear, Bill."

"Agreed." Wiggins took his foot off the brake and drove forward. "Let's see how much mileage we can make by our usual stopping time. I'm starting to feel good about this."

***

Wiggins' good feelings soured just across the New York border. River crossings were their greatest challenge, and as the Appalachian Trail wound its way northward through Connecticut, it hopped back and forth across the meandering Housatonic with frustrating regularity. They decided to take the last bridge the trail crossed, north across the Connecticut border in Massachusetts. They stayed to the west of the river, roughly paralleling the trail as it wound from one side of the river to the other.

Wiggins gripped the wheel tightly and peered at the green landscape ahead, the twisting back roads and range of the NV glasses limiting his speed. But as irritating as it was, he reminded himself they were making miles under cover of darkness they couldn't have made before.

He was driving north on a one-lane gravel track when he noticed his vision improving due to increasing ambient light from the sky in the east. He increased speed.

"It'll be light soon. How far is the crossing?"

"Less than two miles," Tex said.

"Think we'll have any trouble? There seem to be a lot of freelance toll collectors these days."

"The river's narrow here, with a lot of crossings," Tex said. "There are half a dozen just between here and Great Barrington, a few miles north, and they're all in more built-up areas. There's not much on either side of the Kellogg Road bridge we'll be using, so I think anyone going into the toll-collecting business would pick a busier bridge."

Wiggins sighed. "Let's hope so. I've had about all the conflict I want for a while."

"Me too. Turn right ahead on Lime Kiln Road. We follow that half a mile, then turn right on US 7—"

"Whoa! US 7 sounds like a major road."

"Well, 'major' for around here maybe," Tex said. "But relax, we'll only be on it a few hundred yards before turning on to Kellogg Road anyway. The river looks to be a hundred yards from the last turn, max."

Five minutes later, Wiggins turned right onto US 7 and went less than fifty feet before stopping. There were two sawhorses in the middle of the road, supporting a sheet of plywood with a hand-painted sign.

"Keep out or face the Lord's wrath," Tex read aloud.

"Crap! What now?"

"I'd say the Lord doesn't want visitors," Tex said.

"What about the crossings to the north?"

She shook her head. "There are three communities before the first bridge, and we'd have to stay on US 7 the whole way, somewhere between five and ten miles. On the other hand, we're less than a quarter of a mile from the Kellogg Road bridge. Choose your poison, I guess."

"Well, it's still dark, so let's hope the Lord's sleeping in." Wiggins pulled the SUV around the roadblock.

They'd gone less than a hundred yards when Tex pointed. "That's it on the left ahead."

A paved side road led left from US 7, turning immediately in front of a large frame building with a sign reading Believers Tabernacle. Wiggins powered through the turn, anxious to get past the area and over the bridge. The road curved sharply back to the right through a cluster of homes, and he had to slow.

"So far, so good," he said. "But I wouldn't want to try this in daylight—"

A handheld air horn blasted behind them.

"What is it, Tex? Can you see?"

"Two guys just ran into the road behind us. Both armed, but it doesn't look like they have NV, so I think we're all right."

The road veered sharply to the left, and Wiggins cursed and braked hard. A shot rang out, and the driver side mirror disintegrated.

"Unless, of course, you show them our brake lights," Tex said as Wiggins accelerated.

The bridge appeared around the bend, a short distance ahead. There was an obstruction in the road, and Wiggins realized it was one of the sawhorse and plywood barricades, no doubt to warn off anyone approaching the community via the bridge. There was no room to swerve, and he punched the accelerator, intent on knocking the barricade aside.

An armed man stepped from the wooded verge beside the road, peering in their direction, hearing the engine but unable to see the vehicle. They were almost upon him when he fired. There was a loud metallic *whack* at the front of the SUV, and then they were past, smashing through the flimsy roadblock and across the short bridge to race away down Kellogg Road at sixty miles an hour.

"You think he damaged anything?" Tex asked.

"No way of telling, but we need to put some distance between us and them before we stop to check. What's my next turn?"

"This road dead-ends into another one. You'll be making a left," Tex said.

Wiggins made the turn and got two miles up the road before the temperature gauge and the sun began to rise at the same time.

"We have to pull over," Wiggins said. "Start looking for a hiding spot."

Just Off East Sheffield Road
Near Great Barrington, Massachusetts

Day 33, 6:10 a.m.

A dirt track across a farmer's field led to a secluded strip of woods well off the road and bordering the river. In happier times it might well have been someone's favorite picnic spot; now it was Wiggins' impromptu repair shop.

Tex watched as he squatted at the front of the car and peered through the grill. Steam rose from under the open hood, and the distinctive and unpleasant smell of engine coolant wafted up from the engine compartment.

"It's the radiator all right," Wiggins said.

"Can you fix it?"

Wiggins shrugged. "We don't have much in the way of tools, but I may be able to patch it. It won't be pretty, but it will at least get us somewhere to find a ride. No way this baby's making it to Maine."

Wiggins sighed and stood up. "Give me a hand unloading the back so I can get at the tire tool."

"Anything else I can do?" Tex asked a moment later as Wiggins started toward the front of the car with the tire tool.

He stopped and nodded. "Yeah. Find that bag where we dumped all the unused condiment packets from the MREs and pull out those little packages of black pepper. Then go through all that food we just got at the bridge and pull out all the pepper you can find."

"Pepper? What are we going to do with pepper?"

"Plug the leak, if we can find enough. I'll explain later. For now just see how much you can round up," Wiggins said.

Tex looked puzzled, but she nodded and set about the task as Wiggins moved to the front of the Honda. He shoved the chisel-like end of the tire tool into the plastic grill and pried down sharply. The thin plastic of the grill broke with a series of sharp pops, and he moved the tool and repeated the process before reversing the tire tool to hammer at the broken pieces. He examined his work critically then set about enlarging the hole until he could reach the front of the damaged radiator with both hands. He'd just finished when Tex came around the car, holding up a paper bag.

"One pepper plug, as ordered," she said. "What else?"

"Fill up a bunch of those empty plastic water bottles with the river water, if you will," Wiggins said. "We need to replace the missing coolant, and I don't want to waste our drinking water."

Tex collected the bottles and started for the river as Wiggins went around to their pile of gear and fished the multitool out of the backpack Levi Jenkins had prepared. He folded out the needle-nose pliers and returned to the front of the car.

Working through the hole in the grill to mash the damaged tubes of the radiator flat was difficult. He had to first use the chisel end of the tire tool to flatten the cooling fins before he even had room to get the pliers in around the tubes. Then it took both hands locked around the small pliers and all his strength to mash the damaged tubes flat for two inches on either side of the bullet damage.

By the time Tex returned with an armload of water, Wiggins' forearms were bleeding from repeated scrapes against the sharp broken plastic of the grill, and his shirt was soaked in sweat. But the damaged tubes were crimped, or at least as close as he could make them.

Minutes later, the ground in front of the SUV was littered with empty water bottles, and the engine was running as Wiggins and Tex tore open packet after packet and dumped pepper directly into the radiator.

"Is this really gonna work, Bill?" Tex asked.

Wiggins shrugged. "Beats me. I read about it once, but I've never had to do it before."

"You READ about it? Who reads about stuff like this?"

Wiggins grinned. "I'm an engineer, remember?"

Tex laughed. "And I'm glad you are. What next?"

"When we get all the pepper in, we put the radiator cap back on and let the pressure build up. The radiator is still seeping, and the pepper grains will all be sucked to the leak. The difference in pressure will force the pepper into the leak and it will clog up and solidify. That's the theory anyway. If it works, there won't be any water dripping off the bottom of the radiator."

"And if it doesn't?" Tex asked.

"Even if it doesn't work completely, it should slow the leak," Wiggins said. "We'll fill all our empty bottles with river water, and if the engine temp starts to rise, we pull over and let it cool then top off the radiator. Not perfect but it beats walking."

CHAPTER THIRTY

The plug was holding, at least for the moment. They decided to celebrate by pigging out with a big meal from their now ample supply of food, only to discover to their disappointment there wasn't really anything in their stores tempting enough to warrant overindulgence.

They slept in shifts, Wiggins first for a few fitful hours while Tex stood watch. He relieved her around noon, the growing heat and his own anxieties banishing any hope for further rest. He had a map spread out on the hood of the Honda when she awoke in the late afternoon, with the now battered *AT Guide* open beside it.

The Honda rocked a bit as she crawled out of the back. Wiggins looked up and smiled.

"Sleep well?" he asked.

Tex yawned. "Better than you, I think. It's still hours before dark, would you like to try again?"

Wiggins shook his head. "Nah. I'm good."

She nodded toward the map. "Finding a better route?"

"Well, I don't know if it's better, but I've definitely come to a conclusion," he said.

"Which is?"

"Which is, it doesn't make much sense to stick close to the AT any longer." He pointed to the map. "The terrain is getting rougher and the roads follow the valleys. Just look at this stretch through the White Mountains; sure, a road parallels the trail five miles away, but the terrain in between is impassable. It might as well be five hundred miles away, and half the trail between here and Maine is like that. There's no point in sticking close to a trail we can't possibly access. Access and escape is the whole point, right?"

Tex looked doubtful. "Maybe, but Levi's plan has worked so far, and I don't—"

"But Levi said himself this was all theoretical, and he's not from New England. I know this area, Tex, look at the elevation changes in the guide if you don't believe me."

"Of course I believe you. It's just that every time we come into a populated area, we court trouble, that's all I'm saying."

"And I'm saying we have no choice," Wiggins said. "There are four major river crossings between here and Maine, and they put the bridges where the people are. Those are our points of greatest risk, and there's nothing we can do to avoid them, so I can't see wasting time in between. We can run the back roads at night now, with no lights, and that's an advantage Levi never even considered when he made his plan. We can cover the distance between the rivers in an hour or two at most, then hide the car and scout the crossing on foot during the day. If it looks too dangerous, we can wait until dark and go upriver to the next crossing, and keep checking them out until we find a place to cross."

Tex sighed. "It sounds reasonable. I just doubt we're going to find unguarded crossings. It seems to be getting worse the further north we go."

"It is what it is," Wiggins said. "One thing for sure, though, we have to get a reliable ride. The plug is holding, but if we have to run for it, it may leave us afoot at the worst possible time."

Tex snorted. "Reliable ride. At this point I long for a Greyhound or even Amtrak."

Wiggins smiled wanly. "Yeah, well, I doubt that's happening anytime soon…"

He stopped mid-sentence and glanced down at the map a moment, then traced a line with his finger. He looked up, his smile genuine now.

"I have an idea," he said.

SAME DAY, 9:10 P.M.

With great difficulty, Wiggins forced himself to wait until full dark before they started out. They found what they were looking for less than two miles down the road and pulled in to a weed-choked gravel parking lot. They sat for a minute examining the modest frame building. A large sign on the front read The Yogurt Hut and another slightly smaller sign proclaimed Frozen Treats.

"You think this place was even in business before the blackout?" Tex asked. "It looks pretty run-down."

"Well, if it was, I figure the frozen treats melted long ago," Wiggins said. "But as long as they have a phone book, I couldn't care less."

He pulled the Honda behind the building. The back door had a cheap padlock rather indifferently attached to the wooden door frame. It yielded to the tire tool easily.

Wiggins hopes fell when they entered, and it was obvious the Yogurt Hut hadn't been a going concern in some time. Hope was restored when Tex found a stack of dusty phone books in a cabinet.

"What's that thickest one?" Wiggins asked.

Tex shined her light at the cover. "Springfield."

Wiggins grabbed the book and opened it to the yellow pages, then began flipping pages.

"Track Services, Inc., in Westfield," he said triumphantly.

"If it's still there," Tex said. "That phone book is ten years old."

Wiggins was carefully tearing the page out of the book. "We'll find out when we get there, won't we?"

***

As it turned out, their frustrations weren't over. Westfield was on the east bank of the Westfield River, a minor tributary of the Connecticut. Their original route paralleling the AT took them west of its headwaters, but going directly to Westfield meant they had to cross the river or travel almost two hundred miles around, not an option given the jury-rigged repair.

There were bridges in the city of Westfield itself and on the Mass Turnpike west of the city: main crossings likely to be controlled by someone, either government or freelance toll collectors. Their maps showed two crossings upstream, one in the center of a tiny hamlet named Woronoco and a second just upstream of the town.

"What do you think?" Tex asked.

"The one upstream from town might work," Wiggins said. "I've been thinking about our problem back at that last bridge. They probably weren't trying to block the bridge as much as protect the borders of their community." He pointed at the map. "There's nothing much on either side of this bridge upstream, and the road bypasses the town, so the good folks in Woronoco might care less."

It was a bit over sixty miles to Westfield via Woronoco, all on state roads, with no back road alternatives shown on their maps. The unknowns, besides the Woronoco bridge, were what they would find in the more populated areas they had to transit. With little choice, they could only trust darkness to shield them. They left at eleven, shooting for a midnight arrival at the bridge.

Things went smoothly until they rounded a curve approaching the town of Blandford and Wiggins saw two police cars across the road ahead. He stopped in the middle of the road and stared at the roadblock glowing green in his NV glasses.

"Is there a way around this, Tex?"

"Negative. The only road south dead-ends at a reservoir, and there are no roads to the north until a ways further into town. What are we going to do?"

"They look like legitimate cops instead of freelancers. It's probably something like we ran into at Front Royal, but maybe we can talk our way through. We really don't have a choice." Wiggins pondered it a moment. "Take off your glasses and put them under the seat."

Tex complied as Wiggins put the Honda in reverse and backed around the curve they'd just transited. When he was sure they couldn't be seen from the roadblock, he stopped the car and put his own glasses out of sight.

"Practice looking innocent," he said, and turned on the headlights.

He drove around the curve and toward the roadblock. When his headlights illuminated it, he stopped suddenly, as if he were seeing it for the first time. The Honda had barely come to a stop when he was blinded by a powerful spotlight, and an amplified voice boomed from the roadblock.

"KILL YOUR LIGHTS AND DRIVE FORWARD SLOWLY. BE PREPARED TO STOP ON MY COMMAND."

Wiggins held a hand up to shield his eyes and did as ordered. He'd crept a hundred feet when he was ordered to stop, kill his engine, and to keep both hands visible on the wheel. Tex was ordered to raise her hands as well. Totally blinded by the light, Wiggins was regretting his decision when more bright lights probed into the car, one through the driver's side window and the second through the passenger window. The light on the driver's side played over first Wiggins, then Tex, then the gear in the back of the Honda. The light on the passenger side held steady, continuing to blind them both.

"Are you armed?" asked the cop on the driver's side.

Wiggins cursed himself for a fool.

"Seriously, officer? Do you run across anyone traveling these days who ISN'T armed?" Wiggins asked.

"I take it that's a yes?"

"Yes, we're armed," Wiggins said.

"Very well, sir. I would like you both to keep your hands in plain sight. We will open your doors and then you will exit the vehicle, keeping your hands in plain sight at all times. Is that clear?"

"Really, officer. Is this necessary—"

"IS THAT CLEAR, SIR?"

"Yes, officer. It's clear," Wiggins said.

The car doors squeaked open, and Wiggins and Tex stepped out, holding their hands up. They were ordered to put their hands on the top of the car and then patted down.

"Nothing here, Chief," called the cop across the roof of the car.

"Where are your weapons?" the cop behind Wiggins asked.

"On the car seat," Wiggins said. "It's not real comfortable driving with them stuck in your belt or the small of your back."

The cop shined his light into the car and spotted the Sig and the Glock on the seat. He called across to his partner to bring Tex around to the driver's side, and when she was standing beside Wiggins where he could keep an eye on her, told his partner to collect the guns from the car.

Wiggins started to protest but thought better of it. Losing the handguns was acceptable if that was the end of it. They had plenty more hardware under blankets in the back. Best just to smile and get the hell out of here as soon as possible.

"Where are you going, and what's your business?" the chief asked.

"We're merchant seamen. We got stranded down south by the blackout, and we're just trying to get home to Maine."

"Where in Maine?"

"Just outside of Lewiston," Wiggins said.

"IDs?"

"In my back pocket, if you'll let me get it," Wiggins said.

"Go ahead," the chief said, and Wiggins fished his wallet out of his hip pocket, overcoming a sudden impulse to laugh hysterically at just how ludicrous it was that he was still carrying a wallet full of useless cash and even more useless credit cards. Old habits die hard.

Wiggins opened his wallet and removed his Maine driver's license and, as an afterthought, his Transportation Worker Identification and held them both out. The cop took them and backed away, holding the documents in front of the light so he could see both the IDs and Wiggins and Tex at the same time. He stepped closer and handed them back to Wiggins.

"Thank you, Mr. Wiggins. How about you, ma'am?"

"My IDs are in my backpack," Tex said. "Do you want me to get them?"

The cop considered that a moment. "No. I guess it doesn't matter."

"Look, officer," Wiggins said. "We don't want any trouble. We'd go around your town if we could, but the only way we can get where we're going is through town. But I promise—"

The chief was shaking his head, the action casting outsize dancing shadows in the harsh spotlights from the roadblock. "Be that as it may," he said, "I have to ask you folks to turn around and go back the way you came. Nobody's coming into Blandford from any direction, not even to pass through. No exceptions, by order of the town council."

The cop's voice softened. "I wish you luck, but you can't come through here. We'll unload your guns and leave 'em in the car. Then you have to turn around and leave. Is that clear?"

Wiggins nodded, relieved it wasn't worse.

"Warren," the chief said to the other cop, "unload the weapons and toss them and the loose rounds in the backseat. These folks can stop and reload when they get down the road a piece." The cop glanced at Wiggins. "No offense, but you can't be too careful these days."

"None taken," Wiggins said.

The second cop unloaded the weapons quickly and expertly, then tossed the guns and ammo in the back window. The chief nodded at Wiggins and Tex to get back in the car. Wiggins complied and was about to start the car when the chief spoke again, hesitantly.

"My kid brother's at sea. He's on one of the government ships in Diego Garcia. This is probably a stupid question, but I... I don't suppose you heard anything on your ship..."

"Is he on the *Lopez*?" Wiggins asked.

The cop looked surprised. "How did you know?"

"Just a lucky guess. There aren't that many ships at Diego Garcia, and I did a few rotations on the *Lopez* a few years ago. But I'm sorry, we don't know anything about her. Our communications went down right along with everyone else's."

The chief nodded. "Well, thanks anyway. He... he was almost due home on vacation when the blackout hit."

"Then he's lucky he wasn't en route when it happened," Wiggins said. "And if it's any consolation, he's probably better off than any of us here. Those pre-positioned ships have tons of supplies. And no gangbangers."

"Yeah, that's what I've been telling Mom, but it's tough on his wife and kids."

Wiggins nodded, sensing an opening. "So tell me, Chief, if your kid brother was trying to make it home to his family, wouldn't you want someone to help him out?"

The man didn't speak for a long moment, then smiled wanly. "I walked into that one, didn't I? And to answer your question, of course I want to help you out, but I take my orders from the town council."

"So what if it's not helping me out, but making a trade to substantially improve security? I mean, it's the middle of the night, and I doubt the town council wants to be awakened, but neither would they want to miss a great opportunity," Wiggins said.

"And what opportunity would that be?"

Wiggins reached under his seat for the NV goggles and held them out the window.

"Are those what I think they are?" the chief asked.

"State of the art," Wiggins said, sensing the cop wavering. "And for an escort through town I'll let you have these and sweeten the deal with two M4s and a hundred rounds of ammo. Hell, make it two hundred."

The cop examined the NV glasses. "How do you know I won't just arrest you both and take these and everything else you have?"

"First, because if you were going to shake us down, you'd have done so by now, and second, because I think you're still a decent guy trying to make the best of a truly screwed-up situation, and this is the decent thing to do," Wiggins said. "But mostly because you've got a kid brother who's in exactly our situation who will be trying to make it home sooner or later, and if he doesn't, you'll always wonder if it was because there was some guy somewhere who could have helped him but didn't. Karma's a bitch."

The chief shook his head and chuckled, then extended his hand through the open car window. "You missed your calling, Wiggins, you should have had a mind-reading act. You've got yourself a deal. I'm Jesse Walters."

Relief washed over Wiggins as he took the cop's hand. "Bill Wiggins," he said, "but you knew that. This is Shyla Texeira, Tex for short."

The exchange was completed quickly, and as promised, Walters escorted them through Blandford then pulled into the parking lot of an animal hospital at the edge of town. He got out of his patrol car and came over to Wiggins' window.

"State Route 23 parallels the Mass Turnpike," Walters said. "It's only a couple of hundred yards away through the trees. There are all sorts of refugees camped along the turnpike with nowhere else to go. Some are good people and some bad, but all of them are desperate. That's what our roadblock's all about. You're going to be running with your night vision, so you probably won't have a problem, but don't stop for anyone for any reason. There have been a lot of ambushes, and they often use women or children as bait, so trust nothing you see."

Wiggins nodded, and Walters continued.

"In about ten miles, Route 23 crosses the turnpike via a bridge. Hit the bridge at speed and don't slow down. The woods are close to the road, and the ambushers' sometimes throw rocks to distract drivers and make them run off the bridge approach and crash down the bank onto the turnpike. Be warned."

Wiggins shook his head. "Wow! That's hardcore. Thanks for the warning."

Walters reached into his shirt pocket and extracted a folded paper and handed it to Wiggins.

"At the intersection of 23 and 20, you'll hit another roadblock. There'll be a deputy sheriff in charge named Jimmy Jacobs. He's my cousin, and that note should get you through the roadblock and an escort over the bridge."

Walters grinned. "Of course, I suspect one of your 'extra' M4s and some ammo might get you an escort almost into Westfield, especially if you offer to replace the gas they use."

Wiggins grinned back and extended his hand out the window. "I expect that can be arranged. Thank you, Jesse."

Walters took Wiggins' hand and shook it firmly.

"Thank YOU, for what you said about my brother's ship. It might not seem like much to you, but it will mean a lot to my family. It's getting harder to keep hope alive nowadays," Walters said.

He released Wiggins' hand and nodded across the car. "Tex, Bill, Godspeed. I hope you make it home and find your families safe and well when you get there."

Wiggins glanced over at Tex and saw her quickly suppressed flash of pain.

"Thank you, Jesse," Tex said. "I hope your brother makes it home too."

Wiggins nodded his agreement, then flipped down his NV glasses and put the SUV in gear.

TRACK SERVICES, INC.
LOCKHOUSE ROAD
WESTFIELD, MASSACHUSETTS

DAY 34, 2:50 A.M.

Despite Walters' warning, the anonymity of traveling without lights allowed them to reach the next roadblock without difficulty. Once there, Walters' note and a little horse trading got them an escort not only into Westfield, but to the very gates of Track Services, Inc.

The company was located in an industrial area along a railroad spur. The gate to the tall chain-link fence hung open, and the building looked abandoned. The asphalt parking lot was full of equipment the use of which could only be guessed at, but most appeared intact.

Wiggins handed over an M4 and ammo, along with a five-gallon can of precious gasoline. The escort was worth it, and if his plan worked, they had more than enough gasoline. If not, they'd be looking for a plan B anyway. The deputies wished Wiggins and Tex well and left.

They hadn't disclosed the existence of the NV gear to the deputies at the second roadblock, as they no longer had an extra set to barter and were concerned the deputies might not be willing to settle for just guns and ammo if they knew about the NV. That meant running into Westfield with lights, which they extinguished as soon as the deputies' car pulled out of sight. They donned their goggles and moved the Honda out of sight from the road between two large pieces of equipment.

They found what they were looking for at the back of the lot. Backed against the fence were three Ford crew cab pickups. They had customized beds, with toolboxes mounted on each side, but of most interest were the odd units mounted at the front and rear bumpers of each truck. A pair of rail car wheels at each end of the trucks were fitted to a hydraulic power unit to raise and lower them.

"Bingo!" Wiggins said.

"I'm surprised they're still here," Tex said.

"I'd have been surprised if they weren't. I mean, think about it, no one's likely to want one except to ride the rails long distance, and they have to have the gas to do it."

"Presuming they even think about it," Tex said. "This never occurred to me."

Wiggins nodded. "Necessity might be the mother of invention, but desperation is its favorite aunt. I gotta get home, Tex."

"Well, we have a better chance now."

Wiggins nodded at the open hoods. "This place hasn't escaped notice completely; it looks like someone's taken the batteries. I'm betting all the gas tanks have been siphoned dry as well. We'll have to swap the battery out of the Honda."

He moved to the driver's side of the nearest truck and glanced in. "No keys. We'll hot-wire one if we have to, but let's look in the building. We might get lucky."

The building had several large roller doors, with a regular man door to one side. The man door was open, obviously forced. They entered cautiously, guns drawn. The pitch-black interior yielded no ambient light for their NV gear to intensify. They listened, but heard only dead silence.

"We'll need flashlights," Wiggins said softly as he raised his NV glasses out of the way.

When he was sure Tex had done the same, he switched on his flashlight. It illuminated a cavernous maintenance garage served by the large roller doors. To the right was a large office, overturned desks and chairs visible through the open door.

"Let's try the office," he said.

He found a key cabinet on the far wall, standing open with empty hooks, keys scattered on the floor beneath it. Wiggins piled keys on a nearby desk to sort through them. He'd found several Ford keys when Tex spoke.

"Well, well, well. What have we here?"

Wiggins looked up and his face split into a grin. Tex was ten feet away, playing her light over a large route map of New England rail lines, thumb-tacked to the wall.

"Great find, Tex. We'll be taking that."

Tex was already removing it.

Wiggins jammed a handful of Ford keys into his pocket. "I'm going to try these keys. If one of them works, I'll start swapping the battery over and gas up."

"Okay," Tex said. "I'll poke around a bit more to see if I can find anything of use."

Wiggins grunted his agreement and headed for the door. The keys were marked, but the system wasn't immediately obvious, but there weren't that many keys, so Wiggins just climbed into the first truck and tried them one by one. He hit pay dirt on his fifth try and hurried across the parking lot to move the Honda over to transfer the battery.

With the new battery, the pickup turned over smoothly, and Wiggins was filling their new ride with gas when Tex showed up and dumped the folded railroad map and a small plastic bag in the front seat of their new truck.

"Find anything of use?" Wiggins asked.

"The map's the prize," Tex said. "But I did find a portable air horn and refill cartridges. If we're gonna ride the rails in the dark, we might want to sound like a train at some point."

Wiggins laughed, his mood much improved. "Well, you never know. I'll finish fueling, then siphon the gas from the SUV into one of the empty cans. Would you start transferring everything else over?"

"On it," Tex said.

***

Half an hour later they were ready to roll, but hadn't quite decided the best direction to roll in. They grabbed the rail map and went back inside where their lights would be shielded. Wiggins spread the map out on a desk and studied it under his flashlight.

"It's almost four," Tex said. "If anyone saw us come in here lit up like Christmas trees, they might come nosing around come daylight. We need to be well away from here and out of town before sunup. What do you think, maybe an hour or so to get out of town, then another hour to get off the rails and find some place to hide?"

"Agreed." Wiggins traced a line on the map with his finger. "We don't have to plan the whole route now, but if we head north to Greenfield, we can pick up this line running east, which looks like it connects with northbound lines well outside Boston. We'll fine-tune the route when we stop for the day. For now let's just get the hell out of here."

***

Unfortunately, getting the truck lined up on the rails proved to be a matter of trial and error and not nearly as easy as Wiggins anticipated. They used a nearby street crossing with Wiggins driving and Tex giving hand signals, and it took them almost an hour before the truck was centered on the rails with the guide wheels locked in place. Wiggins cast a worried look at the lightening eastern sky as Tex climbed into the passenger seat.

"Let's hope we get better with practice," she said.

"Let's hope we don't have to use it long enough to need much practice," Wiggins said.

Despite the inauspicious beginning, the truck moved smoothly on the rails. Though, Wiggins' dreams of speeding home were dampened by the large safety notice on the dashboard, limiting the top speed on straight track to forty-five miles per hour and dropping that to thirty for curves, and warning of the near certainty of derailment if those limits were exceeded.

They'd just made a sweeping turn to the left under the Mass Turnpike when Wiggins nodded at the sign. "For sure we won't be outrunning any bad guys."

"Which is why we're running in the dark. Speaking of which, it will be full light in a half hour or so," Tex said, her NV glasses flipped up as she studied the map with a flashlight. "The delay is going to cost us. If we follow our original plan, we'll be in a populated area come sunup."

"Plan B?" Wiggins asked.

"We're in it," Tex said. "We're in a heavily wooded area for the next few miles, with no roads or buildings for at least a half a mile on either side of the tracks. Stopping on the track along here is probably the safest option."

"Okay," Wiggins said, tapping the brakes.

CHAPTER THIRTY-ONE

ON THE RAILS
WOODED AREA
NEAR WESTFIELD, MASSACHUSETTS

DAY 34, 4:25 P.M.

They decided one of them would keep watch in the driver's seat in case they had to run. Wiggins volunteered for the first watch, and Tex stretched out in the backseat of the crew cab and was dead to the world in minutes.

Wiggins was poring over the map for the tenth time when he heard Tex stirring. He looked back over the seat and smiled.

"Lazarus awakes."

There was a red ridge down Tex's cheek from a seam in the upholstery, and her hair was flattened on the side of her head. She looked about groggily, then glanced at her watch.

"You let me sleep all day, Bill!"

Wiggins shrugged. "You needed it, and I'm too excited to sleep anyway." He grinned again. "Even at thirty miles an hour, I'll make it home by morning, Tex."

"All the more reason to sleep. You can't drive all night—"

"Oh yes I can, and I'm going to," Wiggins said.

"Okay, but don't forget the river crossings, even on the railroads. There are at least four major—"

"Twenty-nine," Wiggins said.

"What?"

"There are twenty-nine major rail bridges on our route. We'll cross the Nashua River five times, and some big creek I never heard of six times, and several of the rivers twice or three times each." Wiggins grinned.

"Then why are you so happy?"

"Because ninety-five percent of the crossings are out in the boonies without a road nearby, much less anyone likely to contest our crossing, AND I confirmed we can give Boston a wide berth. We still have to transit some smaller cities, but I don't think we should have a problem on the rails in the dark."

"Still, we need to be cautious. For sure some of those railroad bridges are going to be blocked or guarded," Tex said.

"Yeah, but it's like we were talking about before. People guarding the major highway bridges pull cars across the road or make other strong barriers because they EXPECT cars might try to crash the roadblock," Wiggins said. "But where we've seen railroad bridges guarded, have we ever once seen one with a substantial barrier?"

"No, I'll grant you that. But that doesn't mean—"

"That's exactly what it means, Tex. Anybody guarding a railroad bridge is expecting to stop pedestrian traffic or maybe bikes or motorcycles, or at the very most, a car bumping along at slow speed. Nobody will expect a rail vehicle to take a bridge at speed, and it's such an unlikely event they're not likely to waste time constructing a barrier against it."

"I agree, this is our best option by far," Tex said. "I just don't want to see you get your hopes up too high. We're bound to have to go through some rail yards, and we don't know how all the rail switches are set. Or the blackout might have left a train on the track somewhere, blocking our way, or any one of a dozen things—"

"In which case we raise the guide wheels, get off the track, drive around the problem, and get back on," Wiggins said.

"Which we found out last night is not quite as easy as it sounds," Tex said.

"Well, maybe," Wiggins said, his enthusiasm not noticeably dampened.

***

Wiggins' patience was tested almost immediately when he suggested leaving as soon as it was full dark. Tex pointed out they had to transit Holyoke to reach open track, including a section of track running down the center of a city street for a half mile. Wiggins grudgingly conceded the point, and they delayed their departure until eleven.

Once clear of Holyoke and running north at full speed, a new variable surfaced; they were much noisier than anticipated. The guide wheels rode the tracks with a metallic hum and shrieked a piercing lament as they rounded curves. Likewise, there was a clunk at each rail joint, not unlike the clackety-clack of a freight train, but with a different cadence due to the short length of their vehicle and the odd spacing of the guide wheels and the truck tires.

"So much for stealth," Wiggins said. "I'm sure we can be heard for miles."

"That might be a good thing," Tex said. "Nobody's likely to try to stop a train, and by the time they figure out we're NOT a train, we'll be long gone."

Despite Wiggins' determination, he soon realized his goal was unrealistic. Braking of the rubber tires on the smooth steel rails was touchy at best, and every time they came to a rail yard, they slowed to a crawl, fearful they might find themselves switched to a siding and hurtling toward a stationary string of freight cars.

Likewise, the sound they produced at full speed gave far too much advance notice to anyone who might be waiting at a rail bridge. After some discussion, they decided to slow down well in advance of all bridges and creep forward in the dark until they could use their NV gear to see what awaited them.

It was an expenditure of time made all the more grudgingly because Wiggins had been right about most of the bridges. However, on two occasions their caution paid off, and they spotted guards ahead. The first time, they crept close enough in the dark to dash across and escape down the track before the sleepy guard knew what was happening.

On the second occasion, the guard was more alert and raised a powerful flashlight as they barreled toward the bridge. But Wiggins and Tex were prepared. They'd raised their NV glasses, and Wiggins hit the high beams just as Tex blasted the portable air horn in the guard's direction. The terrified guard leaped to one side, and the pickup rushed past. By the time the guard recovered, Wiggins killed the lights, and the pickup sped away in the darkness.

They were through Lowell by three o'clock, and halfway through Lawrence when Wiggins let out a resigned sigh. "We're obviously not going to make it tonight. We need to start thinking about a hiding place. We'll push across the Merrimack at Haverhill and out of the city. The track runs through rural areas north of there."

"The Merrimack is a pretty substantial river," Tex said.

"Definitely not one of the ninety-five percent. It's a major crossing in an urban area, so I expect it's guarded." Wiggins laughed nervously. "I guess we'll see how valid my 'no barricade' theory is, now won't we?"

Tex studied the map. "There's another problem, I'm afraid. There's a commuter train station to the left, then a long sweeping curve. We won't be able to see a thing until we're practically on top of the bridge, and if we take that curve at anything but a crawl, those metal wheels will squeal a warning. Anyone there will know about us before we know about them."

"What're you thinking?"

"I'm thinking we should stop before we round the curve and check it out on foot," Tex said.

***

Wiggins began slowing as soon as he saw the commuter rail station, and they rolled to a silent stop just as the tracks began to curve left. They started down the track on foot, carrying their M4s and moving cautiously.

They reached a viaduct, which carried the tracks over a city street. Tex touched Wiggins' arm and pointed; the street passing below them ran the short distance to the river and onto a car bridge. Wiggins followed Tex's pointing finger to see a roadblock across the bridge entrance, glowing green in his goggles. Three cars blocked the bridge. He could make out people seated in each of the cars, and one man leaning against the hood of one, holding an assault rifle.

"Well, there are definitely toll collectors on the car bridge, so there's probably someone on the rail bridge, since they're side by side," Wiggins whispered.

Tex nodded, and they started across the viaduct, being careful not to miss a step and plunge between the ties. They were halfway across when Wiggins spotted it.

"Well, so much for that theory," he muttered softly, then pointed to a car parked across the tracks a hundred feet away.

Tex studied the scene for a moment before responding. "It looks like there's some sort of little parking lot there, so all they had to do was back across the tracks." She paused. "I see one guy at the wheel zonked out. You see anyone else?" she whispered.

"Negative," Wiggins whispered back. "Stay and watch the roadblock while I take care of the guy in the car and roll it out of the way. If those guys down there hear us, be ready to discourage them from charging to the rescue too quickly."

Tex nodded and Wiggins moved forward. He circled around to the driver's side of the car and studied the man through the open window. His head lolled back against the headrest and he was snoring softly; drool dribbled from the corner of his open mouth. Wiggins put the muzzle of the M4 against the man's head.

"Make a move and you're dead," Wiggins said quietly.

The man's eyes flew open, puzzled at first, then terrified.

"Put both your hands on the wheel where I can see—"

Wiggins saw the movement in his peripheral vision and reacted instinctively, stepping back several steps as the man who'd been sleeping unseen in the backseat raised a pistol. Wiggins silenced him with a three-round burst, then turned back to the driver, who was now bringing up a pistol as well. Wiggins fired a three-round burst through the thin sheet metal of the car door, and the man jerked and fell forward on the wheel. The blare of a car horn split the night air.

Wiggins looked helplessly at Tex, who shook her head in insect-like astonishment. He jerked open the car door and dragged the dead man out, relieved the horn stopped at least. He laid his M4 down and jumped behind the wheel to pull the car off the tracks, then was out and scooping up his weapon to run back towards Tex. He found her crouched behind the short steel wall of the viaduct, watching the men at the roadblock.

They were all awake now, and Wiggins counted seven. All were well armed, but he could see no NV gear at all.

"I think we're all right," Tex said. "They don't know what the hell is going on, and they can't cut us off unless they crawl up that steep slope to the tracks, and it's pretty overgrown with brush. The only other way up here passes under this viaduct, and we have the advantage. I'll hold them off while you bring up the truck."

"I'll stay. You go get the truck," Wiggins said.

"Knock off the Sir Galahad crap, Bill. You know I'm a better shot. Just go get the truck. And hurry, before those clowns get organized."

Wiggins hesitated, then set off down the tracks at a run. He'd just reached the truck and started it when he heard all hell break loose. He could easily distinguish Tex's disciplined three-round bursts from the roar of full-automatic fire from the street below. He mashed the accelerator and sent up a silent prayer for Tex. He had no doubt she was giving better than she got, but the goons on the street below were throwing out a lot of rounds, and they might get lucky.

He rounded the curve and was relieved to see Tex on the opposite side of the viaduct, firing and moving, taking advantage of the fact her opponents could only see her muzzle flash, and making sure she immediately vacated the place they'd last seen it. With the truck on the rails, Wiggins had no need to steer it, so he shouldered his M4 and stuck it through the open window. He smiled when their opponents came into view. Far from advancing, they'd all taken cover behind the three-car barricade, popping up to spray rounds in their general direction then dropping down again. He added his own fire to Tex's as the truck rolled across the viaduct, then belatedly remembered the rather limited stopping power of the rubber tires on the slick rails and slammed on the brakes.

Tex glanced over her shoulder as the pickup flashed past, tires squealing, and she turned and raced after it. It was still moving when she managed to throw open the door and leap inside.

"GO, GO, GO," she yelled.

Wiggins transferred his foot to the gas and they were off, racing over the Merrimack.

HAVERHILL, MASSACHUSETTS
SAME DAY, 4:55 A.M.

They rode in tense silence through the dark city, expecting to be fired upon any moment. Slowly the tension ebbed, and Tex started chuckling.

"What?" Wiggins said.

"The next time the task requires silence, I'm doing it," Tex said. "Seriously? The frigging horn?"

"It's not like I planned it," Wiggins said.

"Obviously," Tex said, and laughed harder.

Her laughter was infectious, and soon Wiggins was laughing along with her, but a glance at the lightening sky to the east killed his good humor.

"We have to find a hiding place, and soon," he said.

Tex looked at a highway bridge towering above the track ahead, then glanced at the map.

"That's gotta be I-495. The area ahead looks to be a mix of rural land and subdivisions. There's a crossing about five miles ahead. We should be able to get off and on there with no problem."

A few minutes later Wiggins started slowing, and as Tex had predicted, the road crossing proved a perfect place to exit the tracks. He pulled into the crossing and raised the guide wheels, allowing him to steer off the tracks and onto the pavement.

"Which way?" he asked.

"Left," Tex said. "But go slow, and let's see if we can find an opening in the woods to the right."

Wiggins had driven no more than fifty feet when Tex yelled and pointed to a dirt track.

"This isn't the SUV, Tex," Wiggins said. "I doubt the off-road capabilities are close to the same."

Tex nodded and opened her door.

"What are you doing?" Wiggins asked.

"I'll walk in front to check things out. I'll walk a bit, then motion you forward. If we run into problems, we can always back out."

She closed the door without waiting for a response and walked forward. She went fifty feet and motioned him forward, then repeated the process. They'd gone about two hundred feet when he emerged on the now neglected green expanse of a golf course. Tex came over, grinning.

"I saw it on the map," she said. "I figure not too many people are playing golf these days, so hiding in the woods off the eighteenth hole should be fairly secure."

GRANITE FIELDS GOLF COURSE
KINGSTON, NEW HAMPSHIRE

DAY 35, 7:25 P.M.

Wiggins didn't argue when Tex insisted on taking the first watch. He collapsed across the backseat of the crew cab and was snoring soundly before the sun was fully up. He awoke in the early afternoon, rested but sweaty, and relieved Tex. She woke near sundown to find Wiggins standing in the fading light, the railroad map spread out before him on the hood of the truck. She went into the woods to relieve herself and came back to stand by Wiggins' side.

"Problem?" she asked.

He shook his head. "I was just going over the route again to see if there were any more blind approaches like that curve back there."

"And?"

He shook his head again. "There aren't any, but I've had second thoughts about our route. Riding the rails all the way to Lewiston means transiting Portland and two long bridges we don't really need to cross. I don't think it's worth the risk, BUT"—Wiggins put his finger on the map—"there's a spur here in Biddeford with its own bridge across the Saco River. It dead-ends in an industrial park less than forty miles from home. I'll feel a lot more comfortable maneuvering on back roads I know well and with a night-vision advantage instead of being stuck on rails in a city."

"Sounds reasonable," Tex said.

They were close now, and as much as he wanted to rush, Wiggins forced himself to be patient. They decided to wait until after midnight to increase the odds the people in the towns they transited would be asleep. They ate MREs and passed the time talking about their lives. Wiggins hadn't spoken much of his home and family, suppressing his worry to concentrate on the all-important task of getting home. Now that goal was in reach, and he felt a need to verbalize his fears. Tex offered quiet encouragement, silent most of the time but asking questions when appropriate.

He smiled when he talked of his wife, Karen, and their three-year-old, Billy, and his own parents who lived nearby. Then he turned somber.

"Karen's folks were killed in a car wreck when she was in college, but my folks love her as much as I do. She had a real hard time when Billy was born, and my folks were right there with her." His face clouded. "But I wasn't and I've never really forgiven myself."

"Why? What happened?"

"Billy came early and Karen had to have a C-section. I planned to work until a couple of weeks before delivery so I could be there and still have most of my vacation left to help out, but I was a day out of port when she went into labor. I practically rode the gangway down when we made port, but by the time I got home, it was all over. Luckily it turned out okay, but this time I was determined to be there."

He shook his head. "Look how well that turned out."

"When is she due?" Tex asked softly.

Wiggins didn't respond. "Five days ago," he said at last. "And she was likely going to need another C-section. But now..." He trailed off, unable to complete the thought.

"I'm sure she's fine, Bill," Tex said, but it sounded lame even to her.

"She has to be," Wiggins said, his face a mask of grim determination.

They lapsed into silence, checking the luminous faces of their watches as the minutes dragged. Finally at eleven, Wiggins could take it no more.

"Screw it," he said, and donned his NV glasses and started the truck.

CHAPTER THIRTY-TWO

They got off to a good start, managing to get the pickup lined up on the rails and the guide wheels locked on the second try. Wiggins started down the track and they were soon at the prescribed safe speed limit and then five miles over it. Tex said nothing as Wiggins stared ahead grimly.

They rolled through Exeter and Newmarket without difficulty and barely slowed through the University of New Hampshire campus at Durham. Movement seemed to lighten Wiggins' mood, and he began to make small talk once again. They slowed for the Cocheco River bridge at Dover but found it clear, but only five miles further down the line, they spotted a self-appointed toll collector at the Salmon Falls River bridge at Rollinsford.

They surprised him with their high beams and air horn technique and were almost across the bridge before the man recovered and fired at them, or rather their sound, somewhat perfunctorily.

Wiggins let out a relieved sigh as they rolled off the bridge on the far side.

"We're in Maine, Tex! That was the border!" he said.

"How far to Biddeford?" Tex asked.

"Thirty miles to the switch for the spur," Wiggins said.

"Do you have any idea how we're going to manage that? Don't they have padlocks or something?"

"We'll figure it out," Wiggins said.

Tex raised her NV goggles and studied the map. "Maybe we don't have to. After the lines diverge, they cross Main Street about three blocks apart. We can follow this line to Main Street, get off and drive three blocks, and get back on the spur at the crossing. That should be a lot faster than messing around with a switch when we don't know what we're doing."

"Agreed. Good thinking."

Tex smiled. "That's why I'm the navigator."

The miles clacked by beneath the truck's multiple sets of wheels. As they entered Biddeford, the track curved to the right, and Wiggins was forced to slow so the screeching wheels didn't announce their presence as they made their brief foray on the city streets. The transfer to the spur was uneventful, and the rail bridge was unguarded. Wiggins picked up speed again, rushing through dark residential areas before plunging again into heavy woods.

Tex looked at the map. "Take it easy, Bill. There's a sharp turn to the left coming up."

Wiggins slowed, but not enough, and the metal guide wheels screeched a piercing lament as the truck rounded the curve at speed, barely managing to stay on the track.

"Oops! Sorry, Tex," Wiggins said, slowing the truck even more. "I guess I need to keep it together. "Any more curves I need to worry about?"

She looked at the map again. "There's a slight jog to the right around some sort of big facility ahead on the left. Then a bit farther there's a sharp turn to the right under the interstate and maybe a quarter of a mile to the dead end."

Wiggins sighed. "Almost there."

He increased speed again as they hurtled through the thick woods, but mindful of the slight curve ahead, he kept the speed well below the prescribed limit. They rounded the curve, and the trees thinned enough for him to catch fleeting glimpses of a huge industrial building through the trees to his left. He saw movement on the track ahead and glanced back toward a large sign on the building. Uh-oh!

The movement resolved itself into two figures standing astride the track, both in full combat gear with helmets and NV gear. Wiggins watched in mute surprise as one raised his hand in a stop gesture.

"Who the hell are those guys, and what are they doing in the middle of the woods?" Tex asked.

"Army, National Guard, or FEMA I'd say," Wiggins replied. "That building is the General Dynamics Weapons facility. It was a big employer here, but I forgot all about it. They make machine guns and ammunition, so no doubt any number of groups want to control it. They probably heard us screech around that curve and sent guys to check the track."

"What are we going to do?"

"Well, I'm NOT letting them stop us this close to home. At a minimum they'll be suspicious about all the guns and how we happen to be riding the rails. Nothing good can come of dealing with them. Get ready to sound that horn and dive for the floorboard."

The men were both raising their assault rifles now, and Wiggins braked, the rubber tires squealing on the slick rails. He saw their body language relax slightly, and one stepped to the side, obviously intent on questioning them, while the other remained in place on the track. They held their rifles ready, but pointed down. The truck was fifty feet away and coasting to a stop when Wiggins raised his NV goggles and told Tex to do the same.

"NOW!" he hissed, and stomped the accelerator as he hit his high beams.

Tex blasted the horn at the now blinded men as the truck tires squealed and spun on the rails. Wiggins realized his mistake and eased off the accelerator, allowing the tires to bite, and the truck shot forward. They brushed aside the man blocking their way, who barely managed to get off the track in time, and a hundred feet away they heard gunfire. A round slapped into the truck, and Wiggins belatedly killed the lights to make them a more difficult target.

"You all right?" Wiggins asked.

"I think so. You think they'll chase us?"

"No clue, but we need to disappear as soon as possible," Wiggins said.

He pushed the truck as fast as track conditions would allow, and less than five minutes later they rolled under the interstate and into the industrial park. There were multiple places to exit the rails where entrance drives crossed the track. Wiggins overshot the first one, but got the truck stopped at the second.

He raised the front guide wheels, freeing the front tires from the rails, but when he hit the control for the rear guide wheels, there was no response. He cursed and they both got out. Oily hydraulic fluid dripped off the back bumper, and a quick inspection found a bullet hole near the bottom of the hydraulic tank for the rear unit.

Wiggins cursed. "We can't raise the wheels without hydraulic fluid."

***

"What are we going to do?" Tex asked, but Wiggins already had the back door open and was pulling out empty water bottles.

"Drain oil out of the front unit and transfer it to the rear. We only have to get enough in to cycle the rear wheels once."

"But the hole—"

Wiggins started toward the front of the truck with an armload of water bottles. "One problem at a time. Grab a bunch of those bottles and give me a hand."

He squatted down and located the drain plug for the front unit and loosened it with the multitool.

"Okay, Tex. There's no valve on this thing, and when I pull that plug, it will be slick as hell. I doubt I can screw it back in without dropping it, especially with hydraulic fluid gushing out. We've only got one shot at this, and if we don't catch enough, we're screwed."

"What can I do?"

"I'm gonna have a bottle in each hand and swap them out one after another. I need you to take the full ones, set them out of the way, and feed me empties. You ready?"

Tex nodded, and Wiggins pulled the plug. Fluid gushed over his fingers and ran down his elbow as he jammed the narrow neck of the plastic bottle under the stream. It filled in seconds and he swapped bottles, trying and failing to capture every drop. They ran out of bottles before they ran out of fluid, and though he tried to get the plug back in, most of the remaining hydraulic fluid ran onto the pavement before he managed to do so.

"Well, let's just hope we have enough," Wiggins said and started toward the back of the truck with an armload of bottles. Tex did the same.

"What about the hole?" Tex asked as Wiggins opened up the fill cap for the rear unit.

"Let's find a plug. It's only got to hold long enough to fill the lines and cycle the wheels once," Wiggins said.

Tex jammed her index finger in the hole.

"Seriously?" Wiggins asked.

"Got a better idea? We're sort of in a hurry here, right?"

"I can't argue with that," Wiggins said, and started pouring hydraulic fluid into the tank.

He finished quickly and moved around to the driver's side. "Let's just hope there's not too much air in the system, because bleeding the lines could take forever," he said as he got behind the wheel.

He hit the switch and was rewarded with the expected whine, followed a long moment later by a clunk as the rear guide wheels locked into their stowed position. He called to Tex, and she crawled in the passenger side, wiping greasy hands on her clothes.

"I feel like a damned engineer," Tex muttered, and Wiggins laughed despite the situation.

"Intelligent?"

Tex smiled. "No, greasy and irritable."

***

There was no need for maps now, and Wiggins pressed the pickup through the inky darkness with a confidence born of familiarity. They took two-lane blacktops and one-lane gravel roads through farm land and forest and across country bridges. At one point they pulled onto a dirt track, and Tex gasped as Wiggins plunged across a wide dark stream of unknown depth. Or unknown to her, anyway, for Wiggins seemed to have no doubts.

They were speeding down a county road through thick forest when Wiggins began to slow. Tex saw two mailboxes beside a driveway, and Wiggins turned up the gravel track and followed it a hundred yards through the trees. He spoke for the first time since they'd left Biddeford.

"My folks have a hundred acres, but they gave half of it to Karen and me. We built our house two years ago, or I guess I should say we started building it. We're doing most of it ourselves, and my mom says you never really finish building a house," Wiggins said.

They'd come to a large clearing in the woods, and the gravel driveway diverged into two separate lanes, each serving a tidy, rustic home built of logs and native stone. They had an honest look about them, and Tex thought they looked like homes Wiggins might build: neat, sturdy, practical buildings.

Wiggins stopped at the split between the driveways.

"What's the matter, Bill?"

Wiggins didn't answer right away, and when he did, there was a catch in his voice. "I'm scared, Tex. For over a month I've been telling myself everything was gonna be okay, but now I have to find out. What if it's not okay? I... I think I just want to sit here a bit." He nodded toward the lightening sky. "It'll be daylight soon anyway. No need to wake everybody up just yet."

***

They sat there silently for almost an hour as the gloom turned to gray. A light flared in a window of the house on the right, the flickering of a flame lighting a lantern. It seemed to be what Wiggins was waiting for.

"That will be Dad," Wiggins said. "He's always the first one up."

He started the truck and turned toward his parents' house. They got out in the driveway, Tex suddenly unsure what to do. She hung back as Wiggins climbed the short steps to the porch and knocked on the storm door. There was the sound of footfalls inside the house.

"Who is it?" asked a cautious voice.

"It's Bill, Dad," Wiggins said.

There was the sound of locks being turned; then the inner door opened and an older man burst through the storm door and enveloped Wiggins in a hug. Then he saw Tex and flushed red, obviously embarrassed by his display of emotion. He straightened and released his son.

"It's sure good to have you home, son." The man looked at Tex. "And who is this—"

"Dad, is Karen here or at our house?"

The joy on the elder Wiggins' face morphed to anguish, and Tex had no doubt as to the cause.

THE WIGGINS PROPERTY
NEAR LEWISTON, MAINE

The lights had been out almost two weeks when Karen Wiggins went into labor early, the same day Tex and Bill Wiggins had left North Carolina. By that time, the Central Maine Medical Center in Lewiston had closed their doors for good, having exhausted not only the fuel for their emergency generator, but all medicine and supplies.

Ray and Nancy Wiggins used the last of their gasoline and braved the chaos of the city to get their daughter-in-law to the hospital, where they'd found the doors shuttered. Desperate, they'd returned to their home ten miles out of town and done the best they could. It had been a breech presentation, and neither mother nor child had survived.

Ray Wiggins told the story in a flat monotone, as if hoping his unemotional presentation could wring the anguish from the tale. Bill's mother, Nancy, sat beside her son and held his hand, mixing her tears with his own on the kitchen table. Tex, feeling very much an outsider, took it upon herself to entertain three-year-old Billy in the living room.

The days took on a sameness after that. The Wiggins' homes were well off the beaten track, and they'd had no problems with marauders as of yet. Tex was made welcome, and the supplies they brought meant no immediate hardship.

The Wiggins were both avid gardeners and home canners, and Ray and Bill were hunters, so they were generally self-sufficient in the way of rural people. They had no electricity for the well pump, but a spring in the woods behind the homes and a few drops of chlorine bleach provided their drinking water. Tex volunteered for water-hauling chores, eager to pull her own weight.

Bill Wiggins became lethargic almost to the point of catatonia and went about his chores with a listlessness that was heartbreaking to anyone who had known him even two months earlier. Ray and Nancy had buried Karen and the infant on a gentle slope overlooking the two homes, and Bill moved a picnic bench from their patio up to the graveside. He was spending more and more time there, sitting alone by the graves and thinking thoughts to which only he was privy.

The elder Wigginses grew equally morose, their joy at Bill's homecoming sapped by the enormity of their son's loss, and their own guilt they'd been unable to prevent it. The only bright spot in the house was little Billy, who viewed life with the wonder and irrepressible optimism of a three-year-old. He took an immediate liking to Tex, and she to him, and he followed her everywhere.

Her chores done for the day, Tex was playing hide-and-seek with Billy in the backyard late one afternoon. She flushed him from his hiding spot and chased him squealing across the backyard before picking him up and tickling him. She set him down on the picnic table and was about to resume her tickling when a solemn look crossed his face.

"Will Daddy always be sad?" Billy asked.

Tex turned to follow Billy's gaze and saw Bill sitting at the top of the knoll on the picnic bench, staring down at the twin crosses.

"He just misses your mom and your baby sister, that's all," Tex said.

"But he never met the baby, and she and Mommy are happy in Heaven and that's a good place. Nana told me so," Billy said. "Doesn't he want them to be happy?"

"Sure he does, honey, but when someone you love goes away, you miss them a lot."

"But we're here." Billy's lip started trembling. "Doesn't... doesn't he love us?"

Tex felt as if her heart would break. She blinked back a tear and folded Billy in a fierce hug. "Sure he does, baby. He just needs a little time, that's all."

"You're smushin' me," Billy said.

Tex laughed. "Sorry," she said, releasing him and holding him at arm's length. "What say we go in and see if your nana might have a little snack for you?"

***

Bill looked up as Tex sat down on the bench.

"Like some company?" she asked.

He shrugged, and they sat in silence.

"What's up, Tex?" Bill asked at last.

Tex took a deep breath. "You have to move on, Bill. Karen and the baby died, and that is truly heartrending and tragic, but there's nothing you can do about it, and there are three people in that house who love you and need you very much."

Bill Wiggins bristled. "You don't get to tell me when it's time to move on. You don't understand—"

"You're right I don't understand. MY family is gone, and yours is right here in front of you, being dragged along to your pity party whether they like it or not. If my folks were still alive or if I was blessed with a great kid like Billy, I sure as hell would be counting my blessings instead of my losses. Do you honestly think KAREN would want this? Do you know Billy thinks you don't love him?"

"You leave Karen out of—" Wiggins stopped mid-sentence. "What do you mean Billy thinks I don't love him?"

Tex took another deep breath and told Wiggins about her exchange with Billy. When she finished, he turned his head away, but not before she saw a tear leak down his cheek. She reached over and took his hand.

"Bill, this is tough. I know that, but you were there for me, and I'm here for you. We all are."

Wiggins squeezed her hand. "I… I just don't know what to do, Tex? Everything is so screwed up."

Tex shrugged. "We do what people have always done. We live, and if we're lucky, we love and laugh a little. Fundamentally, the world hasn't changed that much as far as the basics go, except nobody is hooking up with total strangers on an iPhone or getting their panties in a bunch because someone dissed them on Facebook."

Wiggins laughed and wiped his eyes with the back of his free hand. Then he stood and pulled Tex to her feet and wrapped her in a hug.

"So are you going to hang around to kick my butt when it needs kicking?" he asked softly into her ear.

"I sort of have to," she whispered back. "You got my choo-choo train shot up."

Wiggins threw his head back and laughed again; then he and Tex walked down the hill hand in hand.

CHAPTER THIRTY-THREE

Anderson sat on his makeshift log stool in his skivvies, pants around his ankles, examining his left knee in the flickering light of the torch. A few days' rest had done wonders; the swelling was down, and it hardly hurt at all now, at least if he was careful how he put weight on it.

The last days seemed like paradise compared to the ordeal of his escape and flight. Concerns about food eased somewhat on the second day when the chickens made themselves at home in a corner of the cave and began laying again. Likewise, both Cindy and, under her instruction, Jeremy had proved surprisingly proficient at woodcraft. By the third day, their snares and deadfalls were producing at least one meal a day, the protein supplemented by edible greens Cindy foraged from the forest. Between nature's bounty and the water source at the back of the cave, they wouldn't starve or die of thirst anytime soon.

In fact, Anderson's only real complaint was boredom. Cindy insisted he stay off his knee, a prohibition enforced with the rigidity of a drill sergeant. The result was days of boredom, stretched out on his mattress of evergreen boughs or sitting in the sun in front of the cave, waiting for Cindy and Jeremy to return from checking their traps or gathering firewood. His only pastime was digging insects out of cracks in the rock face, which he tossed to an appreciative audience of chickens.

The evenings were better, sitting around the fire. Jeremy inevitably began to nod and retired to his mattress to snore until sunup, but Cindy, like Anderson, was by nature a night owl. They talked long into the night about everything, and nothing. The more he learned, the more he admired her; and she was definitely easy on the eyes.

"How's it looking?"

Anderson jumped. Cindy stood in the flickering torchlight with an armload of firewood, which she bent to add to the nearby pile without waiting for his answer.

"How do you do that?" he asked.

She straightened. "Do what?"

"Move so quietly," Anderson said. "You're like a cat."

Cindy shrugged. "You have to be light on your feet to dance, and moving quietly over rock isn't very challenging."

Anderson nodded and began to stand to pull up his pants. Cindy waved him back down.

"Leave it," she said. "I want to look at that knee."

"It's fine."

"I'll be the judge of that. Now sit your butt back down," Cindy said.

Anderson sighed and sat back down on the upended log. "Yes, mother."

Cindy squatted and peered at his knee. "Looks like the swelling's gone. Is it giving you any pain?"

Anderson shook his head and was about to say no when Cindy reached out with both hands and began to gently probe his knee. Her touch was electric and totally unanticipated. The fly of his boxers gapped open as his erection rose unbidden.

"Oh geez! I'm sorry, Cindy. I didn't mean—"

Her laughter resonated into the darkness of the cave, and she reached out and wrapped her hand around him.

"Jeremy's checking the deadfalls. We've got at least twenty minutes," she said.

***

As it turned out, they had a bit over thirty, and it was easily the best half hour of Anderson's life in recent memory. Correction, pretty much everything in recent memory sucked, so he amended that to the best half hour ever.

Afterward, he hardly felt the evergreen needles of his sleeping pallet scratching his bare back as he enjoyed the pleasant weight of Cindy's naked body on top of his. He began to stir again, and she lifted her cheek from his chest and grinned.

"There's nothing I'd like more, Romeo," she said. "But I'll have to take a rain check. Jeremy will be back soon."

"So there's going to be a next time?"

She studied his face. "Do you want there to be?"

"Absolutely," Anderson said. "Though I have to admit it took me by surprise."

She laughed. "That was sort of obvious."

"No, I mean that you would... that you wanted..."

Cindy silenced him, her fingers on his lips. "You do realize you're working pretty hard to spoil the moment, don't you?"

Anderson was totally confused.

"You're a decent guy, George. You risked your neck for us when you didn't have to, and let's just say facing death with someone is a pretty intense bonding experience. Add that to the fact we're both single and horny as hell, and the sex was pretty much inevitable," Cindy said.

"Sooo..."

She bent down and kissed him tenderly. "So let's just play it by ear, and see where it goes. But now we better get up and get dressed before Jeremy comes in and decides he needs to shoot you."

***

They'd just gotten dressed and moved back outside when Jeremy's head appeared over the lip of the ledge, followed in short order by the rest of his body. He beamed when he saw them and held up two gutted rabbits.

"Lunch," Jeremy said.

"Good job!" Anderson said while Cindy just returned Jeremy's wide smile.

With no refrigeration, they normally cooked and ate small game as soon as it was killed, and two rabbits made for a bountiful early lunch. Anderson finished his third piece of rabbit, licked the juice from his fingers, and heaved a contented sigh.

"That was really good. In fact, the only thing that could have improved it is a little seasoning," he said.

"I had all my seasonings and spices in big Ziploc bags in the trailer," Cindy said. "Maybe they're still there."

"You thinking we should go look?" Anderson asked.

Cindy nodded. "If anyone was looking for us, I think we would have heard or seen them by now. I think it's safe."

"The current may have smashed and scattered it from here to who knows where," Anderson said.

"And the trailer could be sitting high and dry on the creek bank a half mile downstream," Cindy said. "One thing is for sure; if it's there, it will be in or near the creek bed. We'll just follow it a ways; if we don't find it in a reasonable distance, we turn around and come back."

Jeremy was excited at the prospect. "Let's go today!"

Cindy shook her head. "We should leave at first light tomorrow to give us as much daylight as possible. We don't know what we're going to run into, and we don't want to make the steep climb up to the cave in the dark."

***

They all turned in early for a change. As usual, Jeremy's soft snores were drifting across the dying embers of the fire in minutes. The sleep of the innocent, Anderson thought as he rolled on his side. He was almost asleep himself when Cindy crawled in beside him and kissed the back of his neck.

"Rain check," she whispered. "Presuming you can be quieter than you were earlier."

Anderson smiled in the dark and shifted in place to face her, his smile widening when he discovered she was naked. "Me?" he whispered back. "I seem to remember you might need to take your own advice."

DAY 36, 5:40 A.M.

They rose early to a breakfast of leftover rabbit and eggs and left as soon as there was enough light to navigate the steep slope down to the creek. They traveled light, carrying only water, some hard-boiled eggs for lunch, and their weapons. Anderson and Jeremy both carried M4s, but Cindy stuck to her tried and true shotgun.

The steep climb down put Anderson's knee to the test. There were twinges of pain, and he mentally put his recovery at ninety percent. He caught Cindy watching him, and smiled and gave her a thumbs-up. She gave him a skeptical nod and continued to watch during the rest of the descent. They had their first disagreement when they got to where the Mule was hidden.

"This is premature," Cindy said. "You're still favoring the leg, and this is a good way to reinjure it."

"It's fine. I'll let you know if it starts bothering me, and I'll stop and rest it."

"It's already bothering you; I can tell by the way you're walking. We'll take the Mule," Cindy said.

Anderson shook his head. "Too noisy."

"We're at least ten miles from the nearest house or road," Cindy said. "Unless someone's in the woods—"

"Exactly," Anderson said. "We've got as near to a perfect hideaway as we're likely to find, and we should keep a low profile. If someone hears the Mule in the woods, who tells someone else, who then tells someone else, before long a whole lot of someones know there are people back here. Sooner or later FEMA might get nosy. Besides, we don't even know if we're going to FIND the trailer, in which case, we've made a lot of noise for nothing."

Cindy looked unconvinced. "But if we DO find the trailer, that's a lot of gear to hump uphill to the cave. It's going to be hard enough getting it up this far, without being exhausted by the time we even start."

They argued for five minutes, finally agreeing to make the initial search on foot. If they found anything worth salvaging, they'd assess the most efficient way to get it back to the cave at that time. Anderson considered that a win, though he didn't press the point. From the look on Cindy's face, she was less than thrilled at the 'compromise.'

Descending the creek proved to be much less of an ordeal than reaching it. It was back down to its normal flow, only an inch or two deep in most places, and the stair-step breaks in the slate bottom, which had made the Mule's ascent difficult, had the opposite effect when traveling by foot. Their biggest concern was slipping on the slimy bottom or losing their footing on a loose rock.

They moved down the creek almost as fast as the heavily laden Mule and trailer had crawled up it and, after two hours, reached the spot they'd entered the creek days before. *Was it only a few days?* Anderson thought. It seemed like a lifetime. He stood at the crossing and peered downstream.

"It gets a lot steeper," he said.

Cindy nodded. "The creek runs directly downhill with a considerable drop over just a few hundred yards, then starts winding again with a more gradual incline. If it's down there, it'll be a bitch to get stuff back up this hill."

"What do you want to do?" Anderson asked.

Cindy shrugged. "It's not even midmorning. Let's look a bit further, but if we don't find it soon, it's a lost cause."

Anderson nodded and started downhill. They hadn't gone far when Jeremy let out an excited whoop.

"Mom! I see it!"

They followed Jeremy's pointing finger to where the trailer rested on the creek bank, bridging the gap between two large trees growing in a line perpendicular to the stream. They scrambled down.

The trailer had hit the trees sideways, borne on the raging floodwaters. Its short tongue rested against the upstream side of the tree closest to the creek bed, and the rear end of the trailer was jammed against the other tree. Debris and trash was mounded on the upstream side of the trailer, and as Anderson got closer, he could see the force of the partially dammed water against the side of the trailer had bent the tongue at a significant angle.

"There'll be no towing that even if we managed to get it out of here," he said.

Cindy nodded in agreement. "But everything is still lashed down. It's a miracle it didn't roll over. Now we just have to get the stuff back up to the cave."

She gave Anderson a withering look. "Which would be a lot easier if we had the MULE with us."

"All right, all right," Anderson said. "You made your point. I'll go back and bring it down."

Cindy shook her head. "I can get back up faster than either one of you two, and we're not getting the Mule down this last slope anyway. I'll go get the Mule while you two hump this stuff up to the crossing."

Anderson sighed, then nodded.

"And one more thing," Cindy said. "It's going to be a three- or four-hour round-trip to bring the Mule back, so take your time and don't overdo it on that knee. Remember, we still have to hump all this stuff up to the cave. Jeremy?"

"Yes, ma'am?"

"Keep an eye on George. If it looks like his knee is hurting, I want you to remind him to rest. Can you do that?"

"Yes, ma'am," Jeremy said.

***

Jeremy took his instructions seriously and badgered Anderson the entire time they humped supplies up the hill. But truth be told, the young man also carried far more than his fair share up the steep slope, and Anderson was happy to let him. They finished in a little over three hours.

"How long until Mom gets back?" Jeremy asked.

Anderson shrugged. "I'd say another hour."

Jeremy began to nod, then stopped and grinned. "You're wrong, George. I hear her coming now."

Anderson heard it too, but it was wrong somehow. It wasn't the throaty rumble of the Mule, and it came from the clearing where the cabin once stood, a quarter of a mile away. He put his finger to his lips to caution Jeremy and stood listening. The sound stopped, and Anderson heard the sound of two car doors slamming.

"Someone's at your cabin site, Jeremy. You stay here while I check it out."

Jeremy nodded. "I'll go too. You may need help."

What I don't need is worrying about you getting shot, Anderson thought, but he didn't say that.

"Negative. You need to get up the creek and warn your mom. Okay? If whoever it is hears the Mule, they'll get curious, and we don't want them looking for us."

Jeremy looked scared. "Is it the bad guys?"

"I don't know, Jeremy, but I don't want to take any chances. Now go warn your mom."

CHAPTER THIRTY-FOUR

Jeremy nodded and splashed up the creek at a run. Anderson waited for him to move out of sight, then started for the clearing, moving through the woods parallel to the trail. He slowed as he approached the clearing, then dropped to one knee and slowly parted the foliage.

He suppressed a curse. Cindy and Jeremy's cabin was still standing, though the walls were black and the roof was caved in at one corner. The rain! The same torrential downpour that claimed the trailer had doused the fire they started in the cabin.

A FEMA Special Reaction Force Hummer stood in front of the blackened cabin, and Anderson could make out voices coming from the inside. After a long moment, two black-clad SRF troopers emerged from the cabin, one of them dragging a small black tarp. He threw the tarp on the ground and spread it out. Anderson's heart sank.

"It's a UTV cover all right, for a big unit, probably one of those multi-seat side by sides." The man scanned the ground around the cabin and pointed. "And look at that! Those ain't hummer tracks; there was a UTV here for sure."

The second trooper seemed unimpressed. "UTV, BFD. Who cares, Carr? All I know is we're supposed to be patrolling this section of the Lexington Turnpike, and this wild-goose chase is going to get all of our asses in a crack."

"Yeah, well, you'd feel a bit different if it was YOUR brother that got capped. This never felt right to me. If the patrol visited here first, then got ambushed on the road later, why ain't there any bodies in the cabin?"

The second trooper shrugged. "All right, I'll admit it's strange, but what exactly do you plan on doing about it? We ain't even supposed to be here, and I sure as hell ain't joining no posse to chase ghost UTVs through the woods."

Carr bent and started rolling up the UTV cover. "We take this as evidence. That and the fact you and I both saw there ain't any bodies in the house and there's old UTV tracks all around should convince the captain. I mean, somebody out there murdered three SRF troopers, and we can't let that stand. I'm sure I can convince him to mount a search and destroy mission. And if he won't, I'm gonna round up volunteers and do it myself in my off time. Nobody murders my brother and gets away with it."

Anderson crouched, parsing the possibilities. They were leaving now, but it sounded like they'd be back. He felt his dreams of living the idyllic life of a cave dweller fading. He was debating his next move when the one called Carr looked in his direction and shouted, "STAND DOWN!"

Anderson heard a sound behind him to the left and swiveled in that direction, unable to stifle a groan as an unexpected pain knifed through his left knee. He brought his M4 up, but knew it was too late even before the butt reached his shoulder.

"FREEZE!"

He stared into the muzzle of an M4 less than twenty feet away.

"Ground your weapon very slowly. Then drop to your knees and put your hands on top of your head and face away from me. Do it now," the man ordered.

Anderson did as instructed.

"HEY, CARR. WE GOT A VISITOR. AND HE'S WEARING ONE OF OUR UNIFORMS."

***

Assumptions can get you killed, and they probably already had, Anderson thought as he lay facedown in the grass, wrists tied behind him. Two slamming car doors did not necessarily mean two people. In this case, it meant four, with two on overwatch at the clearing perimeter. It was a bonehead mistake, and he probably had this coming.

The initial beat down had been almost perfunctory. They'd flex-cuffed his wrists and ankles, and two of them held him upright while a third worked him over with fists and feet. The one called Carr had just stood back and watched, a smile on his face, until the men grew tired of the sport and threw him facedown in the dirt and chicken droppings.

Anderson figured he was dead already, and the only question now was whether he could deflect attention from Cindy and Jeremy. If these guys thought he'd taken out their friends alone, they'd take him back to HQ to make an example of him. With the shooter eliminated, the SRF no longer had any reason to be poking around in these woods.

He contemplated the best way to play it. The uniform would help sell his story, but if he confessed too quickly, they might put two and two together and figure he was protecting someone. On the other hand, Cindy was sure to come looking, and if he was still here and alive, she might do something stupid.

He didn't really know how much time had passed, but he grew increasingly desperate for them to either take him away or deal with him quickly, before Cindy arrived. He might have to provoke them.

That was still a half-formed thought when he was jerked to his feet and held erect by a strong hand in each armpit. His eyes had barely focused when the rifle butt struck him in the stomach and doubled him over. The men on either side jerked him back upright, and suddenly Carr was in his face, the man's pockmarked visage mere inches away as his fetid breath washed over Anderson.

"That was just another little love tap, asshole," Carr snarled. "We were gonna take you back to base, but I thought about it and decided we can have more fun here. I'm gonna skin you alive and make it real, real slow. But I'm a fair guy. You seemed real interested in us, so I'll let you have the first question. What would you like to know?"

Anderson smiled through the pain. "I'll take personal for five hundred, Alex. Didn't your mommy teach you to brush your friggin' teeth? Your breath smells like a skunk crapped in a sweaty jockstrap."

Carr flushed and delivered three hard rights into Anderson's gut in the general vicinity of the rifle butt strike, then stepped back with a malevolent smile.

Anderson gasped, and only the men on either side of him kept him from collapsing.

"What was that, tough guy?" Carr asked. "I don't think I heard you."

"I said you hit like a girl, and your mother blows sailors in bus station bathrooms."

Carr reddened again, but this time he pulled a knife from a sheath on his calf and came toward Anderson with blood in his eyes. *I guess I hit a nerve with that one,* Anderson thought as he closed his eyes.

Something warm splashed his face a split second before he heard the crack of a rifle shot. He opened his eyes to see Carr sinking in front of him, his face distorted and bloody. The men supporting Anderson released him to reach for their own guns, and rubber-legged, he did a strategic face-plant in the dirt. There was a protracted roar of gunfire that seemed to go on forever, and in the midst of it, a body landed on top of him. He heard the man curse and attempt to rise, then felt him jerk before the man's entire dead weight crushed him into the ground.

And then it was quiet.

He heard the whisper of rapid footsteps through grass, then the welcome sound of Cindy's voice.

"Cover them with the shotgun, Jeremy. If any of them move, shoot them."

Then he heard her grunt, and felt relief as she rolled the dead man off his back. He rolled over to find her staring down at him, her face a mask of fear.

"Are you hit?"

Anderson shook his head. "This isn't my blood."

He sat up and looked around in amazement. The four sprawled around him, all dead from head shots. Cindy ignored them and grabbed the knife Carr dropped and cut the flex cuffs off Anderson's wrists and ankles. He sat there a moment, rubbing his wrists.

"Where the hell did you learn to shoot?"

Cindy shrugged. "Right here. Tony used to bring his AR out every weekend. Jeremy and I both got pretty good with it."

Anderson shook his head. "That's an understatement."

She shrugged again. "The dumb asses were standing in a tight group fifty feet from the nearest cover. My biggest worry was the body armor and whether I could take them all down before they got there."

"Still, head shots…"

"Only the first one, really. He was about to gut you and I had no choice. I shot the legs out from under the others and finished them when they couldn't move around."

Anderson just stared. She'd said it matter-of-factly, as if she were discussing taking out the trash.

"And you devised this plan on the fly?"

Cindy flushed. "Not completely. I'm a single mom living in the middle of friggin' nowhere, and I couldn't exactly expect to call 911. So yeah, I had a pretty good idea of what I'd do in different situations and just modified one of my imaginary scenarios to fit. The only reason I didn't have an AR yet was because I couldn't afford one, but I was saving up. And you're welcome, by the way."

It was Anderson's turn to flush. "Thank you."

Cindy nodded as Anderson crawled to his feet, unable to suppress a groan as a sharp pain gripped his midsection.

"Are you all right?"

"Nothing serious. He worked me over pretty good, so I'll probably be sore for a few days. But there's no time to worry about that now; we've got to decide what to do."

CHAPTER THIRTY-FIVE

It was obvious they couldn't stay. Elimination of a second patrol in the same area in less than a week was sure to bring a massive response, including dogs and thermal imaging sweeps by chopper. As much as they loathed the idea, they'd have to leave their comfortable cave and flee.

A big unknown was the length of their escape window. The unauthorized nature of Carr's visit would help, but they had no clue whether the patrol was outbound from nearby Buena Vista or returning to the FEMA base there. Sooner or later they would be missed, and it was only prudent to assume it would be sooner.

They couldn't afford the long round-trip to the cave, so they abandoned Cindy's and Jeremy's sleeping bags and left the chickens to their own devices. Cindy and Jeremy went to get the Mule from where Cindy left it upstream while Anderson set about salvaging things from the Hummer.

Forty-five minutes later, Anderson heaved the last of the bodies into the back of the vehicle and closed the door. He then climbed into the driver's seat and locked the differential just as Cindy and Jeremy emerged from the woods in the now-loaded Mule in time to see the Hummer back across the clearing and settle its rear bumper against the cabin.

Anderson floored the accelerator, and the house shook and began to move, then toppled off its cinder-block piers in a cloud of dust to settle upright on the ground. He pulled the Hummer away from the cabin, then threw it in reverse to crash backwards through the cabin wall. He emerged from the ragged hole only seconds later, coughing into his fist from the billowing dust.

Cindy stopped beside the cabin and leaped out. "Are you nuts? What are you doing?"

Anderson shook his head as he finished his coughing spasm. "Buying... a little time," he said at last.

"How?" Cindy asked.

"They seem pretty lax about tracking their patrols; otherwise I don't think Carr would have taken the chance on his unofficial side trip. So even if the Hummer has a working tracking device, I don't think they'll monitor it until the patrol is overdue. And since I'm not real sure where to find and disconnect a tracking device, or if there might be more than one, I figure we just burn up the whole car. That should destroy any trackers."

Cindy grinned. "Pretty smart."

Anderson nodded. "Even if they track it to this clearing as the last known location, they still won't know what's going on. All they'll find is a raging cabin fire, and it'll be too hot to poke around in the ashes for at least twenty-four hours."

"Think it will stay lit this time?" she asked.

Anderson looked up. "It doesn't look like rain, and the cabin is mostly charred now and pretty dry. I've got ten gallons of diesel from the back of the Hummer to help it along," Anderson said, then nodded to a pile some distance away. "Come look at what I salvaged. You guys can load up while I start the fire."

Cindy shook her head as she followed Anderson. "We stopped and loaded the stuff from the trailer, so there isn't much room left, and when we run out of gas, we're afoot."

"How much gas do we have?" he asked.

"I topped up with gas from the trailer, so we've got a full tank plus part of a five-gallon can. Why?"

Anderson grinned as they reached the pile and he pointed to two red plastic containers. "Because now we have ten more gallons. I guess our friends were doing a little scavenging. There's also a box of MREs, several jugs of water, and a couple of boxes of canned goods."

Cindy's initial smile faded.

"I thought you'd be pleased," Anderson said.

"If they have gas and boxes of canned goods, it means they've already BEEN scavenging. Which likely means they were headed back to base, which means for sure they'll be missed sooner rather than later," Cindy said.

"Point taken. I'll get that fire started."

***

Despite Cindy's misgivings, she was able to cram everything into the back of the Mule. They left the clearing twenty minutes later, all jammed in the front bench seat, with the remains of the cabin burning brightly behind them. Cindy was at the wheel, and she cast a worried glance over her shoulder at the rising smoke.

"I didn't think about the smoke," she said.

Anderson shrugged. "I doubt anyone is manning the fire towers these days."

Cindy nodded and turned her attention to the road. Their only real option for going off road and making any time was the Appalachian Trail. However, the Mule left tracks, and they didn't want those tracks leading from the burning cabin to the soft dirt of the AT on the opposite side of Lexington Turnpike. They had to run on the hard pavement a while, a long while preferably, so it wouldn't be obvious they'd taken the AT.

Cindy was familiar with both the Appalachian Trail and the back roads and knew a circuitous route to intersect the AT over ten miles away. The bad news was a two-mile run on Lexington Turnpike, north towards Buena Vista. The good news was the guys tasked with patrolling that road were all now well on their way to well done in the remains of the cabin, presuming no one came looking for them early.

They turned right on Lexington Turnpike, the Mule straining immediately as they crawled up a hill. Anderson looked ahead nervously.

"Is this as fast as this thing will go?"

"It's got a governor. Top speed is twenty-five," Cindy said. "But that's not the problem. We're going uphill with three adults and twice as much cargo weight as we're supposed to carry."

"Is it uphill all the way to the turnoff?"

"No, just this stretch," Cindy said. "Relax, George. We'll be off the highway in ten minutes or so."

"Won't be soon enough for me," Anderson muttered.

It took seven minutes, and Anderson breathed an audible sigh when Cindy turned left on a gravel track and they disappeared into a dark green tunnel of woodland. It was a twisting odyssey she apparently knew by heart, never hesitating at the numerous intersections or forks in the path. They moved slowly but steadily, occasionally climbing hills requiring her to stop and lock the differential before she engaged four-wheel drive to crawl up a steep slope at a snail's pace.

"How far did you say it was?" Anderson asked. "Seems like we've been traveling forever."

"It's eight or ten miles as the crow flies." Cindy looked over at Anderson and smiled. "But obviously we're not crows. We'll hit the AT in twenty minutes or so."

Her prediction was accurate, and twenty minutes later, the gravel track they were on intersected a slightly better state road. She darted across the state road to a footpath through the woods.

"We're on the AT," Cindy said.

Anderson nodded, then noticed a paved road through the trees to the right. "Uhh… what's that road?"

"The Blue Ridge Parkway," Cindy said. "We'll cross it just ahead; then the trail moves away from it. But I think they weave south together for quite a ways. I don't know for sure because I've only been as far as the James River."

"I think that's right," Anderson said. "I remember that from the trail guide…"

He cursed.

"What's the problem?" Cindy asked.

"The trail guide. It's back in the cave."

Cindy shrugged. "We didn't have time to go back for it anyway, so it doesn't matter."

Anderson gave an unenthusiastic nod of agreement just as Cindy emerged from the woods to scoot across the Blue Ridge Parkway. She drove several hundred feet into the woods and stopped.

"It might get a bit hairy here. We're going up Punchbowl Mountain, and I have no idea if the Mule will make it on this trail," Cindy said.

"Do we really have a choice?" Anderson asked.

"No good ones. If we can't make it, we either abandon the Mule and proceed on foot or back down the mountain and try our luck on the Blue Ridge Parkway," she said.

"Then let's hope we make it," Anderson said.

Cindy nodded, locked the differential, and put the Mule in four-wheel drive.

The trail got ever steeper and rockier as the Mule inched up the incline. Halfway up, they had a series of switchbacks, and the mule tipped and swayed precariously as they crawled through them. At one point, the UTV teetered at the very edge of overturning before settling back on its springs.

"Why don't I drive while you and Jeremy go ahead and check out the trail?" Anderson said. "That will take some of the load off the Mule."

Cindy shook her head. "Good idea. But I already know what's ahead and I'm considerably lighter than either of you two, so y'all get out to lighten the load."

Anderson hesitated.

"Go on and get out," Cindy said, "because I'm not stopping. It'll be a bitch to get this thing moving uphill again from a standing stop."

Anderson shook his head and grabbed the overhead handhold to swing out of the slow-moving vehicle, with Jeremy close behind. The Mule was going so slow they passed it in a dozen long strenuous uphill strides, all of which Anderson felt in his knee. Once ahead of it, and unburdened by packs, they easily maintained their interval.

"It's making a difference," Cindy called. "She's not laboring as bad, and the engine temp stopped rising."

They reached the summit fifteen minutes later, and Anderson and Jeremy climbed back in to ride another mile and a half along the ridgeline to Saddle Gap. Cindy said the trail rose another four hundred feet to a second peak before starting an equally steep descent. They decided to stop for the night, both to allow the Mule to cool down and because, if something happened, they didn't want to find themselves on the equally steep descent in the dark.

SADDLE GAP
APPALACHIAN TRAIL
MILE 1398.2 SOUTHBOUND

DAY 36, 8:50 P.M.

The ridge between the peaks was relatively narrow, but they managed to find a wide enough stretch of level ground to allow them to pull the Mule into the trees well off the trail. Anderson and Jeremy cut brush and low-hanging tree limbs to camouflage the Mule in the unlikely event of unexpected company. Cindy got evergreen boughs and piled them behind the Mule before covering them with the camouflage tarp to make a communal mattress.

They decided against a fire and had a dinner of MREs warmed by the chemical heaters included with the meals. Jeremy, as usual, had gone down with the sun, and Anderson and Cindy sat on the ground nearby, sipping MRE coffee as they leaned back against a large fallen log.

Anderson looked over to where Jeremy snored on the makeshift mattress and smiled as he shook his head in the dim light. "I envy him his ability—deep sleep in five minutes flat, every time."

Cindy smiled. "The sleep of innocence. Some folks pity me, but every challenge has its silver lining. Jeremy is a truly good human being, and I doubt he's had a mean or evil thought in his life. How many mothers can say that?"

"Very few, I expect. But I think it may be the sleep of the secure as well. Jeremy knows you're in his corner. Not a lot of people have that either, especially these days."

"Yeah, well, I'm afraid I'm not doing too well in that department lately. Which brings me to the elephant in the room; where the hell are we going, George?" Cindy asked.

Anderson sipped his coffee. "God, this is foul crap!"

"You'll kill for it when there's no coffee at all," Cindy said. "But quit stalling. What are we gonna do?"

"Honestly? Not a clue," he said. "All I really know is what we CAN'T do."

"Which is?" she asked.

"Live out here in the woods, at least when it starts turning cold. It would've been a stretch even in the cave, and there we had a shelter with an even year-round temperature and a protected source of fresh water. All we really had to do there was make sure we got in an ample supply of firewood and that we smoked meat or made jerky from the game we trapped. Out here, we have no durable, weather-tight shelter unless we managed to stumble on an abandoned cabin, and I put that chance somewhere between slim and none."

"I'll take my chances out here before I go to one of those hellhole FEMA camps." There was steel in her voice.

"Well, if you stick with me, that's not an option anyway. I doubt I'd be welcome in a FEMA camp, for obvious reasons," Anderson said.

"Actually, they're not—obvious, I mean. But what IS obvious is that we ARE going to stick together. I think it's time for you to tell me what you're running from."

"It's like I told you, it's better for you if you don't—"

"Would you give me a frigging break? In the last week, I've shot five SRF thugs. I'm pretty sure that qualifies me for a place on FEMA's hit list all by myself. And we're traveling together, for God's sake. Do you honestly think if we get caught, they're going to believe I don't know anything about whatever it is you did before we met? So since we're at risk anyway, I'd at least like to know why."

Anderson hesitated a long moment, then told her the whole story of how he ended up guarding Simon Tremble, Speaker of the House of Representatives, and how that duty caused him to be a wanted fugitive.

"But how did you end up in FEMA to start with? You're not like those other assholes."

Anderson shrugged. "Decent pay, health insurance, and benefits. Look, I went to work for them like five years ago, and it was just a pretty good law enforcement gig. It's not like there were posters of Darth Vader saying things like, 'Welcome to the Evil Empire.' In fact, a lot of the FEMA people are decent folks, or were anyway. It was a job, that's all, and I was pretty good at it. I got transferred to Mount Weather, which was a plum assignment." He shook his head. "Then came the blackout and everything went to hell fast. I didn't particularly like what was going on, but like a lot of people there, I figured I didn't know the whole story, and I certainly didn't want to quit and end up out in the chaos. Then I ended up guarding the Trembles, and I didn't feel right about that at all, but what exactly was I supposed to do? In the end, the decision was made for me, and as tough as it's been, I'd rather be here than there."

Cindy reached over and squeezed his hand. "So they never caught the Trembles?"

"I'd say no, since the guys chasing me thought they were chasing him." Anderson shook his head again and chuckled. "Simon's a crafty bastard, I'll give him that." She heard the admiration in his voice.

"So you're one of the few people who actually knows Tremble is still alive, and who is a firsthand witness to the President's illegal actions?"

Anderson shrugged again. "I guess so. At least one of the few people that's not actively involved with it. But so what? All that's likely to get me is a bullet in the head and a shallow grave. Why? What're you thinking?"

"Wilmington."

"Delaware or North Carolina?"

"North Carolina. Just before those FEMA goons swooped in to confiscate radios, there was a lot of chatter on the ham networks, and Wilmington was the source. They have some defectors from the SRF who were putting out word about what FEMA was actually up to. It sounded like they were doing okay down there, all things considered, and beginning to offer an alternative to FEMA," Cindy said.

"I still don't see what that's got to do with me, or us."

"Don't you think they'd like to have an eyewitness to illegal government actions? They'd probably welcome you with open arms," Cindy said.

"I doubt it makes any difference, and you may not have noticed, but I'm not really hero material. I just want to find a place where everyone will leave me the hell alone, and I'll do likewise. Is that too much to ask?"

Cindy studied him through the gloom. He could barely make out her face. "Yeah, George," she said, "in this screwed-up world, it probably is. I mean, we tried that and it didn't work out. People kept showing up trying to kill us. The way I look at it, our choices are to hide in the woods, hunting and scrounging food and becoming less human every day, or using what resources we have to get to Wilmington, where we can join people trying to make a difference."

"Who you THINK are there trying to make a difference. We haven't had any information in over a week," Anderson said.

"Granted," Cindy said. "Have a better option?"

Anderson shook his head. "So how do we get to Wilmington?"

"Not a clue," Cindy said. "But we're sure not going down I-95. We have to steal a map."

EPILOGUE

1 Mile off the Appalachian Trail
Near Virginia-West Virginia Border

Five Days Earlier
Day 31, 8:25 a.m.

Congressman Simon Tremble (NC), Speaker of the House of Representatives, suppressed a grunt as he grabbed a sapling to pull himself up the steep slope. Fifty feet ahead of him, he watched his son, Keith, top the hill and turn to look back at him with a wide grin.

"Come on, old-timer, you're almost there," Keith taunted.

Tremble laughed and closed the distance with ease, though it took more of his reserves than he'd ever let on. Things had started getting a bit more challenging after he hit fifty, but he was too stubborn to acknowledge it.

He grinned at his son. "Just hanging back in case I had to carry you."

"Hah! That'll be the day. So did I pass?"

Tremble frowned. "I'm sorry, I can only give you fifty percent."

Keith's face fell.

"You don't get the other fifty until you get back to the bottom without reinjuring that ankle," Tremble said.

"You're on," Keith said, starting down the steep slope.

***

Tremble stood in front of the cave, inspecting their gear. He'd lashed together pack frames from pliable green limbs, essentially wicker baskets to hold the black garbage bags they'd mooched from Wiggins and Tex. The pants of their FEMA uniforms were now secured with paracord drawstrings, and the web belts had become pack straps. Their homemade packs each held a supply of squirrel and rabbit jerky, wild onions, and dried mushrooms. Bulging water bladders improvised from a double thickness of condoms rode in the wicker packs but outside the garbage bag liners, in case the condoms burst or leaked.

The one thing that wasn't improvised was their weaponry. They both carried M4s taken from the FEMA cops, and each had a 9 millimeter Sig and ammo for both in their packs.

"How long will it take us, Dad?" Keith asked.

"How long, I can't say, only how far. Wiggins and Tex picked up the AT at Black Horse Gap, but they were paralleling it in a car. By the trail that's a little over two hundred and fifty miles. Then they used the Blue Ridge Parkway and rural roads from this guy Levi's house, they said about five hundred miles, all told. I don't know quite how far his house is outside of Wilmington, but evidently he has a place on the Black River. I'm thinking if we can find a way to get to the Black, we might be able to float down into friendly territory and right into Wilmington."

Keith shook his head. "That's gotta be like twice as far than if we just stayed off the interstates and just took back roads! I still think we should go as direct as possible."

Tremble nodded. "We might not have a choice. They ran into problems northbound at Front Royal, and I doubt things have improved. We'll just have to play it by ear. But that won't be a choice we have to make for a few days yet."

Tremble reached down and shouldered his pack, and Keith did the same.

"Ready?" Tremble asked.

"I've been ready," Keith said. "I just keep thinking about the look on that bastard Gleason's face when we get to Wilmington and you start broadcasting the truth."

Tremble nodded and smiled as they set off up the hill, though he felt far from confident. His mood improved as they plodded up the hill back to the Appalachian Trail. Perhaps Keith's youthful optimism was contagious, or maybe it was just the effect of setting out with a purpose at last, surrounded by the beauty of nature.

That sense of purpose grew with each step, and as they reached the ridgeline and moved onto the trail, Tremble felt the doubts and fears slip away, replaced by grim determination. *I'm coming you bastards. I'm coming at last.* And at that moment, the Honorable Simon J. Tremble of North Carolina, Speaker of the House of Representatives of the United States of America, promised himself as long as there was breath in his body, he'd never stop fighting to put things right—or at least as right as he could make them.

There was a new spring in his step, and Keith looked over and grinned as he matched his father's faster pace. "You gonna run all the way to Wilmington, Dad?"

Tremble grinned back. "I just might at that, so try to keep up. We have promises to keep."

Author's Notes

I guess I'll start with the question I'm most often asked, "When will the next book be available?"

Rather than overpromise like I did on *Push Back*, I think I'll be smarter this time and just say sometime next year (2017). Because the simple truth is I really don't know. I have an outline and I've made a start, but this story seems to have a mind all its own, and I'm pretty sure my outline will be useless before I'm halfway through *Promises to Keep*, the third and final book of the series.

That said, I'm going to do my dead-level best to publish it early in the year.

Part of my problem is structure—I don't have any. Some writers can develop an outline and follow it religiously to produce a book within a certain time window. My method (if I may charitably call it that) is a bit more chaotic. Oh, I try to develop an outline every time and start with the best of intentions, but around about page three, I have a 'better idea,' and I'm off and running. The 'better idea' is often a new plot point or sometimes a new character. I have a lot of 'better ideas,' probably far too many.

All my ideas usually get developed and written, though many are eventually discarded. Then there's always the idea I dream up around page two hundred that requires a substantial rewrite of everything I've written thus far. For every page you read, I often write three or four. What you get to read are the 'keepers,' the polished scenes and plot points that fit together nicely to advance the story. There's a lot of trial and error involved, mostly error, but to date I've always been pleased with the final product.

I avoid deadlines because I never know how long the process will take, and I don't want the artificial pressure of a deadline to nudge me to compromise the quality of a story. Honestly, I could make more money if I wrote faster (probably quite a bit more), but I doubt I (or you) would like the product as much. And the day I'm not proud of my work, I'll choose another line of work.

So there you have it; I'm pretty much stuck in tortoise mode here at McDermott Publishing World HQ (aka our spare bedroom). I console myself with the knowledge the tortoise actually won the race.

I appreciate the patience of all you Dugan fans out there. There will be more Dugan stories, though the timing is uncertain at the moment. I'm still trying to conjure up another semi-realistic scenario involving a middle-aged marine engineer turned ship owner.

Now back to work for me, while I hope you take a moment to consider badgering your friends and loved ones relentlessly until they buy my stuff. Really. I need the money.

All the best,

Bob

Thanks and an Invitation!

There isn't any shortage of thrillers in the world, so I'm truly honored you chose to read one of mine and I sincerely hope you enjoyed it.

If you did enjoy this book, I hope you'll check out my other books (listed below) and consider subscribing to my email notification list. Subscribers receive early notice of new releases, as well as limited time opportunities to buy new releases at deeply discounted prices.

You can learn more about my notification email list on my website at **www.remcdermott.com/mailing-list-sign-up-2016**. There's no obligation, so check it out.

One other point. Given the limited keyboards of many reading devices, it may be easier to learn more by just typing the URL of my sign up page (**www.remcdermott.com/mailing-list-sign-up-2016**) into the browser on your computer.

With that out of the way, let me say I truly enjoy hearing from readers, so if you're so inclined, feel free to shoot me an email via my website contact page at: **www.remcdermott.com/contact**.

And finally, independent authors such as myself live and die on the strength of our Amazon reviews, so for us they're a very big deal. But it's not enough to just accumulate a lot of good reviews, as factors in the Amazon quality ratings also include both the frequency and timeliness of those reviews. Thus a book with a lot of great reviews will tumble in the ratings if reviews don't continue to accumulate on a regular basis.

So the bottom line is, I regularly beg for reviews and appreciate every single one.

Reviews need not be lengthy, and a sentence or so with your opinion of the book is more than sufficient, so please consider returning to Amazon and leaving a brief review of *Push Back* (or any of my other books). It will be most appreciated.

On that note, and whatever your decision regarding a review, I'll close by thanking you once again for taking a chance on a new author, with the hope that I've entertained you at least a bit, and with the promise that I'll always strive to deliver a good story at a fair price.

Sincerely,

R.E. (Bob) McDermott

P.S. Check out my other books on the following page.

More Books by
R.E. Mcdermott

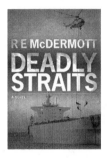

Deadly Straits - When marine engineer and very part-time spook Tom Dugan becomes collateral damage in the War on Terror, he's not about to take it lying down. Falsely implicated in a hijacking, he's offered a chance to clear himself by helping the CIA snare their real prey, Dugan's best friend, London ship owner Alex Kairouz. But Dugan has some plans of his own. Available in paperback on both Amazon and Barnes & Noble.

Deadly Coast - Dugan thought Somali pirates were bad news, then it got worse. As Tom Dugan and Alex Kairouz, his partner and best friend, struggle to ransom their ship and crew from murderous Somali pirates, things take a turn for the worse. A US Navy contracted tanker with a full load of jet fuel is also hijacked, not by garden variety pirates, but by terrorists with links to Al Qaeda, changing the playing field completely. Available in paperback on both Amazon and Barnes & Noble.

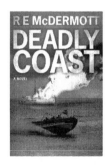

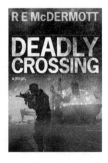

Deadly Crossing - Dugan's attempts to help his friends rescue an innocent girl from the Russian mob plunge him into a world he'd scarcely imagined, endangering him and everyone he holds dear. A world of modern day slavery and unspeakable cruelty, from which no one will escape, unless Dugan can weather a Deadly Crossing. Available in paperback on both Amazon and Barnes & Noble.